DEAD SKIN

DEAD SKIN

Chasing Blue Skies

A. J. Turner

authorHOUSE®

AuthorHouse™
1663 Liberty Drive
Bloomington, IN 47403
www.authorhouse.com
Phone: 1-800-839-8640

First published by AuthorHouse 10/13/2011

ISBN: 978-1-4567-8910-7 (sc)

Printed in the United States of America

This book is printed on acid-free paper.

1

Dark, rain filled clouds lay heavy in the sky; the first spots of rain had started to fall less than a minute ago and small puddles were already forming on the ground. Miranda turned up the collar on her coat as she stood looking down the empty street.

There was a good chance she wouldn't make it to her nineteenth birthday. Why shouldn't she end up just another statistic? No-one cared about her; she wasn't anything special . . . . just another homeless teenager. And if she didn't die young, then she would end up being one of those mad old bag ladies you see pushing a trolley full of crap around, muttering things to herself. She grimaced at the thought. Was that all she had to look forward to in this, so far objectionable, nasty little life? She would rather die; anything would be an improvement on that future.

The darkened windows of the derelict houses seemed to frown down into the empty street as the wet tarmac glistened in the rapidly fading light. The saddest part of the whole affair was that when she did finally die there would be no-one to miss her, no-one to cry at her funeral, no-one to say how wonderful she was and how awful the world would be without her. She sighed and looked around her; this street was as empty as her life.

She didn't see the bright green eyes that watched her every move intently, nor did she see the wicked smile that curved the seductive red lips as she stood there shivering from the cold. "Sad little Miranda, so wet and so cold," a mocking voice said from out of the darkness. She turned quickly and peered into the alley where the voice had come from, but she saw no-one. A figure emerged slowly from the shadows.

"Oh hi, sorry you startled me, I didn't see you there," she said taking a step back.

"I didn't mean to startle you—I mean you no harm," the stranger said quietly taking a step closer. Miranda frowned, this guy obviously knew her from somewhere, but she had no idea who he was. The fact that his face was hidden by his hood didn't help the matter, she tilted her head forward slightly to get a better look at him, but he quickly dropped his head to avoid her gaze.

"Do I know you?" she asked, unsure of what to do. She wondered fleetingly if she should just turn tail and run.

"No you don't know me," he said quietly, "but I would cry at your funeral."

"Excuse me?" she said and shuddered as an ice cold chill ran down her spine. How did he know the thoughts that had been in her mind? Running was starting to sound like an extremely good idea.

The stranger laughed quietly. An arm went around her with lightening speed; the swiftness of his movements stunned her as he whispered in her ear.

"Running really isn't an option. As you see, I'm so much faster than you."

Miranda stood perfectly still. She already knew struggling would be a pointless exercise. His arms felt like iron bars wrapped around her chest, inhibiting her ability to breathe. His strength, much as his speed, was far superior to hers. He laughed again; his head so close to hers that she could feel his icy breathe on her cheek. "I must apologise, because when I said that I meant you no harm I kinda lied."

She tried to draw a breath, but the iron bars made it impossible, and even though it was futile she instinctively struggled against his hard body. Was this how it was going to end, suffocated by a stranger. Suddenly his hold lessened and she dragged the cold air into her empty lungs.

"I'm sorry, I have to remind myself just how fragile you humans are," he chuckled softly in her ear. "Poor little Miranda, I'm sorry for your pitiful life, I'm sorry that you will never age beyond your eighteen years, I'm sorry that you won't ever get the funeral that you wanted, with no-one to cry, but there is one consolation," he paused for a moment as he pulled her coat open, "that being, at least you haven't got to live this hopeless, horrible little life for much longer."

Miranda tried to turn, to see the face of her tormentor, but he seized a handful of her hair and pulled her head back sharply. She was completely helpless; there wasn't anything she could do to save herself.

"Now if you just hold still this won't hurt much—actually that's another lie, it will hurt like hell," he said and laughed quietly again. Something gauged her neck; the pain stole her voice as she tried to scream. Warm blood oozed from her wounds and she could feel it trickling down her neck. So she wouldn't make it to her nineteenth birthday, she hated it when she was right.

Her vision started to blur and her heartbeat seemed to pound in her head, she couldn't hear the wind or feel the rain anymore, everything faded, everything except the pounding of her heart and she knew with crystal clarity that very soon she would be dead. Her life didn't flash before her eyes, as they say it does, there was no white light. All she felt was the feeling of floating, drifting. She was flying, soaring higher, all the pain disappeared, and she couldn't feel anything at all as she slipped into unconsciousness, into oblivion . . . . into blackness.

Nathanael crouched on top of the high brick wall between houses thirteen and fifteen; he glanced to his left and then to his right. His eyes darted to the skyline opposite as a black cat jumped from roof to roof and he watched it until it disappeared out of sight. He frowned and looked down at the body in the middle of the road and breathed in deeply; she was already changing.

He looked around again and then jumped gracefully off the wall, touching the ground silently. It was unbelievably quiet for such a miserable night, the homeless normally flocked to derelict streets like this as they tried to find some protection from the elements. He stood there for a moment and listened intently, nothing but the wind and rain, not even the rustling of leaves as rats and other vermin scurried around looking for scraps to eat. It appeared to be too cold, even for rats.

He lifted his hand to his face and wiped away the raindrops. He stood there for a few minutes more weighing up his options. What should he do with her? He moved suddenly towards the body, and stooped down by her side. The frown he still wore deepened as he brushed the hair away from her face; again he breathed in deeply, and then wrinkled his nose in disgust, as her human scent caught the back of his throat.

"God damn awful!" he muttered, putting his arm up to his nose. At least she wasn't dead, and that should count for something. He examined the puncture wounds on her neck, and rubbed his chin thoughtfully, they looked very amateur, they were not the marks one would expect from someone who had lived and fed like this for centuries. The way the blood had trickled down her neck, the way the puncture marks appeared slightly larger than they needed to be all pointed to the fact this was a newborn, a slight smile crept onto his face.

He looked down the street once more and then stood up, he removed his coat and dropped it onto the body, if he must run all the way home with her over his shoulder he needed something to disguise the awful human smell that still lingered. He picked her up carefully, and threw her over his shoulder, being extremely careful not to breathe in as he did . . . . his lungs had been made redundant over three hundred and twenty years ago, but old habits died hard. He wrapped the coat around her and smiled, he couldn't wait to see his brother's reaction when he got home . . . . he was going to be so mad, no not mad . . . . furious.

2

Suddenly she was being dragged back to consciousness, there was a blinding light and it felt like red hot nails were being driven through her skull and into her brain. There was no floating, no drifting and no blackness, just real unrelenting pain. It felt as if a thousand jagged knives were tearing at her flesh, raking her entire body over and over again, she felt raw.

Flames caressed her, flames over every inch of her, licking, scorching her flesh, burning it from her bones. She wanted the blackness back, her mind begged for the blackness back. She was aware of someone crying, not loudly, hardly at all really, they were the quietest of sobs. But there was definitely the sound of someone crying; maybe it was she herself who was sobbing, through the haze of pain she couldn't tell.

A voice spoke to her. "I know you can hear me," it whispered softly in her ear, "please hold on, it's not going to last forever."

The voice sent a ripple through her body and for the smallest of moments the pain ebbed away and simply licked at the edges of her. It hadn't sounded real; perhaps the voice of an angel, a ghost or a spirit, letting her know heaven wasn't far away. Someone was here with her, so why wouldn't they help her? They were here and they knew she was in pain so why wouldn't they help her? The blackness teased itself closer and closer until it consumed her totally.

There was a slight flickering in her brain; a soft glow crept slowly towards her through the blackness, like wispy, ghostly forms reaching out, steadily, silently moving closer. Fear surged through her as the insubstantial forms of light crawled closer, light meant consciousness, and consciousness meant pain . . . . surely she had been through enough. It circled her for the shortest of moments before it bathed her in its soft warm glow and she realised she had nothing to fear from it.

And then it started to, very slowly, fade. She could feel, she could hear, suddenly she was aware of everything around her. But there was no pain, the pain was gone. Shadows moved in front of her closed eyes . . . . not shadows . . . . people, the people were still here. She was still alive, but something was wrong, she wasn't the same as she used to be, she wasn't Miranda anymore.

"So how much longer have we got to wait?" a male voice asked close by. Miranda's eyes moved automatically, behind her eyelids, to the sound of his voice. She recognised him, he had been there through the pain, but his wasn't the voice that had banished it.

"Not long, she's through the worst of it," a woman's voice answered. Again Miranda's eyes moved to the sound of her voice, she recognised her too. Both of these people had been with her.

"Come on sleepy head, open your eyes," the male voice said as he tapped her lightly on the arm. Miranda didn't want to move, she didn't want to open her eyes, "I can't wait around all night for something to happen," he said impatiently.

"Well go then, no-one asked you to stay," the woman said annoyance tainting her tone. A door suddenly slammed shut to Miranda's right.

She wondered how long she'd been here lying in this bed, drifting in and out of painful consciousness . . . . hours, days, maybe even weeks. Time had meant nothing at all; she could have been here for an eternity. It had felt like an eternity. She couldn't remember how many times she'd gained consciousness and then slipped back into the blackness. How many people had been here with her? Why had they been here? Where exactly was here? How did she get here? She lay quietly listening to the noises around her.

Footsteps, the wind blowing, water dripping, a child humming, a light bulb buzzing, a dog barking in the distance, paper rustling and a piano playing, no, not a piano . . . . a radio, a radio was playing. She opened her eyes slightly and looked around the room. The woman stood at a chest of drawers with her back to Miranda.

There was a coldness that seemed to be travelling through her body, an iciness that flowed through her with increasing rapidity. It suddenly appeared to fold in on itself, drawing back, until it was a small but very powerful, freezing ball of energy in the pit of her stomach. Miranda clasped her arms to her stomach and grunted quietly.

"Oh!! You're awake," the woman said turning and taking a step towards her. The woman's voice caused the energy to expand rapidly within her, and with a sudden painful jolt it seemed too exploded out into the room. Miranda lay there and watched with horror, fascination and disbelief, as a crackling, static charge arced away from her and into the room, the air rippling in its wake. It hit the woman, knocking her backwards into the wall; momentarily stunning her.

In one swift, fluid movement Miranda sprang to her feet and backed away from the bed and the woman. Her eyes darted around the room. She saw the hole in the wall, saw the rumpled bed sheet where she had been lying, her eyes picked out every tiny detail of the room, the chair by the wall, the red lamp on the dressing table, the tree branch that tapped lightly on the window, until they came to rest on the other woman. Miranda shook her head and frowned then she took another step back. She glanced quickly towards the window, "at least there's a way out" her mind said as she stood pressed against the wall.

There was a rich coppery aroma in the air, the scent caused an unbearable burning sensation deep in the pit of her stomach and it suddenly growled like a hungry wolf that hadn't eaten for months. She was hungry, starving and it hurt, it hurt way down. She doubled over in pain and clutched at her stomach, she needed something . . . . but what was it that she needed?

"It's alright, you're quite safe here; no-one will hurt you," the woman said regaining her composure and moving forward slowly.

"Where am I?" Miranda croaked looking up and narrowing her eyes, "and who are you?"

"I'm Morana and you're—home," the woman smiled as she reached the bed, she studied Miranda for a moment. "Why don't you come back and lie down, I'm sure you must feel very weak—you're safe here," she said straightening the sheets and tapping the pillow. Miranda moved cautiously towards the bed, her eyes never leaving Morana's face as she climbed onto it. Morana smiled and pulled the sheet over her, as a mother would do with a child.

She was an extremely beautiful woman, Miranda thought as she studied her face. She noticed her bright green eyes first, they were amazing, and she wondered if she'd ever seen eyes that green before in her life. Her long dark hair shimmered in the light of the room; it was the darkest brown . . . . not black but the closest thing to it, and her face much as the rest of her was slim, and perfect. Her skin was extremely pale, and looked so hard, like ivory marble, she was very feminine, but also very strong.

Miranda leant a little closer and sniffed at her, she didn't smell coppery . . . . where was the smell coming from. The woman smiled at Miranda for a moment then moved away from her.

"How did I get here?" Miranda asked quietly lifting her hand to her neck. Talking hurt too much. Morana looked at her hand and smiled slightly.

"Nathan found you, he knew you'd been bitten straight away, he couldn't just leave you there in the middle of the street, and so he brought you home."

Bitten, Miranda thought about the word, she raised her hand to her neck again; there were two painful holes in the base of her throat. So that was what had happened, the reason why she felt so strange, she frowned, "Miranda is dead, and I have taken her place," her mind said quietly.

A figure stood in the doorway, the young girl shifted slightly. Miranda's eyes darted quickly to the girl.

"I didn't think you were ever going to wake up," the young girl said moving into the room.

"Libbi, not too close, remember," Morana said smiling at the girl. The girl watched the woman as she moved over to the wall to inspect the damage and then looked back at Miranda.

"How are you feeling?" she asked as she hovered at the bed.

"Strange," Miranda managed to say then grimaced. The young girl looked back at the woman and moved down the bed and sat on the end of it, and then she smiled.

Miranda smiled back, this little girl was the prettiest little thing. Her pure blonde hair was braided down to her waist, and tied at the end with a red silk ribbon. Her eyes were also vivid green, and they sparkled when she smiled. Her nose was no more than a button in the middle of her perfect little face, and although she was pale, she maintained a youthful glow. Miranda breathed in suddenly and frowned. This little girl smelt different from the woman, she had a slight coppery smell about her, and the pain in Miranda's stomach intensified a little making her frown.

"I am Libitina, and you're going to be my big sister now," she said in a matter of fact tone. "I've always wanted a big sister, I'm Libitina by the way—oh I already said that didn't I—I'm a goddess of death you know, that's what my name means—and I'm nearly ninety years old even though I only look eight, that was how old I was when I changed you see—well anyway you can call me Libbi, everyone else does, do you like dolls, I love dolls, maybe when you feel better we could play, I'm so glad you're awake," she added quickly.

"Libbi could you please go and let Gabriel know that Miranda is awake," the woman said quickly before the girl had time to start talking again. She moved away from the hole and smiled at the girl.

"Ok," Libbi frowned, unimpressed by the interruption, but she jumped off the bed and skipped from the room. She returned quickly, "I told him—he's coming," she said to Morana then turned to Miranda again. "I will see you later, then we can play dolls, when you don't feel strange anymore, but please, please hurry up—I've waited like forever for you to wake up," she said waving as she skipped from the room again.

"Gabriel will be here shortly, and I won't be far away if there's anything you need, just call," Morana said walking to the door, she turned back with a smile and said, "welcome to our family," and then left.

3

The cursor flashed on the computer screen, not one word had been typed on the blank page. Gabriel sat with his back to it; his head turned towards the window, his unseeing eyes stared out into the night sky. It had been ten days since he'd returned to find her here, and she still hadn't gained consciousness. He stood up, rubbed his head and then sat back down; she should have woken up by now . . . . why was it taking so long?

He stood up again and walked to the window, why wasn't she awake yet, it never usually took this long. He rested his head against the cool glass of the window and closed his eyes. She shouldn't be here. Nathanael should not have brought her here. He pulled his head back, and banged it against the window, and then he looked up and frowned as a crack spread across the pane. She should be awake, why wasn't she awake? He turned to look at the door as it opened and Libbi skipped in.

"She's awake, she said she's going to be my big sister you know, and she is soooo pretty—anyway you gotta go and talk to her," the girl said with a smile. She turned and left the room as quickly as she'd entered.

Gabriel closed his eyes; he didn't want to do this, he'd been waiting for her to wake up and now he wished that she hadn't. Why did it fall to him to tell her what she'd become, to have to explain that the life that she'd known was over. That she was now one of the most dangerous things ever created, that she now had to kill merely to survive. He couldn't handle it.

He left the library and climbed the stairs slowly. Morana met him outside the room. She looked at him for a moment, and then patted his arm. "You'll be fine," she said with a smile then turned and walked down the hall.

Miranda watched the woman leave then lay back against the pillow. Nathanael was the one who brought her here; could he have been the one that had spoken to her through the pain? And who was Gabriel, exactly how many people lived here, exactly how many people had been here with her for the last . . . . Miranda frowned . . . . exactly how long had she been here?

There was a knock on the door, but before she'd managed to answer, it opened and a young man walked in.

"Hi," he said quietly walking over and sitting next to her on the bed, "I'm Gabriel—how are you feeling?"

She sat there blinking rapidly, she opened her mouth but nothing came out, she was having great difficulty forming words, looking at his face literally stole them from her mouth; any intelligent thought deserted her the moment he'd opened the door. He had the most amazing face she had ever seen. She snapped her mouth shut and just sat there looking at him.

His stunning emerald green eyes had the tiniest specks of silver in them. His hair was raven black; it was short, brushed back off his perfect face with not a single strand out of place. He had a small scar underneath his left eye, but it did nothing to mar his perfection, if anything it added to his beauty. Not even the slight shade of stubble hid his handsome features. Her eyes drifted to his claret lips as he smiled, highlighting the dimples at the edges of his mouth; he was quite simply the most beautiful creature she'd ever seen.

She thought her head was going to explode as he reached over and brushed a few strands of stray hair away from her face. His scent was absolutely wonderful, and she breathed in deeply as he leaned towards her. As his fingers touched her skin, something similar to an electric jolt coursed through her and she flinched involuntarily. He pulled his hand back instantly and frowned. "Sorry," he said standing up and moving away from her.

Miranda watched, fascinated, as he glided across the room. His shirt tightened over his broad muscular shoulders as he picked up the chair, and Miranda could feel the heat rising up through her body. She took in every detail of his muscular frame as he walked back towards the bed; his movements were mesmerizingly graceful for someone so obviously strong and powerful. He placed the chair by the bed and sat down. "So how are you feeling?" he asked again.

Miranda put her hand to her throat and opened her mouth but still nothing came out. He looked down at the puncture marks as she moved her hand away, the disgust in his eyes made her wish she hadn't drawn his attention to them.

"Do you know what has happened to you?" he asked quietly. Miranda nodded. "I'm sorry," he said looking away from the marks and down at the floor.

"Who did this to me?" she finally managed to croak.

"We don't know," Gabriel said shaking his head, "when Nate found you there was no sign of him, we don't think he knew what he was doing and from the marks on your neck he is relatively new to this life himself—I'm sorry to say this but I think you were just in the wrong place at the wrong time, a link in an unfortunate chain of events."

"That'd be right," she said lifting her hand to her throat to try and ease the pain somehow. It didn't surprise her because her whole life had been a string of unfortunate events, so why should her transition into vampirism be any different. "But I don't believe in vampires, they don't exist—except in stories."

"Yes we do, you do," he said frowning.

"What am I supposed to do now?" she asked quietly closing her eyes.

"You can stay with us for as long as you need—we're not what you'd call a normal family."

Neither of them spoke for a while and the silence seemed to stretch out for an eternity. Miranda kept her eyes closed, it hurt to look at him, as beautiful as he was, and he seemed quite uncomfortable with the way she was staring at him. Even if she tried to look away her eyes strayed back to his mouth. Yes, closing her eyes seemed like the safest option.

"Is there anything you need?" he asked suddenly breaking the silence.

"I'm hungry," she frowned opening her eyes and as if her words had been an invitation, her stomach growled loudly again. "The thing is I don't like the taste of blood."

"Well that would be a first, a vegetarian vampire," he smiled briefly, "I think you'll find your tastes have changed somewhat," he said then stood up and left the room.

Miranda hardly had time to think before he was back. He ignored the chair, moving it out the way easily with his foot, and sat on the bed next to her. He handed her the cup and frowned as he looked down at the floor, "I'm sorry but it's not the same as the real thing, although it will do for now," he said quietly, his eyes remaining on the floor.

Miranda peered into the cup, the rich coppery scent filled her nostrils, her mouth watered and the burning sensation that had started earlier in the pit of her stomach became almost too much to bear. She put the cup to her mouth and drank quickly.

The crimson fluid was amazing, thick and warm, it surged through her entire body filling her with what could only be described as strength, it was like nothing she'd ever felt before, all her senses seemed to intensify. As she lowered the cup she frowned and looked down at her chest for a moment, there was the loudest sound coming from within her and she quickly looked back at Gabriel.

"What's going on?" she asked looking back down at her chest.

Gabriel looked up at her, his frown deepening for a moment as he watched her, and then a smile crept slowly onto his face, "that is the sound of your heart beating—don't get to used to the sound, it only happens for a short while after feeding, while the blood circulates."

Miranda looked back at him, the smile that he had on his face caused her heart to skip a few beats and she looked away quickly . . . . did he know the effect his smile seemed to have on her. She glanced slyly back at his face, the smile had disappeared and he moved back to the chair. Apparently she wasn't the only one that could hear her heart beating.

"Do you remember anything from the attack, anything at all?" Gabriel asked reaching over and taking the empty cup from her.

She sat there for a while trying to recall that night. She remembered the rain, and walking down a dark street. She remembered arms wrapped around her, not arms, iron bars and she couldn't breathe, she frowned . . . . he had let her breathe for a moment before she'd died.

"It was raining," she said shrugging her shoulders, "and I remember his wrapped around me, but I can't remember his face."

"It's alright—that happens sometimes," he said frowning slightly, "loss of memory is not uncommon for a short period after changing."

"I mean I didn't see his face, he kept it covered with a hood," she frowned as she tried to remember.

"You didn't see him at all?" Gabriel asked his frown deepening.

Miranda shook her head as an involuntary shiver crept down her spine, “I remember that he told me it was going to hurt,” she said quietly and shivered again.

Gabriel’s frown deepened even further at her reaction and he had to look away from her. He couldn’t stand it. “I’ll leave you to rest now,” he said standing abruptly; he walked to the door and turned to her again. “You’ll be safe here—no-one can ever hurt you again,” he said quietly, he stood there for a moment just looking at her then turned and left the room.

She lay back and pulled the sheet up to her chin, the burning sensation that had been coursing through her minutes ago had dissipated slightly, so had the pain in her throat and she felt warm and comfortable. She thought about Gabriel, about his eyes, about his lips and his smile—perhaps being a vampire wouldn’t be so bad after all. She smiled to herself as she closed her eyes and fell asleep.

Gabriel closed his bedroom door and lent against it, he was trembling from head to toe, and it had taken all his strength not to fall to pieces in front of her. He sat on his bed and put his head in his hands.

How could he endure this, how could he deal with what had happened to her and how could she have simply accepted it the way she had. There had been no tears, no screaming and no tantrum. He had expected at least one, if not all of those reactions, but she’d surprised him. She had accepted her fate with dignity and grace.

He frowned over at the window, then stood up and walked over to it and pulled the curtains shut angrily, she shouldn’t be here . . . Nathanael should not have brought her here.

Miranda woke early and looked slowly around the room; yesterday hadn't been some kind of dream. She was still in this house, still with these people; she was still one of the living dead.

Sitting up, she swung her legs out of the bed; she looked down at her chest and listened to the quietness of it, no beating . . . . no pounding . . . . nothing. She walked over to the dressing table and sat on the stool then turned towards the mirror and frowned, if she was a vampire how could she see her reflection in the mirror . . . . was that really her? A stranger sat there staring back. She slowly raised her hand to her face, she looked beautiful. There wasn't a blemish, not a mark to mar the perfect skin, not one freckle. Even her long auburn hair was beautiful; it shimmered and shone as she moved. She hadn't looked this beautiful while she was alive of that she was sure.

She moved closer and peered into the mirror, her eyes sparkled back at her . . . . what colour had her eyes been before being turned . . . . she couldn't remember, they were now vivid green, not as beautiful as Gabriel's, there were no silver specks, but even so green suited her. Her usual sun stroked skin was now deadly pale; in the dying light of day she looked almost translucent.

She looked curiously towards the window, the heavy velvet curtains were parted slightly and a weak shaft of light could just be seen. She stood up and moved towards it, "curiosity killed the cat," her mind said as she inched closer. She stopped with her toes at the edge of the beam, and watched the tiny dust particles for a few moments as they glistened and danced in the light. She considered the shaft of light for a minute, would it really hurt if she were to jump into it. She wondered if she should just do it, but the thought of instantaneously bursting into flames stopped her. She moved away from the light and back to the mirror.

The door opened and Libbi skipped in, she smiled at Miranda as she laid some clothes on the bed then skipped over to her. Miranda moved over slightly as the girl joined her on the stool; she smiled at her through the mirror.

"You're so pretty—you won't bite me will you, Ana said not to get to close, in case you still feel strange—cause you might bite me, but you won't will you?" the young girl asked looking around at her.

"Ana?" Miranda asked slightly puzzled.

"That's what we call Morana, she said you might bite me, you won't will you?" the girl asked again.

Miranda turned to the girl and frowned then shook her head slightly.

"I knew you wouldn't, Ana said that sometimes stuff like that happens, sometimes when a vamp wakes up for the first time they get angry, and just bite, they don't care if it's another vamp or not, sometimes they fight terribly as well, cause they don't want to be one of us—but it's not so bad—she said that sometimes vampires bite other vampires if they're hungry too, makes them crazy she said—Nate and Gabe bite each other when they fight, they get awfully angry with each other sometimes, and fight," the girl said looking back into the mirror.

"I would never bite you, even if I was starving," Miranda said smiling slightly at the girl.

"I knew you wouldn't—Ana said you should get dressed and then come and join us in the kitchen, and she sent you some clothes so you don't have to wear your nightdress—you are so very pretty you know, and your hair is very long—maybe I could braid it for you, Ana showed me how—maybe we could play later, if you don't feel strange anymore—maybe after you've talked or something, Ana said you got loads to talk about, and anyway Jess wants to meet you, she's waited like forever," Libbi finished and looked around at her.

"Who's Jess?" Miranda asked absently running her fingers through her hair.

"She's my best friend," Libbi said jumping off the stool. "The kitchen is down stairs, at the end of the hall," the girl informed her as she skipped from the room.

Miranda looked at the mirror again; she was pretty. She sat looking at her reflection for a few minutes more then turned away from it; she stood up and walked to the bed. She dressed and looked at herself in the mirror again—she definitely hadn't looked this good while she'd been alive. She smiled at her reflection then turned and left the room.

Nathanael lounged in a chair. Libbi played distractedly with a doll, humming softly to herself. Gabriel was frowning over a newspaper, scanning for anything of importance. If it was a young vampire that had attacked Miranda then it wouldn't be long before he made a mistake. He was looking for reports of animal attacks or unexplained deaths, but there wasn't anything unusual. After a while he grabbed the paper, rolled it up into a tight ball and threw it across the room in temper.

"Nothing," he said fiercely.

Nathanael looked up at him; a slight smile tugged the corner of his mouth. "I told you, I don't know why you're bothering, he's long gone."

"We can't be sure though can we?" Gabriel asked looking over at him.

Nathanael rapped his fingers on the table; he'd grown bored of this conversation. It had been the only topic they'd discussed for the last ten days and it was getting on his nerves. He was getting very close to leaving again and would have been long gone if it hadn't been so entertaining. He'd relished his brother's reaction at having Miranda in the house, but now it was getting old. He frowned over at Gabriel, "look, he's gone, end of story."

"What if he is still around?" Morana asked joining the conversation; she'd been standing quietly over by the counter. "A new, inexperienced vampire, running around the city with no guidance is the last thing we need."

Nathanael groaned. "God not you too," he said giving her a withering look, "I told you there wasn't a sign of him—he was long gone by the time I got there, I think I would have known if there was another vampire in the area." He stood up and walked to the backdoor, "I'm off for a walk. Anyone coming with me?" he offered. Libbi dropped her doll on the table and jumped from her seat and walked to the door. Nathanael took her hand with a smile and they left.

Gabriel sat back in his chair. He thought of what Miranda had said last night, she hadn't seen her attackers face, that he'd hidden his identity. But his kind had no need to hide themselves from humans unless there was a specific reason . . . . so what did this vampire have to hide?

A shiver ran down his spine and the hairs on the back of his neck prickled, he had no need to look around to understand this reaction, or the sudden tension he felt in every muscle of his body.

"Hello Miranda," Morana said pleasantly as she walked into the room. "Have a seat," she motioned towards the table. Miranda hesitated and then sat opposite Gabriel.

He was frowning as he pushed back his chair and got to his feet. He muttered, "good evening," in her direction and then turned to Morana, "I'll be in the library if anyone wants me," and with that he was gone.

"So how are you feeling this evening?" the woman asked frowning slightly at the door he'd just hurried through. She opened a cupboard, and produced a bottle of blood which she emptied into a cup and handed to Miranda.

"I'm fine," Miranda answered vaguely, she wondered why Gabriel had left in such a hurry, he'd seemed so nice last night and yet this evening it was as if he couldn't even bring himself to look at her. She looked at the cup then drank it quickly and she glanced down at her chest as her heart suddenly started to beat again.

She noticed the doll lying where Libbi had left it and reached over to pick it up. She absently fiddled with its dress. She didn't know any of them and yet here she was sitting in their kitchen, sleeping in their bed, drinking their blood as if she belonged, but if she didn't belong here where did she belong? The backdoor opened and Miranda looked up as a blond haired man walked into the kitchen. He too, was a very handsome man, with his long blond hair tied back from his perfect face; the usual green eyes sparkled as he smiled at her.

"Good evening, you're finally up," he said as he walked over and kissed her on the cheek. "I'm Michael—welcome to the family."

Miranda was momentarily stunned by this show of affection. She hadn't realised there were more of them and she wondered just how many lived here. Michael walked over to Morana and wrapped his arms around her waist and kissed her. "Hello my love," he said moving away from her. He picked the crumpled paper up off the floor and looked quizzically at Morana, she raised an eyebrow at him, and he chuckled quietly then nodded as he moved to the table and sat opposite Miranda.

She sat quietly watching them with interest. Their act of love towards each other had looked convincing, and yet she couldn't help but wonder if real vampires acted much the same as humans did, they really did look as if they were in love. Morana sat down next to Michael and smiled over at Miranda, "so I'm guessing you have a lot of questions," she stated rather than asked.

Miranda nodded, and wondered where to start, "how different can I expect my life to be?"

"Well—we need blood to survive, that's the one thing that is definite," Michael said as he glanced at Morana. "We can survive on animal blood but not for long, we need a substantial diet of human blood—I hope that won't be too much of a problem," he said looking back at Miranda.

Miranda considered his words for a moment, and then shook her head as answer. She had never considered taking anyone's life when she was human, but she wasn't human anymore, was she?

"You would have already noticed that your senses are more acute, sense of smell, taste, your hearing is exceptional as well, we can literally hear a pin drop in a crowded room," Morana said and winked at her.

"Then there are other differences, we all have special powers," Michael said. "We have vampiric telepathy, it allows us to communicate with each other easily; we can hear each others thoughts, speak to each other, that sort of thing."

"So you can hear what I'm thinking?" Miranda asked looking from one to the other, she felt mortified . . . . did they know exactly what she though of Gabriel.

"No we can't—at the moment you are quite new and therefore not as prone to delving as we are, and as soon as you start to feed properly you will gain the power to block intrusions anyway—that being said you will find that there are some of our kind that can still get into your head easily—and I'm afraid to say that these vampires have absolutely no scruples at all," he said looking at Morana. "Just something you should be aware of," he added looking back at Miranda and smiling slightly.

"We have another power," Morana said shifting a little, "it's much the same as telepathy, all vampires possess it—we call it perfect recall, we remember everything—and when I say everything I mean everything from our human lives too," she said glancing at Michael.

"It can be very unnerving to start off with, it will creep up on you at the most unexpected times until you learn to control it," Michael said sitting back and looking towards the backdoor.

Miranda hadn't realised that the backdoor had opened until Libbi barged past a figure standing in the doorway.

"Hey watch it squirt," he called after the girl as she skipped to the table and picked up her doll. Libbi kissed Miranda lightly on the cheek then skipped from the room, but Miranda hardly noticed, she was too busy staring at the man stood in the doorway. He stayed there for a few moments just looking at her and then he smiled.

Only two things separated this man from Gabriel, the first was the length of his hair, his was slightly longer than Gabriel's and not as neatly kept, the second was the lack of a scar on his face. His attitude however was completely different to his brother's, he possessed an arrogance that she had not yet seen in Gabriel, in the tilt of his head and the curve of his mouth as he stood smiling at her.

"Hi, I'm Nathanael—Nathan or even Nate if you prefer," he said closing the door with his foot and walking to the table. He pulled the chair out next to her and sat down, he didn't seem to have any concept of personal space; he was so close to her that they may as well have been sharing the same seat. He leant even closer, draping his arm around her shoulders and brushed her cheek with his lips, "welcome to the family."

Miranda shifted uncomfortably in her chair, she didn't know this man and his actions made her feel uneasy. She was also acutely aware that Morana and Michael were quietly watching this exchange.

"Thank you," she said not knowing how to react to his over friendly gesture. Nathanael grinned at her; he was enjoying her discomfort she realised. What was wrong with the men in this family? One seemed to find her disagreeable and the other was just . . . . troubling.

"So Libbi and I didn't finish our walk, how about I show you around." He stood up, took her hand and pulled her to her feet without waiting for an answer. "See you two later," he said as he pulled her through the backdoor and out into the cool night air.

5

The middle of winter should have felt colder than it did; but she reasoned, her flesh was dead, so she wouldn't ever feel cold again. The cold wasn't something she would miss, but what about the warmth of the sun, was that going to be something she would miss on her dead skin.

"So we can't go out in the daylight," she muttered to herself more than to Nathanael.

"Not unless you have a death wish," he chuckled glancing at her.

"Do we burst into flames?" Miranda asked looking at him.

"No—actually the whole bursting into flames is a myth, dying for a vampire is not as visually dramatic as they make out—we blister, we dry out, we shrivel up, and then we die, turn to ash and blow away on the breeze," he said the slightest hint of longing in his voice. "I've heard say it's a very drawn out, painful experience, though I don't know where that story came from, in this life when you die you die, ain't no coming back to tell what it felt like."

"I died," Miranda said quietly.

"No you didn't die, you simply transformed, as we all did, and from what I remember that was bad enough."

"Yes, it was bad enough," she said taking in her surroundings. The garden was vast with boundaries that ended with a thick line of trees. To the east was a large pond filled with water lilies, their brilliant white petals shone in the moonlight. The surface of the pond rippled gently as a frog jumped from a lily pad.

Her eyes saw everything; it was quite amazing now that she looked around. Everything was so clear, she could see absolutely everything. The leaves on the trees and hedges, as they swayed in the breeze, even the smallest blade of grass was visible to her as it moved in the wind. She could see colours, greens, reds and blues, in fact the whole colour spectrum. Everything seemed to glow, everything seemed so alive.

She looked up at the sky in wonder; it wasn't as black as it had always appeared to be, more like a clear, deep sapphire blue, with the blackness of space behind it somehow. Did stars really look like that she wondered, not just little lights that twinkled, but bright dots of fire, whose flames reached out like thousands of small fingers gently caressing the night sky.

Nathanael stood watching her for a second, and followed her gaze; he smiled then looked back at her. He cleared his throat quietly and broke the trance she was in and she looked at him for a moment. "You found me," she said, "after I'd been bitten, you brought me here—how did you find me?"

"I could smell you," he said and smiled at her questioning look, "I was a few streets away, feeding, and I knew I wasn't the only vampire in the area—and I knew from the smell that he hadn't killed you—so I didn't have any choice but to bring you home, I couldn't just leave you there, you'd already started to change—once it starts there is no way to stop it," he frowned. "I did consider, for the briefest moment, finishing the job, but who was I to deny you this new life."

Miranda considered his answer for a moment then turned her attention back to her surroundings. She should have been shocked by his disclosure, but she wasn't. She should be grateful that he had allowed her to live, but she would save her thanks until she knew if this new life was any better than her old one. She looked to the other side of the vast garden; it was dominated by two large well kept hedges, which divided in the middle.

"It's a maze; would you like to see it?" Nathanael asked following her gaze, "it's very big so stay close, we wouldn't want to lose you," he said smiling wickedly. She didn't think getting lost was going to be a problem; he hadn't loosened his grip on her hand since he'd taken hold of it in the kitchen.

It occurred to her, as she walked, that vampires weren't anything like she originally thought . . . . not that she'd ever given the creatures in stories any thought at all. In books they were portrayed as cold unfeeling creatures, but it didn't seem to be the case at all, hadn't she already witnessed love, from the two people in the kitchen?

"Books aren't a very good reference, we aren't the way humans portray us," Nathanael said as if reading her mind, she looked at him accusingly, but he carried on unperturbed, "in three hundred and forty-five years of this life, human and vampire, the one thing that I've found, is that we feel far more than humans do," he said as his features darkened. "Love, hate, anger—every human emotion is magnified ten fold in a vampire."

"You're over three hundred years old?" she asked amazed.

Nathanael nodded and smiled, "yeah, Gabe and I have been vamps for around three hundred and twenty years, Morana is two hundred and seventy five, Michael is one hundred and ninety eight and Lib is nearly ninety, we are all pretty old—we all look rather good for our age don't you think," he said laughing quietly.

Miranda smiled slightly, "what else have the books got wrong?" she asked.

"Well, err—take the wooden stake through the heart, hurts like hell, but our hearts are already dead; they don't beat, they don't pump blood through our veins, so how could driving a stake into something that's already dead, kill us—even when we feed it only beats for a short time—yeah good luck trying to stake a vamp that's just fed," he sniggered then leant closer to her for a moment, "that's when we're at our strongest you know."

"What about crosses, holy water and that sort of thing?" Miranda asked as he pulled away from her again.

"They have no effect on us—all stories to help people sleep a little better at night—just imagine if they knew that the things they imagine lurk in the dark really do," he said then laughed again.

Miranda deliberated for a moment, "so you're saying that people don't know that we exist?"

"Did you?" he asked a slight smile curving his mouth. Miranda shook her head. "I know that every story starts somewhere, but they—meaning humans, really don't have any clue, they think they dreamt us up when in fact we have been around since before most of them even came out of the dark," he said slightly annoyed. "I do sometimes get a little agitated at the human race, they are such dirty, depraved creatures, however they inherited the earth I'll never know—the only things that humans think about is money, sex and violence—they are cold unfeeling animals and if I could, I would rid the world of every single one of them—their appetite for destruction is only over shadowed by their greed," he said frowning.

"You were human once too," Miranda said mirroring his frown.

"Yes, that's true, so it kind of makes me an expert on the matter, wouldn't you say—they destroy everything they touch—half of them would step over a dying child to make a quick buck while the other half are responsible for pulling the trigger of the gun that killed the child—they annoy me so much with their pettiness and greed."

"We kill," Miranda said quietly.

"Yes, but unlike them we only kill to survive, they kill for a number of reasons, religion, money, power and on the odd occasion love—tell me what sort of creature kills for love?" he stopped talking again and looked at her and then smiled ruefully.

Miranda smiled and changed the subject, "so apart from drying up in sunlight, is there anything else that can hurt us?"

"There are only two ways to kill a vampire—the first is to drag it out into the sunlight—which really wouldn't happen, the second is to remove its head with a silver blade—you will notice there is absolutely no silver anywhere in the house, it makes us very weak when we're around it too long—oh and sorry about the necklace," he said looking at her neck, "I hope it wasn't important to you, I had to remove it before you completely changed and Michael wouldn't let you in the house with it on—burnt like a bitch I can tell you," he said lifting his free hand to inspect it.

"No it wasn't important," Miranda said shaking her head. She frowned for a second as she tried to remember where the necklace had come from and was met with blackness; she shook her head and looked back at Nathanael, "you said being dragged out into the sunlight wouldn't happen, why wouldn't it happen?"

Nathanael stopped and looked at her, then laughed loudly. "The only thing on this planet strong enough to drag a vampire anywhere is another vampire—like I said it really wouldn't happen—that is, of course, unless the vampire doing the said dragging was feeling suicidal."

"Oh," Miranda murmured feeling stupid, Nathanael grinned and continued walking.

"You have so much to learn, don't be afraid to ask if there is anything you want to know, we don't bite," he said and then chuckled again. "Actually we do but that was just a figure of speech."

"How come I can see my reflection in the mirror?" she asked.

He frowned for a second, "as I've said, books aren't a good reference—but I do have an interesting fact about that, did you know that humans can't see our image at all through reflective surfaces—the amount of times I've had fun with that," he said grinning at the thought, he paused and looked at her, "I think it has something to do with not possessing a soul—humans have one, and we don't so I guess that's why they can't see us." He stopped talking for a moment and then sighed, "it's quite amazing to look at a human through glass, they glow you know, quite literally," he said smiling at her, "I suggest you have a look next time you're around one—it's quite beautiful," he said.

Miranda frowned, "so we haven't got souls?"

"My, you are an inquisitive little thing aren't you," he said smiling at her, then added, "again I don't really know, but the way I see it humans have this glow, and we don't—I think their souls make them shine, but that is just my opinion, I suppose if you asked Gabe, Mike or Ana they would each give you a different answer—I mean the definition of a soul is the pure, incorporeal essence of any living thing—and we are not exactly what you would call living," he said glancing at her.

Miranda considered his answer for a moment, then glanced at him, "what's it like to kill someone?"

Nathanael stopped; that wasn't a question he had been expecting, at least not so soon. He looked down at her for a moment and frowned, he shrugged then started to walk again, "it's necessary, we can survive on animal blood and that disgusting bottled stuff that Ana keeps in the cupboard—but none of it is as satisfying as fresh human blood—human blood keeps us more—human—without it we would just degenerate into blood thirsty zombies, we would kill anybody, anytime without the consideration of consequences—it really doesn't do any of us any good if we deny ourselves what our bodies need—so, we do what we need to do to survive," he said shrugging again.

"Do you ever feel guilty for what you've done after?"

"Never," he said stopping again, "humans are food, nothing more—you'll realise this soon enough Miranda—a vampire's conscience is a very small and insignificant thing." Nathanael remained where he was and smiled at Miranda as she realised they were no longer moving.

She looked around; they seemed to have arrived at the centre of the maze, she had been so engrossed in their conversation she hadn't even realised they had entered it.

Nathanael stood at the base of a large marble statue, situated in the middle of the large square; he stood for a moment staring up at the beautiful face. He had a pensive look in his eyes, and seemed lost in thought for several minutes. He sighed and glanced at Miranda, "lovely isn't she."

Miranda saw sorrow flash across his eyes as he looked back at the statue. "Who is she?" she asked moving closer, she suddenly got the distinct feeling that she was somehow intruding on a private moment that only two people should share.

"A love long lost," Nathanael frowned snapping out of his reverie. He still had a tight hold of her hand but suddenly he released it, as if he was holding something distasteful, and backed away from her. "Now dearest Miranda let's see how good your abilities are—find your way out." With that he chuckled and disappeared.

6

Gabriel backed his chair away from the computer desk and frowned, why he had even contemplated trying to get any work done was beyond him. He had been having difficulty concentrating on walking and talking over the last two weeks, so why had he thought he'd be able to concentrate any better on work. He hadn't even been able to talk properly when she'd walked into the kitchen and looked at him, she most likely thought him an idiot as he'd mumbled and excused himself.

His mind kept conjuring up images of her maker, hiding, springing out on her when she was least expecting it. Of him grabbing her and holding her in his arms, then sinking his teeth into her tender flesh and drinking her blood until she was so close to death. It literally hurt to think of it, it was going to drive him crazy, he needed to go out; he needed to kill something, he left the room and stood in the hall listening for her voice.

He opened the door to the kitchen and Morana looked up at him and frowned, "Nathan and Miranda went into the garden—over two hours ago."

Gabriel shrugged at the woman, "so, what's wrong with that?"

"Don't you care; you know what Nate's like—she shouldn't be left alone with him."

Gabriel walked towards the backdoor and opened it, "Miranda can spend her time with whomever she pleases—it's nothing to do with me," he said walking out into the garden. He stood at the door for a moment and sniffed at the air, her scent still lingered on the breeze, and he glanced over towards the maze as Nathanael emerged alone. Gabriel shut his eyes for a moment then opened them and shook his head; he made his way over to his brother, stopping at his side. "Where's Miranda?" he asked quietly.

Nathanael turned and smiled at him, "she's in there—I'm seeing how long it takes her to find her way out."

Gabriel turned and frowned at him, "you left her in there, alone?"

Nathanael grinned and nodded slightly.

"For god's sake Nate, what are you thinking?" he frowned and then disappeared into the maze. Nathanael chuckled quietly then followed him.

It was an unexpected turn of events; she hadn't been paying the slightest bit of attention as Nathanael had guided her through the maze. She wished she had been, and she guessed that it must have been his plan all along, to distract her. The darkness of the maze seemed to be wrapping itself around her and she had no idea what to do. She had been a vampire less than a day and had no idea of what powers she possessed. With her eyes closed, she listened intently at the noises around her; maybe if she concentrated she would be able to pick up a sign as to where he was.

"Come on Miranda," Nathanael's voice whispered in her mind, Miranda frowned and listened again. "Start moving Miranda, you don't want to be lost in there all night, the sun will be up soon," his voice said then he chuckled quietly. Miranda opened her eyes and looked up at the statue; it smiled serenely down at her.

"Run, Miranda, Run," he whispered quietly. The face of the statue continued to smile down at her.

She suddenly clutched at her chest, as the energy ripped through her body, she was shaking from head to toe as she stood there trying to hold the energy in. It was a different feeling to the one she'd had last night, this energy felt hot, like volcanic lava, bubbling and burning as it moved slowly through her body.

She moved further away from the statue and backed into a hard unmoving object and then it happened again, as before the energy exploded from her, thermal vapours shot out in all directions and seemed to actually scorch the air around her. She was forced further back into the solid object, and she realised that the thing she'd backed into was Gabriel as he grunted quietly.

He too was forced backwards by the power of the energy; he quickly regained his balance and wrapped his arms around her to keep her from falling. She turned quickly in his arms and he looked down at her. She couldn't think straight with his arms wrapped around her, holding her so close to his perfect, hard body. "Are you alright?" he asked quietly.

She nodded; she didn't trust her voice enough to talk as they stood there. If she opened her mouth nothing would come out and she'd just end up looking like a complete fool. Through the fog that had descended in her brain, she realised that somewhere between him looking down at her and asking her if she was alright, she'd snaked her arms around him and was now holding, very tightly, onto his shirt.

"You just have to go and spoil all my fun don't you," Nathanael said walking past them and over to the statue.

"What the hell is wrong with you," Gabriel shouted, the volume of his voice caused her to shudder against his body, and he instinctively tightened his hold.

"God, take a chill pill Gabe, honestly, she's one of us now, and she needs to learn how to look after herself."

"She hasn't even been a vampire a day you idiot, what did you expect—that she would just know how to do everything—for god's sake Nate she only woke up last night, we have no idea of her potential, no idea what she's capable of."

"We're not going to know what she's capable of, if you keep jumping to her rescue every five minutes are we," Nathanael said looking around at the statue, "I got mine, and now you've got yours," he said running his hand down the marble. Miranda couldn't tell if the last statement was meant for Gabriel or the statue. "Happily ever after," Nathanael added moving towards them, as he drew level with Miranda he bent his head towards her. "Ask Gabe to tell you the story of how we became vampires, it's worth listening to," he winked at her then looked meaningfully at his brother.

Gabriel flinched slightly, as if Nathanael had reached out and slapped him. She didn't have to guess what had just happened; the unspoken words between brothers were something she had no desire to listen to, even if she could.

"See you later Miranda," Nathanael said bowing his head to her. "I will leave you now; it seems my brother is desperate for your company," he looked purposely at Gabriel's arms around her, and then he turned and left them.

Gabriel shifted uncomfortably at his words, he hadn't realised just how tight he'd been holding her all this time, but it felt so good. He didn't want to let her go, he could quiet happily stand there with her in his arms for the rest of eternity. But he had to let her go . . . . now if only he could get his arms to comply.

Miranda didn't want to move, it felt good with his arms around her, and although her fingers had started to tingle with the way she was holding onto his shirt, she desperately wanted to stop him as he slowly released her.

"We'd better get back to the house," he said quietly as he moved away from her. "I suppose you're hungry by now—I know I could do with a bite," he looked down at his feet and frowned slightly, "sorry that was just a figure of speech, I didn't mean bite—I meant—oh hell, I did mean bite, but not that way—damn it, I meant I'm hungry," he ran his fingers through his hair then looked up at her. "Let's get back to the house."

7

Dark shadows crept across the ceiling and Miranda lay watching them; as soon as they had arrived back at the house she'd drunk the blood that Morana had handed her quickly, and retired to her room. She had stayed there for the remainder of the night, and had hardly slept at all through the day. Being in his arms had unsettled her completely, and she'd had visions of him every single time she closed her eyes.

She frowned slightly and turned to look at the door as someone knocked lightly, "come in," she called and smiled as Libbi and Morana popped their heads around the door.

"We got you a new room," Libbi informed her, entering the room and jumping on the bed. "I picked it—it's lush and much bigger than this one—Ana said you can have it if you're gonna stay—and we want you to stay—you're a good one and didn't bite any of us—so come and look—I bet she likes it," she said glancing at Morana. "I bet you like it," she added grabbing Miranda's hand and pulling her to her feet.

Morana smiled as Miranda was dragged out of the room and down the hall by the young girl. She stopped Miranda outside the door and jumped deftly onto her back, covering her eyes with her small hands. "No peeking—you can't see yet," Libbi said excitedly.

Morana opened the door and guided Miranda slowly into the room; Libbi jumped off her back and ran to the bed. "What do you think—you like it don't you—I said you would."

Miranda walked over to the bed and sat next to her, "yes Libbi I like it—it's very big." She looked around the room and smiled, it was elegantly decorated in deep reds, the curtains made of the same heavy velvet that adorned the windows in every other room, also adorned the four poster bed. Miranda had no idea that velvet curtains came in such a range of colours. The furniture in this room was old, a large wardrobe, a chest of draws and two bedside tables were all oak as was the bed.

"I knew it, I knew it, I said you'd like it didn't I Ana," the girl said proudly as she jumped off the bed and skipped over to the woman.

"You did Lib," Morana smiled down at the girl.

"See you later," Libbi called dancing from the room.

Morana walked over and sat next to Miranda with a smile, "so would you like the room—you can decorate it if you don't like the colour scheme—that is, of course, if you've decided to stay with us."

Miranda looked at the woman for a moment and then shrugged, "I don't really have anywhere else to go—I do like the room."

"Good that's settled then, I hope you don't mind but Michael and I got some things for you, I've already put them in the draws and wardrobe for you, I guessed that you must be about the same size as me," she said and smiled apologetically.

"Thank you," Miranda said and smiled at the woman, "so I guess I must be ok then—considering I haven't bitten any of you yet," she said and smiled again at the woman's expression.

"I can't believe Libbi said that—I just warned her that it was a possibility, she has never witnessed a turning before and sometimes newborns become difficult—we weren't sure if this life would suit you, and I was slightly worried about the amount of time it took for your transformation," Morana said frowning.

"How long was I asleep for?" Miranda asked, standing up and walking over to the window.

"Almost eleven days," Morana answered, "and that is a long time for a vampire."

"So you weren't worried I'd bite you out of hunger—Libbi said that it sometimes happens," Miranda said looking down at the fountain that stood below her window.

"No I wasn't worried about that, as a newborn you are quite resilient, you can survive on the bottled stuff for a few weeks if you have too," Morana said smiling.

Miranda continued to stare down at the fountain below. She'd decided that she liked this woman, as she liked Libbi. Michael, from what she'd seen of him, seemed nice too, but what of Nathan and Gabriel—Nathan, as she'd thought originally, was trouble, and Gabriel—she didn't know what to think about him, she should leave her judgement on the brothers until she knew them better.

"Would you like to come down, I could show you around—if you have nothing better to do," Morana said breaking into her train of thought. Miranda smiled and nodded then followed her out of the room.

Nathanael opened the door and walked casually over to the desk, Gabriel looked up with his usual frown. "What do you want?" he asked looking back at the computer.

"You owe me bro," Nathanael said resting against the desk.

"Owe you—for what?" Gabriel said pushing him away from the desk. Nathanael chuckled then leant against it again.

"I had to lie for you."

"Lie?" Gabriel asked pushing his chair back and standing up.

"Yes lie—Miranda asked me last night just how I happened to find her," Nathanael said smirking.

"And, what did you say?" Gabriel asked frowning again.

"Don't worry, I didn't tell her your little secret if that's what you're thinking—I told her I was feeding a couple of streets away—told her I could smell her and I knew she wasn't dead blah, blah, blah."

"Did she believe you?"

"Yeah, I think so—I wonder how she would have reacted if I'd have told her the truth, how would she react if I told her my obsessed brother made me watch out for her while he was away," Nathanael said folding his arms across his chest.

"Yeah, if you told her I asked my useless brother to watch out for her," Gabriel said frowning at him, "a lot of good that did, didn't it—tell me again, how was it that you couldn't get to her in time—how is it that he got away?"

Nathanael frowned at him for a moment, and then smiled slightly, "accidents happen bro, what can I say, but at least she isn't—dead, is she?" he looked at Gabriel for a moment then pushed away from the desk. "I would have expected some kind of thanks—I could have just left her there in the street."

"Oh god, of course, where are my manners—thank you so very much for failing at the most simplest of tasks Nate, thank you so much for watching out for her, for keeping her safe and thank you for bringing her here after you'd failed so dismally at the only thing I've ever asked you to do," Gabriel said sarcastically, "let's see, have I forgotten anything, no, I think that just about covers it—now get out of my library before I lose my temper and punch you in the head."

Nathanael walked slowly towards the door then smiled as he turned back to Gabriel, "well that's just charming, I realise I've put you in a bit of a predicament, given the situation, but you realise that was the whole point of bringing her here, so I can watch you squirm," he said.

Gabriel picked up the pen pot off the desk and threw it has hard as he could towards Nathanael as he quickly disappeared through the door. It hit the door with a loud bang then fell to the floor with a dull thud, as Nathanael laughed from the hallway. He popped his head back into the room and chuckled, "hey careful—that could have hit me," he said and then disappeared again.

Gabriel stood up and walked to the window, Nate now had something else to torment him with, something else to use in his war against him . . . . how long would it be before his brother told Miranda everything. He frowned, he couldn't think about it anymore, it was hurting his head . . . . he needed to get out of the house . . . . he needed . . . . he didn't know what it was he needed.

Miranda followed Morana down the stairs but faltered as Morana called out Gabriel's name. She had to will her legs to continue moving as he stopped and turned to look at them. She placed her hand quickly on the stair rail and held on tightly as she descended the stairs slowly towards him.

He stared up at them mesmerised. He should have turned around, he should have gone straight back to the library as soon as he'd seen them, but instead he just stood there unable to move, looking up at her as she glided towards him.

"Finished work?" Morana asked.

Gabriel nodded slowly, "err, uh—yeah, I'm off out," he said and rubbed his head. Why did he always feel so tongue tied when he looked at her.

"Where are you going?" Morana asked then turned to Miranda, "maybe Miranda could join you?"

Gabriel looked from Morana to Miranda and frowned, "yeah, sure," he said quietly.

"I don't want to impose, if you'd rather go alone," Miranda said turning towards the kitchen.

"Of coarse you won't be imposing, will she Gabriel?" Morana said reaching for her arm and stopping her from leaving.

"Yeah, sure—I mean no—god damn it—of course you won't be imposing," he said quietly looking down at his feet, he should stop speaking; he sounded like a complete fool when he opened his mouth in front of her. What was he saying—she would, most definitely, be imposing—he was trying to stay away from her, and yet here he was inviting her to go for a walk—being alone with her twice in as many days was not staying away from her—his brain wasn't functioning properly—he should be running out of the front door, he should be running back to the safety of the library, but he did neither.

"That's settled then, see you later," Morana said disappearing into the kitchen.

Gabriel stood staring down at the floor for a few more seconds, "shall we go," he mumbled walking to the door and opening it. Miranda followed quietly and stood looking around her for a moment.

A long gravelled drive curved down to high black wrought iron gates, with lush green lawns on either side. On the left hand side stood the large fountain that she'd seen from her window. No water ran from the opened mouthed fish and Miranda wondered if they ever used it. "How old is it?" she asked looking back at the house.

Gabriel shrugged. "I don't know—it's quite old," he said absently kicking the stones under his feet.

Miranda looked over at him; this had been a mistake, she should have just walked straight past him as they'd met in the hall, but as he'd stood staring up at her, her mind had gone completely blank. Now they stood here, in this uncomfortable silence, and he didn't even seem as if he could be bothered to try and make conversation. She frowned and looked back at the house.

"I think it was built in the middle of the seventeenth century, they tended to make things bigger in those days—not so many humans taking up all the space," he said, following her gaze back towards the house. If he tried speaking a little slower and actually thought about the words before they poured from his mouth maybe he wouldn't end up sounding like a blithering idiot every time he spoke. He turned and walked towards the gates, Miranda followed quietly.

When they got there he pulled something out of his pocket and aimed it at the gates. He looked down at the thing in his hand and frowned.

"Damn it," he said quietly and put the object back into his pocket; he crouched down and sprung into the air, clearing the gate easily and landing quietly on the other side.

Miranda watched as he opened a mailbox, put the contents under his arm and jumped back over. She looked at him puzzled as he landed beside her. "You get post?" she asked looking at the envelopes stuffed under his arm.

"Sometimes, mainly junk—we also get papers, milk and on the odd occasion yogurt, and fruit juice," he said pulling the envelopes from under his arm and looking at them. "Mainly junk."

"But why, why milk—why yogurt and fruit juice?" she asked frowning slightly.

Gabriel looked at her for a moment, "we have to try and appear normal to the outside world, we have to fit in with their ideals—this is what humans do, they get mail, read papers, drink milk and juice, they eat yogurt—so we go through the motions in the hope that we blend in and they seem to notice peculiar snippets of information like that—who gets milk, papers and mail," he said frowning slightly.

Miranda looked at him for a moment. How could he possibly think, that he'd blend in with humans. He was as far away from normal as God was away from the Devil. There wasn't one single human on the planet that could compare to him; even the frown that he wore so often couldn't hide or take anything away from his perfection. "What do people think when they see you?" she asked quietly.

"I don't know," he said turning away from her; why did she keep asking all these questions. When he'd said she could come with him he hadn't realised he'd be called upon to have a conversation. He started walking back towards the house. "We generally keep to ourselves—that's why we live here, not too many prying eyes as in a big city—of course on the odd occasion we have to deal with people who are too nosy for their own good."

"How do you deal with them?" Miranda asked walking quickly to catch up with him.

"We either clean them or kill them," he said stopping to look at her. "There are some humans that aren't susceptible to cleaning so they have to die," he frowned and then added quietly, "we are killers; never forget that Miranda. Morana, Michael, Nathan, me, you, each and every one of us, even Libbi as sweet as she may appear, is a killer. It's our nature, it's what we are and what we will always be, we do what we need to survive—and on the odd occasion we have to kill for other reasons besides feeding."

"What is cleaning?" she asked frowning slightly.

"We quite literally clean their memories; we remove everything concerning us—but like I said some humans aren't susceptible to it," he said frowning towards the house.

They walked the rest of the way to the house in silence. Gabriel held the door open for her, but as she drew level with him she missed her footing and stumbled forward. He grabbed her in time to stop her fall, but just as before his touch sent a charge surging through her and she flinched. Gabriel frowned and released her as quickly as he'd caught her.

"God damn it, you must be the clumsiest vampire I've ever met," he snapped. He turned away from her abruptly and entered the kitchen. Miranda stood looking after him; why did she have this reaction whenever he touched her. She stood there for a few moments while she tried to compose herself and then followed him into the kitchen.

He was sitting at the table talking to Morana and Michael; he didn't look up, or show the slightest interest as she sat down opposite him. In fact he seemed totally oblivious to the fact that she was even there. Morana smiled at her and handed her a cup, Michael winked at her as she took a chair and she sat quietly listening to their conversation, all the while trying desperately not to look at the man sat on the other side of the table. And yet she still caught herself, staring at his mouth as he spoke.

"If you don't mind, I think I'll go to bed now," she said standing quickly when there was a lull in the conversation.

"Ok sweetie, sleep well," Morana said smiling up at her. Michael smiled but Gabriel didn't pay her any attention at all, he didn't even say goodnight.

She walked slowly to her room and sat on the bed, she had no idea why he seemed to find her so disagreeable. What had she done to make him dislike her, which, he so apparently did? One thing was certain; her feelings towards him were different to what he felt for her. She felt an indescribable pull towards him and it actually hurt when he ignored her.

She walked towards the window; it wouldn't be long before the sun came up. She looked at the lightening sky for a few minutes before she drew the curtains. Gabriel would never be hers that was obvious, his attitude and whole demeanour left her in no doubt as to the extent of his feelings towards her. He was as far out of her reach as the blue skies that she already missed and she wondered just how long she would be chasing blue skies.

Gabriel stood by his bedroom door and frowned at the noises coming from the room next door. He moved quickly and entered the room. Miranda jumped to her feet and looked at him, total shock on her face.

"Excuse me, I didn't realise you were in here—I heard a noise—I'm sorry," he said frowning and moving slowly backwards towards the door. He ran his eyes down the entire length of her body as his back hit the door, he fumbled for the handle for a moment, "I'm sorry," he repeated bowing his head towards her and leaving the room quickly.

He stood outside her door for several minutes with his eyes closed, why the hell had Morana put her in the room next to him, this wasn't staying as far away as possible from her . . . . a wall between them was not as far away as possible . . . . a wall between them was as close as they could be without actually sharing a room. He walked into his room and frowned, he could hear every move she made, the walls might as well be made out of paper . . . . what the hell had Morana been thinking?

8

Nathanael sat at the table and smiled over at Miranda, "so how are you finding this new exciting life?" he asked sitting forward and stroking her hand.

Miranda looked down and frowned, why didn't she have the same reaction when Nathanael touched her. He was to all intents and purposes the same as his brother, they looked exactly the same. But when Nathanael touched her, she didn't feel as if she was going to burst into flames. When he looked at her, her knees didn't threaten to collapse underneath her. The very sound of his voice didn't make her tremble inside. There was nothing about Nathanael that made her wish he'd take her in his arms and kiss her until she forgot her own name.

"So, new life—hello—" he said waving a hand in front of her face.

Miranda looked up at him and frowned, "can we go for a walk?" she asked standing up quickly.

Nathanael sat back in his chair and looked at her for a moment then stood up and followed her out of the door. "Gabriel's not going to like this," he said taking her hand as they walked.

Miranda stared down at her feet for a moment, the last thing she wanted to do was to get into a conversation about Gabriel, especially with his twin brother and especially since she was trying so very hard not to think about him. She ignored his last statement and smiled at him.

"So Morana said we all have powers—what sort of powers do we have?"

Nathanael stopped and looked at her for a moment, and then smiled, "ok, you don't want to talk about Gabe—I get it, he's not my favourite subject either, we'll stay away from all things Gabriel, but I will give you one little piece of advice—his bark is most definitely worse than his bite, no actually I got that the wrong way around—his bite is very bloody painful in all truth, never let him get at your neck because once he sinks those pearly whites in he won't ever let go."

Miranda stared at him shocked, and then frowned as he laughed loudly.

"I'm only joking—god don't look so serious, I was joking—actually I wasn't joking about his bite, it is painful—but anyway, powers, you want to know about powers," he said, sitting down on the grass. He took off his jacket and placed it on the floor next to him for Miranda to sit on. She sat carefully, trying not to sit too close; even so he put his arm around her and pulled her closer.

"Mind reading, cleaning, talking to animals, elemental control, seeing the future, telekinesis, fazing, even talking to the dead, if you believe that—those are just a few of our powers—I have four," Nathanael said. "There's only one amongst us who possesses more."

Miranda looked at him, "who?" she asked after a moment, her curiosity getting the better of her.

"Someone we're not talking about," he said glancing around at her. "He is by far the most powerful vamp I know, even the ancients were afraid of him," he said looking down at the floor.

Miranda turned to him, "who are the ancients?"

"They were the oldest of our kind, the first of our kind, every vampire that exists descended from them," he said watching her from the corner of his eye. "I wonder what generation you are."

"Generation," Miranda repeated quietly.

"We, much the same as humans, were created by someone—there are something like seven generations so far I'd guess, but I don't know for sure—the ancients didn't make too many seconds."

"Why not?"

"Because seconds have all the power of the ancients but not all of their weaknesses—it all comes down to genetics, the joining of our two species resulted in a stronger, faster breed of vampire," he said smiling as he lay back to look at the sky. "They only made eight seconds—Gabriel was never meant to be turned—he was a—mistake."

"Why was he a mistake?" Miranda asked intrigued.

"That is something you will have to ask the one we're not supposed to be talking about," Nathanael said amusement tainting his tone, "he wouldn't like the fact that we're talking about him, he's a very private person."

Nathanael closed his eyes for a while and Miranda sat looking at him, he had stoked her curiosity. Why had he been a mistake? And now she was thinking about him all over again. She shook her head and tried to push Gabriel to the back of her mind. "You said they 'were' the oldest of our kind, what happened to them?" she asked after a few moments.

"They all died—killed," he answered simply opening his eyes. "Anyway you have all the time in the world to find out about the ancients and all things vampire."

Miranda sat quietly thinking for a minute, and then frowned, "what generation am I do you think?"

Nathanael rolled onto his side and considered her for a moment. "We have no idea, considering he just left you there—you are quite baffling—vampires don't normally just turn someone and then leave them—considering the bond between creator and created."

Miranda's frown deepened, "bond—what bond—I don't understand?"

"It's very difficult to explain," he said frowning slightly. "When a vampire turns you, you become bound to him, he gave you this life, this gift, so you kind of belong to him and as your creator he has certain rights as far as you're concerned—but saying that, he did just leave you, we think he was quite new to this life himself, he may have even thought you were dead—some people are so sloppy," he said closing his eyes again. "I think it only fair to warn you, if he does ever come back, he can command you to leave with him."

Miranda sat quietly thinking about what he'd said, as he lay there with his eyes closed. Her maker could come back for her. The dark mysterious man, that had kept his face covered as he'd sunk his teeth into her flesh, could come back and claim her as if she were some sort of raffle prize. She shuddered at the thought and Nathanael opened one eye to look at her. She stood up and Nathanael opened his other eye, "I'm going in," she said quietly walking towards the house. Nathanael jumped to his feet quickly and ran after her.

"Have I upset you—Miranda slow down, I didn't mean to upset you—I just thought it was something you should be made aware of, I mean chances are he won't come back—chances are he doesn't even know you're alive," he said taking her arm and stopping her from entering the house.

She looked up at him and frowned, "what right does he have to come and take me away, if he just left me there—would I have to go?"

Nathanael frowned and then nodded slightly, "look, like I said, he probably doesn't even know you're here, I'm sorry—I wish I hadn't told you now," he said running his fingers through his hair.

"Well you did, but at least it won't come as such a shock when he does turn up to drag me off to who knows where," she said pulling away from him and entering the house.

Gabriel was sat at the table, a mug in his hand, and she faltered for a moment at the sight of him and suddenly wished she hadn't come back to the house. Nathanael walked past her and sat opposite him and smiled. "Shouldn't you be in the library working—or something?"

"Shouldn't you, not be here by now—or something?" Gabriel said smoothly looking across the table at his brother.

Nathanael smiled again and looked over at Miranda as she hovered by the backdoor, "I'm in no hurry, the house seems so much brighter these days don't you think?"

Gabriel looked over at Miranda for a second then back at his brother, "if you say so," he replied quietly. He stood up suddenly and left the room. Miranda frowned, what was it that made him dislike her so much, why did he continually treat her this way?

Her frown deepened as she walked towards the door, she turned back and looked at Nathanael who sat quietly watching her, "I'm going to my room for a while," she said opening the door.

"Ok, see you later," Nathanael said as she left the room.

As she reached the stairs the library door opened and Gabriel walked out. He stopped and stared at her for a second then walked towards her. "I need to apologise," he said looking down at the floor. "I'm sorry, I shouldn't—I mean, it was wrong—I didn't mean too—" he stopped talking and rubbed the back of his neck, he opened his mouth to say something then closed it again, and then he ran his fingers through his hair and looked back at the floor. "I was wondering, do you like to read—um, we have a lot of books and I was just wondering if you might like to have a look at them sometime, tomorrow maybe—if you want to that is," he said as he backed away from her. "It doesn't matter, I'd better—" he said turning to leave.

"Thank you, I would like to read," Miranda said quietly as he reached the door.

He turned to face her and bowed his head slightly, and then he disappeared, quickly, back into the library.

Miranda turned back and walked slowly up the stairs. She couldn't believe that he had just apologised to her, that he'd actually invited her into the inner sanctum of his library. She smiled as she closed her bedroom door. Tomorrow night she would be with him in the library . . . . and now tomorrow night couldn't come quickly enough.

Gabriel sat with his eyes closed, why did he turn into a complete wreck whenever she was around. Every time he opened his mouth complete nonsense came out.

It was quite simple, all he had to do was apologise and invite her to read and when he'd gone over it in his mind it sounded simple. Then he'd looked at her and all his carefully planned words crumbled to dust. He'd ended up sounding like a complete idiot. In over three hundred years he had never felt as tongue tied as he did when he was in her presence, and now he had to deal with the fact that she would be here, in his library, with him.

He did however have an ulterior motive; if she was here she wasn't with Nathanael and at least that would keep Morana off his back; she had made it all too clear yesterday that she thought Nathanael and Miranda shouldn't spend so much time together. He stood up and walked over to the window. He hadn't realised how long he'd been sat there, the sun would soon be up, and yet again he'd done nothing. He was having trouble doing the simplest of things since she'd arrived; it was a good job he didn't need to breathe because he was pretty sure that he'd be dead by now due to lack of oxygen.

He really needed to get a hold of himself. He left the library and walked slowly up the stairs and paused outside her room for a moment; he could hear her moving around. He closed his eyes and imagined her in there, getting ready for bed, combing her beautiful hair in front of the mirror, changing into her nightwear, he opened his eyes and frowned, he had to stop thinking about things like that.

He walked into his room and sat on the bed for the longest time, and just listened to the noises coming from the room next door.

Miranda stood with her hand on the handle for a minute before she opened the door and walked in, Gabriel glanced at her and frowned and quickly looked back at the computer screen, "you can read in here if you like," he said without looking up at her again.

She walked further into the room and looked around, he hadn't been joking when he'd said they had a lot of books. Shelves aligned the walls from floor to ceiling, and each shelf was packed with books. She walked to the furthest shelf and looked up, "won't I be in the way, if you have to work?" she asked reaching up and taking a book down.

"No, I probably won't even realise you're here," he said keeping his eyes fixed on the screen.

Of course he wouldn't know she was here, she thought glumly, why would he? She placed the book back on the shelf. She heard the tapping of keys and realised he was working. So much for conversation she thought, walking silently around the shelves. A name caught her attention, and she took the book from the shelf.

She walked over to the sofa and sat down, she kicked off her shoes and relaxed back, opening the book. Her gaze shifted to the man sat at the desk, she had a perfect view of him, and she could easily see all of his exquisite body from this position. She tried to concentrate on the book but found her eyes drifting towards him time and time again. She watched intently, seeing all the little movements he made as he tapped away on the keyboard.

Now and then he would stop typing and stare at the screen; he'd rub his chin, or run his fingers through his hair and every so often he'd mutter to himself. Miranda was mesmerised by him, at all the little movements he made and all the time he didn't take his eyes from the screen, not once did he even glance in her direction.

She started to feel curious as to what it was he was doing to make him mutter to himself that way. "Gabriel—can I ask you something?" she said quietly.

He stopped typing and frowned, "what is it?" he asked slightly exasperated at the interruption, he sat back and stretched his arms above his head, pulling his shirt taut over his torso, every single muscle looked hard and perfect underneath the thin material, and every thought in Miranda's head disappeared in a puff of smoke.

She felt the heat rising through her body as she tried to tear her eyes away. What had she been about to ask him . . . . she knew it was there, in her mind somewhere. She stared down at her hands for several seconds trying to think of what it was she'd wanted to ask. When she eventually looked back at him, he seemed puzzled by her hesitation.

"I was wondering what you do?" she said suddenly finding the question that had deserted her moments before. "For—work," she added.

He put his hands behind his head and frowned, "I write stories, but it's not a job, it's more of a hobby, I don't do it for money—we have enough money, I do it because I enjoy it—I do it because I need something to do."

"Oh right," she said nodding, "have you had anything published?"

Gabriel looked at the book in her hand and nodded, and she turned the book over to look at the cover, then she looked back at him. "Oh—OH you're N.Pride," she said feeling slightly stupid.

"Yes, I used Nathan's initial for those books—they are, after all, horror stories," he said looking quickly back at the screen. "I hope you enjoy it," he said, starting to type again.

Miranda watched him for a moment, and then turned her attention back to the book. She'd hoped for too much. She thought that maybe their relationship would become bearable after he'd apologised, but after only a short while in his company, she found it wasn't to be. He was still ignoring her; the only difference was that he'd invited her to the library to do so. With her hopes fading, she made an effort to read at least a chapter before sunrise.

As soon as she spoke, every thought in his head disappeared; he sat staring blankly at the screen. The words that he'd typed didn't seem to make any sense at all. In fact the last two paragraphs seemed to consist of random lettering and spaces, several times her name had appeared in a line. He re-read the last two paragraphs, but still he couldn't make sense of the words as they danced and swirled in front of him. He put his finger on the delete button and frowned.

Why had the library become such a small space in a matter of seconds, why had her sweet, beautiful voice invaded his mind, clearing it of every thought and why had the room become so unbearably hot? He undid the top two buttons on his shirt and rubbed his neck, he suddenly felt as if he were on fire.

Why had she sat on that couch, directly in his line of sight, it was driving him to distraction. Even as he sat there, with his eyes fixed firmly on the screen, he could see every single movement she made. Was it too much to ask that she sit on the other couch, at least then he wouldn't be able to see her, at least then he might be able to concentrate a little better. He frowned again . . . . yes, because his concentration was so much better when she was out of sight.

He closed his eyes for a moment, he should un-invite her, now Nathanael had left there wasn't any reason for her to be here at all and yet he'd still reminded her of his offer . . . . was he out of his mind? Perhaps he should find other things for her to occupy her time with. How would he ever get anything done with her here night after night?

He turned off the computer; he was fed up of looking at words that made no sense. He sat there for a few moments then looked over at her, "do you have any interests, or did you have any when you were human?"

Miranda looked up from her book; at least he wasn't frowning . . . . that had to be a good sign. She thought about his question, she'd never had time for a hobby when she was younger; most of her time had been spent looking after her alcoholic mother, after her brother Caleb had left home and abandoned her at the age of eleven. Then at the age of sixteen, when she'd finally had enough of the abuse she'd left home for a life on the streets. The city was a great place to disappear if you didn't want to be found.

"I never had time," she said quietly.

"Well perhaps now would be a good time to find something—eternity is an awfully long time to fill," he said, the frown returning.

Suddenly she had a sinking feeling; suddenly she understood the meaning behind his question. He wanted to get rid of her, if she had a hobby she wouldn't need to be here, in his library. "I like music," she said closing the book.

"Well, maybe you should learn to play an instrument," he said as a slight smile appeared on his face.

"Sure," she said as she stood up and returned the book to the shelf.

"Finished reading?" he asked as she walked back to the couch. She nodded as she picked up her shoes; she left the library without looking at him again.

Gabriel shook his head . . . . what had just happened. He thought the conversation had gone rather well, he hadn't babbled on like a fool, so what had he missed, why had she left? He stared at the door; he hadn't sent her away, hadn't done anything or said anything wrong. But as she'd left the room she'd looked despondent and he suddenly felt a little guilty. He shook his head again; all these years and he still didn't understand women.

Miranda sat at the table, Gabriel had clearly already talked with Morana about giving her a room for her 'interests' and everything was in place. The room was across the hall from the library, fitted with everything an aspiring musician could want. Now she knew the real extent of Gabriel's aversion towards her, he must have moved mountains to get everything in place so quickly.

"It's nice that you have an interest—I do hope you like everything, Michael and I had such a good time sorting things out," Morana said, though Miranda was only vaguely aware that the woman was talking, she nodded anyway. She couldn't shake the misery that wrapped itself around her three nights ago in the library.

Gabriel walked into the kitchen and sat opposite her, but she didn't look up. If he could act as if she didn't exist then she would show him the same courtesy.

"We were wondering if you'd like us to hire someone to teach you how to play," Morana said smiling over at Gabriel.

"Play what?" he asked quietly glancing over at Miranda.

"Whichever instrument she wants to learn first—Michael and I kind of went over the top, lets just say there are a few for her to choose from," Morana chuckled as she joined them at the table.

"The rooms ready?" Gabriel asked with a slight frown. He should be glad that there was something to occupy her time, he should be glad that she wasn't in his library driving him to distraction, but he wasn't. She had been there for all of two hours the other night, just two hours, and yet while he'd sat in there last night, he'd felt lonelier than he'd ever felt in his life.

"Yeah sure," Miranda said still not sure what Morana had asked her; she hoped that "yeah sure," had been an appropriate answer. She stood up and went to leave the room, but Michael reached out and took her hand.

"Would you mind staying a few minutes more, we want to talk to you—it won't take long," he said as she looked at him.

She looked at Morana then back at Michael as they smiled up at her, then she glanced quickly towards a frowning Gabriel. All she wanted to do was get away from them all, she wanted to be alone with her misery, but instead she walked back to her chair and sat down again.

Morana glanced over at Michael then smiled. "You need to start hunting," she stated in a matter of fact tone.

Miranda looked wide eyed at the woman, "hunting—but I don't know how," she said shaking her head.

"That's why Gabriel will be accompanying you," Michael said smiling over at him.

Gabriel stared at the man, and then he looked at Morana and shook his head. "Not a chance," he said quickly sitting back and folding his arms. He glanced at Miranda and shook his head again. "No I'm not doing it."

"Would you prefer us to ask Nate?" Michael asked calmly.

"NO!" Gabriel said quickly then frowned, "I'm not doing it, it's not a good idea—I'm not doing it," he said again.

"Fine, we'll just let her starve shall we?" Morana said raising an eyebrow at him. "She hasn't fed properly since she woke up Gabriel, I'm surprised she is still with us at all—she needs to start hunting properly before the hunger gets too much and you need to guide her."

"You or Michael could show me," Miranda said quietly frowning down at the table.

"Sorry Miranda but that's not possible," Michael said patting her hand, "Ana and I are bound to each other and unfortunately that disables us from doing such things—Gabe on the other hand isn't bound to anyone," he said as if that explained everything.

Gabriel frowned down at the table; he knew the argument was lost. He had absolutely no control over the situation; this was going to be a monumental mistake. And yet he'd always known that this would be down to him, with Morana and Michael being bound. So after all his arguing, after all his words to the contrary he knew that this particular job was down to him. He sat there brooding for a few minutes, well aware of how they were looking at him, well aware of the way Miranda was looking at him. "Ok, we will go tomorrow night," he said quietly as he stood up. He looked at Morana for a moment then shook his head and left the room.

10

Miranda stood looking out of the open door, Gabriel stood at her side. The rain lashed down and the wind howled loudly. "Is Libbi upset?" she asked turning towards Gabriel. He turned and looked at her quizzically. "She told me it's one of her powers, elemental control, she said if she gets upset then it usually rains—I wonder what's upset her," Miranda said quietly to herself.

"Nathan's gone," Gabriel answered shrugging his shoulders. "This will probably last for days."

"Gone?" she asked surprised. She hadn't even realised he was missing, she hadn't seen him for a few nights, but then she hadn't thought anything of it.

"Are you totally oblivious to everything that goes on around you—he left three days ago," Gabriel said impatiently. "I would have thought you, of all people, would have noticed his absence."

"Why?" she asked trying to ignore the harshness in his tone.

"Because you two seem quite close," he said frowning.

"No, I mean why has he gone?" she said looking out at the rain.

"He does it—it's his thing, he leaves for weeks or months at a time, he never tells us, just goes," Gabriel looked at her for a moment. "I'm surprised he didn't tell you that he was going though."

"We're not—" she said and then frowned as he interrupted her.

"I hope you don't have an aversion to getting wet," he said walking out into the garden.

Miranda followed quickly. She was very excited about finally tasting fresh blood; she wasn't going to let a little rain stop her. But she soon discovered it was slightly more than a little rain, because halfway across the garden she was soaked to the skin. As they reached the forests edge, Gabriel turned to look at her, he opened his mouth to speak but snapped it shut and just stood there looking perplexed. She wasn't the only one who was soaked to the skin. His shirt was virtually transparent and she could see every tiny detail of the muscular body underneath. His hair was dishevelled and spiked, the rain drops glistened in it like tiny diamonds. She watched mesmerised as small droplets of water rolled down his skin and disappeared inside the opening of his shirt.

Gabriel blinked rapidly as he tried to tear his eyes away from her. He should have called the whole thing off as soon as he'd seen the rain, but he hadn't, and now he should just run back to the house and leave her to it, but he couldn't. He had turned to look at her with the intention of saying something but try as he might he couldn't remember what it was. The way her clothes clung to her body, the way her hair caressed her face, the sight of rain drops rolling down her skin had stopped him dead in his tracks.

Miranda suddenly looked away from him, "are we still going?" she asked uncertainly, turning her attention to the darkened edge of the forest. The trees shifted and swayed in the wind, their branches appearing like thin sharp fingers reaching out to trap some unsuspecting soul. Even the well kept hedges of the maze appeared wild and unkempt as the wind whipped and whistled through them.

"Err—yes," he said sounding as uncertain as she had.

"Well let's get on with it then," she said as she shot forward, through the dense tree line. She heard him shout her name, but she didn't dare wait for him, she didn't want to look at him for a moment longer than she had to, the sight of him in the rain was more than she could handle.

She darted through the trees; she was going so fast that it didn't feel like running, it felt like she was flying. She stopped suddenly and crouched low to the floor. Different aromas flew up to meet her as she moved slowly across the ground, old tree bark, dead rotting leaves and the smells of new growth, spring was going to arrive early next year and she could smell it above all the other scents, sweet and blossoming underneath all the death.

And there was the scent she had been searching for, floating on the wind and catching her attention. She turned into it, it smelt wonderful, fresh living blood, and the burning in her stomach intensified.

A deer and a stag, stood huddled together by a tree, trying to shelter from the rain. She circled the tree where they stood several times just breathing in the sweet smell, she could hear their beating hearts, could hear the blood pumping around their fragile little bodies, louder and louder. She crouched down and watched for a while, all the time moving silently closer.

She'd waited long enough; she pushed off with both feet and flew through the air towards the animals. The only thing in her head was the heavenly smell that seemed to envelope her. She landed in the middle of the animals startling them; she wrapped an arm around the stag's neck, she felt the sudden flash of fear as it tried to run, and the doe kicked out. But she was too fast, in one lightening movement her arm shot around the doe and with a quick powerful jerk she broke its neck, the stag tried to buck but she held it easily with the other arm.

She felt a sudden change take place as the sharp fangs distended into her mouth, should it hurt like this? Should they throb? She wondered as she felt them with her tongue for a second. But as she lowered her head and sunk her teeth into the soft warm flesh all her pain evaporated. Rich thick blood filled her mouth instantly; she felt the coppery liquid seep into her throat, felt its warmth spreading through every inch of her body. The animal's heartbeat pounded in time to her own suddenly beating heart. She felt alive.

The blood didn't last long enough she thought as the stag fell limply to the floor. She looked down at the lifeless bodies at her feet; she bent down and stroked the fur. She couldn't believe that she'd thought hunting would be difficult, her instincts had taken over completely, and she hadn't even had to think about what she was doing. She heard a sudden movement and looked up quickly to see Gabriel walking through the trees towards her. He looked furious and she was just about to apologise for running off, but he spoke first.

"Why did I even bother coming out tonight? Why did they assume that you needed me to teach you anything? And why is it still god damn raining!" he shouted angrily. Miranda shivered involuntarily at the look on his face as he closed his eyes for a moment. "I knew from the very start that I shouldn't even be here with you—I tried to tell them—but they wouldn't listen, no-one ever listens—and my god—just look at you, standing there, looking so innocently at me—you just don't have any god damn idea do you," he shouted running his fingers through his hair. "It's bad enough that you don't and probably never will need me for anything—I also have the added hell of knowing—" he stopped and ran his fingers through his hair again. "But I don't care anymore—DO YOU HEAR ME, I DON'T GOD DAMN CARE," he shouted at her. He covered the ground between them quickly and she had no time to react as he grabbed her and kissed her.

Miranda melted as soon as his hands took a hold of her, her thoughts deserted her, and her legs buckled beneath her. He groaned deeply in his throat, as she kissed him back wildly. She moved closer, feeling frantic she needed to get closer. She pulled at his shirt, trying to find the buttons, but her hands were shaking too much. He pulled back momentarily and whipped it over his head. He dropped his head to hers and kissed her urgently, he shuddered as she ran her hands down his back, his muscles tensed at her touch and all the time he kissed her.

His hands moved quickly as he stripped her out of her clothes, never once did he lift his head, his lips never once left hers. In seconds they were on the floor, Gabriel moved above her, his hands and lips caressed every inch of her skin, and every place his hands and lips touched felt as if it were on fire.

She didn't feel the wet ground underneath her as they moved together as one, their bodies and movements matched perfectly, like some kind of exotic dance. She had never felt anything so intense, it was ecstasy. Wave after wave crashed into her as she felt his teeth at her throat, and when he bit down into her flesh, she couldn't believe the feeling, there was no pain just total euphoria. She felt as if she was falling, spiralling into blissful rapture, everything else started to fade away; all that she could think about was his skin next to hers.

Everything felt surreal; the world seemed to be spinning out of control. She didn't want it to end; she didn't ever want to let him go. Tears fell softly from her eyes as he whispered her name; he had wanted her all along.

Gabriel had never felt anything like it in his entire life, he didn't want to move, he didn't have the energy to move; he wanted this to last for as long as possible. How did he ever think this could be wrong? She was always meant to be his.

She gently stroked his hair as they lay together, if he died right here, right now he'd die happy. Time seemed irrelevant as they lay there together, the rain had stopped, and the wind had turned into a light breeze. Miranda watched as the first rays of dawn, crept slowly towards them across the ground.

Gabriel lifted his head; he looked towards the trees where the light had started to seep slowly through the branches and sighed. "We have to move," he said as he kissed her shoulder and got to his feet.

Miranda didn't want to move she lay perfectly still while he dressed, she watched every single movement as he did so; she was in awe of him. He gathered up her clothes and stood over her and still she didn't move. He looked towards the trees then back at her naked body, and shivered involuntarily.

"We really do have to move," he said quietly dropping her clothes beside her. He turned his back to her as she dressed. He couldn't look at her; he closed his eyes and clenched his jaw painfully. How could he have done this, how could he have placed himself above her maker and taken what was never meant to be his. Worst of all he hadn't even told her the consequences for what they'd just done. He'd just taken what he'd wanted; he might as well have just killed her himself.

Miranda didn't understand the feeling that suddenly descended on her. She felt tense, anxious. It was something she couldn't explain, but the look on his face as he'd dropped her clothes on the floor and turned away had filled her with dread. "Gabriel, what's wrong?" she asked quietly when she'd finished dressing.

"We need to get back, or haven't you noticed the sun's coming up," he said impatiently walking away from her. "If you're ready let's go," he said, breaking into a run. Miranda stood there for a second looking at the light that continued to creep slowly across the ground. The sun wasn't the reason for his sudden change of mood, so what had happened?

"Come on," he shouted angrily from somewhere in the forest.

Miranda followed and found him at the boundary waiting for her; he stood with his hands in his pockets and didn't look up as she approached. As she drew level with him he turned and walked towards the house. She walked behind watching him, every muscle in his body seemed tight, close to snapping as he pushed open the door and walked in.

Libbi had been watching them from the window and pounced on Miranda as soon as she entered the kitchen. "Did you have fun," she asked quickly, "did you like it, what did you kill—was it a deer, no a stag—it was, wasn't it, oh I wish I'd have been there, I bet you were good—was she good Gabe—oh she was, I knew she would be," the girl said excitedly.

"Yeah she was great," Gabriel muttered.

"That was cutting it bit fine," Morana said frowning as she closed the heavy curtains behind them. "I was about ready to send out a search party."

"Hope you left some for us," Michael said glancing over at them and smiling.

"Plenty," Gabriel said frowning, "excuse me won't you?"

Miranda moved uncomfortably as he rushed from the room. She looked nervously from Morana to Michael, as tears threatened to spill from her eyes, and she blinked rapidly.

"The trouble with forests, I find, is that they are awfully muddy, perhaps you'd like to freshen up dear," Michael said looking back at the paper he'd been reading. Miranda simply nodded. She didn't trust her voice well enough to speak. She ran upstairs, along the hall, and into her room. She managed to close the door before the tears started to fall.

He'd made her believe he wanted her and then treated her like a pariah. What had she done that had been so wrong? She fell onto her bed as sobs wracked her body.

11

Miranda looked over at the door as it opened slowly. Libbi popped her head into the room and smiled. "Ana wants you to come down," the young girl said dancing into the room. "She says you can't stay up here forever—no matter what you and Gabe fell out over, she said he should apologise—cause he's an idiot—and she wants you to come down and sit in the lounge with her and Michael—until Gabe says sorry."

Miranda frowned, "Ana said all that?" she asked as the young girl sat next to her on the bed.

"Well not exactly—she didn't say all the stuff about Gabe, but she thought it—which is really the same as saying it, don't tell her I told you though, else she'll get mighty mad with me," Libbi said frowning. "You won't tell will you?"

Miranda smiled and shook her head, "no I won't tell, promise."

"I do wish you wouldn't cry so," she said leaning over and stroking Miranda's cheek. "I think Gabriel should apologise—did he shout at you, he shouts a lot lately—I heard him shout at Nate—and Ana when you came—I mean he always shouts at Nate anyway—and Nate shouts back—but I never heard him shout at Ana or Mike before you came," she said and jumped off the bed "anyway come down."

Miranda watched as the girl danced from the room. She'd always known Gabriel didn't want her here and now Libbi had confirmed it, but why, it wasn't as if he even knew her, it wasn't as if she'd even done anything to make him dislike her in the way he did. So what reason was there for his behaviour?

As she walked down the stairs the library door suddenly opened and Gabriel walked out. He stopped and looked up at her, the look on his face made her knees go weak and she grabbed hold of the handrail to steady herself.

"We need to talk," he said then turned and walked back into the library.

Miranda stumbled down the last few steps and then hovered there for a few moments. She knew that this conversation was inevitable and she had to face him sooner or later, so she might as well get it over and done with. She walked into the library and closed the door quietly behind her.

Gabriel was standing by the window, bathed in moonlight and she felt the burn of desire in the pit of her stomach as she turned to look at him. She took in every single detail, the way his hair had the slightest hint of blue to it in this light, how his eyes shone as he stared up at the moon. She also noticed how his shirt pulled tight across his shoulders, and his trousers pulled tight across his hips as he stood there with his hands in his pockets.

"Sit down, please," he said without turning. It had been more of an order than an invitation, but she did as he said. She sat looking down at her hands as he walked over and lent against the desk, she couldn't bring herself to look at him, she was too afraid to see the expression on his face.

"I've been thinking about last night—I mean, I've been trying to think of an easy way of saying this—I need to—what I mean to say—" he stopped talking and frowned down at the floor. "Last night should never have happened," he said quietly then turned his back to her and slammed his hands down on the desk, making her jump slightly. "I'm sorry," he said, "that didn't come out right—what I meant to say was—god damn it—last night was."

"I understand," Miranda said keeping her eyes on her hands. It was exactly what she'd been expecting and yet every single word had hurt, every single word felt like a knife being driven into her dead heart.

He turned to look at her, she knew he was frowning without having to look up and see it. She couldn't look at him; his words caused so much pain that she was sure it would be apparent on her face. She couldn't let him see how much this was hurting her. "No you don't understand," he said quietly, "I need to explain."

"No you don't," Miranda said quickly standing up. She needed to get out of the room; she needed to get away from him. The walls seemed to be closing in on her, the room had become so small, and she was feeling slightly claustrophobic. She didn't want to hear anymore, she didn't need him to explain why he thought last night had been a mistake, she turned towards the door. Suddenly he was in front of her, between her and her means of escape.

"Miranda, will you look at me please," he said quietly, but she couldn't, her whole world was crumbling around her, and if he saw what this was doing to her, he'd know how she felt about him.

"It's ok, I understand. You don't need to say anymore," she said trying to move away from him. Why was he doing this, he had no right to treat her this way. She frowned down at the floor as the anger started to build inside her.

"Miranda!" he said again.

"I said its ok," she snapped trying to push past him, but he grabbed her arm quickly and pulled her back.

"I need to explain—there are things that—" he began but she cut him short.

"It's as you said, a mistake—and it won't happen again," she said, finally looking up at him. She hoped that this new found anger she felt would disguise her true feelings, she hoped that he couldn't see in her face that her heart was breaking. He looked stunned for a second, as he scanned her face, and then he released his grip and moved back as she walked quickly from the room.

How could she have been so stupid, she'd actually thought he'd wanted her, last night she'd thought he'd felt the same way she did. But now she knew without a shadow of a doubt that he would never feel that way. Suddenly there was an ache from deep inside, from where her dead heart lived. How could you break a vampire heart . . . . if they didn't have one to break?

He had lain, for the most part of the morning, listening to Miranda, as she lay crying quietly to herself. He tried to ignore it, he had even buried his head under several pillows in order to block her out, but he could still hear the quietest of sobs that escaped her. Until finally she had stopped . . . . she wasn't asleep, he knew she wasn't . . . . she had just run out of tears.

While he'd lain there, listening to her, he'd made a decision. He was going to explain everything, but the conversation hadn't started the way he'd hoped, his mouth started talking before his brain was in gear, and now he was left in no doubt that she didn't share his feelings at all.

He'd been completely shocked by the look on her face, she had displayed an icy indifference which had been so unexpected that it had completely stunned him. That look on her face had told him all he needed to know. It told him that she had no real feelings for him, last night he'd fooled himself into thinking that she felt the way he did. He had hoped for a split second, as she lay in his arms, that she did, but it was all just wishful thinking on his part. He was a pathetic excuse of a man, he had actually thought that she was crying because of him, but he knew by the look on her face that she was just disgusted and sickened by the events of the previous night.

At least he hadn't made a complete idiot of himself, and that was something to be thankful for. At least he hadn't got as far as to confessing his undying love for her. Imagine the pain he'd have suffered when she had rejected him then; imagine the look on her face as he'd told her he loved her with all his heart. He sat down heavily in the chair and buried his head in his hands.

At least now he knew, without doubt, the extent of her feelings towards him. Now all he had to do was to try and put the whole thing behind him, bury it deep and never think of it again. But he didn't know how to achieve that, he still loved her, still wanted her, no matter how much pain she'd caused him.

"I can't do this," he said quietly into the empty room.

12

Miranda turned off the stereo and frowned, she lay back and closed her eyes and listened to the voices coming from the kitchen. Gabriel had apparently given up on spending his nights in the library, she had been waiting several hours for him to leave the kitchen, and yet he was still in there. She was hungry—starving in fact and she'd waited long enough. She stood up quickly and walked to the kitchen, before she had chance to change her mind. She hesitated for a moment before she pushed the door open.

He was in the middle of a conversation with Michael, but he stopped talking mid-sentence as she stood behind him. She saw how the muscles in his back became almost ridged with tension before she looked away from him towards Morana.

Morana looked up at her with a smile. "Well hello stranger," the woman said moving towards the cupboard. "I wasn't sure if you were still with us sweetie," she joked as she opened the door, "no-one has seen you for days—I thought you'd done a Nathan—so what's your poison."

Miranda looked at the bottle in her hand then back at Gabriel as he turned slightly to look at her, and she realised that bottled blood just wasn't going to do the job . . . . she needed to kill something. She needed fresh blood. She shook her head and frowned, "no thanks."

Morana raised an eyebrow at her as she turned quickly towards the backdoor. She was aware that Gabriel was watching her as she stood there with her hand on the handle so she turned back to look at him as she pulled the door open. The look on his face caused her to waver for a second.

"I wish you would make up your mind what it is you want," she screamed silently in his direction. "See you later," she said quietly as she turned and walked out into the cool night air.

"Whoever would have though she'd take to this life so easily, she is quite divine—don't you think Gabriel?" Michael said leaning back in his chair.

Gabriel sat staring at the door, he heard Michael's voice, knew the man was talking to him, but his brain was having great difficulty processing the words. He was too busy trying to contain the pain deep within him to concentrate on what the man was saying.

"I wish you would make up your mind what it is you want," her voice had screamed at him. He'd heard it so clearly. As if she had actually said the words, but she hadn't because her lips hadn't moved, and he knew this as a fact because he'd been looking her in the face.

Michael frowned over at him then looked at Morana, as she walked over to the table. "Gabe, are you alright?" she asked leaning over and looking at him.

He heard Morana speak, was even aware that she was looking at him, but he couldn't answer. Her words echoed in his head, "I wish you would make up your mind what it is you want," she'd screamed, but he didn't need to make up his mind, he already knew what it was he wanted . . . . and the thing that he wanted had just walked out of the backdoor.

Morana turned to Michael, "what's wrong with him?" she asked a worried expression on her face.

"GABRIEL!" Michael shouted. He jumped at the sound of Michael's voice, and blinked rapidly as he took in the concerned faces in front of him.

"What's wrong?" Morana asked.

"Nothing, I err—I need to go and um—I have to—" he frowned and stood up quickly, "something has to be done—I have to do something," he said as he moved towards the backdoor. He lifted his hand to the handle then stopped; he stood there for a moment staring at his hand. What was it that he had to do? Go after her? No, that would be a huge mistake, he couldn't follow her. He dropped his hand and moved away from the door, he turned to Morana and Michael who sat looking rather puzzled by his unusual behaviour.

"I need to go out—that's what I need to do, but not that way," he stood and frowned down at the floor for a moment. "Hunt—I need to hunt," he said quietly walking quickly from the room.

Morana and Michael sat in stunned silence for a moment. "Could you please tell me what, on gods green earth, was that all about?" Michael asked looking over at Morana.

"I have absolutely no idea," Morana frowned.

Miranda had felt rather relieved when she'd returned from hunting to an empty kitchen; she didn't think she could face him again tonight. The blood that ran around her veins had eased the pain of seeing him a little but if he had still been here sat at the table, she wouldn't have coped.

She walked to her music room and stood outside it . . . . she didn't want to spend the rest of the night alone, there were still several hours until the sun came up. She stood outside the shared room, "what if he was in there?" her mind asked, "so what if he is," she answered herself quietly. "Isn't this the first sign of madness, talking to oneself," her mind said quietly. "Yes and the second one is answering oneself back," she said as she pushed down on the handle.

Michael and Morana were sitting together on the couch as she opened the door; Michael tossed Miranda the remote control as she entered the room. "Nothing on—we are quickly approaching the realms of day time telly," he joked as she caught the remote. "Only a few more hours until sun rise."

Never in a million years would she'd have guessed that vampires would spend their time sitting in front of a TV. She placed the remote on the table without even bothering to look, she had no interest in television; she had no interest in anything. She was restless, she was bored . . . . this life wasn't all it was cracked up to be.

"Why don't you read?" Morana suggested seeing the expression on her face. "Gabriel isn't here but I don't suppose he'd mind you going and getting a book."

Miranda nodded, "I think I'll take it to my room," she said getting up and walking to the door. She said goodnight and left. She paused outside the library, reading wasn't what she wanted to do; she didn't know what she wanted to do. She walked through to the kitchen and stood at the backdoor for a second then opened it. She stepped out into the cool night and looked over at the maze. She wondered if she should go and have a look at it, she made her way quickly to the opening and peered in.

It looked even more daunting tonight, maybe because she was here alone. She stopped and smelt the air. She dropped down to a crouching position as she'd done in the forest and picked out Gabriel's scent. She reasoned if she stayed low she should be able to traverse the maze and be able to find her way out easily. When Nathanael did come back, she would beat him at his own game, at least she'd have beaten one of them she thought wryly. She wouldn't need Gabriel to save her ever again.

She weaved in and out of the hedge rows confidently and it wasn't long before she'd reached the centre. She stood next to the statue looking up into the sky. Both looked like beautiful pale sculptures and Miranda wished she was this woman stood silently in the dying light of the moon, sculptures didn't suffer; sculptures didn't ever feel the pain of rejection. She moved away from it and frowned, "god damn you, Gabriel Pride."

She walked back through the maze slowly, she had no interest in going back to her stuffy old bedroom; she had no interest in going back to the house at all. She found the opening of the maze easily and chuckled quietly to herself.

She didn't notice Gabriel striding towards her until he shouted. "Where the hell have you been?"

She frowned up at him, as he reached her quickly, he was angry at her . . . . what had she done this time? "I went for a walk," she said trying to walk past him, but he moved to block her way.

"Didn't you think to tell someone? You've been gone nearly two hours. I come back and the house is in an uproar, no one can find you—but apparently you just decided to go for a walk—have you even noticed the sun is rising!" he shouted looking down at her. For a moment she was stunned by his anger.

"I'm sorry, I didn't notice," she said quietly looking over towards the trees where the sun had started to rise. "I'm sorry," she said again as she tried to walk around him, but his hand shot out grabbing her arm.

"Don't you dare walk away from me Miranda, are you deliberately trying to get us killed?" he said through gritted teeth. "Have you got a death wish—good god you're just so stupid sometimes!"

"Yes Gabriel I am stupid—stupid, foolish Miranda," she shouted angrily up at him, "if that's all, let me go," she said pulling herself free; she pushed past him and ran back to the house.

Gabriel stood staring after her; he clenched his fist tightly and closed his eyes, then his eyes snapped open and he stormed back to the house after her.

Miranda ran to her room and closed the door. She needed time to get control of this sudden anger that burned within her and she should give him time to calm down too . . . . yet more time spent trying to stay out of his way. He had looked so angry that she'd actually felt a little frightened of him. She could easily understand why he and Nathanael fought all the time with his temper the way it was.

Her door flew open and Gabriel barged in. He looked even angrier. "How dare you walk away from me when I'm talking to you!" he raged.

"Haven't you heard of knocking? Get out of my room," she shouted as she moved forward to push him back towards the door, but he didn't budge an inch.

"You owe me an apology," he grated.

"I already said I was sorry—I won't say it again—now get out of my room," she shouted trying to push him again. He grabbed her hands and held her still.

"I could have died out there trying to find you and all because you didn't have the decency to tell anyone where you were going," he shouted back at her.

"I didn't ask you to come looking for me, and I certainly don't expect you to die for me, I thought you would have realised by now that I don't need you for anything Gabriel," she said, trying to pull her hands from his.

"Well next time I'll just leave you out there," he said tightening his hold slightly, "but until the next time you could perhaps start thinking about someone else other than yourself and have a little consideration for the people who took you in and put a roof over your head, instead of being so god damn selfish," he said trying to contain the pain that her words had caused him. He released her hands and turned away from her.

"Selfish," she repeated the word and frowned. "You're calling me selfish, of all the nerve—you're hardly in any position to pass judgment on anyone—you're hardly a picture of perfection yourself—well just maybe I should remove my god damn inconsiderate, selfish self from your house," she yelled, "then you wouldn't have to put yourself in life threatening situations would you."

Gabriel lost control of his anger; he turned around quickly and lashed out at her, slapping her hard across the face. Miranda stumbled back onto her bed; she blinked up at him as tears filled her eyes. He turned and strode towards the door then stopped and turned back to her. "You are unbelievable—you ungrateful little—fine, leave—it's not like I wanted you here in the first place—I have far better things to do with my time than to babysit an unappreciative brat like you," he shouted then he turned and left slamming the door behind him.

Miranda sat stunned looking at the door. She couldn't believe he'd hit her. She had given him the perfect chance to get rid of her and he'd taken it, he couldn't wait to be rid of her. She buried her head in the pillow and cried.

The moon shone down through the library window, lighting up his face as he sat there with his eyes closed. He didn't know what to do. He wanted to go to her and apologise but how could he, there was nothing he could say that would make up for what he'd done. He'd just been so angry and hurt by her words that he'd lashed out at her, he'd wanted to hurt her as much as she'd hurt him.

She had cried nearly all morning, and he'd had to lie there in his bed listening to her sobs, which he had, yet again, caused. How could he ever look at her again?

When he'd returned Morana had been frantic, Miranda had said she was going to bed, but when Morana had gone to check that she was alright she was nowhere to be found. They had searched the house and Michael had gone into the forest to search for her there. In the two seconds it had taken him to run from the house and join Michael in the search, a thousand images of what life without her would be like had run through his mind. He had felt sure that after his behaviour she had simply had enough and left.

Then as he'd stood by the house considering his next course of action, she'd appeared around the hedge of the maze. He hadn't even considered the maze after the last incident in there; he had just expected the worst. He knew he should have just let it go, he should just be thankful that she was alright. But then as they'd stood arguing in her room, and she'd actually threatened to leave, he'd lifted his hand and slapped her so hard it had stung his palm for the rest of the day. What type of apology was there for that?

The library door flew open and Libbi ran in, panic in her eyes. "You gotta go and stop her," she screeched pulling at his sleeve. "Come on, you gotta tell her you're sorry and you gotta make her stay."

Gabriel frowned down at the girl.

"She's packed some clothes and she's gonna leave unless you go and stop her—Gabriel please don't let her leave—go and tell her how sorry you are," Libbi cried pulling him to the door.

"Ok," Gabriel said as the girl pulled him frantically into the hall.

"Hurry up—go and stop her," she said pushing him up the stairs.

"I'll try but I'm not promising anything Lib," he said walking up the stairs towards her room. He stood outside, not knowing what to do. He knocked the door and waited for her to answer; when she did he walked in.

She was standing with her back to him, doing the zip up on the bag in front of her. "What do you want Gabriel?" she asked without turning to look at him.

"Libbi told me you were packing," he said quietly.

"Do you want me to leave in just the clothes on my back," she said dropping the bag to the floor.

"You don't have to leave," he said.

"I could have sworn you told me to leave, don't you remember, you said it this morning, right after you slapped me around the face."

"I'm sorry," he said looking down at the floor.

"Oh well, that's fine then—as long as you're sorry—let's just forget the whole thing ever happened—but what if I should make you angry again Gabriel? What will you do next time?" she asked turning to look at him.

He looked up at her, and frowned at the slight mark she still had on her face. He moved towards her slowly and gently brushed her cheek. Miranda pulled back instantly and frowned at him.

"I promise I will never touch you again, just please don't leave," he said moving back slightly.

"Why, Gabriel, because you want me to stay so much—tell me, would it really break your heart to see the back of me?"

"We don't want you to go," he said looking back down at the floor.

"We?" she questioned.

"I don't want you to go; I didn't mean what I said last night—I was just—I was just," he stopped talking as he tried to find the right words and then frowned.

"I think I'd better, if I'm not here your life will be so much easier, with no unappreciative brat to baby sit," she said sarcastically picking up the bag, she threw it over her shoulder and turned towards the door. He moved in front of her to block her way.

"Please Miranda—I don't want you to go—please—please stay," he said reaching out for her hand. She pulled back quickly before he had chance to touch her, he frowned but dropped his hand quickly.

Miranda stood looking at him; she had been so ready to go, resigned to the fact that he didn't want her here. She was so angry with him right up until he'd walked into her room this evening. As soon as she'd turned around and looked at him, all the anger seeped out of her, and now she just wanted to forget the whole thing.

"So will you stay?" he asked as she turned away from him again.

"I don't think I should," she said although she dropped the bag onto the bed.

"Please don't leave," he said quietly.

She stood looking down at the bag, and then undid the zip; she didn't want to go anyway. "Ok, I'll stay."

Gabriel watched her for a moment as she started to unpack her things. He'd been ready to drop to his knees and beg her to stay if that's what it took, he would have dropped to his knees and begged and pleaded for the rest of eternity, if that's what it took. "I'll go and tell Libbi," he said quietly turning towards the door, "she'll be so happy that you decided to stay."

Miranda stopped what she was doing and turned to look at him as he disappeared out of the room. She just knew it was too good to be true. How foolish of her to believe he wanted her to stay, how foolish to believe he was truly sorry for what he'd done . . . . when it was all for Libbi.

She turned around and sat down heavily on the bed. It didn't matter what he did to her, she would always forgive him, he would say sorry and he would win. She was destined to spend the rest of her life in misery, hoping that one day he'd want her, hoping that one day he'd love her. She was destined to chase her blue skies for the rest of eternity.

13

Morana linked her arm through Miranda's as they walked down the street, and smiled slightly as a young man whistled at them from a shop doorway. "These humans are so easily impressed," Morana said quietly as Miranda glanced at the man.

Miranda frowned and looked around. She had hated this City when she was human and she was still far from impressed as a vampire. At least on the outskirts where they lived there were colours, not just deepening shades of grey and miserable. The buildings here held a certain uniformity that she'd never even noticed as a human, every other shop was boarded up and every few steps there seemed to be another darkened alley down which to drag ones meal for the night.

"So are you feeling confident sweetie, you know you can ask me questions and I can answer, I'm just not allowed to help you with the kill," Morana said frowning a little.

Miranda shook her head, it had been decided that Morana would have to accompany her on her first ever human kill, Gabriel had probably refused outright, and for that she was thankful . . . . she didn't trust herself enough to go hunting with him again if the forest was anything to go by.

Morana patted her hand gently, "I have the utmost faith in your abilities," she said and smiled.

Miranda stopped suddenly and turned to look back down the street, she tilted her head slightly as she listened to the whispered voice of a young girl. "Please stop—let me go, I won't tell anyone I promise," she said between quiet sobs.

Miranda frowned and looked at Morana, "do you hear that?" she asked as she turned in the direction of the girl's voice again.

"Yes, but it's none of our business, come on," Morana said trying to pull her in the opposite direction, but Miranda pulled herself out of the woman's hold and walked slowly towards the sobs. "Miranda, it's nothing to do with us—leave it alone."

"Please don't, don't—don't," the voice said again.

Miranda watched the scene for a moment, she took in every detail of the darkened alley in front of her, from the fire escape on the right hand building, just five foot above the girl's head, to the boarded up windows of floors two and three of the building on the left. Hardly any light shone on the two people down at the furthest end, but Miranda could see them with crystal clarity. The man towered over the girl, her clothes were ripped and muddied, her hair was tangled and dirty, and tears streamed down her face as the man stood there with the knife to her throat.

The girl turned her head slightly and looked at Miranda, with pleading in her tear filled eyes. The man was too busy undoing his zip to even notice Miranda as she moved silently towards them. She stopped just behind the man.

"Get away from the girl," she said quietly.

The man spun around, startled by her voice. He seemed stunned as he stood there staring at Miranda. She moved forward slowly and reached out for the knife, she took it from him then threw it to the floor. She turned back to him and grabbed him around the throat forcing him against the wall, at the same time she grabbed the girl and pulled her away from the man and into her body.

The girl gasped for breath, as Miranda's vice like grip forced the air from her lungs. Miranda lessened her hold; she kept forgetting how strong she was compared to the feeble humans. She looked down into the young girl's face for a moment then smiled. "The street isn't the place for a pretty young thing like you," she said looking into her eyes. "There are a lot of people who really don't care whether you live or die—there are also things here that are far more dangerous than he is," she said nodding towards the man. "I don't care what made you leave home, Charlotte, but you really should go back—nothing about being there could be as bad as being here," she said and smiled. Then she looked deep into the girl's eyes. "Now when I release you, you will turn around and walk away from this alley, you won't remember me, you won't remember him; you won't remember anything about this."

Charlotte looked into Miranda's eyes and nodded. Miranda released the girl slowly and reached into her pocket and pulled out a note. She handed it to Charlotte and smiled, "a nice hot meal and a drink—oh and Charlotte, be a little more careful in future," she said stepping back slightly. Charlotte took the money and smiled, then walked quickly from the alley.

Miranda turned back to the man, his face had turned a purplish blue as she'd been talking and she suddenly realised that she was strangling him, she lessened her grip and chuckled. "So what am I going to do with you?" she pondered as he gasped for air.

"Let go of me you bitch," he said trying to pull away from her.

"Now, now, there is absolutely no need for language like that—I probably saved you from a long stretch in prison," she said as the man tried to claw at her arm. She moved closer to him, and smiled. He tried desperately to get away when she removed her hand from around his neck, but she held him easily between her body and the wall.

"Get away from me you bitch!" he shouted still struggling against her.

Miranda slapped her hand over his mouth quickly. His eyes started to water and Miranda watched slightly mesmerised, as blood trickled from his nose and down the back of her hand. "I'm sorry, I realise that I've probably just broken your nose, but I already said there's no need for language like that."

"GUT TA FK F MI U FK BIT," he yelled against her palm.

Miranda chuckled at his attempt to speak then frowned, "well I'm definitely not letting you go with language like that—you're a regular little potty mouth aren't you."

"LE MO GU—U HTIN MI," he said renewing his efforts to escape.

"Oh I'm nowhere near to hurting you yet—you really haven't got a clue about how much I can hurt you, have you? when I told pretty little Charlotte that there are more dangerous things here than you, I meant myself—you really think you're a dangerous little man, but you're nothing compared to me—and now I'm going to show you just how dangerous I can be," she said grabbing his arm, she jerked it back at an unnatural angle and grinned as the bone snapped loudly in the quietness of the alley.

The man howled in pain against her hand, tears streamed from his eyes, and he choked slightly on his own vomit. "Ples li mi go," he begged against her hand, "LI MI GO!" he begged as his eyes started to close and his head lobbed to the side.

Miranda frowned and then shook him vigorously. "Don't you dare pass out on me—I haven't finished with you yet—I was under the impression you liked it rough," she said a wicked smile curving her lips, "it is a little unfortunate for you that I'm in a bad mood—I would have made this quick and as painless as possible, but you disgust me—you are a disgusting excuse for a human being, you make me sick—you and your kind—preying on the weak, but compared to me you're the weak one," she said smiling as the fangs distended into her mouth.

"NOOOOO!!" he shrieked against her hand as she dropped her head to his neck.

"And just so you know I never had any intention of letting you go—now hold still and take it like a man," she whispered as she sank her teeth into his flesh.

His struggling only lasted for a few seconds more as the blood flowed freely into her mouth, his heartbeat pounded in her head as she sucked every last drop of the warm coppery fluid from his body. It crept slowly through her veins causing her flesh to tingle; a slight thrill ran down her spine as her heart sprung to life, it faltered for a split second as it altered its rhythm to that of the dying man's until his last heartbeat exploded in her head and the heat filled her completely.

She lifted her head slightly to look at his face as his head lobbed to the side. She stood there for a few seconds more then moved away and watched with amusement as he slid down the wall. His head hit the floor with a dull thud.

Morana drew level with her and frowned down at the body for a moment, "well maybe not the best of starts—but I must say finely executed nonetheless," she said stooping down quickly and picking up the body.

Miranda turned slightly to look at the woman as she threw the corpse over her shoulder, she hated this city—she hated the reeking stench of the humans that lived in it—Nathanael was right, she felt absolutely no guilt at taking the mans life—a vampires conscious was after all a small and insignificant thing.

Gabriel sat frowning down at the table as Miranda walked into the kitchen. She hesitated for a moment at the sight of him, as he looked up at her.

"We need to talk," he said turning his attention back to the table.

Miranda walked around the table and sat down, she knew she should have gone straight to her music room. Morana had obviously told him about last nights hunting expedition and now he was no doubt going to shout at her again, and get angry at her, again.

"What the hell did you think you were doing?" he said as she sat there looking at him.

Miranda frowned there was nothing like getting the pleasantries out of the way first, but what had she expected . . . . did she think he'd start the conversation by asking how she was . . . . hardly likely since he didn't even seem to be able to look at her these days.

"I didn't think I was doing anything," she replied quietly.

"And that's the whole point—you didn't think—you never think," he said annoyed. "Miranda listen, we don't get involved with humans and their problems, ever—why do you think we have survived as long as we have—it's because we are so very careful in everything we do—what do you think would happen if they ever found out about us? You think they would just sit back and let us carry on regardless? No they wouldn't—they would hunt us down and kill us—and they wouldn't stop until we were all dead—we may be strong and powerful creatures, but not even we could take on the entire human race—they outnumber us thousands to one."

He sat back in his chair and looked at her for a moment then rubbed his head, "it isn't our job to save them, it's our job to feed on them."

"I wasn't trying to save anyone," she said quietly looking down at her hands.

"So why is the girl still alive—surely killing her would have been an easy task—the point is that you let her go, you saved her—what do you think would happen if she goes and tells someone?"

"There was no need to kill her—I cleaned her," Miranda said looking up at him.

"Oh really—and tell me are you sure it worked?"

"Yes I am sure it worked," Miranda said annoyed at his lack of confidence at her abilities.

"But what if it hadn't worked—not all humans are susceptible to being cleaned—I've told you this before," he said frowning at her again.

"Yes, I remember quite clearly what you told me Gabriel, and it did work so there's no point discussing it—I'm not as incapable as you think—I know that I haven't been around as long as any of you and I know you don't pay much attention to my existence—so I should point out that I have progressed astoundingly, since the last time you raised your head enough to look at me—and I know that the cleaning worked," she said standing up, she frowned down at him for a moment, "is that all?" she asked.

Gabriel looked at her for a second then nodded slightly, "yes, that's all," he said quietly looking back down at the table.

He sat there with his eyes fixed on his fingers as the door closed behind her and frowned. She thought he didn't pay much attention to her existence . . . . he paid the utmost attention to her existence; she was the only thing he ever thought about. Every single second he was awake he thought about her, then he would go to bed and dream of her all day. He closed his eyes for a moment as the memory of how her skin felt against his ran through his mind.

Miranda sat down heavily on her couch; it hadn't gone as bad as she'd expected it to. He had frowned several times, but he hadn't raised his voice, so all in all it hadn't gone too badly. His lack of confidence hurt almost as much as his ability to totally ignore her existence. She sat back and closed her eyes as she remembered how his hands had felt on her body.

14

Gabriel popped his head around the door and smiled slightly at Michael as he looked up, "do you mind if I join you?" he asked as he entered the room.

"Of course not, I'd be happy of the company," Michael said frowning slightly.

Gabriel took the seat opposite and stared over at him for a moment, "what's wrong—you seem a little tense?"

"Ana and Miranda hunting again," Michael said shortly, and Gabriel grinned. Michael always got himself into a state when Morana went hunting without him. "You just know she'll pick a man because I'm not with her, and I'll smell him on her—and then we will argue for days—I should have gone with them," he shook his head and frowned over at Gabriel. "So how come you're not in the library tonight?" he asked sitting forward.

Gabriel sat forward and looked over at Michael, "I need the company—to tell you the truth I can't concentrate on work, so what is the point of trying—I just sit there staring at the screen—I spend all night just thinking about, well you know what I think about," he said frowning slightly.

Michael smiled and inclined his head, he looked at Gabriel for a moment and sat back, "what are you going to do when she remembers everything Gabe, I mean—you know it's only going to take one misplaced word."

"Cuimhnigh Orm are hardly misplaced words Mike," he said sitting back and closing his eyes.

"Yes you have a point, but I hate seeing you like this," Michael said folding his arms. Gabriel opened his eyes and looked at him and frowned. "Just tell her—take her to the library, sit her down and just tell her everything—if not for your own sanity then for mine and Ana's."

"How exactly do you suggest I start the conversation?" Gabriel asked frowning. "Oh by the way Miranda I've been watching you since you were a baby, and when you were seven I had to clean you—I've been stalking you for the last seventeen years, watching you nearly every single night of your life—oh and another thing, if having a vampire stalker for nearly two decades wasn't bad enough, I've probably sentenced you to death, after our first night in the forest, because I wasn't able to control myself around you—but not to worry, because having your head hacked off with a silver sword shouldn't hurt all that much—if indeed that is all your maker will do to us."

Michael looked over at Gabriel with wide eyes, "Oh!"

"Yeah, oh! I told you and Ana it was a bad idea, but neither of you listened, and I am trying so hard to stay away from her, so hard—and every time I look her I just want to—" he stopped talking and buried his head in his hands.

"You have to talk to her Gabe, you have to try and make a start," Michael said.

"Yeah, but how? I mean she can hardly bring herself to look at me—can you imagine the look on her face if I were to try and explain things to her—after the last time we spoke she's hardly said a word to me, and if we meet in the hall she quickly disappears into her room, or runs up the stairs—even when I do try I just make a mess of everything—the night after the forest I tried to explain things, but I just got everything wrong—and even if I hadn't, she didn't want to know—the look on her face, god the look on her face Mike," he shuddered at the memory, and the sudden pain in his chest caused him to clutch at his ribs.

Michael looked at him for a moment, and then shook his head, "you have to start talking to her—I don't think it will be as bad as you think Gabe."

Gabriel stood up slowly, "I don't think I can—you didn't see the look on her face Mike—I just don't think I can," he said then walked out of the room.

The light in the restaurant was almost non existent; the candles on the tables lent a certain ambience to the eatery. Miranda stared into the candles flame as her 'date' ate his meal. She looked up at the youth as he moved to attract her attention and smiled at him; he smiled back and leant towards her.

"I want to thank you again, this is absolutely the best meal I've had in months," he said putting another meatball into his mouth, he smiled again. Miranda looked at his mouth, he had a beautiful smile, but now she looked at him closely, he was as different to Gabriel as any man could be. How could she ever hope to find him amongst these mortal beings?

"So why aren't you eating? These meatballs are to die for," the young man said stuffing another in his mouth. She felt like laughing at the irony of his statement, but instead she frowned.

"I don't like Italian, it doesn't sit well," she said patting her stomach, his eyes followed her hand down to her perfectly flat midriff, and he stopped chewing for a moment as his eyes wandered over the rest of her body.

He sat up straight and tilted his head for a moment, and then asked, "are we going somewhere after this?"

Miranda smiled, "I don't know, is there anywhere you would you like to go?"

He thought for a moment and then grinned, "I haven't slept in a bed for over a year, and it would be good to take a shower, maybe a hotel for the night."

Miranda smiled, but said nothing.

The young man popped the last morsels from his plate into his mouth then sat back and sighed loudly.

Miranda raised her hand to the waiter and asked for the bill. She turned towards Morana and she nodded as Miranda silently though, "I'll meet you back at the car in half an hour."

Miranda heaved the body into the boot of the car, with ease. She slammed it shut and then rested against it for a while. The young man had tasted alright when she'd stopped gagging on the overpowering smell of damp human flesh, she maybe should have taken his advice and let him take a shower, but at least he didn't have that overpowering stench of humanity to him any longer—now he just had the bearable stench of death. She smiled as Morana sped around the corner; she moved away from the car and opened the boot. Morana brushed herself down after she'd dropped the corpse in and slammed it shut. She smiled at Miranda as they both leant against the car for several minutes.

"Ana, can I ask you about something?" Miranda said after a moment.

"Sure, you can ask me anything sweetie?" Morana said turning slightly to look at her.

"I think there may be something wrong with me," Miranda said uncertainly, "I know you said I'd have difficulty with my powers to start with—but my power of recall doesn't seem to be working properly—it's so strange—I don't seem to have any memories from my childhood, I can remember most of it but—I don't seem to have any memories until the age of seven."

Morana smiled slightly, "Sweetie, you're far too impatient; you haven't even been a vampire four months yet, give it time."

"So you don't think there's anything wrong with me then?" Miranda said still a little uncertain.

"Of course there isn't anything wrong with you, it will all come eventually—four months in this life is a blink of an eye, trust me you'll be fine," Morana said reaching out and patting her hand, she moved away and got into the car.

Miranda remained where she was for a moment and tried hard to remember something from her childhood, but there it was, that blackness that swirled around in her mind, that solid brick wall, that no matter how she tried she couldn't see through. She got into the car and glanced at Morana, she wished she could be as confident as the woman seemed to be about her powers, but she was sure there was something wrong with her.

Michael opened the front door as they pulled up outside, he walked out to the car and opened Morana's door and looked curiously at her, "hello my love," she said putting her hands on his shoulders and jumping out of the car, "Aww you've missed me haven't you—well I'm back now my lover, no need to worry," she chuckled lifting her head for him to kiss her, "my GIRL was absolutely gorgeous—I might share her with you, if you promise that you've stopped sulking," she laughed wrapping her arms around his neck.

Miranda turned away from them quickly and walked into the house, she couldn't bear to see the love they had for each other. A sudden hopelessness engulfed her; she was never going to experience the kind of love that Morana had with Michael . . . . and yet all she had been focusing on was the fact that her recall wasn't working properly . . . . what good was recall to her, when all her memories would be filled with Gabriel frowning . . . . and arguments with Gabriel . . . . or Gabriel shouting at her . . . . what good was recall when all you ever felt was misery. She sighed and walked into the kitchen.

Gabriel was leaning against the counter as she entered the room, the sight of him sent her legs weak, and she sank deeper into misery as he looked at her and frowned. She was about to turn around and leave when he spoke. "Is it raining?" he asked moving slowly towards her. Miranda shook her head and frowned. "Then what is that smell?" he said wrinkling his nose.

Miranda lifted her arm to her nose and sniffed then wrinkled her nose too, she smelt so bad. Gabriel moved closer to her and smiled his dazzling smile. "I guess dinner was a little damp," she said and stiffened slightly as he undid the button on her jacket and pulled it off her; he threw it into the washing basket and sniffed her again then smiled.

"That's a little better," he said turning away from her and walking back towards the table. "So how was—"

Miranda turned quickly and left the room, she couldn't stay and listen to what he'd been about to say, his closeness had disturbed her equilibrium and she was in fear of collapsing into a heap right in front of him. She hurried to her room, undressed quickly and got into her bed. There were still a few hours before the sun came up, but his actions had thrown her into turmoil.

It had been some time since he had stood that close to her and her heart had missed several beats as he pulled the coat off her. Even as she lay there it pounded rapidly, and she tried hard to calm herself. She needed to get control of her emotions; she didn't want to feel like this anymore. She turned her head into her pillow and moaned.

Gabriel stood looking at the door; he shook his head and sat down on the chair. What had he done to make her run away this time?

After his conversation with Michael he had decided to at least try and talk to her, and he'd thought now would have been the perfect time. She had already fed, so she had no need to run through the backdoor as soon as she saw him and there were still a few hours until the sun came up, so she didn't need to run off to bed . . . . or so he'd thought.

As she entered the kitchen she had frowned as she'd seen him, but she hadn't pulled away as he'd helped her out of her coat, and he had, apparently mistakenly, taken that as a good sign. But as he'd turned away from her, she'd bolted from the kitchen; she hadn't even afforded him the courtesy of staying to listen to what he'd been saying.

Was this the true extent of her feelings towards him, were they such that she couldn't even stand to be in the same room as him? He knew she didn't want him but he was starting to accept the fact and move on. He shook his head . . . . who was he trying to fool? Whenever the thought crept into his mind, his world crumbled a little more and the pain that gripped him threatened to reduce him into a blubbering idiot.

Perhaps he should face the fact that they would never be anymore than this, strangers that did their very best to avoid each other. He put his head in his hands; this wasn't what he wanted, he had to do something about it.

Morana watched Miranda disappear quickly up the stairs and frowned, what had Gabriel done this time. She walked to the kitchen and smiled at a slightly perplexed looking Gabriel. "What did you do?" she asked joining him at the table.

"I have no idea," he said shaking his head.

She reached over and took his hand in hers, "I hate to be the bearer of bad news, but Miranda has started asking questions about recall—she thinks there is something wrong with her Gabe."

Gabriel closed his eyes and shook his head; he'd known this would happen sooner or later . . . . though he had hoped it would be later.

"I think I managed to put her mind at ease for the time being—but sooner or later she's going to need to be told," she said letting go of his hand.

He put his head in his hands and sat there for a while and Morana watched him. "I tried to talk to her, but she walked out, I don't know what to do anymore, Ana—I realise that I haven't exactly been, friendly, towards her since she's been here, but even when I try she just—I don't think she can even stand to be in the same room, what am I supposed to do?" he said running his fingers through his hair.

Morana sat looking at him for a moment then smiled, "find a common ground, find out what she's interested in and talk to her about it—it's a start at least."

Gabriel frowned slightly, "I don't suppose you have any idea what she's interested in do you?"

Morana shook her head, "seventeen years and you're asking me what she's interested in?" She chuckled suddenly and reached out and tapped his hand, "I do know that she was thinking about the ancients—and don't you give me that look—you can't tell me that you've never read someone's thoughts without them knowing," she said as Gabriel gave her one of his reproachful looks.

He looked at her for a moment then smiled widely, "perhaps all the time spent studying the ancients could pay off after all—I mean I am an expert in the field of all things ancient aren't I," he said sitting back in his chair.

"Indeed," Morana said standing up, "now I need to get back to Mike, would you believe he's still sulking," she said and chuckled again as she moved away from the table.

"Yeah, I know," Gabriel said laughing quietly, "thanks Ana, I sometimes wonder what I'd do without you."

"You are very welcome sweetie," she said kissing him lightly on the head as she walked past.

Gabriel walked into the library and stood there for a moment looking up at the bookshelf, the ancients could prove invaluable to him after all.

15

She walked slowly down the stairs, pondering the thought of spending another lonely night in her music room when the door to the library opened and he walked out. He looked up at her and smiled. She wondered briefly if she should turn around and go straight back to her room, but the sudden pain in her chest stopped any kind of movement and he appeared to be waiting for her. She forced her suddenly heavy limbs to carry her the rest of the way down the stairs and he smiled again as she reached the bottom.

"Morana said that you seem interested in the ancients, we have the original tomes if you would like to read them, they are quite interesting," he said.

Miranda frowned for a moment, last night he'd spoken to her, had acted almost friendly for a change and now was he actually inviting her into his library? What had happened . . . . had she been so lost in her own misery that she hadn't even noticed it when their relationship had shifted?

He turned and walked back to the library and opened the door, and then turned back to look at her. He stood watching her for a moment and frowned slightly, he'd been sure this would work, but as he waited for her, doubt started to creep into his mind. She looked uncertain, as if she was going to turn around and run away, but suddenly she moved towards him, and entered the library.

As she drew level with him she thought she heard him mutter, "see that wasn't so difficult was it." She turned quickly to look at him and as with every other time she was in his company, she lost all control of her limbs and stumbled into him. His arms were around her in a split second.

"Are you ok?" he asked looking down into her face.

She looked up at him for a moment then nodded. He looked down into her face for a few seconds more then released her gently, he moved away from her to the nearest bookshelf with a slight chuckle, "as I've said before, the clumsiest vampire I've ever met."

Miranda grabbed the bookshelf, as he stood with his back to her; she needed to hold on to something while she regained control of her legs. She watched slightly enthralled as Gabriel rose upwards into the air to retrieve five rather large, rather heavy looking books from the highest of the shelves.

"These," he said touching the floor silently, "contain much of the ancients history, from the time they arrived in England, these notes date back to the thirteenth century, but no-one really knows how long they'd existed before then—it's a good job you enjoy reading, these will keep you busy for a while," he said dropping them onto the couch. He looked over at her, as she remained at the bookshelf and frowned, "I suppose you could take them to your room if you'd prefer to read them there," he said bending to pick them up again.

"No, I'll read them in here," she said quickly. She moved over to the couch and sat down. She didn't trust her legs to support her weight a moment longer, every single time he looked at her and smiled her knees went weak. He stood looking down at her as she looked at the books.

The gold lettering stood out against the blood red leather of the cover, as she ran her fingers over the words she realised they were sunken and not raised as she first thought. 'Vampire Tome I' the letters read.

"Where did they come from?" she asked looking up at him.

"The council gave them to me after the ancients died," Gabriel answered a slight frown on his face.

"The council?" Miranda repeated mirroring his frown.

"Yes, there is a vampire council—though they aren't as powerful now as they used to be, the seconds joined together to form a group, they made their own rules to try and govern our kind—we have to have rules too—but we are, I'm glad to say, left to our own devices nowadays."

Miranda nodded slightly then turned her attention to the first page of the book. There was a list of ten names, unusual names she thought as she looked down them. Decastell was at the top of the list followed by Ambrose, there was a slight gap then eight more names were scrawled underneath. Anouk, Zeke, Cormack, Freya, Vania, Carad, Shavaun and lastly Ariel. She was so engrossed in the names that she hadn't realised that he'd sat down next to her. She looked up at him as he started to talk.

"This book belonged to Decastell and Ambrose, each of the tomes are written by two of the ancients, they all liked to keep notes on different things—Decastell and Ambrose were the most powerful of the ten—when they arrived in England, Decastell and Ambrose stayed together throughout their lives, the others seemed to go their own ways for a short period, but after a while they discovered there was safety in numbers."

Miranda smiled slightly, "because we were so much stronger than they were."

"Yes," he said looking questioningly at her for a moment, he frowned and looked down at the book, "just imagine creating something that was far superior to the creator, that's what they found when they created the second generation—there are only about eight or nine of us in the world," he said and again he frowned. "And there were only ever two firsts as far as I know."

Miranda looked down at the book and then back at Gabriel, "I don't understand—weren't the ancients the first generation?"

Gabriel smiled and shook his head, "no the ancients were a different breed of vampire to us—they were pure vampire—they weren't bitten, as we were, they weren't transformed—I don't think they were ever human."

"So what is the difference between firsts and seconds?" Miranda asked again.

"It's kind of difficult to explain—first generations, as the ancients called them, were created from their letters, but they found that the first were ridiculously strong—a lot more powerful than they were, hence there were only ever two made," he said and smiled as she frowned again.

"What are letters?" she asked feeling more confused by the second.

"The ancients chose a family, for blood letting—they weren't the best hunters, they weren't as fast or as strong as us—so they, more or less, brain washed humans into giving up their blood freely," he said frowning at the thought. "They would get many rewards for their consent of course, for example financial gain, exceptionally good health, a long life and so on—the ancients would stay with their family of chosen ones for centuries, moving on to the next generation when they needed too," he explained.

Miranda closed the book and moved it off her lap then turned to face him, "why didn't they change, if the ancients kept feeding from them?"

"Well, the ancients were able to control the flow of venom, it was one of their gifts—seconds can also do it and I assume that the firsts could too, though neither of them lived long enough to find out," he said and mused over the idea for a minute.

"So you don't actually kill people?" Miranda asked frowning at him.

"Actually yes, I do, I said I could do it, not that I do, do it—it is a little difficult to control and takes all the enjoyment out of feeding—and I enjoy feeding—the only pleasure I have in this life," he said quietly looking down at his hands, "and anyway letters were outlawed by the council after the demise of the ancients—they saw them as a liability, and with the ancients gone, letters were no longer needed."

"So you were explaining why they didn't turn," Miranda said returning to the original conversation.

"Yes," he said looking up at her again, "when an ancient fed from their letter only the smallest amount of venom would have entered the body—that initial surge, as their teeth punctured the skin—but it was the smallest amount, it wasn't enough to change them—and after so long, they built up a resilience to it anyway," he said and smiled at her. "They also discovered that it was passed on from generation to generation—they were still human, just a little different, each generation showed different abilities like speed, strength, intelligence—nothing so obvious as to draw unwanted attention, but most had very good lives," he said then sat back and rested his head on the back of the couch. "Vampire venom is responsible for nearly all human advancements over the last thousand years," he said smiling slightly. Miranda tilted her head and frowned slightly as she tried to figure out if he was joking.

"As the ancients moved onto a new letter, the venom in the old letter would slowly diminish over the years, they would die a natural death and that would be an end to it—but, if during that time, they were bitten with the intent of changing them, they would become first generation vampires," he said turning his head slightly to look at her.

"So exactly how much venom does it take to turn a normal human?" Miranda asked curiously.

"When we break the skin, we have about twenty seconds, after that the damage is done—when you were bitten, do you remember the feeling of floating?" he asked frowning slightly. Miranda nodded, she remembered she'd felt as light as a feather. "Well as soon as that feeling starts, its the point of no return—that is unless of course all the blood is drained from the body—when we drain all of the blood we are also draining the venom out, kind of how you would with any kind of venomous bite," he said the frown still on his face, "that's why feeding seems a little euphoric—we are not immune to the effects of vampire venom—even our own."

"So we can affect other vampires with our venom," Miranda stated looking down at her hands, remembering all too clearly the night in the forest when Gabriel had bitten her.

"Yes, I would imagine it acts pretty similar to the way a narcotic would to a human—it can also be used as a weapon, disabling an enemy—enough venom renders us unconscious," he said and smiled again as she looked up at him.

Miranda considered the answer for a few seconds . . . . whoever thought a vampire's venom would be so complex . . . . then she frowned slightly. "So the first—first—what happened to him?"

"Her, she was an experiment—Decastell and Ambrose were curious about the effects being turned would have on the letters, a trial took place, and they soon discovered they had absolutely no control over her, she was apparently so strong that it took six of them to kill her—you would think after all the years they were alive they would have learned from their mistakes—Anouk paid the ultimate price for her mistake," he said a slight grin on his face.

"Anouk—why, what happened to her?" Miranda asked a little puzzled.

"She decided to turn her letter, but it didn't quite go to plan—the change had a detrimental effect on his mind, he may have loved Anouk while he was human, he may very well have agreed to it, but the change was too difficult for him, from what they wrote about Nadia—I assume that the power they possessed was to difficult to handle, physically and mentally—and as I said it didn't quite work out the way Anouk hoped, soon after he'd changed he killed her," Gabriel said and smiled again.

"But how did he kill her?" Miranda asked feeling even more confused by his statement.

"I suppose he ripped her to pieces—there were lots of ways in which one could kill an ancient, but I don't really know, it doesn't go into detail of how it was done in the tome," he said looking down at the book.

"No, I mean how could he kill her, if he was bound to her?"

Gabriel turned towards her; "did Nathan tell you about that?" he asked frowning.

"Yes, he told me about it, and that one day he will return to collect me," she said quietly looking down at her fingers.

"What else did he tell you?" Gabriel asked. Miranda looked back at his face and was a little taken aback by his expression.

"Nothing, just that I'm bound to him," she said quietly, she couldn't stop the shudder that ran down her spine at the thought of her maker coming back to claim her. She looked down at her hands again; she had made him angry again for some reason. His frown had deepened and his jaw was suddenly ridged with tension.

"Err, well firsts and seconds aren't ruled by the ones that make us, we are—" he couldn't finish what he was saying and turned away from her for a moment. He felt that familiar, crippling pain sear through his body at the mention of her maker, and it took all his strength not to cry out in agony.

"I'm sorry—I have to—do you mind if we carry on with this later, I have to—excuse me," he said suddenly standing and leaving the room.

Miranda sat staring after him. The night had been going so well, he hadn't frowned as a direct result of something she'd said or done and they were having a proper conversation, but as it had veered in the direction of her maker the atmosphere had suddenly changed, the tension in the air had seemed almost palpable and Gabriel had looked as if he were in pain as he'd rushed from the room. She frowned down at the book for a moment then snapped it shut.

He kicked the dead deer at his feet so hard that it flew through the air and hit a nearby tree with a loud crack. Everything had been going so well, then the conversation of her maker had started and the world started to crumble around him. The pain still throbbed through him now.

He had to try and get control of this and he had to do it quickly, before it ruined everything again, how could he possibly form any kind of relationship with her if he had to keep running away. He still couldn't stand the thought of her maker touching her, of sinking his teeth into her, of owning her.

He walked slowly back to the house and realised the sky was already showing signs that the night was drawing to an end. He'd spent at least the last two hours in that clearing, just lying there thinking of the time they had been there together. He'd thought about it until it had driven him mad and he'd had to kill something.

As he entered the library he saw she was sleeping, he walked quietly over to the desk and sat down. He wondered for a moment if he should wake her, but she looked so peaceful and serene that he just wanted to look at her. He smiled to himself as he felt the usual feelings stir deep within. She was so beautiful she made him lose control of all his senses, physically and mentally.

She started mumbling quietly and he was totally mesmerised. She said something about someone without a shirt, about being in the rain. He didn't want to listen but he couldn't stop himself. But then he froze as she said his name, at first he wondered if he'd imagined it, but he knew that he hadn't, it was crystal clear. She had definitely said Nathan. She'd been dreaming of his brother and that had hurt more than he could ever have imagined. He sat there stunned for several seconds as, yet again, the pain threatened to rip him to shreds.

She opened her eyes and sat up quickly, she looked lost for a moment and then her eyes focused on him, "oh hi, I didn't realise you were back," she said seeming confused.

"Obviously not," he said curtly looking at the computer screen.

"I'm sorry, I fell asleep," she said uncertainly.

"Yes I noticed—do you know you talk in your sleep?" he said abruptly. "You have to excuse my ignorance, but I didn't realise that you and my brother were quite so close," he said glaring at her.

"We're not close—we're—" Miranda began to say but she closed her mouth as he stood up quickly.

"Oh really, not close, but close enough to have seen him without his clothes on, and I was thinking I was special—my god, I am so stupid," he almost shouted walking towards her quickly. "Was he as good as me I wonder or was I better—did you enjoy being able to compare the two of us? Tell me which did you prefer Miranda—me or Nathan?"

Miranda shrunk back into the couch; she noticed how tightly his fists were clenched as he looked down at her. He grabbed hold of her arm and pulled her roughly to her feet and stood staring down into her face.

"Perhaps you need a little reminder as to how different I am compared to my brother," he rasped lowering his head to hers. His mouth claimed hers; the kiss was aggressively hard as he bit down angrily on her bottom lip.

Miranda tasted the blood seeping into her mouth, as he forced her back against the couch. Her legs buckled beneath her and they fell down onto it. His hands moved swiftly finding the bare skin under her blouse, and she tried hard to suppress the moan that escaped her as his fingers dug savagely into the tender flesh of her breast. He forced his body between her legs and she shuddered as he dropped his head to her neck, his teeth grazing her skin.

"Tell me Miranda, am I as good as my brother," he said quietly running his lips down to the opening of her blouse. Suddenly he jumped to his feet, and grabbed her roughly by the arm, he pulled her up and then grabbed the books; he thrust them into her arms so hard that it took all her strength to remain standing.

"I think it might be a good idea if you read these in your own room after all," he fumed. "I don't want you here, I can't stand the sight of you a moment longer—you make me sick—I mean my brother for god's sake."

Miranda stood looking at him stunned for a second and then turned quickly and walked to the door, arguing was useless, he had already made up his mind on the matter. She could tell he wasn't going to give her chance to explain. "And in future, if you need any answers try asking your lover," he shouted as she left the room.

She sat on the floor by the bed as tears fell from her eyes, and she wiped them away angrily, only for a fresh wave to fall. Her dream had started as it usually did with her running in the forest, of her feeding, of Gabriel taking off his shirt and then of him taking her in his arms and kissing her. The rain pelted against them as they lay naked on the ground. But as the dream had ended an image of Nathanael had appeared in her mind.

"Miranda Bombanda," he had chuckled. "Are you missing me?"

"Where are you, when are you coming home?" she'd asked.

"So you are missing me then?" he'd grinned then reached out to stroke her cheek.

"No I'm not—Libbi is," she'd answered as his hand skimmed her face.

"Well in that case I won't bother coming back, what's the point," he'd said as his image started to fade. "I won't come home until you ask me to, oh please Miranda do ask me, I miss you and Libbi so much—I'd even endure my brother for you."

"Come home Nathan," she'd heard herself saying as his image flickered then disappeared completely.

She'd woken suddenly and couldn't quite remember where she was, until she saw Gabriel frowning angrily over at her. She had no idea that she talked in her sleep, she had no idea that he had been sitting there listening to everything she'd said. His reaction had come as quite a shock, as had the way he'd accused her of doing things she hadn't done.

The way he kissed her had also come as a surprise, and although it had been slightly painful when his teeth had broken the flesh on her lip, she'd had that feeling of euphoria. The way he'd pressed his body against hers and the feel of his hands on her skin had made her head spin. She crawled into bed and lay there as more tears fell from her eyes, and she stayed there as night turned into day and then into night again. She stayed there as another day arrived and departed and finally she fell asleep.

16

She became aware of a loud rapping; someone was tapping at her door, someone wanting to know if she would ever come out of her room again. Maybe Libbi, or Morana she thought as she sat up sleepily, before she had chance to answer Nathanael walked in. He smiled and jumped onto the bed next to her. "I can't believe you're still in bed, sun's been down for hours," he said making himself comfortable.

"When did you get back?" she asked as he moved closer and put his arm under her head.

"Oh," he said looking at his watch, "about two minutes ago." Miranda moved away from him slightly, but he tightened his hold so that she couldn't get up completely. "So how are you?" he said putting his free arm behind his head.

"Fine," she said.

"Only fine," he said quietly, "what's wrong?" he asked turning to look at her.

Miranda shrugged, "nothings wrong—I'm fine."

"I know what it is, you're bored aren't you—I suppose my brother has been wrapping you up in cotton wool, smothering you," he said sitting up. "Well I'm back now so come on get up, get dressed and we'll go do something fun." He jumped off the bed and left the room.

Miranda dressed quickly and opened the door, Nathanael was stood leaning up against the door frame waiting for her, and he smiled as he took her hand and pulled her down the stairs.

Gabriel was in the hall, outside the lounge, as they walked down the stairs. He looked at Nathanael and frowned then he glanced at Miranda.

She didn't have time to decipher the look on his face before he looked back at his brother. "I didn't realise you were back," he said quietly.

Nathanael smiled broadly and glanced at Miranda for a moment, then turned back to Gabriel, "we're off out, you want to come?" Gabriel shook his head and looked down at the floor. "Your loss, bro," he said pulling Miranda through the kitchen door.

Gabriel stood there and watched them leave and frowned again. The lounge door opened and Morana walked out stopping level with him. "When did he get back?" she asked frowning. Gabriel shrugged and walked to the front door. "Gabriel, you have to do something about this—she shouldn't be spending time with him," Morana said following him.

He turned back and frowned at her, "what exactly do you suggest I do? If you hadn't noticed we're not even on speaking terms—you think she'd listen to me if I told her to stay away from him?" he said angrily.

"How do you know if you don't try," Morana said irritated.

"I don't need to try when I already know the outcome of the conversation," he said opening door, "I'm going out," he said walking out and slamming it behind him.

Morana shook her head and frowned again, she knew how difficult the situation was for him . . . . but it seemed as if he'd already given up . . . . in all the years she had known him, she had never seen him looking so defeated.

Gabriel stood looking at the house for several second, then took a step back and jumped over the gate. He walked slowly up the drive and frowned as he heard Miranda laughing, the sound rung in his ears and made his insides twist painfully, he'd give just about anything to be able to laugh with her like that.

He walked into the kitchen and smiled at Michael as the man dropped the paper on the table, "I haven't looked yet," he said referring to the nightly routine of scanning the pages for anything out of the ordinary.

"It will give me something to do," Gabriel said and frowned as he sat down at the table and opened paper.

"Happy reading," Michael said walking from the kitchen and leaving him alone.

Miranda collapsed in a heap on the ground, as Nathanael dropped down beside her and frowned. She turned and looked at him and started laughing all over again when she saw the frown deepen slightly.

"You've been practicing," he accused lying back and looking up at the stars.

"No I haven't, I've been wrapped in cotton wool remember," she laughed turning on her side to look at him. They lay there for a few minutes in silence, and then Nathanael turned to face her, his eyes sparkling in the moonlight.

"So why didn't you tell Gabe I was coming back?" he asked raising an eyebrow at her.

Miranda frowned at him, "I didn't know you were coming back."

"I can quite clearly remember you saying come home Nathan," he said smiling slyly, "so of course I'd come home considering you asked so nicely."

Miranda's frown deepened, "why is it that you find it so easy to do that—stop it—I don't want you in my head all of the time." Nathanael glanced at her and smiled. "I mean it Nathan, stop it," she said angrily.

"Ok, I promise from now on I will only do it with your strict permission," he said holding up his hands up. "Anyway, come on I'm hungry, let's get something to eat and then I might take you back into the maze and show you how we really track," he said pulling her to her feet and dragging her back towards the house.

Gabriel was sitting at the kitchen table as they entered, looking down at a paper, and she instantly tried to pull her hand out of Nathanael's but he tightened his grip and led her to the table. He still didn't release her as they sat down, even though she tried several times to pull away from him.

"So what have you two been up to while I've been away?" Nathanael asked smiling over at Gabriel.

"Nothing much," Gabriel said without looking up.

"Oh come on, I've been gone so long—you trying to tell me that you haven't done one single thing together—I don't believe that for a second."

"Believe what you want, you usually do," Gabriel said quietly.

"What have you done to my brother Miranda?" Nathanael asked smiling at her wickedly.

Gabriel raised his head slightly to look at Nathanael, "it's obvious you have something on your mind, so just get on with it—or is this just another one of your pointless conversations," he said quietly.

Nathanael looked at Gabriel for a moment and smiled, "no it's not at all pointless Gabe," he said sitting forward slightly. "My guess is that you're being your usual pragmatic self brother—and poor Miranda here doesn't know if she's coming or going because of your inability to act in an appropriate manner while you're around her—I bet you've never even took the time to talk to her have you—to find out what goes on in that beautiful head of hers," he said glancing around at Miranda and grinning, "but I know what goes on in her mind bro, I know what she thinks about," he said putting his arm around her and pulling her closer.

"Nathan, don't," Miranda whispered.

"It's ok Miranda we're all friends here—I think it's only fair that he knows how you really feel about him and I could tell you what he thinks of you too—you want to know how he feels about you don't you Miranda," Nathanael said grinning at her.

"Shut up," Gabriel growled glaring at him.

"Life would be so much easier if you both just talked to each other," he said smiling over at Gabriel. "So let me get the ball rolling—Miranda, I bet you'd be surprised if I told you that Gabe has spent the last seven—" Nathanael didn't get chance to finish what he was about to say, Gabriel jumped across the table at him sending them crashing to the floor as the chair slipped underneath their weight.

Gabriel jumped up and grabbed hold of Nathanael's shirt and pulled him to his feet; he pulled back his fist and smacked it hard into his jaw.

"Shut your mouth now, our relationship has nothing to do with you," Gabriel hissed and brought his fist back to hit him again but Miranda jumped up and grabbed his arm.

"Please don't fight," she said moving quickly in between them, "please," she said looking up into Gabriel's face. She placed her hands gently on his chest and ignored the pulses that raced up her arms, "please don't fight," she repeated quietly.

Gabriel was stunned for a moment, she had actually touched him without shrinking back or flinching, and even though he already felt tense, he still felt every muscle in his body wind a little tighter. He looked at her for a moment, then up into the grinning face of his brother as he stepped back. He frowned at Nathanael for a moment then turned and walked from the room without another word.

Miranda turned to face Nathanael and frowned and then turned quickly and almost ran through the backdoor. He smiled slightly then went after her. "What the hell was that—what were you trying to do?" she shouted turning on him.

"I wasn't trying to do anything," he said innocently smiling at her.

"Yes you were, I told you to stay out of my head, how dare you read my thoughts and then try and use them against me—you are—" she stopped talking, she couldn't think of a suitable enough word without using bad language.

"I have stayed out of your head, like I said I would," he shrugged nonchalantly.

"So why did you do that—why did you tell him you knew what I thought about him—that was just—you are just—" she said turning away from him. She started to walk towards the forest; she wanted to get away from him.

"Miranda, I'm sorry, I didn't mean to upset you," he said walking after her, "stop, look I'm sorry—I just wanted to get some sort of response out of one of you, instead of that uncomfortable silence that seems to have developed between you, I mean it's obvious that something has happened while I've been away."

"Nothing has happened," she said turning and frowning at him.

"Of course, nothing at all has happened, that's why he can barely look at you, and you don't seem to want to be in the same room as him—I just thought if I got you two talking it might help," he said taking her hands in his.

"Well it wouldn't, so stop trying—there is nothing going on!" Miranda said pulling away quickly and turning back towards the trees.

"Nothing at all?" he asked stopping her again.

Miranda glared at him. "I thought you could read my thoughts."

"And I thought you didn't want me too," Nathanael said and smiled slightly.

"I don't, so—don't," Miranda said frowning at him.

"Ok—I promise, never again," he said placing his hand over the spot where his heart should have been. "Friends," he smiled offering her his other hand.

"I don't know yet—I'm still angry with you," Miranda said turning away from him again. Suddenly she was unsure of where she was going, she didn't want to go into the forest, and chances were that Nathanael would just follow her anyway. She turned to him again and frowned, "do you intend following me all night," she asked sarcastically.

"Do you want me too?" he asked amused at her tone.

"No I don't, go away."

Nathanael considered her for a minute then laughed. He stooped low to the ground in an elaborate bow and chuckled, "as you command, ma-lady," he turned quickly and strode away leaving her staring after him. She soon heard the sound of a car engine disappearing off into the distance and wondered fleetingly how long it would be before he came back.

Gabriel sat with his head rested against the high back of his chair, his face tilted towards the ceiling, his eyes moving rapidly behind his closed eyelids . . . . replaying the scene from the kitchen over in his mind. He should have ripped Nathanael to pieces, he should have beaten him to a bloody pulp but Miranda's intervention had put an abrupt stop to that.

His chest was still burning from her touch and his whole body ached with being so close to her, he wasn't at all surprised by his reaction, but hers had completely baffled him . . . . it was the first and only time since the forest that she had voluntarily touched him and it had totally thrown him.

He opened his eyes and frowned, it appeared that he hadn't been far off the mark when he'd accused her of being with Nathanael . . . . after the events in the kitchen it was blatantly apparent that she had feelings for him, why else would she have jumped in and stopped the fight.

He closed his eyes as tears started to well in them, how would he cope if she had fallen in love with his brother . . . . he had never even contemplated the though until now, even after the other night . . . . and if that was the case how long before he confessed undying love for her . . . . how long before they left together . . . . how long until Nathanael finally took his revenge.

17

Miranda circled the garden a few times, before she felt able to go back to the house. She still felt so angry at what Nathanael had done, how could he be so nice one minute then a complete ass the next. She stood looking at the house for a moment and frowned as she wondered what Gabriel was doing, would he have calmed down by now?

She walked to the door and pushed it open, to her surprise Gabriel was sat at the table; she'd been sure she wouldn't see him for the rest of the night. He looked up and smiled as she walked in, it dazzled her for a second, and it took all her strength to move. She wished that he wouldn't do that, or at least give her some sort of warning before he did. "What sort of warning should you give someone before you smile at them?" her brain asked.

"Can we talk?" he asked sitting back in his chair. His eyes stayed on her face as she tried to decide what to do.

She should just ignore his request and go to her room. They hadn't said so much as a word to each other since the last incident, but she was fed up of trying to avoid him all the time. She walked over to the table and sat opposite him.

"I need to apologise," he said looking down at the table. "And not just for what happened with Nathan—I need to apologise for the other night—I was—" he stopped talking and frowned up at her. Did he dare to say any of the words that ran through his head, hurt . . . . devastated . . . . jealous? "I'm sorry—for the way I treated you, for the way I acted," he continued, looking down at the table again. "It seems that I'm always apologising to you for something—and I don't know about you, but I don't want things to be this way between us all the time—I was wrong to accuse you the way I did—I had no right, whatever you do with my brother is entirely up to you," he said rubbing at his forehead as he frowned again.

Miranda looked at him for a moment, "you know that Nathan and I aren't—that we haven't—" she said shifting uncomfortably as he looked up at her.

"It's none of my business," he repeated but his frown disappeared slightly, "I have a problem controlling my temper as far as my brother is concerned and Nathan loves to make my life as difficult as he possibly can," he stopped talking for several minutes and then sighed and looked up at her again, "has he told you anything about how we became vampires?"

Miranda moved uncomfortably in her chair as she remembered the night Nathanael had mentioned it. She shook her head and looked down at the table.

"And you're not in the least bit curious about it?" he asked.

"I didn't think it was any of my business," she said shrugging. She was curious about it, but she also remembered his reaction that night. The memory seemed to cause him pain and she didn't want to do anything to cause him pain.

"You're part of this family now so it is your business," Gabriel said sitting back. "You will hear it from someone sooner or later, and I think that I'd better tell you before my brother does, he tends to be a little colourful in his version of the facts, and it may also shed a little light on the nature of our relationship." He rubbed his chin for a moment and sat forward again, "I don't suppose you'd believe me if I told you that Nate and I were very close when we were human," he said quietly. Miranda simply shook her head as answer.

"Well, we were, I was the eldest—by sixteen minutes and miraculously we both survived child birth," he moved uncomfortably in his chair. "When our parents died we were fourteen. It fell to me to look after us both—Nate didn't handle our parents sudden demise very well, so I took care of him—anyway when I got to about eighteen I grew curious about the world, I wanted to travel—Nate did not, he was in love with Sophie by then—after five or six years I was summoned home again to attend their wedding," he stopped talking for a minute and rubbed his head.

"We were quite well off and we inherited our parents house, but I wanted to travel, so I gave Nate my share of the house and left shortly after the wedding, but I was summoned back after another seven months—Sophie was pregnant," he stopped talking and closed his eyes for a moment, "while I was home I went out with a few friends, and while I was out I was attacked," he said flatly, sitting back again, "as I stumbled drunkenly from the tavern they grabbed me, pulled me down a darkened alley—and the rest as they say is history."

"Who were they?" Miranda asked quietly.

"Shavaun and Ariel," he answered frowning. "I didn't stand a chance, not against two of them—anyway I changed within a couple of hours, it was the worst pain I'd ever felt in my whole life, they had pumped me so full of venom that I changed almost instantaneously, I didn't know what had happened to me when I regained consciousness, I was totally disorientated and I was in so much pain that I just wanted to go home," again he stopped talking and dropped his head.

When he looked up again Miranda was shocked by the tears in his eyes. "Nate didn't notice the change in me, he let me in—and the pain was unbearable—I wanted it to stop—I would do anything to make it stop—and I did make it stop. I killed Sophie—I sank my teeth so far into her neck that she wasn't even able to scream with the pain—and she tasted so—good."

Miranda remembered the pain well, she hadn't been able to scream either; she hadn't been able to do anything.

"I could hear Nate screaming, begging me to stop—but I couldn't—she tasted so good," he said wiping the tears from his face. "When I finished Nathan attacked me—he broke, I broke nearly every bone in his frail human body—I couldn't control myself. As he lay there sobbing, next to Sophie, slowly dying from the injuries I'd bestowed upon him, the thought occurred to me that I was going to have to live for eternity without my brother—and I couldn't stand the thought of being alone—so I decided to turn him," he said and shook his head.

"I didn't know that he'd bring all those feelings into this life, the love he had felt for Sophie, the anger and hate he felt towards me for what I'd done—I sat with him as he changed, and he never once lost consciousness. He lay there calling her name, and telling me how much he hated me—three days I had to listen to him, three days of hatred, three days of agonised screams as the broken bones repaired themselves—three days of tortured screams and broken sobs."

Miranda frowned; she could understand Nathanael's animosity towards him. She knew the power of perfect total recall. He had lived all this time with those memories, her heart ached for his pain. But Gabriel also hurt, because didn't he also have the gift of perfect recall too—it was still so apparent on his face even after all these years.

"Nate didn't want this life, he would have happily died along with his wife and unborn child—he has never and will never forgive me for what I did—he takes every opportunity to remind me of what happened and how much he still hates me, he uses everything he possibly can to hurt me—and that includes you," he said quietly then stood up quickly and left the room.

Miranda sat staring at the door as it slammed behind him. How did Nathanael use her, she shook her head, she didn't understand the meaning behind his last statement.

The backdoor opened and Nathanael walked in, he stopped suddenly and frowned at her. "Miranda what's wrong?" he asked hurrying to her side. She hadn't even realised that she was crying until he wiped a tear from her cheek.

"Nothing, I'm fine—it's just—Gabriel told me how you became vampires and—" she stopped talking then as the words caught in her throat. She rested her head on his chest as he tightened his hold. "I'm so sorry," she whispered.

"Please don't cry," he said his voice cracking and she lifted her head to look at him as the first tears fell from his eyes.

"Nathan," she whispered as he lowered his head to hers. She froze as his lips touched hers. The shock vibrated through her body in reaction; her head screamed at her to pull away from him, but she couldn't move as his pain wrapped itself around her, as the things he felt ran through her mind—his pain was still so raw and it made her whole body ache with sorrow.

She wasn't aware of the kitchen door opening until Nathanael pulled away from her, she stared up at him for a moment, she wasn't aware that Gabriel was stood watching them from the doorway, until he spoke. "I err—I'm sorry—I didn't realise—sorry," he said. He stood there momentarily stunned looking at them both then shook his head. "Sorry," he repeated again then turned and left.

Gabriel stood pressed up against his bedroom door with his eyes closed. He couldn't move, his limbs felt heavy and painful and his head was spinning. He felt sick to his stomach.

Everything he'd done since she'd arrived had been wrong, he'd stumbled blindly into one mistake after another and now he'd actually succeeded in pushing her into the arms of another man. Not another man . . . . his brother. He dropped to the floor and clutched his chest . . . . was this how it felt to have your heart ripped out? It was pure agony.

He managed to crawl over to the bed and drag his heavy aching body onto it. He now knew what it felt like to see her in his brother's arms . . . . it was absolute torture.

He couldn't stay and watch Nathanael take away the only woman he had or would ever love, he couldn't sit back and simply watch them together . . . . it would kill him. He curled himself into a ball; the pain that gripped him was so unbearable that he simply didn't have the strength to move.

He lay silently for the longest time, until the shaking stopped, until the agony lessened enough for him to think properly. He sat up and wiped angrily at his face. He needed to leave because if he stayed he would kill Nathanael and quite possibly Miranda too. He leaned over and took a small note book out of his draw, he had to write Morana a note, she would only worry if he took off without a word.

But what was there to say? Should he tell them why he was leaving? Should he say that his heart had finally died its last death . . . . that everything he'd waited for, everything he'd ever wanted had been stolen away from him? Should he tell them everything and give his brother the satisfaction of knowing he had finally won . . . . no, he wouldn't do that, although he was pretty sure that Nathanael would know the reason for his sudden departure.

He simply wrote; I have to leave, don't worry about me, I don't know when or if I'll be back, he signed it and dropped it onto the bed.

Miranda walked down the stairs, she hadn't slept at all, her head felt clouded and she couldn't think straight. She had wanted to talk to Gabriel before she'd gone to bed; she'd even stood outside his door for a while.

But what could she say to him? How would he have reacted if she'd have told him the truth, that none of it mattered because she loved him—yes she loved him, not that the thought had been any kind of revelation, she knew she loved him from the very first moment she'd seen him.

"It says he might not come back," Morana said looking at Michael and then at Nathanael as Miranda entered the room. She looked at their frowning faces, and remained at the door.

"It's just not like Gabriel," Michael said turning to look at Morana, "did it say where he was going?"

She took a piece of paper out of her pocket and read it aloud. "I have to leave, don't worry about me, I don't know when or if I'll be back. Gabriel," she said folding the paper again. She glanced over at Miranda a worried frown creasing her features.

Miranda stood quietly in the doorway looking from one face to another, they all looked so serious, they weren't joking—he had left.

"It's just not like Gabriel," Michael repeated. "He didn't even say goodbye."

Miranda couldn't move, she heard their words but she didn't believe them, why would he leave, it didn't make sense. Why would he go? She felt panic rising up from the pit of her stomach, she wanted to scream. She felt a crushing pain in her chest, where her dead heart lived, as if it was crumbling into dust. She could feel the desolation spreading through her body, the sadness and despair threatened to tear her apart.

Her head started to pound and she lifted her hands to her face. He'd left, how was she supposed to face life without him here? The room started to spin, and the energy started to grow. But it hurt so much, it was pounding in her head she couldn't contain it; she didn't want to contain it.

Nathanael glanced in her direction and frowned again, she was only vaguely aware of putting a hand out in front of her, as she did he slid across the floor on the chair. She brought up her other hand to Morana as she started to move towards her; she too was forced backwards as if some invisible energy was pushing her. She was aware that Michael was saying something to her, but his words made no sense. "Let them go—you're hurting them!" he shouted.

She looked from Nathanael to Morana as their faces contorted in agony, how was she hurting them? She pulled back her hands instantly and released them from whatever power held them. A strangled scream escaped her as she clutched her head again; the pain was unbearable as the energy seemed to explode from her brain. She was propelled upwards into the air and hovered a few feet above the rest of them as another wave of energy enveloped her, and then the pain in her head returned, burning, searing, and pounding. As unconsciousness swept over her, Nathanael jumped to his feet and quickly moved towards her.

She became aware of Morana whispering somewhere beside her, but she didn't want to open her eyes. Her head was still pounding. She felt Nathanael's hand on hers but she didn't even have the strength to move away from him. She didn't want him touching her.

It was his fault Gabriel was gone; hers and Nathanael's fault . . . . between them they had managed to drive him away . . . . and even though she couldn't understand why she knew they were to blame. She could feel the tears trickling down her face, she opened her eyes.

Nathanael sat beside her; he lifted his hand to her cheek and gently wiped away a tear with his finger. He said nothing as he lifted his hand and watched the tiny droplet roll down into his palm. The door opened and Morana walked in, she handed Miranda a cup and smiled.

"Drink up while it's warm, it will help," she tilted her head and smiled again, and then she reached out her hand and stroked Miranda's hair gently. Miranda did as she said and handed the cup back to her; Morana took it with another smile and then turned to Nathanael, "don't keep her talking to long, she needs to rest," she said then left the room.

Miranda looked at him, "has he really gone?" she asked as a fresh wave of tears burned at the back her eyes.

"Yes, he has," Nathanael shrugged. "But he won't be gone for long—I'm not that lucky."

"How can you be like this," Miranda said suddenly angry. "How long can you stay that angry at him?"

Nathanael shrugged, "oh I'm not angry at him; anger doesn't even cover what I feel for him—I hate him—he did tell you everything, didn't he, about what he did, did he include the fact that he was in love with my wife, that he was jealous because Sophie loved me and not him—did he tell you that he was jealous because Sophie chose me and not him—turning me into this and killing her was his way of teaching me that I should not have taken what he wanted," he said calmly.

Miranda frowned; he hadn't told her that, not that it mattered. It didn't matter what Nathanael said about him, because she loved him. "Can you please leave," she said turning away from him.

"I'm sorry, I don't mean to upset you, but this is the way it's always been between us—nothing will ever change that Miranda," he said taking her hand. "I don't want us to fall out over it—I never meant to hurt you."

Miranda turned to look at him again and he smiled at her. "I'm sorry that my actions forced him to leave—it wasn't my intention—if you want me to, I'll go find him and bring him back," he said looking at her hand.

Miranda didn't answer.

18

Gabriel opened his eyes and sat up quickly. He rubbed his eyes and looked around the room, he was completely disorientated. It took him several minutes to realise he was lying in bed, in the hotel he'd resided in for the past month, one week and six days, and not sat with Morana and Michael at the kitchen table at home. But the dream had felt so real.

Miranda had been there, and she'd smiled at him and kissed him. Everyday he dreamt of her, every single time he closed his eyes and each night he'd wake a little later than the night before, just so he could see her beautiful face and hear her sweet voice. If he could he'd sleep for the rest of eternity, just to be with her.

Nothing was right . . . . he was broken, damaged in ways he didn't understand . . . . he wanted to go home. But what would be waiting for him at home. Miranda would be waiting, Miranda . . . . happy in the arms of his brother. He closed his eyes against the pain the thought caused him, he folded his arms across his chest to try and stop the ache there. It throbbed through him and he couldn't stand it.

He needed blood, the only thing in this life that gave him some semblance of peace. But in order to get what he needed, meant that he had to leave this room, he had to interact with people. That meant he would start looking for her all over again, and then he would have to endure the pain of not being able to find what he was looking for.

He stood up and dressed quickly and then left the room. He managed to smile at the young couple who walked past him, and he didn't need to look to know that the young woman had watched him all the way to the lift. As he reached the lobby, the concierge looked up at him.

"Good evening sir," he said smiling.

Gabriel nodded slightly and dropped his key onto the counter. "I will be leaving at the end of the week," he informed the man.

The man inclined his head slightly, "certainly, have a good evening sir," the man called as he turned and walked out into the cool night air.

Miranda walked slowly through the forest, she had no interest in feeding; she wasn't hungry. But Morana had been watching her all night and she'd needed to get out of the house. Two months, one week and two days had passed since Gabriel had left, and the pain was still so unbearable. Miranda wondered if she didn't have a heart, why was she in so much agony.

Why, every time she thought of him, did this pain start in her head, why did this blackness cloud her senses and envelope her completely. She was having a hard time functioning properly; she had no interest in anything. She didn't even know why she bothered getting out of bed at all.

She stopped and looked around, this was the place, this was the place right here. The place that he'd held her, the place where he'd kissed her. The place that she'd thought that he loved her for that one brief moment.

The pain washed over her and she fell to her knees, as the images flew through her mind . . . . she couldn't stand it. So much for being an all powerful vampire, so much for living for eternity, how could she face an eternity without him? How could she live forever with this pain as it threatened to rip her apart piece by painful piece? Every part of her hurt, inside and out.

"Please come back," she whispered as tears fell from her eyes. "Please, I need you to come back—please I love you, come back," she begged clutching at her chest. The pain ripped through her and she closed her eyes.

"GABRIEL!!!" She screamed at the top of her voice, lifting her head towards the sky. The pain again tore through her and she fell to the ground, "please, please—I can't live without you—please come back, please," she sobbed quietly as the blackness took over and rendered her helpless. She lay there for the longest time, and as the blackness started to slowly creep away she turned her head towards the rising sun.

"We really do have to move," Gabriel said turning away from her and disappearing into the forest.

"Please don't go," she said jumping to her feet, "please come back—don't leave me—Gabriel please," she sobbed as she stumbled after him through the trees, she could hardly see where she was going as the tears streamed from her eyes and several times she slipped and fell to the ground.

"As I've said before, the clumsiest vampire I've ever met," he chuckled quietly moving away from her again.

"Please come back," she cried, remaining on the ground for a moment as the agony washed over her again.

"Come on!" he shouted angrily from somewhere in the forest. Miranda jumped to her feet and ran towards the sound of his voice, but as she came to the edge of the forest, she realised that it was just a memory . . . . his image, his voice . . . . were all just memories from a time already passed . . . . he wasn't here, he wasn't real. The pain again forced her to her knees and she doubled over in agony, but she couldn't stay there the sun was rising; she needed to get back to the house.

"We really do have to move," Gabriel's voice whispered in her mind.

She looked towards the house; Libbi was stood by the backdoor, waiting for her. The girl waved as Miranda slowly stood up and made her way across the garden towards her. "I was getting worried that you wouldn't come back," the young girl said frowning.

"Sorry Lib, I lost track of time," Miranda said frowning down at her muddied clothes; she took the girl's hand and they walked into the kitchen.

Morana looked up and frowned but said nothing.

"I'm going to bed," Miranda said quietly releasing Libbi's hand and leaving the room.

Morana looked at Michael and shook her head; Michael reached over and took her hand as a single tear rolled down the woman's cheek.

Gabriel smiled at the young girl in front of him, he could just see her eyes above the rim of the cubical, and every now and then she would duck down and pop her head up and smile at him. She must have been about three or four Gabriel guessed. He heard her mother telling her to leave the nice man alone and get on with eating her burger, he laughed quietly as the little girl took absolutely no noticed and carried on with, what seemed to her to be, a very good game of peek-a-boo.

The waiter walked over and placed the order in front of him, he looked down at the mush on the plate and he swallowed instinctively, it smelt awful and looked worse, he slid the plate over to the woman sat at his side. "Is there anything else, sir?" he asked as he handed Gabriel a knife and fork.

Gabriel glanced up at him and shook his head. The woman beside him took the knife and fork from him. "This looks absolutely delicious, don't you think?" she asked.

Gabriel simply nodded and turned his attention back to the young girl, but she'd gone. Suddenly someone tapped his arm; he frowned and looked around into the little girl's smiling face. "Well hello little one," he said replacing the frown with a smile.

"Ello, who's your name?" she asked and smiled brightly.

"I'm Gabriel—what's your name?" he asked amused.

"I am randa—ello Gabel," she said with a wide smile.

"Miranda Philips you get back here right now!" her mother said approaching the table and grabbing the girl's hand. "I'm so sorry, I only looked away for a second—honestly you have to have eyes in the back of your head," the woman apologised and smiled.

Gabriel blinked up at the woman, he knew she was talking to him, but as she'd called the girl's name the agony and emptiness had threatened to swallow him whole. The woman suddenly frowned at him. He frowned too mimicking her expression.

"It's fine, no problem," he said, suddenly realising she was waiting for a response. The woman nodded curtly then turned away quickly pulling the young girl behind her.

"Bye-bye Gabel," she called back to him, as she was dragged from restaurant.

He stood up quickly and his legs threatened to buckle beneath him as he stood there trying to decide what to do.

"Is something wrong?" the woman beside him asked.

He turned to look at her, "no, nothing's wrong," he said sitting down again. He couldn't stay here; he needed to get away from this place. But his insides had twisted so tight that he didn't think he'd be able to walk if he tried. He sat there for several minutes, as the woman next to him ate the food, and the watery feeling in his brain subsided.

He turned to the woman and tried, unsuccessfully he guessed by the frown on her face, to smile, "excuse me for a few minutes," he said and then stood up again.

He had intended to go to the men's room and then return after he'd regained control of himself, but instead he walked over to the waiter, he placed an ample amount of money on the counter and the waiter looked at him puzzled. "Give her anything else she wants, then take the rest as a tip—god knows you deserve it," he said as he glanced around at the other diners.

"Would you like me to tell the lady anything sir?" the waiter asked bemused.

Gabriel stood thinking for a moment then shrugged his shoulders, "tell her whatever you want."

Miranda pulled up the collar on her coat and followed Morana down the street. She still had no interest in hunting but Morana had insisted, and if she hadn't accepted she was in no doubt that they would have all sat frowning at her for the rest of the night.

"So do you have any preference to which street you want," Morana asked turning and linking her arm through Miranda's. Miranda shook her head and Morana stopped walking and looked at her for a moment. Miranda pulled away from her and turned to look down the darkened street to the left of their position, she looked back at Morana and smiled.

"I'll take this way," she said moving further away from the woman and closer to the scent that had attracted her attention, "see you in about an hour—back at the car," she said quietly as she started running.

She stood silently staring down the alley, she could see right to the end of it and there was nothing frightening about it . . . . it wasn't at all like the alley from her memory, but she hadn't been a vampire when she first stood looking down this alley, she had been a human, with all the frailties of a stinking human. She closed her eyes and breathed in deeply . . . . it was still there, just faintly hanging on the air . . . . her human scent, long gone by the time she'd changed, but still a faint whisper of that life remained here, in the darkest part of the city.

Why had she been so stupid, she had never ventured to this part of the city until that night, what had possessed her. She moved further into the alley and looked up at the sky, a single tear escaped and rolled down her cheek, "why did you leave me here, why did you turn me and just leave me here alone," she said crouching down and clutching at her stomach. "It's all your fault, if you hadn't turned me and left me here I wouldn't even know of a Gabriel Pride, if you had taken me with you I would never have met him, or fallen in love with him . . . . I wouldn't be in all this pain now," she sobbed quietly as tears streamed down her face.

"WHY DID YOU LEAVE ME HERE!" she shouted sliding down the wall, the pain in her chest became too much and she clutched at her ribs. She stayed there for a few minutes as the pain washed over her, she couldn't fight it anymore. She wouldn't fight it anymore because pain was the only thing she had to prove she was still alive.

She looked up suddenly as a scent caught her attention; a figure stood watching her from the opening of the alley.

"Sorry, I don't mean to disturb you, but are you alright—do you need help," the young man asked uncertainly. Miranda breathed in deeply and closed her eyes, "sorry, I'll leave you alone, I didn't mean to frighten you," he said moving away slowly.

"NO!" Miranda said opening her eyes quickly, "don't go, I do need help—it's my leg," she said putting her hand on her ankle and holding it protectively.

"Ok, don't worry, I'll help you," he said advancing slowly towards her, "how did you do it," he asked kneeling down by her side. He leant in towards her to take a closer look at her face.

"I slipped—I'm a little lost too, I haven't got the slightest clue where I am—I don't think it's broken, maybe sprained that's all," Miranda said smiling up at him.

He moved slightly and took her foot in his hand and gently stroked her ankle, "how long have you been here, you're frozen to the bone," he said frowning, "shall we see if we can get you up on your feet," he said dropping her foot carefully to the floor. Miranda moved quickly grabbing his head and pulling it towards her. Her teeth sliced into his skin as easily as cutting butter with a hot knife. The young man shuddered slightly and moaned in that slightly euphoric tone as his blood seeped into her mouth, she pulled back to look into his face, his eyes had soon taken on that far off look, he was close to death and he looked so peaceful. Miranda frowned slightly as she wondered if she too had had that peaceful look at this stage, in that spilt second before she'd started to change.

Had she ever felt that kind of peace in any of this wicked, unkind life . . . . she looked into his face for a few more moments then she wrenched his head back and sunk her teeth into him once again.

19

There wasn't a cloud in the sky; it was as blue as she ever remembered seeing it. She missed this colour, sky blue; when it all ended today at least she'd seen it one last time. She wouldn't be chasing blue skies for the rest of eternity. He'd been gone four months, three weeks and a day, and she couldn't stand it anymore. The pain was too much for her to handle.

She'd left the house as soon as it had become quiet; she'd walked out to the fountain and lay down beside it. The trees had shaded her for a little while, and she'd watched as the light had crept slowly across the grass towards her. All the time her brain screamed at her to get up and run back to the house, but she wasn't moving, she wanted to burn, she wanted to turn into a pile of ash, anything would be better than this hollow empty existence that she was forced to live everyday since he'd left.

She lifted her hand to look at it; tiny blisters were starting to form under the skin. She wondered fleetingly exactly how long it would take before this miserable life was over, how long would it take to reduce her to dust and for her to blow away on the breeze?

Why couldn't vampires be how books portrayed them, they walked out into sunlight and death was instantaneous, but no such luck. Nathanael had explained it gets very uncomfortable very quickly but it could take four or five hours to bake a new vampire. She had been lay here for just over two of the five.

"Nothing in my life could ever be that easy," she muttered to herself. Her skin felt as if it was on fire, she felt as if she were bubbling, the blisters were starting to hiss and pop. She lifted her hand to her face, it hurt to touch as the blisters exploded under her finger tips. How much longer until she started to dry out, she wondered as a fresh wave of pain washed over her body.

The blackness was threatening to cloud her mind, licking away at the edges of her consciousness; it was ready to pounce at any moment, to take her away from everything one last time. Maybe it wasn't such a bad thing, when the end came at least she wouldn't be aware of it. Another wave of pain hit her and energy exploded out and upwards into the blue sky.

The faint sound of trickling water caught her attention and she turned her head towards the fountain. She watched in amazement as with a deep gurgling, groan and a long hiss it spluttered into life. Water flowed freely from the mouths of the fish. She closed her eyes for what she hoped would be the final time and a vision of Gabriel appeared in her mind.

"Gabriel," she whispered as the blackness clouded her senses for the last time.

Gabriel sat bolt up right, he blinked rapidly and looked down at his arms; they felt as if they were on fire, his whole body felt as if it were on fire. He looked over at the closed curtains and frowned. He raised his hands to his face, it was smooth, but he could have sworn there were painful blisters all over it, he'd heard them hiss and felt them pop. He lay back against the headboard and closed his eyes. He could smell stagnant water, it was vile and he put his arm in front of his nose for a second to mask the smell, and why could he hear trickling water, he frowned slightly.

"Gabriel."

His eyes snapped open again and he looked quickly around the room. He was going insane. Her whispered voice had been so clear, as if she was in this very room with him; as if she was lying right next to him. He glanced at the clock. 8:25 A.M, she was at home, no doubt in Nathanael's arms. Gabriel shook his head, she was at home, she would always be at home with Nathanael and he would be here alone with just the memory of her voice to haunt him, the memory of her voice disturbing his sleep. He lay down and closed his eyes, as a tear escaped and rolled down his cheek.

Nathanael stroked her hair as she opened her eyes slowly; she looked at him for a moment and frowned.

"Did you really think that was going to work?" he asked quietly, smiling slightly. "If you ever make me do that again I will kill you myself," he added just as quietly as the smile disappeared from his face. He moved away from her and inspected his blistered arms and then looked back at her. "Three hundred year old skin doesn't take a lot to burn, I could have died trying to get to you—so next time you think of anymore idiotic stunts, be warned, I won't be so eager to save you," he said moving over to the dressing table.

"I didn't ask you to save me," Miranda said frowning at his back.

Nathanael turned his head and looked at her. "And if I had just left you there, what do you think would have happened—what do you think would've happened to me? Let me tell you what would happen to me—I'd get the blame, I don't know whether you've noticed but I'm not exactly Mr Popular around here."

Miranda's frown deepened, as he turned to face her again, "god you can be so selfish sometimes, you're not the only one who has ever suffered in this life—can you just imagine what Gabriel would do to me, he would kill me and not think twice about if any harm came to you, actually he'd probably kill the lot of us for not taking better care of you—do you really want to be responsible for so many deaths?"

Miranda shook her head, she couldn't imagine for one minute that Gabriel would be in the least bit bothered about her demise. At least if she was dead he could come home.

"Now be a good little girl and drink this," he said walking back to the bed, he handed her a cup. "Rest now, I will be back later to check on you and I think it best if we never talk of this again," he said, he looked down at her for a moment then he turned and left the room.

Nathanael shut the door to his room quietly; he walked over to the bed and stripped off his tee shirt. He examined the blisters on his forearms for a moment, and then walked over to the mirror to examine his face. In hindsight he should have changed into a shirt before playing the hero, but by the time he woke up tonight there would be no trace of them.

He'd felt slightly uneasy all night, not that she'd done anything to arouse suspicion, since his brother had left she'd been no company at all. He had lain in bed and suddenly a feeling had descended on him, a feeling that something wasn't quite right. So he'd got out of bed, dressed quickly and gone to her room—and she hadn't been there. He'd panicked momentarily as he'd searched for her and he'd wondered for a second if he should alert the others, when he'd caught the strong scent of stagnant water, he'd stood listening for a second and realised he could hear trickling water. He'd parted the curtains carefully and looked out at the fountain and there she was lay, fully exposed to the sun.

He stood looking at his reflection for a few minutes before taking the rest of his clothes off and getting into bed, he was getting soft; he was spending too much time around her. He turned over and smiled at the portrait and then frowned slightly, "Oh shut up, I know it's my fault—yes I was wrong—but how was I to know he'd turn tail and run." He turned onto his back and closed his eyes, "I don't know, I guess I just have to hope he comes back, he will eventually, he loves her, he'll come back." He threw his arm over his eyes and sighed, "yes I can hear you, please shut up—I've got to get some sleep, we'll talk about it later, yes—yes—SHUT UP!"

Then there was silence, he did hate it when she kept talking, it was bad enough he had to listen to the other voices in his head, at least he could block them out, but she just kept on and on driving him to distraction. He wondered how long he was going to have to endure hanging around this dull, drab old house, and how many times would he be called upon to save the pitiful damsel in distress. It was too much to expect his brother to be back anytime soon, though he knew he'd had big part to play in Gabriel's disappearance.

How was he to know that his brother would turn tail and run so easily, how could he have known one little kiss was going to be all it took. How could he have known that one little kiss would awaken feelings in him he'd thought dead for so many years?

20

Libbi jumped up and down excitedly. “Oh please Miranda—I won’t get in the way—oh please let me come with you—I promise I’ll be good—oh please, oh please, oh please—say I can.”

“Alright you can come,” Miranda shrugged then smiled as the young girl squealed and ran from the room.

Nathanael frowned at her from across the table; he wasn’t at all impressed by the fact that Miranda was allowing Libbi to go hunting with her. Miranda stood up ignoring the looks he was giving her and walked to the backdoor. Libbi skipped back into the room and over to her side.

“See you later,” she shouted towards Nathanael as she continued skipping out of the door.

Miranda followed her out into the darkness; she hadn’t been able to refuse the girl as she’d begged her to go hunting. The only person she’d ever hunted in the forest with was Gabriel, since that night she’d only ever been by herself. The idea of going with anyone else filled her with dread.

Libbi grabbed her hand as they reached the trees. “Thank you for letting me come—you are the best big sister, and I don’t mind if you want to cry—I promise I won’t tell if you do,” the girl said smiling sadly. Miranda opened her mouth to speak but Libbi continued. “I know that you miss him—I cry all the time when Nathan goes—I miss Gabe too—but I miss Nathan more when he leaves—he found me you know.”

“Found you?” Miranda asked with a frown.

“Yep, he found me and brought me home—my maker left me too—but Nathan looked after me and taught me things and he loves me,” Libbi smiled fondly. “I know you love Gabriel, don’t you—but it’s ok I won’t tell that either—I’m good at secrets—but I do wish you wouldn’t cry so, I hate it when you're upset—I think it upsets Nathan and Morana too," she said quietly then released Miranda's hand. She dropped down to the ground and flashed Miranda a wicked smile, and then she disappeared quickly through the trees.

Miranda stood there for a moment staring at the place where she'd disappeared, then shook her head and followed quietly. She found Libbi standing in front of a large stag. She stood watching the girl as she spoke quietly to the animal. It was an amazing sight. There was fear in the stag's eyes but it made no attempt to escape, it just stood there staring into Libbi's eyes.

"Et corruc dut saint dut erogog tasssk toout ee ee du," Libbi whispered to the animal.

The girl lifted her hand and stroked its fur gently; she glanced over towards Miranda and chuckled quietly. She pushed off with both feet, and in less than a second she landed squarely on the animal's back. Her impossibly quick movement startled the stag, the animal reared up and Libbi clung on tightly. The girl howled with laughter as again and again the stag tried to throw her. Miranda couldn't help but chuckle at the girl's delight.

Libbi lowered her head to the animal's ear and whispered quietly to it, "eun tai nix tasin sia tou laesta." Suddenly it became subdued again. Miranda watched in amazement as the stag walked calmly over to her. "It's ok you can stroke him if you want to, he quite likes it really," Libbi smiled.

Miranda reached out and ran her fingers over the coarse fur, "what were you saying to him?"

"I told him he had nothing to fear, and then I told him my beautiful sister wanted to stroke him." Libbi said smiling sweetly.

Miranda smiled up at Libbi for a moment then looked sternly at the girl, "haven't you been told not to play with your food."

Libbi giggled then opened her mouth, her sharp little fangs shone in the moonlight for a moment before she lowered her head to the stag's neck. Its whole body shuddered and trembled as the girl drunk every last drop of its blood. She jumped deftly off its back before it hit the floor.

"All full," she smiled patting her stomach.

Miranda caught the scent of a nearby deer; she was a lot quicker than Libbi had been, draining the blood from her prey quickly.

"You looked scary when you did that, did I look scary too?" Libbi asked innocently taking her hand again.

"Very," Miranda said as they started walking back towards the edge of the forest.

"I think I should hunt with you in future, you didn't cry at all this time," the girl said proudly. "Morana gets very worried when you're out all night."

Miranda stopped and looked at the girl; she had no idea they worried about her. The only thing she ever thought about lately was her own misery; she never even considered the effect it had on anybody else. "Well they needn't worry anymore, what could possibly happen to me when I've got my little sister to look after me?" she said squeezing Libbi's hand. "And from now on you can come with me whenever I go hunting, ok."

"Really, I can?" Libbi squealed with delight.

"Really," Miranda smiled as they left the forest, and made their way towards the house.

Gabriel paced back and forth, as the girl sat reading on the bed. He was hungry, he'd missed feeding last night because of this stupid human, and she was starting to get on his nerves. Why had he brought her back here? What had possessed him? Bad company was better than no company at all.

"What's wrong Gabriel?" the girl asked, breaking into his thoughts.

Gabriel considered telling her for a second, he wondered how she would react if he told her that he was a real live vampire and that he needed to feed, that he was very close to ripping her god damn throat out and he didn't have an ounce of guilt at the thought of doing so. He sat down on the bed and frowned, he couldn't kill her here, too many witnesses. She came and went as she pleased and even though he made sure that they weren't seen together too often, he was pretty sure they'd remember who she was here with if she suddenly turned up dead.

"I have to go out for a while," he said finally, as he stood up again.

She sat up and smiled, "where are we going?"

"No not we, I, I have to go out for a while," he said tersely.

She frowned and then sighed, "you want me to stay here again," she stated rather than asked.

Gabriel could feel the anger rising up from his stomach like bile and he had to look away from her. Didn't she realise just how very close to death she was. Didn't she realise just how little taking her life would mean to him? He grabbed his jacket and moved towards the door.

"Please don't leave me, I promise I won't get in the way," she begged jumping up from the bed and grabbing his arm. It took every ounce of control he had not to turn around and sink his teeth into her flesh. He turned slowly to look at her after a moment.

"Louise, please," he said, wrapping his arm around her waist and pulling her into his body, "you will stay here, because I need a break from you, do I have to go wherever you go, do I kick up a fuss when you're out all day," he said looking deep into her eyes, "you should maybe have a bath to get rid of your god awful stench—not that there's enough water in the world to wash away that stink, and then you should go to bed—it's getting late, and you need your beauty sleep—actually no-one could sleep that long, and stop being so god damn clingy—because if you don't I won't be held responsible for my actions."

The girl blinked at him then pulled away, "well, I'm going to have a bath and go to bed I think, I'm so tired," she said stretching.

"I won't be long," Gabriel said turning back towards the door.

"Take all the time you want, I'll probably be asleep by the time you get back," she said pulling her tee shirt over her head. Gabriel watched her for a moment as she undid her jeans and wriggled out of them, she dropped them onto the bed and turned to look at him as she wrapped the towel around herself.

"See you later," he said quietly as he left the room.

He left the building and found a meal quickly. He didn't bother with the usual offer of food or a drink; instead he pulled the girl down the alley and got it over with quickly. As the body hit the floor he became aware of someone watching him and he smiled as he turned around.

"Well that was unusually quick for you Gabriel," the man said walking up to him.

"In a bit of a rush tonight," Gabriel smiled then stuck his hand out to the man. "How have you been Mike?"

"Not too bad all things considered," Michael said shaking his hand. "I would feel a lot better if you were to consider coming home—can we hope for that to happen?"

Gabriel considered the question for a few seconds and frowned, the last five months had been such a struggle; all he ever thought about was going home. "How is everyone?" he asked changing the subject.

Michael shrugged, "some handled your departure better than others," he chuckled suddenly then added, "Morana is mighty mad with you."

"I suppose Nathan is still there?" Gabriel said. He folded his arms across his chest to contain the deep throbbing pain there, as images of Miranda in his brother's arms sprang to the forefront of his mind.

"Unfortunately yes, we all live in hope that sooner or later he'll take off again, but as of yet—"

"How is Miranda?" he asked quietly looking down at the body by his feet.

Michael considered him for a moment and frowned, "she's alright," he said quietly slipping his hands into his pockets. What else was he supposed to say?

Gabriel shifted uncomfortably; he wanted to ask so much more. How had his disappearance affected her, did it seem as if she was missing him. Did she ever talk about him, did she ever think about him—but he couldn't ask them—he was too afraid of the answers. He suddenly wished he'd chosen a different alley down which to feed. This chance meeting with Michael was making him wish for home even more. "Are you going to tell them that you've seen me?" he asked after a few minutes.

"Are you joking, I'm a firm believer in self preservation—if I tell Morana I've seen you and I go home without you she'll hit the roof, no I think this little meeting should be kept strictly between you and I."

Gabriel felt the relief wash over his friend; Michael seemed as uncomfortable talking about Miranda as he felt. He looked at Michael for a few more moments, and then pushed away from the wall; he looked down at the body then back at Michael. "I don't suppose you'd get rid of this for me would you?" he asked kicking the corpse.

Michael raised his eyebrows but smiled. "Sure," he said stooping to pick the body up, he looked at Gabriel for a moment then frowned, "I really wish you'd consider coming home Gabe—we all miss you," he said turning away from him.

"Well, see you then," Gabriel said quietly as the man started to walk away.

"Yeah, see you Gabe," Michael said quietly disappearing around the corner.

Gabriel stood there for a while longer, resting against the wall, clutching at his aching chest—something was wrong. All the time he'd stood with Michael, the man hadn't once thought about Miranda. What had happened for Michael to guard his thoughts the way he had, he hadn't called to mind one single thing about her even as he'd answered Gabriel's question. Gabriel pushed away from the wall and shook his head. He had finally had enough, he needed to go home.

21

Miranda sat looking out of her bedroom window watching Libbi skipping around the garden; her dolls were all sat in a row, obediently watching the elaborate dance that she was performing for them. The flowing water from the fountain glistened in the moonlight; it looked beautiful now that it was working. The young girl turned and waved towards the drive, as the black car pulled in through the gates.

Miranda put the unopened tome down and went to meet Nathanael as he walked through the door. Libbi pushed past him and headed for her playroom, all the dolls hanging out of her arms.

"She is an ungrateful little brat," he shouted as the door closed behind the girl. "Gabriel always gets me dolls, what do I need with a baby book," he said imitating Libbi perfectly. "Does she know how difficult it is to find a doll shop open at this time of night?"

Miranda felt her stomach twist painfully at the mention of his name. It had been five months three weeks and three days since he'd left. And she'd missed him every minute of it. She had given up hope of him ever returning. The blackness that clouded her mind was the only means of escape she had from the sadness. It would sneak up on her and consume her totally, but over the last month even the blackness had deserted her, and she had to find ways to occupy her time.

"So I'm leaving tonight," Nathanael said then turned to look at her.

Miranda blinked, "Sorry what were you saying?"

"I said I'm taking off for a while," he frowned, "weren't you even listening to me?"

"Sorry, so you're going away?" she said only vaguely aware of the conversation.

"Yeah, for a while," he said still frowning.

"Well have fun and bring me something nice back," she said walking towards the door.

"Where are you going now?" he asked as she opened the door.

"I'm going to bed," she said and shrugged.

"Bed, but its hours until dawn," Nathanael said shaking his head.

"I'm tired," she said walking up the stairs. "See you when you get back."

She stood at her window and watched as the car speed down the drive and narrowly missed the opening gates. Nathan didn't seem very pleased with her.

She undressed and reached under her pillow, she pulled out Gabriel's shirt and slipped it over her head. She stood there for a moment with her eyes closed; she lifted the sleeves to her face and breathed deeply. His scent had all but disappeared, but as she stood there breathing in, she imagined it smelt of him, somewhere underneath her scent. She opened her eyes and pulled back the sheets and got into bed.

Shortly after he'd gone she'd stood alone in the kitchen, trying to think of the reason for her existence, and the shirt had caught her attention. She'd picked it up and stood there holding it to her face just breathing in his scent. She stood there for the longest time just breathing in and before she realised it, it was soaked in tears, so she'd taken it to her room and slept in it every night since.

She breathed in deeply and closed her eyes, she couldn't cope anymore; she needed him, she couldn't bear this life without him, death would be kinder. So as she lay there, waiting for sleep, she wished for death.

Gabriel picked up the limp lifeless body and looked down into the girl's dead face. He threw her over his shoulder, picked up the large boulder and waded out into the lake.

He held the body on the lake bed with his foot, and then dropped the boulder on top of it. Even with the rush of water in his ears, he could make out the sound of her bones cracking under the pressure of such a huge weight, he smiled suddenly as the thought occurred to him . . . . maybe a slightly smaller boulder would have served the same purpose. He stood and listened to her bones breaking for a few more seconds then he turned and walked from the lake.

As he approached the Harley, he stooped down and picked up his back pack and took out a new set of clothes. When he'd dressed he rested on the bike and looked out across the water. He was going to miss a few aspects this life, he'd grown use to it over the last six months, and he was going to find it extremely difficult to start drinking animal's blood again.

He'd killed nearly every night, which was more than he'd killed over the last decade, at that rate he'd soon clear the human race of all its homeless and then some. He'd had a lot of time to think things over and he'd realised that he didn't want to live without her anymore; nearly six months had been long enough and the pain was becoming unbearable. He needed to see her, how had he thought that he could spend eternity away from her.

He realised he'd given up too easily . . . . he'd walked away without even trying . . . . he'd ran away instead of fighting . . . . he wasn't going to run anymore. He frowned slightly as a vision of Miranda kissing Nathanael ran through his mind, but he didn't flinch at the pain it caused . . . . he simply pushed it to the back of his mind.

He also realised that he hadn't thought things through enough before he'd left . . . . would his brother really risk losing his head over her; he doubted it very much . . . . even if it was the perfect way for Nathanael to have his revenge. He opened his eyes and smiled. This time tomorrow he'd be home.

Miranda became aware of someone moving around her room, they were being extremely quiet, but not nearly quiet enough. She opened one eye slightly; Libbi was sitting on the stool, she was swinging her legs back and forth, looking around the room. She would occasionally look at Jess, who was propped up against the dressing table mirror, and nod or shake her head, as if the doll had spoken.

Miranda opened her eyes and smiled at the girl, Libbi jumped off the chair and onto the bed in one fluid movement.

"Good you're awake, you really sleep a lot you know, that much sleep isn't good for you—you should come outside and get some exercise—or how about we go and play some music," she said excitedly, bouncing on the bed.

"Give me a chance Lib, at least let me wake up first," Miranda laughed at the girl's enthusiasm.

"But it's after twelve you know—I've waited all night long for you—Morana said I should just let you sleep—I'm not even supposed to be in here." She stopped bouncing and frowned at Miranda, "you won't tell will you?"

Miranda shook her head, "It's our little secret," she said pulling the girl forward to kiss her head. "Look, give me ten minutes to wake up and get dressed and then we'll go play music and dance and sing and whatever else you want to do."

The girl nodded and smiled, she hopped off the bed and collected Jess from the dressing table. She skipped to the door and then turned back to Miranda, "you are the best big sister ever," she said flashing Miranda her sweetest smile.

"And you're the best little sister ever," Miranda smiled back.

Libbi left and she got out of bed, she stripped out of the shirt and held it to her face for a moment and then frowned as she pulled the shirt away and looked at it. She walked over to the bed and lifted up the pillow, her frown deepened as she examined it. She looked down at the sheet for a moment and sat down heavily . . . . she hadn't shed a single tear last night, the shirt, the pillow, and the sheets were all bone dry. She closed her eyes and dropped her head . . . . she hadn't dreamt of Gabriel at all last night . . . . the last place she would ever see him had gone . . . . her memories of him joining her memories of blue skies . . . . abandoned to the darkest parts of her mind.

The wind blew gently through the trees, stirring the scents around him. He had missed this smell, he had missed this place. He lifted his hands to the wrought iron gates and wrapped his fingers around the bars. He stood there with his eyes closed for many minutes just breathing in.

She was in there right now. What was she doing? Was she with his brother? He didn't care anymore; he just needed to see her—he needed to be close to her.

He looked towards the house and frowned slightly as he realised that water now flowed from the fountain. It had been some years since he had seen it working; actually it had been ten years since he had pulled the plug on it. He stood there for a while longer watching the water as it glistened in the moonlight before he slipped his hand in his pocket and retrieved the small black remote, he pressed it, and the gates started to open. He pushed the bike quickly up the drive and into the garage. He hesitated at the front door before he pushed it open and entered.

22

Music blared out of the stereo and Libbi giggled as Miranda spun her around, this was the tenth track in a row they had danced to, and Miranda was starting to get dizzy, as the song ended she flopped onto the couch while Libbi continued to dance around, the girl stopped suddenly and turned to Miranda. "Can I play the guitar?" she asked jumping onto the couch beside her.

"Sure if you want, I'll be back in a minute," Miranda said leaving the room; she smiled to herself as she opened the bottle and poured it into the cup. She hoped Libbi wouldn't want to play the guitar for too long, she'd heard the girl's attempts before and she didn't think her ears could take it again. She heard the front door open and close and frowned, she hadn't heard Morana's car come up the drive. She waited for the kitchen door to open and for Morana and Michael to walk in and when it didn't happen she frowned again.

She put the cup down and walked out of the kitchen towards the lounge, she opened the door and popped her head in, but Morana and Michael weren't in there. She closed the door and stood there looking a little perplexed for a moment, she shook her head and moved towards her music room.

She lifted her hand to the handle and faltered as the slightest hint of a scent attracted her attention. She frowned, her mind was playing tricks on her . . . . she hadn't smelt that particular aroma for such a long time.

Suddenly the door burst open and Libbi grabbed her hand pulling her into the room, "look Miranda, he came back—Gabriel came back," she squealed dragging Miranda over to the couch, "and look at all the pretty dolls he brought me," she added releasing Miranda's hand to scoop up three new dolls. Libbi ran out of the room leaving them alone.

Gabriel moved suddenly and grabbed her hand pulling her down onto the couch next to him and smiled, "hello Miranda," he said after a few seconds.

She opened her mouth but nothing came out, "you should say something," a little voice said trying to prompt her. She closed her mouth then opened it again but still nothing.

"I think what you're trying to say is, welcome home Gabriel it's nice to see you," he said raising his eyebrows slightly as his smile widened. She tried again but the lump in her throat just wouldn't let the words out. "Well if that's the way you feel I suppose I should leave again," he said standing up, "I won't stay where I'm not wanted."

Miranda reached out and grabbed his hand. "No don't—I want you—I mean—it's nice to see you," she finally managed to say quietly.

He looked at her for a moment then sat back down. He sat there looking down at her hand in his for a minute then lifted it to his mouth and brushed the back of it with his lips, Miranda felt as if she was about to burst into flames at his touch. He looked at her face before lowering her hand, "I always thought you had a real aversion to my touch—but now?" he said then he released her and sat back, "how are you?"

She did her best to sit still under his gaze, but his closeness was making it difficult, her hand felt like it was on fire where his lips had touched her skin and every muscle in her body had started to ache. "Fine," she answered quietly looking down at her hands.

He rested his arm on the back of the couch and tilted his head. "You look a little pasty, have you been hunting enough?" he asked genuine concern on his face. Miranda nodded but she could tell he wasn't convinced. He turned and looked around the room. "So where is that pain in the ass brother of mine?" he asked glancing at her. "I felt sure he'd be glued to your side," he said then reaching over and touching her hair he added, "if you were mine I wouldn't leave you alone for one second." Miranda frowned down at her hands.

"What's wrong, Miranda—don't you like compliments?" he asked smiling.

"No, I—" she said shifting uncomfortably.

He raised his hands and his smile widened, "ok, no compliments—I have no wish to make you feel uncomfortable, I came back with the hope that we could start afresh—maybe even become friends," he said, as he took her hand again. "So, you still haven't answered me, where is the son of a bitch."

"He left yesterday," she said quietly looking down at her hand in his.

"Oh damn, and I was so looking forward to seeing him," he said sarcastically as he sat watching her.

She looked up at him as he lifted her hand to his lips and kissed the back of it gently. As he lowered it he looked back at her face for a moment before releasing her and sitting back. "Curious," he said closing his eyes, "it's so good to be home."

Miranda watched him, sitting there with his eyes closed, for a while and wondered if he'd fallen asleep. He looked so peaceful and so beautiful, that she started to wonder if it was she who was still asleep and merely dreaming of him. She heard the front door slam and then heard Morana's voice; Gabriel opened one eye and smiled at her, then opened the other and grinned.

"Uh oh I'm in for it now," he said standing up; he took her hand and pulled her to her feet. "Come with me—then I can use you as a shield if she starts on me," he joked pulling her out of the room and towards the kitchen door. "If I were you I'd brace myself—things could get a little loud," he said as he opened the door to the kitchen.

The look on Morana's face as she looked from Gabriel to Miranda and then back again nearly made her laugh, but the piercing screech did actually hurt her ears for a moment. Gabriel let go of her hand for a few moments as he hugged Morana and shook Michael's hand, but he quickly took hold of it again and pulled her over to the table to sit next to him.

She sat there quietly and listened to the conversation, as he told them about the places he had stayed the people that he'd met and consequently killed. Several times she tried to pull her hand from his as they'd sat there and every time his hold had tightened, so much so that her hand started to ache a little.

Morana got them all a cup while they sat there talking. Libbi joined them; she sat on Gabriel's lap and showed them her new dolls. "Can I please call this one Miranda? She's so pretty and she looks like you," Libbi said thrusting one at Miranda.

Miranda stared at the doll for a moment and smiled. "I'm not nearly that pretty Lib, but I don't mind if you call her Miranda."

"Oh you are as pretty—more pretty in fact—isn't she Gabe?" the young girl said.

"Most definitely," Gabriel said smiling at the girl. "In fact that's why I bought the doll because it reminded me of Miranda—she's just so beautiful," he said glancing over at her.

"Well, if you don't mind I think I will get off to bed, I'm so tired," she said pulling her hand from his and standing up.

"Yes that's a good idea, I'm tired too; I actually think I could sleep for a month," Gabriel said stretching his arms over his head as Libbi jumped off his lap. He stood and walked to the door and opened it, he looked at Miranda as she hovered by the table and smiled, "are we going to bed?"

She looked at Morana and Michael who sat there smirking at each other, and then she turned and walked past Gabriel quickly. He caught her up halfway up the stairs and took hold of her hand again, "I'm sorry if what I said about the doll embarrassed you."

Miranda shrugged as they stopped outside her room, "why would I be, the doll is beautiful, though I don't think it looks remotely like me."

"No I agree, you're far prettier—good night Miranda," he said gently pushing her back against her door with his body, he dropped his head slightly and kissed her cheek and then slowly pulled away from her, "sweet dreams," he added quietly and then disappeared into his own room.

Miranda remained pressed against her door for several minutes after Gabriel had disappeared, her eyes closed tightly together. She peeled herself away from the door and managed to get into her room before her legs buckled and she started to shake from head to toe. She couldn't believe he was back.

The curtains billowed into the room as the wind blew through the open window, and the moon shone brightly has he lay down on the bed. He'd forgotten just how very comfortable his own bed was compared to the ones in the hotels he'd slept in over the last six months. He'd forgotten how clean home smelt.

He turned to look at the wall that separated their rooms and smiled, she was in there right now . . . . just a wall separated them . . . . she was so close that he could smell her sweet scent if he breathed in deeply enough, he did so and closed his eyes and rolled back onto his back.

He was a little surprised at the fact she hadn't pulled away the instant he'd taken her hand. The feel of her skin against his would have caused his pulse to race and he was slightly relieved that he hadn't stopped to feed on his way back. She seemed different to the girl he'd left six months ago . . . . not that he was complaining, he liked touching her, he liked being able to hold her hand without fear of her pulling away abruptly. Those six months away had improved their relationship, absence, they say, makes the heart grow fonder. Perhaps her aversion to him wasn't as bad as he'd presumed.

He had also been extremely surprised when she'd told him Nathanael had left. He frowned for a moment as he wondered what could be so important that Nathanael would just leave her. Surely there was nothing more important than being with her. He turned onto his side and looked at the wall again, and imagined her lying in her bed and smiled; it was so good to be home.

23

Before he'd disappeared into the library, he'd asked her if she was still reading then he'd invited her to change her book whenever she wanted to. She had lied when she'd said she'd just finished one, when in all truth the last book that Libbi had taken to her lay unread just gathering dust on her bedside table.

Now she hesitated outside the door, should she knock, should she just walk in. Would he be expecting her to go so soon? What was she doing? She should wait a few days at least before she went to him . . . . before she went to change her book. She swallowed the lump in her throat and pushed the door open; she popped her head in. He was frowning intently at the screen, in the same way as he used to. "Is it still ok to change it?" she said uncertainly holding the book up.

"Of course it is, come in," he said and smiled, he glanced back at the computer screen for a second then sat back in his chair and watched as she walked over to the bookshelf.

Miranda faltered and nearly tripped over her own feet, she felt so self conscious as he watched her walk the entire length of the room. She was acutely aware that he was sitting there watching her as she stood looking up at the books.

Suddenly he was standing behind her and she hadn't even heard him move. The closeness of his body rid her of every single thought in her head, in exactly the same way as it used to.

"Having trouble deciding?" he asked softly in her ear. She could feel his cool breath on her bare skin and she suddenly felt naked in the strappy top she was wearing. He reached above her head and took a book down.

"What about this one?" he asked positioning the book so that she could see the title.

Miranda shook her head, "read it," was all she managed to say. She heard a thud as he dropped the book to the floor, he reached out again but this time he trapped her between his body and the bookshelf and he made no attempt to move away from her.

"This one?" he asked almost inaudibly dropping his head to her shoulder.

"No, I—I want—" she stammered, struggling with the words as his lips grazed her shoulder. It sent ripples of pleasure racing down her spine and she closed her eyes.

"What is it you want?" he asked quietly as he raised his head slowly, following the contour of her neck. His lips skimming her flesh, and she held onto the bookshelf as her legs threatened to buckle beneath her.

He dropped the book to the floor again and spun her around to face him; the intensity in his eyes made her head spin. This new Gabriel scared her more than the old one had.

"So what is it that you want?" he asked again. His lips were so close to hers that she felt what he'd said rather than heard him. She wanted him to kiss her, that's what she wanted, she wanted to rip his clothes off and feel his body against hers.

He touched her lips softly with his and closed his eyes, he ran his tongue along her lower lip and groaned quietly, "I'd forgotten just how good you tasted," he whispered. He pulled his head away slightly and looked into her eyes, he sighed quietly and then suddenly moved away from her completely, leaving her holding onto the bookshelf for support.

He walked to the desk and leant against it, he ran his finger through his hair and folded his arms across his broad chest and then smiled at her. "I seem to have great difficulty keeping the promises I make when I'm around you don't I," he said looking down at the floor. "I seem to remember swearing, at the beginning of the year, never to touch you again, and not even a day ago in the music room I swore never to pay you another compliment, and here I am in the space of a minute, breaking both of them."

Miranda simply stared at him, she couldn't trust her legs to hold her up yet, and she couldn't trust her voice to speak.

He shook his head and stood up straight; he walked over to her again but stopped a safe distance away. "I will re-make both promises, but I can't promise that I won't just break them all over again."

Gabriel paced back and forth across the bedroom; he'd stop occasionally, and listen for any movement next door. It sounded very quiet.

He shouldn't have kissed her so soon, he should have waited, but he hadn't expected for one minute that she would go to the library. He thought she would be wary of him, he thought she may be wary of spending time alone with him, but it didn't appear to be the case.

As soon as she'd walked into the room, he couldn't contain himself. He watched her walk over to the shelf, he watched every single step she took and as she'd stood there looking up at the books, with her head tilted slightly, he felt his stomach knot. Before he'd realised what he was doing his mouth was on hers, it wasn't by any means the way he wanted to kiss her, but it had blown his mind all the same.

It had taken all his strength to drag himself away from her, and she'd just stood there looking so god damn tempting. If she hadn't grabbed a book and left when she had, he would have lost all control and had her then and there.

He walked to the wall that separated their rooms and rested his head against it. What was she doing? What was she thinking? Was she thinking about him? He closed his eyes for a moment and remembered how her lips had felt against his, how she hadn't flinched or tried to push him away. Perhaps her feelings towards him had altered while he'd been away.

He remained at the wall just listening for any movement for a very long time.

Miranda sat on her bed, staring out of the window, it was still hours before sunrise, and she wasn't in the least bit tired. All she could think about was the man in the room next door.

He was so different to the man who had left here months ago, so different that it frightened her. He hadn't frowned at her once; he held her hand, paid her compliments and he'd kissed her. All things that the old Gabriel would never have done. So what had changed him so dramatically?

Not that she was complaining; she liked the way he looked at her, she liked the way he kissed her. The feel of his skin next to hers still had the same effect, still made her feel as if she were on fire and she guessed it always would. But she wasn't going to pull away from him again, she'd let him touch her and kiss her whenever he wanted, just as long as she was close to him.

She stood up and walked quietly over to the wall that separated their rooms. What was he doing at this very moment? What was he thinking about? Was he thinking about her? She rested her head against the wall. It sounded very, very quiet and she stood there for the longest time, just listening for the slightest movement.

24

"One of my shirts is missing, do you know where it is?" Gabriel asked as he entered the kitchen. He glanced over towards Miranda as she lifted the cup to her mouth, and flashed her one of his irresistible smiles as she lowered the cup to the table.

"Which one is it?" Morana asked walking over to him.

Miranda stared down at the table, she knew exactly which shirt it was he was searching for; at least she'd had the insight to bring it down in the early hours while everyone else was sleeping and put it in the wash basket.

"The white one, granddad collar, with the seam down the—" he said as Morana pulled it out of the basket. "Yeah that's the one."

"How did this get in here?" she said examining it. Gabriel took it from her and held it to his face, he sniffed at it and smiled, he glanced over at Miranda as she looked up at him and he held her eyes for a moment before turning to Morana.

"It's ok, I'll swap you," he said pulling the shirt off that he was wearing and dropping it into the basket.

"But it's dirty," Morana frowned watching him, "and it's creased."

"It looks and smells fine to me."

Miranda felt her stomach knot as she stared at his bare torso, the muscles flexed in his broad shoulders as he pulled the shirt on and she was mesmerised by every movement he made. He turned to her, doing up the buttons and she caught a glimpse of his tight muscular stomach, she was thankful that she didn't suffer the affliction of blushing; as she realised he'd caught her looking at his body. She saw the grin spreading across his face as she tried to drag her eyes away from his beautiful frame.

He pulled a chair out opposite her and turned it around; he straddled the seat and rested his chin on the back of the chair, "so what were you doing with my shirt?" he asked silently and smiled. It took Miranda a minute to realise his lips hadn't moved. She looked at his mouth then back into his eyes.

"I can hear you," she thought.

"And me you," he thought raising his eyebrows at her. "So—my shirt?" he asked again.

She was so shocked that she was finding it easy to communicate with him this way that she hadn't yet come up with a good excuse as to why she'd had his shirt. "I don't know what you're on about," she thought looking away from him.

"Yes you do, it has your smell all over it—maybe you wore it?"

"I don't know what you're on about," she insisted silently.

Gabriel looked into her eyes for a moment then grinned. "Lying is not one of your strong points Miranda—tell the truth."

"I don't know what you mean," she said again and looked away from his grinning face.

He chuckled quietly into her mind, "ok, whatever you say—you don't know what I mean." He sat there grinning at her for a moment and she wondered how she could stop him from listening to her thoughts. "Please don't do that, I've waited such a long time to get inside your mind," he thought and she looked up at him as he frowned slightly, "don't shut me out again," he said silently and stood up. "Are you busy Miranda?" he asked aloud.

"Not really," she said shaking her head. He walked around the table to her and taking her hand he pulled her to her feet.

"Good," he said smiling down at her, and then he turned to Morana, "we're off out, we'll see you later," he said pulling Miranda behind him.

The night air washed over her, as he led her through the garden. He was taking her towards the forest she realised and memories of the last time came to the forefront of her mind. He pulled her towards the trees, but she pulled back suddenly hesitant. He turned to look at her. "I'm not really dressed for hunting," she said looking down at the dress she was wearing.

Gabriel ran his eyes over her body, and shook his head. "No I don't suppose you are—you look absolutely stunning." He turned back towards the trees but stopped suddenly and shook his head again. "Well I didn't do so great with that promise again did I?"

Miranda bumped into him as he stopped and would have lost her balance if he hadn't grabbed her around the waist. "Ha nothing ever changes—still so clumsy," he laughed.

"You stopped right in front of me," she protested. She was never clumsy when he wasn't here; he was the reason for her clumsiness. He laughed again as he let her go and turned towards the trees again. She realised with dismay that he had also heard that thought.

"I bet I can get one before you do," he said as he started running. She watched him as he disappeared through the dense tree line; she had absolutely no chance of winning on foot but she smiled and then followed him.

She dropped down to the ground for a moment then stood up quickly and turned to her left, "Et corruc dut saint dut erogog tasssk toout ee ee du," she said quietly towards the small clearing, "Et corruc dut saint erogog tasssk toout ee ee du," she whispered again. The small deer appeared through the clearing and Miranda smiled, "Nocc dut erain sai ee ee dut bue dut," she whispered holding out her arms towards the deer. It moved cautiously towards her. "Nocc dut erain sai ee ee dut bue dut," she repeated a little louder.

The deer moved forward a little quicker, until Miranda was looking down into its face, it turned and pressed its body against hers. "Erbdut erosue corruc dai," she said gently stroking its fur then she wrapped her arm around its neck and lowered her head. Within a minute the dead body lay at her feet.

"Someone has been having lessons off Lib I see." Gabriel said with a smile. "Though I must say I'm more impressed at seeing you do it—Lib does tend to play with her meals."

"Yes, I'm quite fluent in deer, so much easier to call them than chase them," she said as she turned to look at him. He looked totally relaxed leant up against the tree, one foot brought up to rest on the trunk, his arms folded across his chest as he looked up at the sky.

"So who won?" Miranda asked moving closer to him.

"I did of course, I think I should get a prize, for being the winner," he said turning towards her.

He reached out and pulled her over to the tree. He stood in front of her, trapping her between his body and the trunk. She stood looking up into his eyes as he lent forward and brushed the corner of her mouth with his tongue. "You missed a bit," he whispered against her mouth. "Mmm—yours tasted much better than mine."

"What do you want as a prize?" Miranda asked trying to ignore the rapid beat of her heart against her ribs.

Gabriel considered her question for a moment then smiled, "I do have something in mind, but now is not the time—and here I am breaking my first promise again," he said his smile widening into a grin. He considered her for a moment and then pulled away from her slowly. "Do I really have to re-make them—it does seem pointless, when you and I both know that I'll just break them again."

"Pointless," she said moving away from him quickly; her heart felt as if it could burst out of her chest if she had to stand that close to him for too long. Gabriel smiled and took her hand and they ran back to the house.

Why hadn't he kissed her, he'd pulled her over to the tree and as he'd licked the blood away from her mouth she'd felt sure that a kiss would follow. She had wanted a kiss to follow.

He wasn't acting at all like the old Gabriel. She had waited so long for him to come back, but now that he was she didn't know whether she was coming or going. It was all very confusing.

He was so different—how had he changed so much over six months, in many ways he reminded her more of Nathanael than of the Gabriel that had left. He was so relaxed, and so much sexier than before.

She wanted to touch him, she wanted him to touch her, but most of all she wanted his lips against hers. She wondered what he was doing alone in his room, was he thinking about her as much as she was thinking about him. She rolled onto her side and stared at the wall.

Gabriel lay on his bedroom floor; his heart felt as if it were actually trying to pound its way out of his chest. As they'd stood under that tree, so close together, he'd felt her heart beating against his body. And he'd realised a little too late the effect her closeness was having on his own beating heart—it seemed to be beating as fast if not faster than hers had been.

He'd tried to stop himself as the blood had trickled from her lips but the temptation had proven too much. He'd bent his head and licked it away and realised, slightly dismayed, just how provocative it was when his heart had skipped several beats. And then he'd had to try even harder not to kiss her. If he had kissed her that would have been that, he knew for sure that he wouldn't have been able to stop at just one kiss.

His heartbeat finally slowed and he stood up. He undressed quickly and got into bed. As he lay there he wondered again what she was doing, alone in her room, was she thinking about him as much as he was thinking about her. He rolled onto his side and stared at the wall.

25

The second hand on the clock went around slowly, he should be in the library but he was waiting. He wondered what was taking her so long; she was normally down by now. He tapped his fingers lightly on the table and Morana turned to look at him. “Waiting for something—or someone?” she grinned.

Gabriel glanced over at her and grinned back, “why would you think that?” he asked innocently glancing back at the clock; time had slowed down so much while he’d been away that a night had seemed like a year. Now he was back a night seemed to fly by, as he tried to think up new ways to get her to spend more time with him.

“And isn’t it about time you changed that shirt?” Morana asked narrowing her eyes at him.

“It’s still clean, and I have a certain attachment to this shirt—I like wearing it, Mom,” he said then smiled. He looked up at the clock again, he was going to have to think up an excuse to go and find her if she didn’t hurry up. Morana was already eyeing him suspiciously. He was trying to think of a good enough reason to go to her room when she walked into the kitchen.

“Good evening sweetie,” Morana smiled as she sat next to him at the table. She placed her hand on his shoulder for the briefest of moments as she sat down next to him and the sensation made the muscles in his stomach tighten involuntarily.

“Good evening,” she replied as she leaned in closer to him. “Well this is a surprise, I though you’d be in the library by now,” she smiled as he looked at her.

"I'm in no rush; it gets quite lonely in there sometimes," he said smiling back at her, "who wants to spend all night in a stuffy old library anyway."

"So I'll be in there alone tonight—only I was thinking that I would make a start on reading the tomes, I did think that maybe you could answer any questions I might have, I heard you were the expert, but I suppose if you're not going to be there—" she said pushing her chair back.

Gabriel watched her as she stood up and smiled, "and you want to start reading them right now—this very minute?" Miranda nodded; she remained at the table looking down at him, and then smiled again as he stood up. "Well I suppose, if you insist, I'd better come and keep you company—after all I am the expert," he said glancing over at Morana, the woman smirked and turned away from them.

Libbi ran into the kitchen and grabbed Miranda by the hand, "can we go and play please—please—please?" she asked dragging Miranda to the door.

"Sure, do you think we should ask Gabe to play too?" Miranda said glancing over at him.

"Oh yes, come on Gabe, you come and play too," Libbi shrieked, then she turned back to Miranda and whispered in a conspiratorial way, "we can gang up on him if you want—he's very fast—and the best tracker—he won't stand a chance against both of us though—we'll win."

"Err Lib, I can hear you—I'm stood right here," Gabriel said then chuckled as the girl stuck her tongue out at him.

She grabbed Miranda's hand and pulled her quickly out of the backdoor. Gabriel looked over at Morana and smiled, "I suppose I should give them a head start," he said glancing at the door.

Morana smiled, "I don't think it really matters."

"Right—see you later," he said as he followed them out of the backdoor.

Gabriel stood at the opening of the maze and closed his eyes; he drew in a deep breath, and then frowned. He opened his eyes and looked down at his shirt; he lifted his arm and again breathed deeply. How could he hope to catch her when she was all he could smell? Her scent was all around him; her scent was all over him. He had no hope of catching her by smell.

He entered the maze and closed his eyes and smiled; "I can hear you Miranda, so you and Libbi split up," he chuckled silently. Suddenly there was silence and he chuckled again, he shouldn't have reminded her that he could hear her thoughts, but it wouldn't be as much fun if he found her too quickly. Libbi was close, she hadn't gone far . . . . but where was Miranda?

He kept his eyes closed and raised his face towards the sky. She was sly, she had jumped . . . . several of the hedges, it seemed. Gabriel stood silently at the end of the row and listened intently . . . . she was in the middle . . . . no close to the middle. He crouched down and pushed off with both feet; he cleared every hedge and landed silently in the middle of the maze.

He looked to his left, as Libbi giggled somewhere in the maze. He smiled, Miranda was just around the hedge to his right, he didn't need to smell the air, and he didn't need to listen for signs. He could just sense that she was close. Every time she was near he got a tingling sensation down his spine and every muscle in his body ached . . . . should he do the gentlemanly thing and let her catch him. As he stood there debating Miranda sprung at his back.

He turned quickly and caught her pulling her close. She wound her arms around his neck and her legs around his waist as he stumbled back slightly. "I though you were supposed to be good at this," she whispered against his cheek. She lightly skimmed her lips across his skin and then she released him and jumped to the floor.

"Catch me—if you can," she said smiling slyly, and then she turned quickly and disappeared into the maze again.

Gabriel stood looking after her as she disappeared around the hedge. He lifted his hand to his face where her lips had touched it. What had happened to the Miranda he knew? Was she actually flirting with him? She had kissed him, well not actually kissed him, because if she had actually kissed him, she would still be here now in his arms with his lips on hers. He shook his head; he didn't understand what was happening.

Miranda picked up the tome and walked slowly towards the library. He looked up and smiled as she walked in and dropped the book on the couch, she walked over to the desk. She stood there for a few seconds looking at the screen. "How's it going?" she asked reading what he'd written.

He didn't answer so she turned to look at him, his eyes scrutinised her for a moment then he reached over and turned the computer off and sat back. "It isn't going very well at all," he said looking up at her.

She turned around, and rested on the desk, then she slipped her hands into her pockets and his eyes dropped instantly to her midriff, she saw the muscles in his jaw tense but he immediately looked back at her face. "Is there something wrong?" she asked smiling slightly, "you seem awfully tense."

Gabriel shook his head, he was trying so hard to keep his eyes on her face, but every time she moved her blouse opened slightly and revealed the slightest bit of her pale stomach and he could feel his eyes drifting down to the beautiful soft flesh. He stood up quickly.

"Are you sure everything's alright?" she said moving in front of him so that he was trapped between her body and the desk.

Gabriel faltered, she was so close that he couldn't think straight, every muscle in his body tensed to the point of snapping, he felt as if he was going to explode into tiny pieces. His legs threatened to give way and he had to put a hand on the desk to steady himself. He managed a slight nod of his head.

Miranda stood looking at him for a few seconds more. Her eyes lingered on his lips for a second as she imagined his reaction if she were to kiss him, and then she turned and walked over to the couch.

She looked down at the tome and then glanced in his direction, "is it still alright to read in here?"

Gabriel nodded; he couldn't talk for a moment he was still trying to gather enough of his senses to move, he couldn't decide what to do. He knew what he wanted to do, he wanted to walk over and have her right there on the couch, he wanted to lose himself in her and everything else be damned. He sat down in his chair again and stared at the screen, the door opened and Libbi ran into the room.

"Miranda—you gotta come quick, I lost Jess, I just can't find her anywhere—oh come and help me Miranda—please," the girl said putting her hands against her head and jumping on the spot.

Gabriel looked up at Miranda as she stood up and walked towards the door, "ok Lib, calm down—we'll find her," she said calmly taking the girls hand, she turned back towards Gabriel and winked, "see you later, don't work to hard," then she was gone.

Gabriel frowned. There wasn't a chance in hell he would be working at all. He turned his chair towards the window. If his resolve had been a visible entity, it would now be broken rubble lying at his feet. Several times, as they'd ran around the maze he'd felt as if his self control had abandoned him, as she'd caught him and skimmed his flesh with her lips. He had to fight so hard to contain himself, and now he ached from head to toe with the strain.

As if that hadn't been bad enough, when she'd entered the library and stood so close to him, when her blouse had opened and he'd had to concentrate so hard on looking at her face, his head had actually started to spin. He had a sick feeling down in the pit of his stomach, as her eyes lingered on his lips for several seconds . . . . he'd actually thought she was going to kiss him.

He needed to get control of these feelings, he was so very close to just taking what he wanted again; he frowned at the thought, he couldn't do that. He had to do something to regain the little sliver of control he possessed . . . . but what?

26

Five days had passed since Miranda had last been to the library; she had hardly seen Gabriel in those five days. He would smile at her as she joined them in the kitchen every evening, he would chat with her for a few minutes, and then he would disappear into the library. Not once did he ask if she would like to join him.

She frowned; she couldn't go to the library without an invitation and every night she hoped he would ask, but he hadn't. She spent every night in her music room, alone, just thinking about him and she'd had enough of just thinking about him; she needed to spend more than a few minutes a night with him. She had to go to him, invitation or no invitation. She opened the door to the library and frowned, the room was empty. Where was he, she was sure he'd be here. She sat down and ran her fingers over the gold lettering of the tome.

"I've been looking for you—you're quite elusive when you want to be aren't you?" Gabriel said as he walked into the room.

Miranda jumped at the sound of his voice and looked up quickly, "I was just coming to get the tomes," she lied. She opened her mouth again but then snapped it shut and looked at him puzzled for a moment, "you were looking for me—why?"

"I'm bored, like I said it gets quite lonely in here—I thought perhaps we could do something together."

"Sure, what do you want to do," she asked casually standing up, her legs started to shake a little as she walked towards him.

"I think it's about time I had my revenge in the maze," he said resting his hand against the door frame.

"Well you can try," she said confidently as she ducked under his arm and walked to the kitchen. She hadn't even realised that it was raining until they stood together looking out of the backdoor.

"Well looks like we'll have to call it off, a rain check as they say," Gabriel said turning back towards the table.

"For goodness sake it's only a little rain, honestly you're such a baby," she said stepping out into it. It felt cooling against her skin. She opened her arms out and raised her head towards the sky; it felt wonderful as the raindrops washed over her and cooled her suddenly hot flesh.

Gabriel stood in the doorway and stared at her, the rain glistened on her skin and the feelings started to surge through him again. She turned and looked at him as he walked out into the rain and mimicked her, he opened his arms and looked up at the sky. He stood there for a minute then turned to look at her as she spoke; "It's only a little water you know, it won't kill you—what have you got against rain anyway?" she asked lifting her head skywards again.

"It gets you wet," he said watching her.

"Aww poor Gabriel doesn't like getting wet," she said glancing at him. She grinned then set off running towards the maze. She couldn't understand why he had such an aversion to rain, she loved it. She loved the way it rolled down his skin, she loved the way it soaked his shirt and plastered it to his immaculate frame, and the way it shone in his hair and glistened like tiny diamonds in the light.

She had misunderstood the meaning behind his statement, he didn't mind the rain at all, but when he looked at her and saw the way the raindrops trickled down her skin, it was more than he could handle. He sunk his hands into his pockets and followed her.

The rain continued to pour as she ran around the maze; she was enjoying it more than she ever would have imagined. Gabriel was trying so hard to catch her, but to his annoyance she kept evading him. She had caught him twice, nimbly jumping onto his back and kissing his neck when she did, then running away as soon as her feet touched the ground.

She was close again, and he chuckled quietly into her mind. He was just around the hedge to her right; he was waiting for her to make her move. She tried not to think about what she was doing, he was close enough to hear the slightest whisper. She crouched down, and momentarily thought about jumping the hedge, but she ran instead.

She sped around the corner taking him completely by surprise, her ploy had worked . . . . he had expected her to jump. As he turned to look at her, with a shocked expression on his face, she lost her footing and slipped sending her skidding into his hard body. She hit him with such a force that it knocked him off his feet, the sound of their bodies clashing echoed around the maze.

He wrapped his arms protectively around her as they fell to the ground. Miranda lay dazed for a moment, cocooned in his arms. She put her head on his chest and breathed in his scent.

"Need I repeat the word clumsy—so, just to clear it up, who won that point," he asked after a few minutes. Miranda wondered if she was imagining the tremor in his voice as he spoke. "I think technically, I caught you," he added as she lifted her head to look at him.

"I think you'll find technically I'm the winner three-nil," she smiled down at him, she didn't want to move from this position and he didn't seem to be in any rush either, his arms were still around her, holding her close.

"Well I don't think that's fair, I mean my arms are wrapped around you, so the evidence clearly shows that it was I who caught you," he said rolling her over so that she was more or less underneath him.

Miranda considered him for a moment then smiled, "ok, but even if I admit that you caught me and give you the point you still lose, two-one."

"Fine, I'd rather lose two-one than three-nil," he said shrugging.

Miranda smiled then rolled him so that she was on top again, "well as the winner, I think I should get a prize—don't you?" she said smiling down at him.

"Sure what is it that you want?"

"Um, there is something I want," she said smiling slightly, "but now is not the time, the sun will be up soon—so this will have to do," she said quickly lowering her head. Before he realised what was happening her lips were on his, her tongue softly probing the inside of his mouth, and then, she was gone.

He'd purposely stayed out of the way for the last couple of days and he thought that he'd regained at least some of his self-control . . . . until now that was.

His body's reaction had been bad enough, feeling her soft warm body pressed so close to his as they lay there, but then as she'd kissed him he'd suffered a complete physical breakdown. He hadn't even been able to stop her retreat, and considering what the consequences of stopping her from leaving would have been, it was quite fortunate. He closed his eyes.

He let the rain wash over him as he lay there; he needed to cool down, his skin felt as if it were on fire. He should have grabbed her; he should have held her tight and never let go. He still didn't understand what was going on, he was so sure that she felt nothing for him, the look on her face that night in the library, the way she'd always acted around him, her inability to even look at him had all pointed to the fact that she felt nothing for him.

But now he was so confused, would she have kissed him if she felt nothing towards him. Sure she was acting totally different to the way she used to . . . . and why had she had his shirt? He still didn't know the answer to that little puzzle. He stood up slowly and looked at the lightening sky and then walked quickly back to the house, on legs that were still very unsteady.

He paused outside her music room for a moment; he was going to find out the answer to the puzzle as soon as he'd changed. He ran quietly up the stairs and into his room.

Miranda lounged on the couch, the music playing quietly in the background. She was thinking about how Gabriel's mouth had felt against hers earlier in the maze, of how the taste of him still lingered on her lips. He hadn't put in an appearance since, she hadn't caught a glimpse of him, and she wondered with slight amusement if he was still lying there in the maze.

The door opened and he popped his head into the room, he smiled at her then disappeared again. Before she had time to wonder what he was doing, he reappeared. She could smell the coppery aroma coming from the mug he had in his hand and smiled.

He lifted her legs carefully and sat down lowering them on to his lap, "fancy a little company?"

"Sure," she said trying to ignore the sensation of his skin on hers.

"What are you listening to?" he asked frowning towards the stereo.

"Not sure, it was already in there, one of Libbi's favourites I think—change it if you want too," she said shifting slightly to look at him. Her foot jerked as she moved and caught his arm, the cup seemed to jump in his hand, and the blood that spilt from the cup splashed, in slow motion, down the front of his shirt. He looked down as the crimson liquid spread rapidly over the fabric.

He sat forward and pulled his shirt off quickly and then turned slowly to look at her and grinned, "if you wanted me to take my shirt off you only had to ask, there was no need to throw blood all over me."

"It was an accident, I didn't do it on purpose," she said indignantly.

"Well of course you didn't," he said laughing at the expression on her face. He stood up and left the room again, before she had chance to protest further. Miranda listened to him moving around in the kitchen and then run up the stairs.

He walked back into the room wearing a clean shirt; he stayed by the door and smiled at her, "you wanna throw this one over me too—or can I drink it?" he asked putting his free hand in his pocket, as he did his shirt fell open and Miranda eyes dropped instantly to his beautiful tight stomach.

"I will if you carry on, it was an accident," she said quietly, trying to drag her eyes away from his torso. It seemed he had become incapable of doing his shirt up lately, not that she was complaining.

Gabriel chuckled but remained where he was as he drained the cup. He walked over to the stereo, placing it on the table as he passed. He stood there for a minute looking through various discs, and selected one. He grinned slightly at Miranda's questioning look, when he walked over and stood in front of her, and then he took her hand and pulled her to her feet.

"Dance with me," he said pulling her into his body. He looked down at her and smiled, "I don't know if you know this, but you're supposed to hold a person when you dance with them," he said quietly wrapping his arms around her. Miranda followed suit and put her arms around him. She was slightly shocked when her hands found bare skin and not the cotton of his shirt. "This is fun," he said dropping his head to her shoulder and resting it there.

Miranda didn't feel the need to say anything; she already knew that nothing would come out even if she did try to answer.

"It's been so long since I danced with anyone—we should do this more often shouldn't we," he said quietly against her skin as he drew in a deep breath, as he exhaled it felt like a cool caress on her flesh. Miranda simply nodded . . . . her voice still hadn't returned, and if he kept doing that she was in no doubt that she would be speechless for a very long time.

"So why did you have my shirt?" he asked quietly as he lowered his head to the base of her throat, several times his lips touched her skin. Miranda closed her eyes and tried hard not to let the sensation have any effect on her, and she was trying so hard that she hardly realised that they'd stopped moving or that he'd stopped talking and was stood grinning down at her.

She opened her eyes slowly and then frowned, she knew he'd asked her something, but she had no idea what it was.

"So my shirt?" he said raising his eyebrow at her.

"What about your shirt?" she asked trying to control the tremor in her voice.

"You know what I'm on about; don't try and act as if you don't—what were you doing with my shirt?" he asked.

"Thank you for the dance," she said pulling away from him, but he swung her around and back into his arms.

"The song hasn't finished yet," he said grinning, "so are you going to answer my question?"

"No," she said pulling away from him again before he managed to gain to tight a hold on her, "I'm so tired; I think I'm going to go to bed—goodnight Gabriel," she said turning and walking towards the door.

Gabriel laughed quietly as he ran in front of her, blocking her means of escape, "oh no, you're not running away from me—not until you answer the question."

"I don't have to answer anything, I'm going to bed," she said pushing forcefully past him. Surprisingly he let her past without a struggle, but as she left the room and ran up the stairs she realised he was right behind her.

"I'll just follow you—I have all the time in the world, eternity in fact—and you don't have the key to your door." She could hear the laughter in his tone as she rushed into her room and slammed the door shut before he got there, she stood with her back to it and he knocked lightly.

"Let me in Miranda," he said then laughed quietly. "Open the door and let me in, you can't stand there all day," he said and laughed again.

"I am not opening the door, I can stand here all day if I need too," she said turning to face the door, "eternity in fact."

"Please Miranda," he said quietly, "are you going to make me stand out here for all of eternity?"

"Yes I am—you're not coming in."

Gabriel grinned, and then stood back from the door, "ok you win, but be warned, I don't give up this easily all the time—we have an eternity to discuss this topic—I won't forget Miranda and one of these nights you will have to answer the question—so for now, sleep well and sweet dreams my love."

She stood there listening intently, she was sure he was bluffing. She could hear him in his room moving about, but still she remained at the door. She listened to him for what seemed like an eternity until finally she heard him get into his bed. Perhaps it wasn't a bluff, perhaps he had given up. She remain at the door a while longer until there wasn't a sound coming from his room, it seemed as if he had indeed given up . . . . because as he'd pointed out, they had the rest of eternity to discuss the topic.

She moved slowly away from the door, undressed quickly and got into her nightgown, then moved over to the mirror, she'd just picked up the hairbrush when her door flew open and Gabriel walked in. She jumped up and turned to face him as he chuckled quietly and closed the door. She ran her eyes over his body as he turned back towards her, she had always wondered what he wore to bed and now she had her answer, shorts, just shorts and nothing else.

"Get out of my room," she said forcing herself into action. She moved forward and put her hands on his chest and tried to push him back towards the door.

"No I'm not leaving until you answer the question—I told you I don't give up that easily," he laughed as she continued trying to push him.

"I knew you were bluffing," she said annoyed at herself for believing him. "Get out of my room."

"I thought you were going to stand by the door for eternity," he said wrapping his arms around her and picking her up. Miranda realised, with growing dismay that they were moving towards the bed.

"Gabriel put me down," she said desperately pushing at his chest.

"Your wish is my command," he chuckled as he dropped her onto it, "now I'm only asking once more—and you'd better tell me the truth, or else we're going to be spending an awful lot of time together—and I don't just mean all night, I'll be here when you go to sleep and I will be here when you wake up, and I'll be here for all the bits in between, that could be interesting—I seem to remember that you talk in your sleep—so do you want to tell me what you were doing with my shirt?"

Miranda shook her head slightly, and tried to scramble, very unladylike, over to the other side of the bed, but he moved at speed and was around the other side, blocking her escape, before she'd moved very far. In an instant he was lay next to her, his arms around her pulling her close.

"There now, isn't that comfortable," he said quietly moving his head down to the base of her throat, "I think I'm going to enjoy spending eternity in your bed," he whispered against her skin.

"Gabriel—you can't sleep here," she said closing her eyes against the sensation of his lips on her skin.

"All you have to do to get rid of me is answer the question—then I will leave you in peace, until then I'm not moving—but please don't answer just yet because I am rather enjoying myself," he said as he lightly skimmed his lips across her flesh.

"I had it because you left and I missed you, I took your shirt so that I had something to remember you with, it smelt of you and I slept in it every night," she said suddenly.

He pulled away from her slightly and smiled, "I said I didn't want you to tell me yet—you're such a killjoy," he lowered his head and resumed kissing her neck.

"But I told you the reason," she said desperately trying to push him away, "please—I told you the reason."

"I know—but I'm pretending—that I didn't—hear you," he said in between kisses.

"But I told you, please—stop."

He pulled away from her and rolled onto his back, "you missed me so much that you slept in my shirt every single night and yet here you are telling me to go?"

Miranda lay there unable to answer, she didn't want him to go . . . . but if he stayed?

He turning his head to look at her, "so, shall I go?"

"I think, I don't—yes—you should go," she stammered as he lay there looking at her the slightest of smiles tugging at the corners of his mouth.

He looked at her for a few more seconds then kissed her gently on the head. "Ok, but I'm only going because you asked me too—I'm not going because I want too," he said pulling the cover back and getting out of the bed, he looked down at her for a moment and moved to the door. "Oh and another thing," he said turning back to her, "the reason I came back, the only reason that I came back, was because I missed you too," he said and then left the room.

The sun shone outside the window, a shaft of light peeked through the small gap in the curtains. He lay listening to the noises coming from the bedroom next door. She seemed to be making an awful lot of noise for someone who was supposed to be asleep. But then shouldn't he also be asleep.

He was trying to sleep but his recall seemed to be in overdrive, reminding him of how it had felt to hold her, of how her scent had filled his dead lungs and caused them to ache, of how soft her skin felt against his lips, of how she filled his senses completely.

He started wondering exactly how much longer it was going take for him to completely crack. As he'd held her it had crossed his mind several times that he should just say the words . . . . tell her that he loved her . . . . that he'd always loved her. He turned away from the wall and frowned it was inevitable that it was going to happen sooner or later, especially if he found himself in a similar situation as he'd been in tonight. He sighed and threw his arm over his eyes, as his brain replayed the scent from her room all over again.

27

Gabriel walked into the kitchen and frowned at the sight of Nathanael sitting at the table, but he wasn't going to let the fact that his brother was back ruin his good mood. He smiled at Michael as he looked over uncertainly, "evening Mike," he said sitting opposite Nathanael, "evening Nate," he added as an afterthought.

Nathanael frowned at him, "when did you get back?"

"Yeah it's nice to see you too," Gabriel grinned, "I got back eleven days and—twenty two hours ago," he said consulting his watch for a moment.

Nathanael sat back in his chair, the frown still on his face, "where's Miranda?"

"Still in bed I suppose—we were up a little later than usual, it must have been around ten this morning when I left her to get some sleep," Gabriel said smiling over at Michael.

Nathanael looked at him for a moment then smiled slightly; he wasn't at all convinced by his brother's statement, if anything had happened between them he was pretty sure Gabriel wouldn't have left her room at all. He sat forward and frowned again, he couldn't let the thought sidetrack him. He had returned for a purpose. "Well considering you're such good friends now, maybe you could go and wake her—I need to speak to her—to all of you in fact," he said and then smiled again as Gabriel frowned suddenly.

"What about?" Gabriel asked eyeing him suspiciously.

"Go and get Miranda and then I'll tell you," Nathanael said smiling again.

The moon was bright in the sky, as Gabriel pulled open the curtains, Miranda closed her eyes tight as he walked over and sat down beside her.

"It's time to get up sleepy head," he and smiled down at her as he gently traced his finger down her arm. "Nate's back—he wants to talk to us," he added frowning slightly.

Miranda opened one eye and looked at him. "Nathan wants to talk to—us?" she asked opening the other eye to look at him properly, "what about?"

Gabriel shrugged, "I have no idea, he's full of intrigue—it must be something really important, Nate never wants to talk to any of us normally—maybe he's leaving for good and he wants to say his heartfelt goodbyes," he chuckled as he stood up. "Come on, he won't talk until you're there."

Miranda swung her legs out of the bed, and walked to her wardrobe. Gabriel leant against the door and watched her as she took out her clothes. She turned to look at his grinning face and frowned. "Do you mind? I need to get dressed."

"No, I don't mind—you carry on—take all the time you need," he said his grin widening.

"I know I keep saying this, but get out of my room Gabriel."

"You spoil all of my fun—are you sure you don't want me to stay and—help," he said running his eyes slowly over her body.

"Get out!" she ordered trying to ignore the thrill of excitement that ran through her at his gaze. He laughed and then turned and left the room, and she made a mental note to ask Morana for the key to her door.

As Miranda entered the kitchen Nathanael looked up and smiled at her. She hesitated for a moment as she tried to decide who to sit by. She walked around the table and took the seat next to Nathanael; he put his arm around her shoulder and kissed her on the cheek. "I missed you," he said then looked over at his brother and smiled.

Miranda looked over at Gabriel too but his face showed only mild amusement, as if he were enjoying the show. He sat back in his chair and stretched his arms above his head bringing his hands down behind his neck, he grinned as Miranda's eyes dropped to his torso then quickly back to his face. He winked at her as she looked away.

Why did he repeatedly do that, didn't he know the effect it had on her, of all the things that ran through her mind as his shirt pulled tightly across his body. Of course he did—he knew exactly what he was doing, and he was enjoying it. She started to regret her choice of seats—however would she concentrate on the conversation?

"Will you please get on with it," Gabriel said looking from Miranda to his brother. "Some of us have a life."

Nathanael frowned, "where's Michael?"

"Oh forget Michael," Morana said impatiently, joining them at the table.

Nathanael frowned at Morana for a moment then looked at Miranda again, "well the reason that I left was because I was puzzled," he paused and sat back in his chair. "How could our little Miranda here possess such incredible power, what with the levitating, the energy bolts, the telekinesis, the void and everything, I mean I know we don't know what generation she is, but even so—incredibly powerful for such a young vamp."

"Yeah so," Gabriel said impatiently. He glanced at Morana for a second and frowned, no-one had even mentioned the void until now, he had no idea that anyone apart from he himself could call on that particular power.

"I bet none of you even thought of the possibility that she could be a descendent did you?"

Morana gasped audibly, and Gabriel's frowned deepened. "A descendant," he repeated as if not believing the words, Nathanael nodded.

"You're sure about this?" he asked looking from Nathanael to Miranda.

"Absolutely, I went over it a few times."

Miranda frowned, "descendant—what does that mean?"

"Are you absolutely sure?" Morana asked the shock apparent on her face.

"As I've just said I went over it a few times," Nathanael said exasperated by the woman's question.

Silence fell in the room as Miranda looked from one face to another. They all seemed shocked into silence, lost in their own thoughts. "Will you please explain what you're on about, I don't understand, descendant of what—and why do you all look so shocked?" she asked looking towards Gabriel.

"Shocked is a bit of an understatement," he said rubbing his eyes. He looked at her for a moment, "you are descended from a long line of letters—you're a first generation Miranda."

"A first generation—how? I can't—I don't understand," Miranda said frowning.

"Who's letter?" Morana asked looking over at Nathanael.

"Ambrose," Nathanael informed her.

"Ambrose?" Morana said her eyes widening. Gabriel frowned down at the table, as Michael walked into the kitchen and sat down next to him.

"But he's dead—they're all dead," Miranda said frowning then she looked up at Gabriel again. "I was never—I didn't ever see—how could I be I couldn't—" she stopped talking as Nathanael placed his hand on hers.

"You come from along line of letters Miranda—you were born with the venom already in you," he said glancing over at Gabriel.

Miranda's eyes opened wide as she too looked back at Gabriel, "you mean my family—oh my god—my family?"

Gabriel nodded, "numerous generations of your family actually—Ambrose never changed his chosen family, so that would've included your great grandmother, your grandmother and your mother."

"My Mother—but how? When did Ambrose die?" she asked confused by his statement, she thought they'd all died centuries before.

"About seventeen years ago," Nathanael said smiling over at Gabriel. "Isn't that about right Gabe," he said more to Gabriel than anyone else. Silence took over again as they sat there, there were so many things she needed to ask, so many things she needed to know.

"Well it's just as well that Gabe here is the ancient expert," Michael said patting him lightly on the back. "Not so bad having one of the oldest living vamps in the house after all, is it," he said with a smile.

"I can answer her questions too," Nathanael said frowning, "I've been around as long as him."

"For god's sake, don't start this now Nate, Gabe knows far more than you and you know it," Morana said irritated.

Nathanael considered her for a moment then looked at Gabriel. He pushed his chair back and stood up, "fine whatever," he said as he left the house. They sat in silence as they heard a car engine roar into life and disappear into the distance.

Gabriel stood after a few moments, "we'd better go to the library."

Once in the library, Gabriel took the couch opposite her. She pulled the first volume onto her lap and opened it to the first page. She looked at the names again then back at Gabriel, she closed the book and went to sit next to him. He smiled as she pulled her legs up and crossed them; she looked like a little girl waiting for a bed time story.

"Whoever would have thought you'd be a first generation—how did I not know—all this time," he said sitting back and closing his eyes. Miranda watched him as he sat there, so many questions had been swimming around her head, but now sat looking at his perfect face she couldn't think of one. Gabriel smiled then opened his eyes slowly to look at her.

"Why were the ancients all so afraid of you?" She asked opening the book.

Gabriel frowned slightly, "they were afraid because I was stronger than they were—I'm the strongest of my generation, I was also very angry for what they'd done to me—for how they just left me there, I blamed them for all that I did—and they were worried that I would have my revenge," he said looking away from her and down at the floor.

She looked at him for several seconds and then turned to look at the book, she read down the names again then looked back at him, "and I take it they had just cause to worry that you would take your revenge."

Gabriel looked back at her and nodded, "yes they did have just cause—and I did have my revenge."

The second page of the first tome had been written by Decastell, telling of how they came over to England.

September, 1267.

I think England will suit us very well . . . . It is a good place to settle down. Anouk, Cormack, Zeke, Ambrose and I have already secured our letters and I am confident that the others will soon follow our example Ambrose and I have also acquired a peaceful residence a few miles from the manor out of sight of the general populous. London town itself seems a dirty, flee infested place . . . . full of homeless, uncaring creatures . . . . I think we will have a trouble free life in this place. Yes I think I could call England my home.

She closed the book and turned over onto her back; she lay on her bed and thought about her earlier conversation with Gabriel.

He'd gone after Shavaun and Ariel first, he'd tracked them halfway across the country, and they knew he was following, several times they'd doubled back on themselves trying to throw him off their trail, they had been around for centuries and thought they knew every trick in the book, they had no idea that Gabriel was the best tracker of his generation. But they soon realised there was no trick they could use to lose him so they decided their only option was to try and ambush him. Only he was so much quicker than them and had cut both their heads off before they'd even realised he was close.

"I wasn't really in any rush to kill the rest, I mean I was going to get them all eventually, and to be truthful I liked to think of them cowering, wondering just when I'd appear to remove their heads, but I met Decastell quite by chance on my way back home—he knew who I was straight away—so we agreed we should just do away with the pleasantries and get on with it," he'd said sitting back and smiling at her.

"Decastell was strong, well stronger than the rest—he was really quite something—and even though I felt nothing but hate for him, I couldn't help but wonder at his beauty," he said quietly then frowned, "him and his kind didn't belong here—but to be in his presence if only until I removed his head was something, like being in the presence of an angel, kind of like being in the presence of god." He sat forward and rubbed his head for a moment, then frowned again, "every second felt it when an ancient died, it was like we were all still connected to them in some way—we felt the blade across our skin, felt the burn of silver slicing through our flesh, felt the emptiness that was death rise up through our bodies—it felt as if I was actually dying too."

She'd asked him why he'd felt the need to kill all of them and he'd frowned then changed the subject quickly. She couldn't understand the sudden change in his mood as he'd shifted uncomfortably at the question, and she decided to leave it at that, even though there was so much more that she wanted to know. As the conversation had drawn to an end she'd left him to do some work, even though she could've stayed and talked to him all night.

She turned onto her side and looked down at the book; why didn't he want to tell her why he'd killed them, it didn't matter to her why he'd done it; it wouldn't make her feel any different towards him. She frowned slightly; Nathanael would know . . . . maybe she should ask him. There was a soft tap on her door; Gabriel popped his head around the door and smiled.

"Come in," she said. He had brought her a cup, and her mouth started to water the instant she caught the aroma of the rich warm liquid, but although she was hungry, the sight of his open shirt made it impossible to think of anything else other than running her hands over his body.

"I thought you might be hungry," he said handing her the cup; she took it and gulped down the fluid in a single mouthful. She put the cup down and instantly looked back at his chest. Gabriel chuckled and sat down next to her on the bed. "I can't believe you're still reading," he said looking at the book.

"I've finished for now" she said sitting up and crossing her legs, "but I have a lot of questions."

"Ask away," he said lying across the bed. Miranda stared at him as his shirt fell open exposing more of his beautiful flesh. Only last night he'd been here in this room with her, in this bed with her, kissing her. Suddenly all the questions she wanted to ask disappeared from her mind.

Gabriel turned his head to look at her when she didn't speak; he grinned for a moment and looked back at the ceiling. He knew what had caused her sudden silence; he knew the thoughts going through her head, because he had the exact same thoughts in his head. Thoughts of how it had felt as his lips had trailed down her skin, thoughts of how she had felt in his arms. "In your own time," he said, the humour in his voice snapped her out of her reverie.

"You'll have to move," she said moving up the bed to lie down. Gabriel sat up and looked at her then moved to lie down beside her with a slight grin.

"Is this acceptable now?" he said raising an eyebrow at her. She seemed to consider the question for a moment, and then she smiled and nodded her head. She rested her head on her hands, and he smiled then moved a little closer.

"The first thing I wanted to ask has nothing to do with the ancients—it's about something Nathan said after you left," she said. Gabriel frowned and his body tensed slightly. She moved a little closer and then put her arm around him, "you have to promise you won't get angry," she said as he moved closer still and put his arm under her head.

"I—promise," he said a little doubtfully.

She looked at him for a moment, "Nathan said that you loved Sophie—you were in love with her, and the reason that you killed her was because she chose him and not you," she said quietly.

"Do you believe him?" he asked frowning.

Miranda shook her head, how could she possibly admit that she had wondered for a moment when Nathanael had said it. Looking at his face now, she knew it wasn't true.

"I didn't love her—but Nate believes what he wants to believe, because what he believes makes his life a little easier, there were a lot of things Nathan didn't know about his wife—no I never loved her," he said quietly. "Next question."

"Well there is something else, again not ancient related—it's something that has been on my mind for a while—but what with one thing and another—" she said frowning.

"Ok, what is it?" he asked mirroring her frown; he didn't care for all these unrelated questions very much.

"The thing is, I think there may be something wrong with me," she said laying her head on his chest.

"Something wrong with you—why would you think that there's something wrong with you?"

"Well, my recall isn't working properly—I mean I remember mostly everything, but—" she lifted her head again to look at him and frowned slightly, "there are things that I can't remember—it's as if I didn't exist until the age of seven, but it's strange—because there's this kind of darkness—like seven years of darkness, and then there's me—I asked Ana about it, and she said not to worry, but that was a while ago and it's still not working."

Gabriel smiled; it surprised him that it had taken her so long to ask about it again—but then a lot had happened since the last time she'd asked.

"You don't know what I'm on about do you, I suppose you think I'm a real strange sort now—a first that can't even use recall properly—perhaps Nathan got it wrong, perhaps I'm not even a real vampire," she said returning her head to his chest. "Do you think there is something wrong with me," she said stifling a yawn.

"No I don't think there's anything wrong with you," Gabriel said pulling her a little closer. "I'm quite sure it's nothing to worry about." Miranda yawned again; she was so comfortable in his arms that sleep wasn't far away. "Are you tired?" he asked stroking her hair.

"Yes a little."

"Do you want me to go?"

"Not yet—I'm comfortable," she said yawning again.

Gabriel laughed softly, and continued stroking her hair. She didn't want to fall asleep, she wanted to talk to him all day . . . . because she knew as soon as she fell asleep, he'd leave and she didn't want him to leave. But as he lay there stroking her hair, she just couldn't keep her eyes open. She succumbed to sleep with a smile on her face.

Gabriel watched her with fascination as she slept. He couldn't help but smile as she muttered away to herself.

She had said his name, and he'd answered thinking she was still awake. Then when no question had followed, he'd pulled away slightly to look at her and was surprised to see she was sleeping.

He knew he should leave, but he just lay there watching her, she was so beautiful. He lifted his hand and gently stroked her cheek and she momentarily tightened her arm around him. He frowned and lowered his hand.

He wanted to kiss her so very much, it felt like infinity since her lips had last touched his. He reluctantly pulled his arm out from underneath her and carefully moved off the bed so that he didn't wake her. He stood looking down at her for a moment, and he just couldn't stop himself, he bent over and kissed her lightly on the lips. As he pulled away, she whispered his name.

He turned quickly and left her room. He shut the door to his room quietly, got undressed and got into bed. It wasn't going to be too long before he had to tell her everything, he should have told her tonight, when she'd asked him about recall . . . . he should have just thrown caution to the wind and told her everything. It was going to happen anyway . . . . and pretty soon it seemed.

28

Gabriel opened the library door and was surprised to see Miranda already sat on the couch with the opened tome on her lap; he smiled at her as he walked over to the computer and turned it on. "Reading again?" he asked as he sat down.

"Yeah—do you think the council know about me?" she asked looking up at him.

Gabriel looked at her for a moment and considered the question, "yes, they know about you, they kept records of all the letters, that's where Nathan got his information I suppose—and if Nate showed interest in it I've no doubt that questions would have been asked—I suppose they are very curious about you—I suppose we should expect a visit sooner or later," he said with a slight frown. Miranda looked at him wide eyed, and he smiled. "You have nothing to worry about, they won't arm you Miranda—I wouldn't let any of them hurt you," he said quietly and smiled again.

Miranda smiled back uncertainly, and they sat there looking at each other for a few moments, then she reluctantly dragged her attention back to the book in her lap. Again she was highly aware that he was still watching her as she read the entries made about the first ever first generation.

October 1372,

I do not think Decastell is very taken with my idea of actually trying to turning one of the letters, although I am sure he is as curious as I as to the outcome of said experiment . . . . I wish to know if they will turn out as we have . . . . that being the case were we also experiments . . . .

were we all once human and simply cannot remember . . . . we all think that we are a pure breed . . . . and nothing like the humans that surround us . . . . but if one was changed what is to say they would not be exactly as we are . . . . I see that I must argue my point a little longer with my brother.

January 1373,

Ambrose goes on and on . . . . trying so desperately to get me to agree on the changing of a letter . . . . I am close to agreeing . . . . if only to stop his relentless drone on the subject . . . . if I did not love him so I would remove his head myself . . . . I too am rather intrigued as to the effect our venom would have on humans . . . . but this must not be taken lightly . . . . there are so many unknown factors to this experiment . . . . and although I grow tired of the conversation, we must talk more on the subject before we decide on anything.

March 1375,

After many more discussions and much to Ambrose's delight . . . . we have indeed decided to try our experiment . . . . although I have told Ambrose in no uncertain terms that we will not be doing this alone . . . . we do not know what to expect so I have asked my brothers and sisters for aid . . . . we are safer as a whole . . . . we do not know the result and therefore I think it prudent to involve each and everyone of us.

Unfortunately Anouk refuses to leave her home therefore it is left to Ambrose, me and our seven other brothers and sisters to try our experiment . . . . though I would feel much happier if we were all involved I realise that the decision is Anouk's.

June 1375,

She sleeps . . . . and she sleeps . . . . and I wonder if she will ever wake up . . . . Nadia . . . . perhaps our venom is after all lethal to humans in larger *doses . . . . we are meant to be alone on this earth . . . . we are not meant to repopulate the planet with our kind . . . . I feel the experiment has failed.*

June 1375,

At last she as awoken . . . . we thought she never would . . . . though I am concerned . . . . she does not appear to be as we are, she appears to be so much stronger . . . . and apparently so much faster . . . . and her powers are on a par with ours . . . . we have revised a plan to contain her . . . . until we can decide what to do with her . . . . Decastell is not at all happy at losing his letter . . . . though I have no doubt that he will soon secure another.

Miranda read the last two entries again then looked over at Gabriel; he looked over at her and smiled.

"So do you think that was the reason I slept for so long after I changed, it says in here that Nadia also slept for a long time," she said looking back down at the book.

Gabriel frowned slightly, and then nodded, "it never even occurred to me—I mean why would it?" Miranda looked over at him and he smiled, "well that's another mystery solved," he said looking back at the computer.

Miranda watched him for a moment as he sat staring at the screen, and then looked back at the book.

August 1375,

We cannot control her for much longer, I fear her rage gets worse with every passing day, we cannot allow her to hunt and I fear she is starving . . . . the longer she goes without feeding the worse the lust becomes for her . . . . we will soon have to dispatch her . . . . she is quite insane and though it pains me . . . . she will have to die . . . . the problem we face is how to do it . . . . she is so much stronger than us . . . . and again I have a feeling of foreboding . . . . there is nothing more than this for us . . . . we are meant to be alone in our life . . . . to walk alone for the rest of eternity . . . . our makers plan I fear.

September 1375,

The deed is done, Nadia is no more, my beautiful letter . . . . gone, she should never have been turned . . . . and yet I find I am now curious to the effects of our venom on a normal human . . . . surely a normal human would react differently than a letter . . . . perhaps a second generation would turn out much as we have . . . . perhaps this is why . . . . because she already had my venom in her body . . . passed down from her ancestors . . . . perhaps I should just leave my curiosity simply as it is . . . . a curiosity!

She turned several pages and read the mundane entries concerning venom and powers, none of which interested her, but then she found Ambrose's and Decastell's fears for Anouk and the entries they'd made concerning her death.

April 1415,

I have just arrived home from visiting my beautiful Anouk, and I am sorry to report that I am extremely worried by her behaviour, I fear the worse . . . . she has fallen hopelessly in love with her letter. She referred to him often during my visits with her; I have never experienced behaviour quite like it. I pray that she doesn't do something foolish . . . I think she gets lonely now that she and Zeke have parted ways. I left her with a stark warning . . . . and yet I fear she still does not realise the true and real danger she faces if she turns Thomas . . . . having not been there when we carried out our experiment on poor Nadia she has no idea about the effects of changing a letter . . . . I have tried time and again to instil the severity of such an undertaking on her . . . . but I fear she thinks I am just being too cautious . . . . I pray she will take heed and will not do any thing foolish.

Decastell had made an entry about her demise.

June 1417,

My poor Anouk is sadly no more, we tried to warn her, Ambrose, I know, tried time upon time . . . . but alas she did not heed our words . . . . she died in the most cruel of ways at the hands of her letter . . . . she will be sadly missed, now all we have to do is find Thomas and dispose of him before he becomes too much of a problem to us . . . . I will truly miss my dear sister.

Then he had made another entry shortly after.

July 1417,

Thomas found, wondering the streets of London, luckily he was not noticed by many in his short Vampiric life . . . . I can hardly believe the strength of him . . . . Ambrose brought Cormack, Vania, Zeke and Ariel for support . . . . and with good reason, we know only too well the strength of the firsts . . . . I very often thought my own demise was close during the ensuing battle . . . . alas it is with heavy heart that I report that my brother Cormack did not make it . . . . Thomas laid him to waste in the most undignified way . . . . but I will remain eternally grateful for his help . . . he fought hard and well . . . . I will truly miss my dear brother.

August 1418,

I am a little worried for my brother Decastell, after our failed attempt at turning Nadia and then Thomas and with the loss of Anouk and Cormack; I fear he has fallen into some kind of depression. He will not even speak of turning a normal human, and if I and my other brothers and sisters discuss the topic he simply frowns and walks from the room . . . . and yet we are still intrigued by the idea of this next experiment. He still misses Anouk and Cormack so very much . . . .

so very much that I can feel his grief wrap itself around me, In those moments the tears flow and I wish I could join them . . . . my poor Decastell suffers more than any of us . . . . and I do not know how to help him.

There were several more pages filled with woeful entries about the loss of Anouk and Cormack, Decastell for the most part seemed to miss them the most. He also made several observations about the health of Zeke, who for a short period had stopped feeding and refused to leave his bed. Miranda leafed through the pages until something else caught her attention.

September 1587,

They have discussed this at length, it seems, without involving me . . . . my pain so great that I did not want to be included . . . . but now it seems the conversation has reached its finality . . . . I am out voted seven to one . . . . so I have no choice but to allow my brothers and sisters to try this new venture . . . . and I must admit, with my pain now becoming bearable that I myself am tempted . . . . if Ambrose creates himself a partner I feel I may have no choice . . . life would be extremely lonely without anyone to keep me company.

February 1588,

We assumed . . . . I assumed, wrongly, that they would turn out better than the firsts . . . . but they did not. Zachariel had us all fooled with his compliance . . . . and it was decided to turn others . . . . Evangeline, Raphael, Saraph, Sammael, Azrael, Uriel and Anngela . . . . it was not until they all woke that we realised our mistake. They too are extremely powerful . . . . we thought that we may be able to control them better than we could Nadia . . . . but alas, to my vexation, we can not . . . . and although they do not appear to be as gifted as Nadia they do possess a strength and speed far superior to ours.

They have left . . . . all gone . . . none were willing to stay with us, their makers . . . . they see us as weak and feeble . . . a crutch in their new powerful lives . . . . I should have trusted my own mind after Thomas . . . . and stopped this idiocy before it had started.

January 1603,

I have just met with Sammael, Vania's creation . . . . I was quite surprised when he appeared at my door. I was quite convinced that I would never see him again. He has informed me that he and the other six second generations have formed a council . . . . he wanted to know if we would be creating anymore of his generation . . . . in fact he warned me against it . . . . how easily they turned on us . . . . and now they are deciding to impose laws on our kind . . . . for our own good . . . . we have created monsters!

June 1603,

The council have set their laws . . . . I was astounded when Sam informed me that they would allow me and my brothers and sisters to keep our letters . . . . of all the nerve . . . . and if you believe it we also have to disclose the identities of our letters . . . I am disgusted with these laws . . . and yet in some sick way I believe it is only what we deserve . . . . I fear for our way of life now . . . . Sammael gave me a short list of their laws for me and my family . . . the penalties for breaking any of their laws range from incarceration to death.

There were several more pages with entries made about the council, Decastell's anger seemed to grow with each one, but he also knew that he was powerless against the seconds and they knew it too. Miranda wondered why he hadn't written about the laws. She turned the pages to see if he'd written them down anywhere, when Gabriel's name caught her eye.

March 1691,

I am fearful of this second . . . . Gabriel . . . . I am very angry that he was made.

I do not know what possessed Shavaun and Ariel, with the law that was passed, forbidding us from making anymore . . . . they are stupid . . . taking it upon themselves in such a foolish, lustful way . . . . I feel it was not their intention to kill him . . . . they did not intend just feeding on him . . . . I can not understand the reasoning for this . . . . and although I ask . . . . they, of course, will not tell me . . . . they are extremely secretive on this subject . . . . they did not even consider the consequences . . . . so alas the damage is now done. I feel they will pay for their mistake.

It pains me to think that they turned him and simply left him there without guidance, without the knowledge of what he had become.

I fear the council will have a lot to say on this matter . . . . I know that Shavaun and Ariel have brought this upon themselves . . . . but I have sent them away and I think it wise that they stay away indefinitely . . . not only because of the council but because of Gabriel . . . with this one foolish act they have made many enemies . . . I wonder if we should go and find Gabriel . . . . if we sort this mess out ourselves maybe the council will not get involved . . . . perhaps if we find him soon enough we could kill him before the council even discover his existence.

She shut the book quickly and glanced over at Gabriel; he looked over at her and frowned. “What’s wrong?” he asked standing up and walking over to sit beside her.

“The ancients were planning to kill you,” she said a little shocked at the revelation.

Gabriel grinned, and then nodded. “Yes they planned to kill me—a lot of good that did them—the only one worth anything was Decastell, I was almost sorry when I tore his head off,” he chuckled at the look on her face.

"So what happened with the council, didn't they get involved?" she asked.

"No, they wanted me to succeed—with the ancients having letters the council saw them as a liability—I was visited by several of them, shortly after I'd killed Shavaun, Ariel and Decastell—Azrael, Raphael, Saraph and Anngela, they asked me if I intended to kill the rest or if I was simply going to stop at three—I told them that I did intend to kill all of them and if they or any of the other seconds had a problem then they should all come and try to stop me," he said frowning then chuckled slightly. "I make myself sound like a real hothead, don't I—I suppose in my younger years I was."

He looked at Miranda and frowned as an image of the time he'd slapped her ran through his mind. "Well I suppose I can still be a little hot headed sometimes," he said quietly. "Anyway they assured me that they had no intention of stopping me, they were very nice actually, we even went hunting together, when they left they wished me luck—I met Zachariel shortly after I'd killed Ambrose, he is the elected leader of the council, he brought me the tomes—I think they classed me as a brother, being a second—I think they were all a little intimidated by me—turns out I'm stronger than all of them."

"Stronger? How if you're all second generations?" Miranda asked trying hard to keep her eyes off his lips as he spoke. Every time her eyes strayed to his mouth, all she could think of was kissing him.

"I think, but I'm not sure about this, that it had something to do with the fact that I was bitten by two of the ancients, I got twice the power—there was also some kind of residual bond between the other seconds and the ancients, they were unable to harm them in anyway, and again I think because I was bitten by two of them it negated that bond somehow," he said getting to his feet, he walked back to the computer and sat down; he glanced over at her as she stood up and picked up the tome.

"I will leave you to work now, I'm going to my room for a while," she said. She walked to the door then turned to look at him with a frown, "does it bother you, me being a first generation?"

Gabriel looked at her for a moment then shook his head, "it's the best news I've ever heard," he said looking back at the computer.

Gabriel looked up at the door as it closed behind her then sat back in his chair, he normally had better control of recall, he'd learnt the art of suppressing certain things over many, many years of practice. Why was it still so surprising that he lost control while she was around?

As the image appeared, he'd felt slightly shocked . . . . as a rule, perfect recall shouldn't be like that, if you had complete control over it as he did. Images didn't just appear, hence the name recall. Usually you had to think of the specific memory before it appeared; it was all quite unnerving and unusual. Gabriel frowned, he knew there was something else unusual about it, and the images had seemed slightly flawed, something was wrong but he just couldn't quite put his finger on it.

He looked over at the door again and his frown deepened, why had she left so suddenly, why would she think being a first generation would bother him? He wasn't bothered in the slightest, because now she would not be held accountable for his actions. If he could pluck up the courage to tell her how he felt, if he told her how much he loved her, how much he wanted her and if she reciprocated his feelings, he knew that no harm would come to her.

So what was stopping him, he had the green light as far as her heritage was concerned . . . . her maker wouldn't have any power over her and he was pretty sure the council would protect her. He also knew the effect he seemed to have on her lately, when he kissed her she became slightly speechless, the way she couldn't help but stare at him if his shirt was open . . . . she wanted him. So what was stopping him . . . . one small thing was stopping him . . . . just one small thing . . . . he wanted her to love him.

29

July 1693,

Shavaun and Ariel slaughtered, reduced to ash, my sisters murdered by the one they made, I am too sick for words . . . . I can not express my anger enough for what he did to them . . . . ripped apart . . . . torn limb from limb . . . . and now Decastell is hell bent on revenge . . . . I have never witnessed him in such a rage . . . . I would compare his temper to that of Nadia . . . . I do not fancy Gabriel's chances were he to meet Decastell at the moment . . . . I even found myself cowering in his presence.

August 1693,

My brother Decastell laid to waste . . . also dying in the most undignified way . . . . my heart aches for this loss . . . . he was my brother . . . my protector . . . . how will any of us survive . . . . this Gabriel is the strongest second I have ever known . . . I cannot hate enough for what he has taken from me . . . . what chance do any of us have if Gabriel was able to beat him so easily . . . . oh my pain and suffering . . . . I cannot bear it.

April 1725,

I live on with this deep unforgiving ache . . . . and since Decastell died I've prayed for death several times . . . . my only solace that he will come and join me to my brother again soon enough . . . . I keep warning my remaining brothers and sister to be vigilant . . . . for I know he intends to end us all.

October 1795,

She did not heed my warning. Vania dead at the hands of Gabriel . . . . I am hoping my words did not fall on deaf ears with my other brothers and sister . . . . I hope they realise that Gabriel is indeed very serious in his mission to rid the world of our family . . . . he will not stop until he has wiped us off the face of this earth . . . . Decastell was worried for our way of life . . . . I am worried for our very existence.

January 1820,

It seems my only entries in this damnable book will be about death and heartache. Carad's demise has come as no real surprise; Gabriel removed his head with such speed that my brother would not have had time to feel it . . . . I hope that he will be as kind with the last of us. Freya is heartbroken at the loss of her mate . . . . and has already expressed a shocking desire to join her beloved Carad. I feel she will go willingly to death should Gabriel find her, his job made easier by her longing to be reunited with the one she loves.

February 1820,

Farewell my sister, I hope your suffering was short and that you are now joined with our family again . . . . my heart is too heavy to write anymore.

October 1875,

I am the last of my race . . . . Zeke dead . . . . my family . . . . all disposed . . . . all blown away on the wind . . . all dead . . . . all nine gone. I know he will come for me soon enough . . . . his anger knows no bounds . . . . he is fierce and resolute in his hunt to wipe out my family . . . . and I am next . . . I should run . . . . but what is the point in that . . . . I feel that it would not matter where I went . . . . he would find me . . . . all I can do is wait for death . . . . and hope that when he does find me it will be swift.

Miranda closed the book and glanced over at the window, still a few hours until sunrise, still a few hours to spend with Gabriel. She stood up and looked down at the tomes, she had eternity to read them right now she wanted to look at Gabriel's gorgeous face; at his sexy, hard body . . . . the tomes could wait.

She walked down the stairs and opened the library door and frowned, he wasn't there. She closed the door quietly and walked to the kitchen.

Nathanael sat as still as he could at the table, he looked over at Gabriel and frowned, Gabriel mirrored his look. Nathanael's frown deepened and so did Gabriel's. He had been sitting there for the last hour and everything that he did, Gabriel did . . . . and it was getting on his nerves.

He leant forward and glared at his brother, "this is a little childish don't you think."

Gabriel leant forward and glared at his brother, "this is a little childish don't you think."

Nathanael sat back and folded his arms and so did Gabriel.

"Stop it," Nathanael said frowning at him.

"Stop it," Gabriel said frowning at him.

Miranda walked into the kitchen and looked at Gabriel and then at Nathanael, and smiled as she carried on over to the cupboard. She took out a bottle and opened it and turned to look at the brothers again as Nathanael moved slightly and Gabriel copied him.

"For god's sake, stop it now or else I'm going to punch you," Nathanael frowned over at him.

"For god's sake, stop it now or else I'm going to punch you," Gabriel repeated frowning over at him.

Miranda watched the exchange and had to sympathise with Nathanael, her brother used to do the exact same thing to her before he'd abandoned her all those years ago. Miranda frowned as his image appeared in her mind . . . . her brother used to go home on the odd occasion just to check up on her . . . . just to make sure she was still alive . . . . but his visits had become infrequent, until they stopped all together. Miranda's frown deepened . . . . she'd though her brother had just had enough of the abuse, and that was why he'd disappeared . . . . but now?

Gabriel looked away from Nathanael and frowned at her, "Miranda—what's wrong?" he asked getting to his feet quickly and moving towards her.

"I have a brother—Caleb," she said her frown deepening, "if he was bitten he'd be a first too wouldn't he?"

Gabriel mimicked her frown, "yes he would be—why are you worried about him?"

Miranda shook her head as Nathanael stood up and moved towards her too, "what if it was Caleb—what if he found me—he knew me, spoke to me—what if he did this to me," she said feeling the energy start to bubble in her stomach.

"The chances of that are slight at best Miranda," Nathanael said stopping at Gabriel's side.

"Why are they—I mean he knew my name—what's to say Caleb wasn't turned years ago, what's to say it wasn't Caleb who found me," she said backing away from them. The energy started to spread through her body and she didn't want either of them to get hurt.

"Miranda, please calm down—I'm pretty sure it wasn't your brother," Nathanael said taking a step closer to her. She shook her head and she moved back further until she was pressed against the kitchen wall.

"Miranda—calm down," Gabriel said moving with Nathanael.

"I'm trying, it's too late," she said closing her eyes for a moment. Her whole body felt as if it was bubbling, she opened her eyes quickly and blinked rapidly as Gabriel started to disappear before her eyes, and even though she knew it was useless she reached out for him, instead of grabbing him her hand simply floated through him. He was right in front of her and yet she couldn't reach him.

"Gabriel!" she shouted but her voice was no more than a whisper, then she was forced further back. Pulled away from him and she closed her eyes. For the shortest of moments she felt ice cold and she had the feeling of falling. She jerked violently for a split second and then she opened her eyes slowly. "This is not the kitchen," her mind whispered as she looked around the room.

There were various pieces of furniture, all covered in white sheeting, and she looked slowly around the room. There was a rather large fire place to her right, the walls showed signs of where pictures once hung, and old wall lights that looked as if they hadn't seen a bulb for decades. Cobwebs hung undisturbed from the corners of the ceiling and Miranda wondered distractedly about the size of the spiders that had made them.

"Miranda are you ok?" she heard Gabriel shout from the other side of the wall. She felt unusually calm, considering she'd just passed straight through a solid wall.

Gabriel looked at Nathanael and frowned. "Find the keys," he said as he walked to the wall. He put his hand to the place she'd disappeared and closed his eyes. He concentrated on the energy willing it into his body, and he started to vibrate as the wall trembled slightly under his hands. He pushed against the wall and shivered involuntarily as the coldness passed through him and then he was in front of her.

Miranda stood staring at him, she moved slightly to look at the wall behind him, and then she looked back at his face as he moved towards her. Her knees gave way as he lifted her gently into his arms; he carried her to the nearest chair and sat her down, kneeling beside her.

"Are you ok?" he asked concern clouding his face.

She nodded and attempted to smile, "I feel a little weak," she whispered. She heard the key in the door and turned to see Nathanael standing there. Gabriel stood up and lifted her into his arms again.

"I'm taking her up to her room, could you bring her some blood."

Nathanael was in the kitchen before he'd even finished the sentence; Miranda closed her eyes and wrapped her arms around his neck as he climbed the stairs.

She didn't want to let him go as he placed her gently on the bed, but she had no choice but to release her grip as he prised her arms from around his neck. He chuckled quietly as he sat next to her. "I thought you said you were feeling weak?"

Before she could answer Nathanael walked in with a cup, he said nothing as he handed it to her. He looked at Gabriel for a second then walked from the room.

Miranda finished with the cup and Gabriel took it from her and stood up. "I'll leave you to rest for a while."

"Don't go," Miranda said grabbing his hand. He stood looking down at her for a minute, and then placed the cup on the bedside table; she moved over to give him room to lie beside her.

He smiled at her then lay down, "are you feeling alright now?" he asked quietly as she moved closer and snaked her arm around him. She nodded and laid her head on his chest and then yawned.

"I'm perfectly fine," she whispered tightening her hold for a second, "don't leave," she said quietly, she didn't hear his answer as sleep overcame her.

Nathanael walked slowly to his room, he stood outside the door and hesitantly pushed down the handle, her portrait was the first thing he saw as he entered the room, and he averted his eyes quickly from the painting. She smiled at him silently, as he walked over to his bed and sat down. The chattering in his head was starting to hurt.

"Please shut up," he whispered closing his eyes for a second. He stood up and walked to the wardrobe, he opened it and took out a clean shirt, "she fazed tonight," he said into the empty room, and then glanced towards the portrait. "Yes I know, she seems to get stronger day by day," he said walking back to the bed and stripping his shirt off, he frowned down at the clean shirt and then picked it up and put it on. "I don't know why it's taking so long, what do you want me to do about it," he said rubbing at his head for a moment. "Yes I know—it doesn't help with you going on all the time—yes I need to feed, I'll see you later," he said quietly as he picked up his jacket and left the room.

"You say she fazed, well I'll be damned," Michael whispered shaking his head slowly.

"Is she ok?" Morana asked quietly.

Gabriel nodded. "I think so, she's been asleep since it happened—to tell you the truth, I think I was more shaken than she was, I mean I know I can do it—but to actually see it happening," he shook his head and frowned. "She was virtually transparent, it was really quite unsettling, and the sound as she passed through the wall—I've never heard anything like it—that sound actually hurt my ears," he said and frowned again.

Miranda felt Gabriel stroke her hair gently; she opened her eyes slowly and was met with the smiling faces of Michael and Morana.

"How are you?" Morana asked leaning over and touching her cheek.

"I feel fine," Miranda smiled at the woman, "is that what it's called, fazing?" she asked looking up into Gabriel's face.

He nodded then smiled at her, "yes."

"We're off to bed now, we will see you later sweetie," Morana said moving away from her. She took Michael's hand and they left her and Gabriel alone again.

"What time is it?" she asked laying her head on his chest.

"It's gone nine," he answered after consulting his watch. "Time for bed."

"You're already in bed," she said tightening her arm around him.

"Technically I'm on top of the bed, in the clothes I've been in all night," he said.

"I don't want you to go," Miranda said quietly.

"Well I need to go and change at least," he said raising an eyebrow at her when she looked up at him.

"But you'll come back, won't you," she said pulling away a little but not releasing him totally.

"Yes, if you want me too," he said and smiled.

Miranda nodded then pulled away from him and he got up and left the room, Miranda changed quickly and got into bed. He walked back into the room and her stomach flipped as she looked over his bare torso. He lay down and she lifted her head so that he could put his arm under it. She instinctively snaked her arms around him as she settled down.

"So do you think it could be Caleb—I mean I know Nate said that the chances were slight—but what do you think—what about the way he spoke to me and knew my name," she said yawning into his chest.

"I would think it highly unlikely—you find it amazingly easy to read a humans mind don't you, so why should the fact that he knew your name be in the least bit surprising—I'm not saying that it's a complete impossibility—but why would your brother hide from you, why wouldn't he have been to see you already and why would he have just left you for dead in the street," he said frowning at the images that jumped into his mind.

Miranda considered his words for a moment and then yawned again, "I'm sorry if I worried you earlier with the whole fazing thing—I really do have to learn to get a hold of these powers don't I—I mean it's not as if he could actually do anything if it was him is it—I'm not bound to him am I, so even if he did come he couldn't make me leave, could he," she said moving as close as she could get to Gabriel. He stroked her hair absently and she looked up at him when he didn't answer. "Well he couldn't could he?"

Gabriel shook his head slightly, "no he couldn't—he has no hold over you," he said quietly as she lowered her head to his chest again.

"Good because I don't want to leave," she said yawning one final time, "goodnight Gabriel," she whispered as her eyes started to close.

"Goodnight my love," he said quietly tightening his arms around her. And as sleep overcame her she didn't see the tears in his eyes or the pain on his face.

30

Miranda was already up when Gabriel opened his eyes; she was sitting quietly, on her dressing table stool, looking at him. He smiled sleepily and turned onto his side to look at her.

"Good evening," he said and then stretched.

"Evening," she replied turning away from him quickly and looking at her reflection in the mirror; she picked up the brush and ran it through her hair. She could still see him in the mirror and the way he lay there with the covers only covering his bottom half, had the heat rising rapidly up her body.

"Is it really time to get up already?" he asked rolling onto his back; he turned his head to look at her when she spoke.

"I'm afraid it is—in fact we over slept."

She saw him throw back the cover, get out of bed and walk up behind her. He stooped down and looked at her through the mirror and she couldn't help the shudder that passed through her as his chin touched her bare shoulder.

"I'm not complaining, a lie in does you good now and again," he said smiling at her, "did you sleep well?"

"Yes thank you, very well—and you?"

"Best night's sleep I've had for centuries—in fact I'd say the best night's sleep I've ever had," he said standing straight and stretching again. "I think I should spend more time in your bed if this is the effect it has on me."

Miranda turned and looked at him, "maybe we should swap rooms," she said standing up and walking to her wardrobe. "My bed is obviously more comfortable than yours—and with you being so much older than I am—perhaps it would be better for you."

As she turned to look at him, the strength of his body forced her back against the wardrobe. Even thought she had spent the whole night in his arms, she faltered slightly at his closeness.

"Are you calling me old?" he asked quietly placing his arms either side of her to block any attempt she might make to escape.

"No, I—yes, you're several centuries older than I am—so yes, I am calling you old."

"In human years I'm only about five years older than you," he said moving closer to her, he dropped his hand to her face and softly brushed her cheek. "One of these nights I might just remind you of how agile I can be for my age," he added dropping his head, so that his lips were so close to hers. He breathed in deeply and then he breathed out slowly. The sensation of his breath on her skin made her tingle from head to toe.

She closed her eyes as images of the way he'd touched her, of how he'd kissed her, raced through her mind. She remembered every single detail from that night in the forest, every single feeling, but she would be more than willing to let him remind her again.

Gabriel froze as the images ran through his mind, his body tensed as the feelings washed over him, he looked down into Miranda's closed eyes for a second and frowned . . . . that wasn't the way he remembered it . . . . his memories shouldn't be like this? He continued to stare at her as she opened her eyes slowly . . . . it was completely wrong . . . and as she stood staring up at him, he knew why . . . . they hadn't been his memories at all . . . . they had been hers. "I think, you can remember quite clearly," he said quietly, "excuse me I need to go and get dressed," he added as he pulled away quickly and left the room.

Nathanael looked up as Gabriel walked into the kitchen. He sat back and smiled as Gabriel sat down opposite him, "did you sleep through your alarm brother?" he asked politely.

"It would seem so, yes."

"I suppose it's very difficult for you isn't it," Nathanael said still smiling at him. "I mean this kind of relationship can't be an easy thing to accept when you want her so much."

Gabriel shrugged, "I'm managing so far."

"Yes but even so—" Nathanael sat forward and stared at his brother for a minute, "how tempting it must be sharing a bed with her."

Gabriel sat back and looked over at Nathanael for a moment then smiled slightly, "I think you're the one having difficulties with it Nate, I mean it can't be nice having to watch us together, considering your feelings towards her."

"You don't need to worry about my feelings brother—oh that's right, sorry I forgot, you don't give a rats arse about my feelings do you," Nathanael said sarcastically.

Gabriel considered him for a moment then shook his head, "I'm not in the mood for this right now Nate—I have more important things to think about other than your stupid insecurities, so if you don't mind, shut up and leave me in peace."

"Is it all becoming a little too much for you—how much longer before you crack—not too long by the look of things, let me just remind you if I may, she may not be bound to her maker, but he still has rights—would you really give your life for her Gabe?"

Gabriel frowned over at him, "I've told you this conversation is over, give it a rest."

"Perhaps you should find a way to get rid of all this pent up tension bro—I'm more than willing to offer my services—come on, it's been ages since we last had a real good fight," Nathanael smiled sitting forward again.

"I am not going to fight you Nate; I am not going to argue with you—hell I don't even want to talk to you, so just go away."

The door opened and Michael walked into the kitchen, he hesitated at the sight of the two of them sat at the table. They appeared to be in the middle of some sort of quarrel and it could quite easily turn into a brawl at any moment. He walked over to the cupboard quickly and took out a bottle.

Gabriel looked over towards him. "Mike I was wondering if I could have a word with you," he said standing up.

"Sure what's up?" Michael asked turning to face both of them again.

Gabriel looked at Nathanael, "in the library, if you don't mind."

Michael glanced from Gabriel to Nathanael and nodded then followed Gabriel from the room. Nathanael sat back and frowned as the door closed behind them.

Miranda saw Michael disappear into the library, closely followed by Gabriel. He had turned and smiled up at her as she walked down the stairs and then closed the door behind him. She looked at the door and frowned as she carried on towards the kitchen. He had acted so strange earlier in her room, he'd left her wondering what she had done to make him disappear so quickly. As she pushed the door open she was met by a grinning Nathanael.

"Good evening," she said smiling, "I was wondering if you might like to come for a walk with me?" she offered moving towards the backdoor.

Nathanael looked a little surprised by the offer, but stood up and followed her anyway. He wanted to spend a little time alone with her before he left again, and with Gabriel safely tucked away in the library with Michael, he couldn't pass up on the opportunity. He put his arm around her shoulder as they walked, he knew she wanted something, why else had she asked him to come for a walk. "So what's on you're mind?" he asked turning to her.

"Nothing really," she smiled.

"You're not the most convincing liar that I've ever met," he said raising an eyebrow at her.

"Ok, I have got something on my mind—it's nothing important, it's just that Gabriel won't tell me why he killed all the ancients, I mean I can understand why he would feel the need to kill Shavaun and Ariel, if like he said it was about revenge—but why the rest," she said stopping and frowning down at the floor.

"If you can't get the story from the source get it from someone who was there is that it?"

"Yes," Miranda said quietly. She suddenly felt guilty, if Gabriel didn't want to tell her then she had no right to go behind his back . . . . when he found out she'd asked his brother he was going to be mad. But the question had been asked, she couldn't take it back now.

Nathanael stood looking at her for the longest time then frowned, "ok, I'll tell you, but before I do, I want something from you first," he said moving slightly closer.

"Ok, sure—what is it you want?" she asked cautiously. Suddenly his arms were around her pulling her into his hard body. She couldn't move; her body seemed to melt into his as his arms closed around her. The kiss was hard against her lips and she tried so desperately not to kiss him back. He forced her lips open with his tongue and licked the inside of her mouth and her head screamed at her to move away from him, but as with the first time he'd kissed her, her body disobeyed. Then Nathanael pulled away from her abruptly.

She could tell by the look on his face that he hadn't planned his own reaction to the kiss; he was trying hard to regain his composure. "He looks like a man who should be gasping for breath," her mind said quietly as she stood watching him.

"I don't know how he can stand it," he said shaking his head. "He's stronger than I ever gave him credit for." He stood there frowning down at the floor for a moment then looked up at her, "he did it for me," he said his frown deepening slightly; "he killed them all for me."

Miranda stared at him for a moment, "why?"

"Because I asked him to do it, he thought that if he could prove how sorry he was by killing them we could just simply forget about what he'd done—that I'd forget what he'd taken from me."

Miranda shook her head and frowned, "he did it for you?"

He stared at her for a moment, "god damn it, he didn't do it for me—he never needed or wanted my forgiveness."

"So why did he even bother, why would he risk his life, if not for your forgiveness, they could have killed him Nathan," Miranda said angrily.

"Yeah, they could have killed him, but they were too weak—far too weak for one as strong as Gabe—weak vile creatures who couldn't even put right the mistake that they made," Nathanael said angrily.

"Oh my God—you hoped that they'd kill him, didn't you?" she said moving away from him. "You wanted them to kill your own brother—how can you hate him so much?"

"How, very easily, look at what he did to me!" Nathanael shouted. "He killed the only person I ever loved and turned me into this—I have had to live for centuries without her—and all because my dearest brother wanted what I had."

"He didn't love Sophie," Miranda shouted suddenly so angry that she wanted to hit him, "he loved you—he couldn't let you die—he didn't want to live without you Nathan."

"Oh my god—you'd believe everything he told you wouldn't you," he said turning away from her in disgust, "you're just like the rest of them—you all think you've felt pain, but not one of you has felt anything like this—imagine how it feels, remember that pain you felt when Gabriel left Miranda, how it twisted your insides—how it felt as if someone had ripped your heart out, and then imagine living with that pain for over three hundred years, I wonder if you could imagine that, all that pain, for all those years—without one days rest from the images that bombard you over and over again, relentlessly day after day, night after night—even in your dreams," he said quietly turning towards her again. "The visions of your brother, the one person in the world you thought you could trust—the one person you would give your life for—taking away the only thing you'd ever wanted, the only thing you'd ever loved—just imagine that Miranda," he shouted.

"Nathan you need to let go of it—he's your brother, it all happened so many years ago," Miranda said reaching out to him.

Nathanael pulled away from her and frowned, "so many years ago, but it could have been just yesterday Miranda, because it's still all here, every single moment engraved into my memory, tormenting me every second of everyday," he said tapping the side of his head; he closed his eyes for a moment. He couldn't decide what hurt more, was it the fact that she loved Gabriel so much that she just didn't care about what he'd done, or was it the fact that she cared so little for him that she wasn't even willing to imagine what his life had been like. "I will never let it go for as long as I live—as far as I'm concerned my brother died over three centuries ago—that thing in there has never been my brother," he said quietly after a minute, "and I won't be happy until he's as dead as my Sophie."

Miranda flinched at the expression on his face, it was pure hatred. "Well why don't you just leave then, you have no ties here, there's nothing to keep you here considering your brother is dead," she said calmly turning away from him.

He grabbed her arm and pulled her into his body again. "Don't you walk away from me, I haven't finished yet—do you love him so much that you can overlook everything he does, you don't know what he's really like, he'll never love you Miranda—his heart is dead and I don't just mean that in the clinical sense, he doesn't understand the concept of love."

"Let go of me Nathan, I have nothing left to say to you," she said trying to push against him, but once again his arms tightened around her and his lips clamped down on hers. So much for all her powers, she thought, as she stood there in his vice like grip, no matter how hard she fought she couldn't control her body, it melted into his as soon as his lips touched hers. Suddenly he released her and moved away.

"Go on—run back to your dear Gabriel, I'm sure he's wondering where you are," he said turning his back to her. Miranda turned and ran back to the house without looking back.

He had never planned on wanting her; the thought had never crossed his mind before the first time he'd kissed her. But now there was a burning deep within him that he didn't know how to control. So many years of anger and rage had disappeared as her body had melted into his.

Tonight he wanted to prove to himself that he didn't want her but as his lips had touched hers he'd known the truth, he did want her. As her body had melted into his, he'd known the undeniable truth; he was in love with her.

He walked slowly back to the house, he needed to get away from this place. He needed to try and regain some sort of distance, before everything crumbled, before it was too late. As he entered his room he dared not look up at the portrait, he didn't want to see her eyes staring down at him. He walked straight to the bed and picked up the bag he had packed earlier and walked back to the door, he hesitated for a moment as the voice whispered in his head, "you stupid, stupid man."

Gabriel sat staring blindly out of the window; he'd sat there nearly all night thinking about the images that had run through his mind earlier in Miranda's room. He'd wanted to speak with Michael; he remembered reading that the ancients could project thoughts, feelings and images into the minds of others, but it was something none of them had ever experienced.

Michael had helped him go through the tomes and after an hour of searching they found what he'd been looking for. "Here it is," Michael said looking at him, "Zeke wrote about it briefly, apparently Decastell and Ambrose were the only one's who possessed this power—he say's that it's quite an unnerving power and that they could do it whenever they pleased, making others feel and see what they wanted them too—he say's that it is extremely worrying," Michael said frowning.

Gabriel took the tomb off him and read it, "well—that proves it then—Miranda has the power to project," he said snapping the book closed and frowning slightly.

"Wow—she really is a powerful little thing isn't she," Michael said a hint of admiration in his tone, "what was it she showed you?"

Gabriel smiled and shook his head, "I can't tell you that Mike—god," he said raising his hands to his face and rubbing his head. He sat there for a moment lost in thought and then he frowned and shook his head again, "Thanks for the help Mike," he said standing up.

"I'll leave you to it then," Michael said somewhat bemused as he left the room.

Gabriel sat back in his chair and rubbed his eyes. He'd actually felt worried about his apparent lack of control over recall, but it all made sense now. She had projected her memories into his mind, and now he really thought about it she'd done it before.

All this time he'd thought she didn't feel anything towards him . . . . but the feelings that she'd projected, the visions that had ran through his mind as he'd stood looking down at her proved different . . . . she had wanted him as much as he'd wanted her . . . . and she still wanted him.

He groaned quietly and looked back towards the window . . . . he'd been so stupid . . . . he'd wasted so much time. He wasn't going to waste anymore.

Morana looked up as Gabriel walked into the kitchen, Michael shifted uncomfortably as she stood up. He looked at Morana then at Mike and sighed, in truth he'd been waiting for this conversation since he'd arrived back and he was surprised that it had taken Morana so long.

"We need to talk," Morana said motioning to the seat in front of her and sitting down again.

Gabriel looked at Mike and smiled slightly, then obediently sat opposite the pair. Mike smiled weakly back at him and looked down at the table.

"Could we just hurry up and get this over with, I have things to do," Gabriel said then shrunk back slightly at the look on Morana's face.

"What, in god's good name, did you think you were doing Gabriel—leaving the way you did—what was it you were hoping to achieve," Morana said frowning at him.

"I wasn't—I needed—" Gabriel said then frowned at the woman as she interrupted.

"We understand that things were difficult for you Gabriel—given the way things happened—given the way you feel about her, but do you have any idea the mess you left behind when you disappeared, you left that poor girl in such a state," Morana said sitting back in her chair, "she fell apart, and there was nothing we could do to help—nothing we could say—she hardly fed, she was an empty shell most of the time—I have never seen anything like it Gabriel—she was a mess."

Gabriel looked at Michael and the man smiled apologetically at him then looked back down at the table. "I didn't know—I had no idea," he said shaking his head.

"Well of course you didn't, and why was that Gabriel—it was because you were to caught up in your own misery to even notice anyone else's," Morana said angrily standing up again, "if you'd have taken the time you'd have realised what most of us knew from the start—Miranda is in love with you Gabriel."

Gabriel looked up at the woman, the frown on his face slowly fading as the realisation of what she was saying hit him, "she's in love with me," he repeated quietly as if he didn't believe Morana's words.

"Oh for heavens sake—are you completely blind—of course she loves you, she always has—what, you really think she just stayed here because she had no other choice—you really think she would put up with the way you treated her because she had too—I'm ashamed of the way you acted towards her Gabe—she's had every opportunity to pack her bags and go whenever she wanted to, but she didn't—and you really never wondered why?" Morana said sitting down again.

"She's in love with me," Gabriel repeated standing up.

"She's really in love with you Gabe," Michael said quietly and smiled at him.

"Thank you," Gabriel said moving quickly towards the door.

31

Gabriel stood outside her room and raised his hand to knock the door, but then lowered it again. It had taken the rest of night for him to find the courage and go to her, his head was still reeling with the revelations from earlier that evening and now that he was stood here with just the door separating them he didn't know if he could face her. Morana's words had run through his head over and over again and even though she had tried to convince him that Miranda loved him, he still had so many doubts.

He raised his hand again and frowned at his lack of self-confidence as his hand shook for several seconds then dropped back down to his side, he needed a reason to go to her room. He smiled suddenly and sped down the stairs to the kitchen.

Miranda lay reading the tome but she couldn't concentrate so she snapped it shut, and frowned. She wanted to see Gabriel so much; she hadn't seen him since he'd disappeared into the library with Michael. She wanted to go to him, but she still felt angry. She sat up and crossed her legs then frowned again. There was a light tap at her door, Gabriel popped his head into the room and smiled.

"Do you know what time it is?" he asked. He hesitated for a moment, and then he frowned and walked into the room without waiting for the invitation he'd been hoping for.

Miranda ran her eyes over him, his shirt was open showing the slightest bit of flesh, but it was enough to start the heat rising up her body, and her stomach did a somersault as he sat down next to her.

"Have you been reading all this time?" he asked putting the cup down on the bedside table.

Miranda shook her head and took no notice of the blood he'd brought her.

He frowned again, there was something wrong . . . . he suddenly felt uneasy. He looked at her for a moment, she was angry, he could feel it, "ok—so what's wrong?"

"I asked Nathan why you killed the ancients," she said quietly and stood up.

"I'd already told you why I killed them," he said his frown deepening.

"I know you think I'm stupid Gabriel—but I'm not—sure, you'd feel a degree of anger towards the ones that turned you—but not all of them," she said turning away from him.

"So I guess Nate filled you in," he said standing up too.

"Of course he did—what were you thinking—you could have gotten your damn fool self killed—and what for Gabriel?" she said turning around to face him.

Gabriel felt a little puzzled as he stood looking at her, "are you—angry with me?"

"Yes I am angry with you—what were you thinking—they could have killed you, he asked you to do it with the hope that they would—and I guess that you already knew that, but you went and did it anyway—I just—" she said then frowned as Gabriel cut her off mid-sentence.

"I could understand it if I'd actually done something wrong—if I was the one sneaking around behind your back," he said suddenly angry himself.

"What do you expect if you insist on keeping things from me—you could quite easily have told me when I asked, but you chose not to—so I'm obviously going to find out from some other source," she snapped, as she realised that control of the discussion was rapidly falling from her grasp. She wasn't supposed to be the topic of conversation, he was . . . . he and, what she considered to be, his lack of consideration for his own life . . . . but that apparently was another argument for a later date.

"But why Nate, you know what our relationship is like—oh, I bet he just loved the fact that you went sneaking to him—I will never hear the last of this now," he said growing angrier by the second.

"Why Nate, because I knew he'd tell me, because unlike you, he's never led me to believe he wanted to be friends and then kept secrets from me, and I was hardly sneaking—I asked him and he told me, instead of changing the subject," she shouted.

"Of course, I'd forgotten what good friends the two of you are—well I'm sorry I'm not as perfect as my god damn brother, yet another comparison for you to make," he shouted, moving towards the door.

"I have never compared you to Nathan in any way and I have never said Nathan was perfect," she said moving with him, "don't you dare make this all about Nathan—this about you Gabriel and your lack of confidence in me—what—did you think I wouldn't be able to handle your past—that it would make the slightest bit of difference to me what you'd done?"

"Oh well lets see, I seem to remember quite clearly your reaction the last time I told you something about my past—you handled that really well didn't you, so well in fact that you ended up in his arms, pressed so close to him that you might as well have been sharing the same skin, so well that you ended up in a lip lock with him," he shouted down at her.

Miranda's reaction surprised her, as she reached up and slapped him as hard as she could across the face. A slight cut appeared underneath his left eye, and little blood seeped down his cheek but Gabriel hardly flinched, he turned towards the door again and opened it, "I think I'd better go before I do something I'm really going to regret," he said quietly.

Miranda moved quickly slamming the door again before he could leave, "oh no, you're not going anywhere, how dare you accuse me of things I haven't done—for your information Nathan kissed me—and while we're on the subject—Nathan and I are nothing more than friends—that's all we have ever been and all we will ever be."

Gabriel grabbed her quickly and pulled her between the door and his body, "did you enjoy it, when he kissed you?" he asked quietly.

Miranda frowned up at him for several seconds, and then shook her head, "no I didn't—I—"

"So you don't have any feelings for him whatsoever?" he asked interrupting her. He dropped his head slightly and stared into her eyes.

"Yes, no—I mean we're friends so of course I have some feelings for him—but I don't feel the same way about him as I feel about—" she stopped talking and frowned.

"As you feel about whom—you don't feel the same way about him as you feel about whom Miranda," he whispered against her lips. But she couldn't answer.

Gabriel stared into her eyes for a moment longer, then pulled her closer and kissed her passionately.

She had no idea how it happened, one minute they were arguing, the next minute they were naked on the bed. The only thing in her head was the way his body moved against hers, how his lips scorched her skin as he kissed every inch of her, of how good he tasted as she kissed every inch of him.

Gabriel pulled away from her slightly, "are you sure this is what you want—because if you don't tell me now, before it's too late."

Miranda looked up into his face then pulled him closer again, "it's all I've ever wanted," she whispered as he kissed her again, but she pulled back and looked up at him, "are you sure this is what you want?"

Gabriel didn't answer; he just lowered his head to her neck and sunk his teeth into her flesh. She felt instant warmth spreading through her body . . . . and again she felt light, as if she were floating and she held onto him tighter through fear of actually drifting away. This was how they were always supposed to be . . . . together. She belonged to him.

Gabriel suddenly became aware that Miranda was no longer lying next to him, his eyes snapped open. He was still naked and he was still in her bed. He looked on the floor; his clothes were exactly where he'd dropped them, next to her nightdress. So it hadn't been a wonderful dream he'd had. He really had spent most of yesterday making love to her. He turned onto his side as the door opened.

Miranda smiled as she closed the door quietly behind her, "I brought you breakfast in bed," she said handing him the cup. He took it from her and drank it quickly; he put the cup down, and then ran his eyes over her body, he reached out and grabbed her around the waist and pulled her down next to him.

"You look so much better in this than I do," he said slowly undoing the buttons on the shirt.

"Yes, well I think that you look better without it," she giggled as he ran his lips over her stomach.

He lifted his head and frowned slightly, "well obviously I think you look better without anything on—" he stopped talking and continued running his lips across her stomach.

She grabbed his head and pulled him up to face her, "I'm sorry," she said.

"For what?" he asked slightly puzzled.

"For slapping you," she said gently stroking his cheek. There was no sign of the cut anymore or the small trail of blood; she had already kissed away any traces of it.

"I suppose I deserved it," he said turning his face and kissing the palm of her hand. "Mind you, you do have a bit of strength in those delicate arms of yours—I think you should at least kiss it better for me."

Miranda reached up to kiss his cheek but he quickly turned his head. "Hey that's cheating," she chuckled then kissed him deeply.

He pulled away quickly and looked at her, "I need to talk to you about something—before we start—that again."

"Who said we were going to start—that again?" Miranda asked raising her eyebrows at him. He smiled then lowered his head to hers and kissed her passionately. She wrapped her arms around his neck and her legs around his waist, but he reluctantly pulled away from her.

She laughed quietly, "ok—so before we start that again what did you want to talk about?"

He considered her for a moment then grinned, "I found out, not so long ago, that you possess a power that you may not know about," he said pulling away from her.

Miranda looked at him puzzled, "what do you mean?"

"Well the other night in your room, you kind of showed me images from that first time in the forest," he said then grinned.

"I did—oh my god," she said covering her face with her hands.

Gabriel chuckled, "yeah, I got a lot more than I bargained for when I was trying to kiss you."

Miranda lowered her hands slowly to reveal a smile, "you were trying to kiss me?"

Gabriel laughed loudly, "I'm trying to tell you that you have this extraordinary power and all you focus on is the fact that I was trying to kiss you?"

"Yes—but I think about kissing you all the time," she said pulling his head closer to kiss him again.

"Don't you—even want—to know about—this—power," he said as she kissed him several times in quick succession, "you—possess—the power—of projection—it's very—unusual—it's a very—rare power," he said slightly amused as she repeatedly kissed him.

"I don't care," she said biting his bottom lip, "I just want to kiss you," she said quietly.

"Well, by all means, don't let me stop you doing the things you want to do," he said laughing as he rolled onto his back and pulled her on top of him.

"Oh, you wouldn't stop me," she said confidently, pulling away from him slightly, "I don't think that you'd stop me doing this," she said lowering her head again and kissing him deeply. "Or this," she said running her tongue down his neck. "Or even this," she whispered as she sunk her teeth into the flesh at the base of his throat.

He had meant to work, but as the hours passed he was finding it increasingly difficult to find a reason to leave her arms. Work meant nothing compared to this, life would mean even less if every minute wasn't spent with her. He was losing himself in her but it didn't even matter.

Three days they had been in bed, the only time they had moved had been to feed, it was a good job that they had an almost endless supply of bottled blood; he didn't think he'd have the energy to hunt even if he had to. Miranda opened one eye and looked at him; she slipped her arm round him and wriggled her body as close as she could get.

Gabriel smiled and put his arm around her and whispered, "if you don't stop wriggling we're never going to get out of this bed."

"I tried to get up last night but you wouldn't let me," she said raising an eyebrow at him. He chuckled quietly as he remembered her half hearted attempt to get out of bed; she hadn't even managed to put both feet on the floor before he'd grabbed her and pulled her back into his arms.

"And I don't know if I'll let you tonight if you don't stop wriggling," he said as he ran his teeth down her neck.

Miranda shivered involuntarily at the feeling of his teeth on her flesh, and then she laughed, "well stop making me wriggle then."

He chuckled quietly but pulled away from her. Miranda moved to the edge of the bed, Gabriel turned his head to watch her as she dressed. He loved watching her.

"Do we really have to get up—I mean it's not as if we have anything important to do—come back to bed Miranda," he said trying to grab her arm as she stood up.

She pulled away quickly and frowned, "no I am not coming back to bed, get up Gabriel."

He considered sulking for a moment, as she stood looking at him, but he did as she said and got out of bed. He stood there looking at her as she ran her eyes over his perfect naked body, and he laughed quietly as she seemed to reconsider getting back into bed with him.

"Oh, for heavens sake go and put some clothes on," she said suddenly, turning away from him.

Gabriel laughed loudly, and then disappeared through the door.

32

Miranda picked up her nightdress and straightened the bed then collected the tomes. He was already waiting outside his door as she left her room. She looked him up and down and frowned. The tight black tee shirt and jeans he wore stirred all sorts of images in her mind.

He looked down at his clothes puzzled at her expression, "what's wrong, don't you like my choice of clothes?" he asked as she drew level with him.

"I like your choice of clothes very much; the trouble is, the only thing I can think of now is a how to get you out of them again," she said walking past him.

Gabriel smiled and followed her; he took the books out of her arms and held her hand as they walked down the stairs together.

Morana smiled her usual smile as they walked into the kitchen and handed them both a mug, Miranda smiled as the woman looked her over.

"Well you don't look too bad considering," Morana said smiling as she turned to Gabriel.

"I don't feel too bad at all really—maybe a little tired but apart from that," he joked taking the cup from her.

Morana chuckled and then looked at Miranda, "I think you should know Nate's gone again."

Miranda frowned as thoughts of their last conversation ran through her mind; the memories of how his lips had felt on hers took her a little by surprise, as did the intensity of the feeling that had surged through her while she was in his arms.

Gabriel tensed as the images ran through his mind . . . . again all wrong . . . . they were her thoughts . . . . her thoughts about Nathanael.

"God damn it," he said loudly as he moved away from her. He slammed the cup down on the table, and as it shattered into several pieces, the remainder of the red liquid spread across the table. Miranda looked quickly at Morana's stunned face and then back at Gabriel, he looked furious. "I'm going to rip the son of a bitch to pieces—he's going to regret ever touching you—I'm going to kill him—why the hell didn't you tell me about this," he yelled storming out of the room.

Morana frowned as Miranda sat at the table; she joined her and tapped her hand. "I don't know what's going on, but I bet if you let him calm down for a while things will be fine."

"I can do this projecting thing—and I guess I showed him Nathan kissing me—I don't know how to control it—oh what a wonderful power it is," Miranda said angrily standing up again. She didn't know what to do, should she go after him and try to explain. Should she do as Morana suggested and give him a while to calm down? She walked round the table then sat down again, what should she do?

Gabriel stood with his back against the door and closed his eyes for a second, he was so angry he could feel himself vibrating. He was going to kill Nathanael . . . . he was going to rip him to shreds when he got his hands on him . . . . how dare he lay a finger on her. He lifted his hands and looked at the deep cuts his nails had made in both of his palms; he watched the blood as it trickled down to his wrists and closed his eyes again.

Why was he letting Nathanael do this, why was he letting his brother destroy the only good thing he'd ever had in his life . . . . he knew Miranda loved him . . . . he hoped Miranda loved him. It was time he told her everything. He opened his eyes and pushed the kitchen door open a little more forcefully than he intended and stood there for a second looking at Miranda as she sat at the table with her head bowed. He moved forward quickly and grabbed her hand, he had to do this now before he lost his nerve—he should have done this the moment he'd found out her true feelings for him.

"I need to show you something," he said glancing quickly at Morana before dragging Miranda from the kitchen.

Miranda pulled back quickly as they stopped outside his room, "what do you need to show me?" she asked moving further away from him . . . . she couldn't understand the feelings that radiated from him as they stood there . . . . he was still so angry, but there was something else there too, a feeling she couldn't quite put her finger on.

Gabriel rubbed his head, "I need you to remember Miranda—please remember."

Miranda looked at him for a moment and then moved closer again, "remember what Gabriel?"

"Remember me," he said quietly pushing down on the handle and opening the door to his room.

"Remember you?" she asked slightly puzzled as he stood back for her to enter the room. She walked in and looked back at him as he hovered by the door. He seemed so tense as he stood looking down at the floor and Miranda frowned.

She did a quick scan of the room, it was just as she expected, elegant, and she looked at him again. She didn't understand what he wanted to show her for a moment, not until she looked around for a second time. There were several framed pictures scattered around the room and one larger photo on the wall, and Miranda froze as her eyes came to rest on it. She frowned as she walked slowly over to it, the girl was around sixteen or so, her pretty image filled the whole of the photo.

"It's me," she said quietly.

Gabriel looked up at her as she stood staring up at the picture. He moved slowly into the room, and closed the door. She looked at him, "it's me," she repeated.

"It's you," he said simply.

"But I'm human—Gabriel—what—?" Gabriel moved over towards the bed and she moved with him, "you have a picture of me as a human—why?" she asked quietly.

"I have loved you for a very long time—nearly eighteen years," he said turning to face her and then he closed his eyes, "Cuimhnigh Orm," he whispered.

It was as if a lock clicked somewhere in her mind, suddenly images bombarded her, the first time she'd seen Gabriel's beautiful face, the way he sang lullabies to her, the way she fell asleep in his arms every night. She remembered this house and the fountain, the way he would bring her here when everyone else was asleep and they would play in the water, while the moon shone down. She remembered everything . . . . the way her necklace had burnt his skin as he'd put it on for her, the way he had cried when he'd told her that he wasn't real, that he was a make believe friend and that she didn't need him anymore, and of how she'd woken the morning after and thought there was something missing.

"I remember," she whispered as the first tears fell from her eyes. "I remember you—Gabriel I remember everything," she said quietly reaching for him. He pulled her into his arms and kissed her frantically.

Miranda rolled over onto her stomach and frowned, "how could I have forgotten everything about you?"

Gabriel looked at her and smiled slightly. "I cleaned you, I stopped you remembering—I wanted to protect you—the only way I knew was to wipe your memory—I've wanted to tell you so many times since you've been here—but up until now I've been so terrified of your reaction that I just couldn't do it."

Miranda smiled, "Cuimhnigh Orm—what does it mean?"

"It's Irish for remember me—I had to chose the words carefully, and I had to chose a dialect that I knew you'd probably never hear—and remember me seemed quiet apt at the time," he said thoughtfully. "Of course when we clean people we don't normally leave a trigger switch—or words in your case."

"So why did you do it with me?" she asked turning on her side to face him.

"Because I knew that one day I'd want you to remember it all—I wasn't sure when, or how—but one day I was going to turn you myself—you were always supposed to be mine Miranda—I'd waited over three hundred years for you, and then another seventeen while you grew up—only I was beaten to it," he said frowning at the thought.

"So why did you wait so long, I mean my life was so bad," she said wrapping her arm around him.

"I was scared," he admitted truthfully, "turning people can turn out one of two ways—they will either except their fate with dignity and grace the way you did, or they will hate you for the rest of eternity—the way Nathan does—I wouldn't have been able to handle that, after waiting for you for so long," he said and frowned again, "and anyway I had to wait for you to develop," he said running his eyes down her body and grinning, "I was going to wait until your twentieth birthday then I was going to come to you, and tell you everything—I was going to make you remember me and then I was going to turn you."

"Good job I turned out to be a first generation then isn't it?" she said smiling. Gabriel nodded and rolled onto his back, he tried to keep the frown off his face, but wasn't at all sure he was successful.

"So how did you find me in the first place?" she asked.

"Ah well I was hungry—" he started to say turning his head to look at her again.

"You were going to bite me?" she asked lifting her eyebrows.

"No, of course not, you weren't even a year old—hardly a mouthful," he said then laughed quietly, "I had just killed Ambrose, and I admit I was looking for someone—but then as I walked down your street, I could hear you crying, I stood under your window just listening to you and it was the strangest thing—I just needed to see you, I needed to see the little human that was making all the noise, I climbed up the drain pipe and in through your window and there you were, screaming, your little face all red and swollen," he said and smiled. "I loved you instantly."

Miranda smiled, he loved her . . . . he had loved her for so long. She wriggled closer and put her head on his chest.

"You were such a sweet little thing—and you were so funny, several times a night I had to bury my head into your pillow to silence my laughter," he said chuckling at the thought, "you used to tell me jokes, you always got them the wrong way around, telling me the punch line first, and you used to hold onto me so tightly as you fell asleep."

"I didn't want you to go, I though if I held on tight enough you'd still be there when I woke up. It always felt as if you were a dream in the morning, my Garb—who would only ever come out at night when everyone else was asleep," Miranda said slightly saddened at the memory.

"That's why I had to leave you in the end—you were such an inquisitive thing, always asking questions," he said frowning a little.

"But I never told anyone about you—I just knew you were a secret, you were my secret—after you cleaned me I woke up in the morning and I had the strangest feeling, as if something was missing, as if I'd lost something—but I couldn't remember what it was or where I'd lost it," she said frowning.

"I'm sorry—I didn't realise—I didn't want to leave you but I shouldn't have even come to you in the first place—and after that first night I'd found you, I should have just left you alone, but I couldn't, it was so difficult—I was so in love with you, but you were a human baby and you didn't belong in my world," he said and then tensed as she ran her hand down his chest, he shuddered at her touch. "Of course, you realise that I've only told you all this because of the assumption that you, maybe—feel the same way as I do," he said quietly.

Miranda looked up at him for a moment then a smile spread across her face, "you want to know if I love you?"

Gabriel looked a little uncertain for a moment then nodded.

"I can't believe you need to ask Gabriel—from the very first moment I saw you—you were the only one I ever wanted, the only one I will ever want," she said lowering her head to his, she kissed his lips tenderly as his arms tightened around her, "I love you Gabriel."

The sun was just starting to set in the sky as Miranda opened her eyes, she was starting to lose track of time, she wondered for a moment exactly what the date was, how many days, and subsequently nights, had they spent in bed . . . . she couldn't remember. All she knew was that she could quiet easily spend the rest of eternity lying here in his arms.

She looked at his peaceful sleeping face and wriggled closer to him. He smiled briefly.

"Stop moving," he moaned keeping his eyes closed. She stretched her body so her mouth was level with his. "Please stop moving," he whispered.

She teased her tongue across his lips and he moaned deep in his throat. He moved to put his arm around her but she pulled away quickly and jumped off the bed, she pulled the sheet with her as she went and wrapped it around herself.

Gabriel's eyes snapped open and he frowned, "what are you doing?"

She turned and looked at his naked body, stretched out before her, she was so tempted to go back to him, to feel that hard beautiful body next to hers and it took every ounce of control she had to resist the temptation.

"We can't stay in bed all night, we have to get up," she teased backing away from him.

He turned onto his side to look at her.

"Come here—now," he commanded, but Miranda shook her head. She squealed as he jumped off the bed and chased her around the room, he was so much faster than she was and he caught her easily, and dragged her back to the bed and threw her down onto it. He was soon on top of her, ridding her of the sheet.

"Don't ever disobey me like that again," he chuckled into her ear, "when I tell you to come here, you better do it and quick or else you will have to suffer the consequences."

"Then I shall suffer the consequences," she laughed as they rolled over, she looked down at him for a second and then kissed him deeply, he rolled her over again but instead of carrying on the kiss he pulled away from her, his face taking on a sadness that hurt her heart.

"I need to apologise—I never meant to hurt you—everything I did when you came here was so wrong—I just tried so hard to stay away from you and then—when I left—" he didn't finish what he was going to say, instead he pulled away from her and rolled onto his back.

Miranda turned to look at him, she watched him for many minutes before she spoke, "when you left I wanted to die, I felt so empty and—but it doesn't matter now," she said reaching for his head, she pulled it around so that she could look into his eyes and then smiled, "I'd forgive you anything Gabriel."

He looked at her for a moment then turned his body towards her, "I'm so sorry that I left you—but I saw you in Nathan's arms and I was so sure that I'd lost you forever—the pain was unbearable—I thought you'd fallen in love with him, if I'd stayed it would have destroyed me—if I'd stayed I'm quite sure I'd have ripped you both to pieces," he said frowning.

"Gabriel—please shut up and kiss me," she said pulling him closer.

33

Miranda sat with the tome on her lap, she watched Gabriel as he frowned at the screen. It had taken every ounce of strength she'd had to drag him out of bed, and now as she sat watching him all she wanted to do was drag him back upstairs. Suddenly a wide grin spread across his face and he looked over at her. "I don't mind if you want to drag me back upstairs, not that you'd have to drag me, you understand, I will come of my own free will—but I thought you wanted to read?"

"I am reading," she said opening the book quickly. She looked down at the page she'd opened it at and she read the last entries that Ambrose had written.

February 1842,

I went to the council . . . . but they are unwilling to give me any kind of protection against Gabriel . . . and while he does nothing against them they are not interested . . . . I think that they are rather pleased that my family have, all but, been wiped out . . . they seem to be willing to let Gabriel do as he pleases . . . . I fear that they have already made an alliance with him.

November 1888,

I am still here . . . . though . . . . my life is not even worth living . . . . my brothers and sisters all gone . . . . I hardly have the will to live anymore . . . . my reliable source tells me that the pride 'family' still thrive in their out of town dwelling . . . . Gabriel still seems filled with anger towards me and I wonder why I am still alive . . . . I still miss Decastell so very much . . . . oh the pain that thinking of him still causes me . . . . and I have had to abandon the beautiful home that Decastell and I shared together . . . . it pained me to have to leave the place where we lived for so many years.

June 1905,

I grow weary of my life . . . I have dropped out of sight of the council . . . I do not doubt that they would inform Gabriel of my whereabouts if they knew . . . . I am growing tired of having to look over my shoulder . . . . of having to hide in shadows . . . . I have to rely more and more on my hunting abilities as it is too dangerous to visit my letter every night. I wonder how much longer it will be before the council disclose her identity to Gabriel . . . one day I expect him to be waiting for me.

March 1915,

Sewers are such dirty, depraved places . . . . even though I have collected a few things from my old home it is cold, damp and uncomfortable . . . . the smell lingers in my nostrils long after I have gone above . . . . the stench is embedded in my very pores . . . . I know that although I have not heard anything of Gabriel for a while, he is still out there . . . watching for me . . . . waiting . . . . I am still in hiding . . . . still looking over my shoulder . . . . still weary of this life.

April 1945,

Still I live . . . . though this is not living . . . . I feel I am close to losing my sanity, in this underground labyrinth I call home.

I dreamt of heaven yesterday . . . . all my brothers and sisters were there . . . waiting for me . . . smiling down on me as I made my ascension . . . . and it felt like I was going home.

May 1975,

How the world has changed since Decastell died, and yet sometimes I still hear his voice in my head . . . . he warns me of my impending demise, I feel it may be closer then I am willing to realise . . . . I know Gabriel has not given up on me . . . . and I have to keep renewing my routines in the hope of avoiding him . . . . and it appears to be working . . . . I have to remain on my guard always . . . . will there ever be a time when I can again walk freely in the world . . . . that is my one wish . . . . though I know without doubt it will not come to pass.

January 1992,

My letter informed me of her pregnancy tonight . . . and I can't hide any longer . . . . I will not hide any longer . . . if Gabriel still has revenge in mind let him find me . . . . Let him reunite me with my beloved brothers and sisters . . . . I have lived a hard life since they died . . . . I do not wish to live it anymore.

July 1992,

My letter had a beautiful daughter . . . the irony of it is that I will not get to taste the sweet blood that races around her beautiful body . . . . I can feel that my time will come soon.

April 1993,

My source tells me that Gabriel has seen me several times since I came out of hiding and I wonder why I am not already dead . . . . what manner of game is this that he plays . . . to have seen me and to not have *killed me . . . . I do not, for one second, believe he has given up . . . . so why am I still alive . . . . could it be that he wishes to instil fear in me . . . . I will not succumb . . . . I will not show an ounce of fear towards him . . . . he may kill me reduce me to ash as he did with my family . . . . but I will not allow him my mind . . . . I will not.*

He is coming, I can feel it . . . . my life is drawing to an end . . . . the cold breath of death is upon me . . . . and my letter's daughter is . . . . beautiful . . . . I am dying . . . . dying . . . . soon I will be dead . . . . oh Decastell, I will join you soon my brother after so long alone . . . . again I dreamt of heaven.

There were no more entries after that, she knew that Gabriel had indeed killed him. She closed the book quietly, and glanced over at him. She had no interest in the tomes anymore she'd read everything she needed to. "Where does this go?" she asked running her hand over the tome.

He looked away from the screen and smiled, "the shelf behind you, at the very top," he said as he stood up and walked towards her.

"Get back to work," she ordered.

"I'll do it for you."

"I'm quite capable of doing it myself," she said raising her eyebrow at him, "get back to work."

"Yes ma'am," he said saluting her, "I do love it when you're forceful."

Miranda glanced at him and smiled, then turned her attention to the book. She spread her fingers out over it and then lifted her hand slightly; the energy wrapped itself around the book and lifted it off the couch. Miranda stood slowly and looked over to the shelf that she needed to get it to, the gap was so small.

She turned her palm upwards and the book rose higher, she turned her hand again as the book became level with the shelf she was aiming for and she flicked her hand towards the shelf. The book wobbled above her head for a moment then flew towards the bookshelf quickly. It hit the shelf with a crack and then fell to the floor with a thud.

She looked towards Gabriel who sat there looking at her with a slightly baffled expression on his face, "would you mind not throwing the thousand year old books around the Library."

"Ooops, I guess I should have pushed, not flicked," she said walking around the couch and retrieving the tome from the floor. Gabriel chuckled quietly as she dropped it back on the couch.

Again she turned her palm up and the book rose higher. She turned her hand towards the shelf and pushed gently then stopped as the book hovered a few inches from its destination. She looked over towards Gabriel, who was sat quietly watching her, with his chin resting in his hand. "So what do I do now . . . . It's the wrong way around," she said looking back at the book. She lifted her other hand palm up level with the base of the book and twisted her hand around. The book spun in the air for a second then dropped to the floor with a thud.

"God damn it," she said quietly, and then went to retrieve the book again.

"Maybe you should try a less valuable book," he said as she glanced over at him again. "Or a lighter one at least," he added as she frowned at him.

"Oh you're full of good advice aren't you," she said. "I don't want to get a less valuable or a lighter one back on the shelf—I want to get this one back on the shelf," she said blowing the hair out of her eyes.

She looked back at the book; again she went through the motions, but this time instead of using her hands she just concentrated on where she wanted the book to go, she imagined that she'd carried it over to the shelf and slipped it into its place. And the book did all the work turning in the air then sliding into its spot.

"Ha, I did it," she said happily, pleased with herself. She looked towards Gabriel triumphantly, and he smiled.

"You completely amaze me," he said as he stood up. "A year old and you already have all these powers, I'm so glad you're my woman."

Miranda smiled up at him as he drew level with her, "well I am a first you know—very powerful—so watch you're step," she warned as he put his arms around her.

"You wouldn't hurt me," he said chuckling and kissing her lightly on the head, "anyway I'm hungry; starving in fact—whoever thought staying in bed would take up so much energy—how about we go hunting?"

"I'll race you," she said pulling away from him quickly. She walked to the door and opened it then looked back at him and smiled wickedly before she ran from the room.

Gabriel stood there for a minute and laughed quietly; he gave her a few seconds head start and then followed her. He grinned at Michael and Morana as he flew through the kitchen and out of the backdoor.

34

Miranda glanced over at Gabriel then rolled over to him. She ran her fingers over his chest as he lay beside her, "so, I was thinking of asking Ana to go hunting in the city tonight."

"Ok," he said stroking her hair absently.

"That is unless you would like to come with me?"

Gabriel moved uncomfortably and she looked up at him, "I would love to take you to the city—but it really isn't a good idea—I have witnessed Michael and Morana when they get back from the city, I've never heard of some of the names they call each other—not even Nate and I argue that bad, I can't argue like that with you," he said tightening his arms around her.

"We wouldn't argue," Miranda said frowning at him.

"Oh yes we would, in fact we'd be worse—Miranda you know what my temper is like, I'd only have to see one of them touch you and that would be it, I'd kill the lot of them and then we'd have to go on the run because I'd exposed us to the world, and all because I can't control myself while I'm around you—there would also be several hundred very angry vampires that we'd have to try and avoid," he said frowning a little.

"God ok, if you don't want to come just say so," Miranda chuckled as she rolled away from him and got out of bed.

"It can't be time to get up already," he said running his eyes down her body.

"Yes it is, now get out of bed," she said walking to the wardrobe.

"No I don't want to get out of bed—I want you to get back into bed."

Miranda turned to face him and shook her head, "we have eternity together and I won't spend all of it in bed—get up Gabriel."

He remained where he was and folded his arms across his chest and frowned sulkily. Miranda laughed quietly and visualised slowly undoing his shirt and stripping it off him, then she visualised slowly trailing her lips down his chest until she reached the top of his trousers, and then she stopped and turned away from him.

Gabriel smiled broadly and got out of bed; he glanced at her as he pulled his shirt out and smiled at her, "this one?" he asked holding it up to show her.

"I just knew that would get you out of bed," she chuckled, "yes, now put it on and then when I get back I can strip you out of it."

Gabriel put it on quickly and looked at her expectantly, "why wait till later, come and take it off me now."

Miranda chuckled again but moved away from him and finished dressing. She turned to look at him and laughed again at the look on his face as he stood there waiting.

"Get dressed," she ordered and he dropped his shoulders in defeat.

"You're a cruel woman," he grumbled as he put the remainder of his clothes on, "how can you make me wait—you'd better not be too long or else I just might start without you, and you better do it exactly how you thought it because there will be trouble if you don't," he said as they walked out of the room.

Morana looked up as they entered and smiled; she stood up and then sat back down. Miranda frowned at the woman's odd behaviour, she seemed uneasy. "I think you should know Nathan's back," she said uncomfortably.

"Oh wonderful," Gabriel said sarcastically.

"The thing is, he asked where you were Miranda—and I told him," Morana said smiling apologetically.

"So—what of it?" Gabriel asked before Miranda had time to speak.

"Well he got angry and stormed out of the house."

Gabriel frowned.

"I don't think I'm going to go to the city," Miranda said silently to him, he looked at her for a moment then shook his head. He pulled her towards the door, and then turned back to Morana, "when he gets back tell him we're in the library if he wants us."

Morana nodded and smiled nervously.

Gabriel sat down next to Miranda on the couch and held her hand. "I didn't think he would be back," she said distractedly looking down at their entwined fingers, "why is he still angry, do you think its because of what I said to him, I really did say some bad things," she said frowning and looking up at Gabriel.

Gabriel considered his answer for a few seconds, "it has nothing to do with what you may or may not have said to him Miranda, I think the reason he's so angry is pretty obvious—he's in love with you."

Miranda shook her head, "don't be ridiculous—Nathan in love with me—that isn't the slightest bit funny."

"Oh I know it's not funny—I wouldn't joke about something like this," he said closing his eyes.

"Then why even say it?" Miranda said releasing his hand and standing up.

"Because it's the truth—that night I walked in on you, I saw it in his eyes—the look on his face said it all, I didn't think I'd ever see that look again after Sophie." Miranda looked down at him as he opened his eyes slowly to look at her. "I know how it felt when he kissed you—how it felt in his arms—projection you see, not only did I see it, I felt it too," he said quietly.

Miranda was mortified; she sat down next to him and closed her eyes. "Gabriel I—"

"It doesn't matter," he said her taking her hand again. "I realise that when I left Nathan was the one who was here for you, he was here when I wasn't and it's ok—I should thank him for taking care of you."

"But I—" she said as tears started to form in her eyes.

"I know you don't love him Miranda, I know that the feelings you felt were completely unexpected—they weren't feelings of love, they were some fleeting fancy that his lips teased out of you," he said pulling her closer. "I'm not going to lie and tell you that it had no effect on me, because it did, it hurt like hell—but I came back because I couldn't live without you, because I knew that if I wanted you I had to fight for you—and I will fight for you for the rest of my life if that's what it takes," he said then kissed her head.

"I'm yours and always have been—you never had to fight for me," she said wiping the tears from her face.

They sat there in silence for a few minutes, in each others arms until Gabriel finally pulled away from her and smiled, "I'd better do something—I'm not going to sit around all night just waiting for him to show up—I won't give him the satisfaction," he said getting to his feet and walking over to the desk.

Miranda stood up too and walked over to the shelf and pulled down a few books.

"You're never going to read all of those, that is, unless you've mastered the art of speed reading too," he said as he watched her walk back to the couch.

"No I'm practicing," she said stretching her finger over the book, she looked over at him for a second and imagined undoing his shirt slowly, imagined trailing her lips down his chest until she reached the top of his trousers and then she stopped again and turned her attention back to the pile of books.

Gabriel blinked rapidly for a moment and then looked over at her and grinned, "well you definitely have that power down to a fine art—but don't stop I was enjoying it."

"Well, you might get the real thing later," she said glancing over at him again and he chuckled quietly as he turned his attention back to the computer screen. She kept all thoughts of Nathanael out of her mind as she practiced pulling and pushing the energy around her and it wasn't until Gabriel touched her lightly on the shoulder that she realised how long she'd been doing it.

"I'm hungry—what about you?" he asked as she turned to kiss him. She nodded. "Will you be alright in here—I won't be too long," he said uncertainly.

"Of course I'll be alright—if you hadn't noticed I'm quite a powerful little thing," she joked kissing him lightly again.

"Ok" he smiled walking to the door, "I won't be long."

Miranda sat down and frowned slightly as something attracted her attention, the slightest glimpse of red could be seen jutting out from underneath the couch. She bent forward and pulled out the third tome. Her frown deepened as she picked the book up, what was it doing there. She stood up and walked over to the bookshelf, as she moved forward her feet left the floor and she drifted higher until she was at the required height to put it back in its place.

This levitating thing came so easily now that the merest thought had her floating through the air. Even the landing was easy she mused as her feet touched the floor lightly. She walked back and sat down as the door opened, she looked up expecting Gabriel, but Nathanael stood there smiling at her.

"Miranda bombanda—have you missed me?" he said smiling at her. He moved at speed and sat down next to her before she even had time to move. She tried to stand up but he grabbed hold of her quickly, stopping her retreat. "Did I leave you in such a state that you can't even bear to be in my company?" he said pulling her back onto the couch. He smiled at her for a moment, his fingers digging painfully into her shoulder as he held her still.

She recoiled slightly as she sat there looking back at him; he didn't look the same man he'd been before he left. His mouth looked thinner, crueller. He had a hardness in his eyes that made her feel uneasy; his whole demeanour was cold and detached. Even the clipped tone in which he spoke sent a slightly shiver through her, this new Nathan was daunting and a little intimidating. Had she ever really known him at all?

"So did you miss me?" he asked again. Miranda moved uncomfortably. "No—I can see by the look on your face that I wasn't missed in the slightest," he said quietly taking her hand and raising it to his mouth, he kissed the back of it lightly, and then smiled as he tightened his grip painfully. "I must say, I am very impressed with the way you've settled into this life—everything seems to come so easily to you doesn't it, levitating, telekinesis, hunting—sleeping with my brother—I suppose that's the easiest part of all isn't it?" he said pulling her closer.

"That is none of your damned business," Gabriel said angrily from the doorway. "Get your hands off her," he said, striding into the room. He took her hand and pulled her to her feet and away from Nathanael.

Nathanael sat there and looked up at them both, a slight look of amusement danced across his features for a moment then he rested back into the couch, "you are actually willing to die for her aren't you?" he asked looking directly at Miranda.

"Shut up," Gabriel said frowning down at him.

"Why dear brother, surely Miranda knows the penalty for your relationship?" he said. He looked from Miranda to Gabriel and smiled widely, "could it be that you haven't yet told her the price that will be paid for all of this happiness."

Miranda turned to Gabriel, "what price?" she asked, a worried frown creasing her face.

"Ignore him," Gabriel said putting his arm around her.

"OH MY GOD—you haven't told her, have you? The most important of things—and you haven't even told her," Nathanael threw his head back and laughed aloud. "I don't believe it."

"What price?" Miranda asked again looking up at Gabriel.

"It's nothing for you to worry about—I'm warning you Nathan, one more word—"

Nathanael stood up quickly so that he was face to face with Gabriel and smiled slowly. "One more word and what Gabriel? You'll kill me? Don't make me laugh, you having a little bit of trouble with your memory bro? You tried that already, but you couldn't could you. Kill my wife—easy, kill my unborn child—easy, but when it came to me—let's see," he said tapping his chin. "Nope, I'm still here—so apparently you couldn't, didn't have the strength, so what the hell makes you think you'd be anymore successful at it this time?"

"Get out!" Gabriel shouted, trying hard to keep control of his temper.

Nathanael laughed again, "or you'll throw me out. Is that the plan—come on then, throw me out."

Miranda reached out her hand and touched his arm gently. "Nathan don't—"

"Don't you touch me you whore," he spat, shrugging her hand off.

Gabriel lost control his temper; he pulled back his fist and drove it hard into Nathanael's jaw, sending him flying over the couch and across the room. He hit the bookshelf with a deafening crack, several books fell from their place and several more threatened to. Nathanael recovered quickly from the blow and ran at Gabriel at full speed, his teeth bared.

Gabriel had just enough time to push Miranda out of the way before he caught the full force of Nathanael's attack. It sent both of them flying backwards through the air, they landed on the desk with a loud crash, and the sound of the wood splintering underneath their weight got lost in the sound of Gabriel's cry of pain as Nathanael sank his teeth into his chest. Gabriel quickly grabbed a handful of his hair and pulled his head back forcefully and Miranda thought that she'd actually heard Nathanael's neck snap.

Nathanael growled deep in his throat as Gabriel bared his teeth, he sunk them deep into Nathan's shoulder, and blood erupted from the wound turning his white tee-shirt a beautiful shade of crimson.

"Please stop it," Miranda said finally finding her voice. But neither of them heard her plea.

Gabriel quickly produced a ball of fizzling energy, from the very centre of him it appeared, and Miranda shrunk further back against the wall as he flicked it towards Nathanael . . . . Nathanael, quick to react, gracefully leapt into the air, leaving the ball to explode against the far wall.

Miranda felt her own energy growing deep within her, as she stood pressed close to the wall. Nathanael ran at Gabriel again. The growl, coming from within him, sounded more like a roll of thunder, as this time he sank his teeth deep into Gabriel's abdomen. Gabriel quickly brought his knee up and caught Nathanael hard in the chest. As Nathanael stumbled backwards Gabriel produced another ball of energy, this time it crackled and hissed and Miranda could feel the heat off it from where she stood. It hit Nathanael square in the chest, pushing him towards the door.

Gabriel ran towards him at full speed, his lips pulled back unnaturally, his bloodied fangs protruding from his mouth. He crashed into Nathanael, and the sound as they collided was deafening. He wrapped his arms around him and again bit down hard into Nathanael's shoulder. Blood flowed freely from both men's wounds but neither gave up, they snapped and snarled and bit each other like savage dogs.

"Please stop!" Miranda shouted as Nathanael punched Gabriel hard in the chest. Gabriel seemed to have forgotten she was even in the room, in the throes of rage he quickly produced a third energy bolt and flicked it towards her. Nathanael shouted at her to move, but instead she raised her hand out towards the ball as it hurtled towards her. She closed her eyes and waited for the impact, sure that the ball was going to hit her, but it didn't. It came to a halt and hovered at her hand and remained there, fizzing and crackling.

She opened her eyes slowly and looked from Gabriel to Nathanael then back again. As several energy balls fizzled and died. "I asked you to STOP!!!" she shouted as the energy exploded from her. It appeared as a visible wave that arched out into the room. It surged towards both men, several finger like strands broke away from the wave and coiled around each of them, forcing them to their knees, while the main wave carried on towards the window, the tinkling of broken glass was only just audible, above the pained cries of both men, as the wave hit the far wall and then exploded into a thousand sparks and died.

Gabriel lay still, unable to move, as the pain gripped him, the energy pinned him to the floor for several minutes before the agony subsided. He slowly turned his head and looked over at her, standing pressed up against the wall, the shock and pain etched into her frowning face. He got unsteadily to his feet. He was totally astounded. All of the fight had been knocked out of him; it had been absolute torture. He had never in over three hundred years felt anything like the energy contained in that wave, his whole body hurt, his hard marble skin showed several scorch marks where the fingers had touched, he examined the deep grooves for a second then raised his head to look at his brother.

Nathanael lay where he was for a moment, he couldn't even gather enough strength to turn his head. The force of those strands had all but crippled him. The pain had thrown him completely, he closed his eyes for a moment as the last remnants of pain faded then got slowly to his feet. He shook his head and blinked over at his brother. Her energy had hurt him far more than anything Gabriel had thrown at him in the last five minutes; he couldn't quite believe how powerful she was.

Gabriel looked away from him and towards Miranda; he frowned and moved very slowly towards her. She stood there just looking between the men, looking at the blood that soaked their clothes, looking at the wounds they both bore. She looked around at the devastated library, then back at Gabriel as he approached her.

"I'm sorry," he said quietly stopping as her eyes came to rest on him.

"I thought you were going to kill each other," she said quickly covering the ground between them and wrapping her arms around him.

Nathanael stood there for many minutes watching them. Miranda looked at him as he spoke. "What a powerfully little creature you have there Gabe—who knows she may even be strong enough to save you—but don't count on it," he said then smiled slightly. He turned and left the room before either of them had a chance to reply.

Miranda ran her fingers gently over the red puncture marks on Gabriel's chest, they looked painful, but he didn't flinch at her touch.

"Do they hurt?" she asked lowering her head to kiss them softly.

"No not really, but I don't mind if you want to kiss them better," he chuckled.

"But they look painful, how many have you got?"

Gabriel shrugged, "I don't know, I don't usually count when Nate bites me, I don't have as many as I usually do, we normally fight until neither of us can stand—I normally feel much weaker than this," he said stroking her head.

"So you don't feel weak?" she asked looking up at his face.

"No—why what do you have in mind?" he asked tightening his arms around her. But she moved away from him.

"Well to start with, you can explain to me what the consequences are for our relationship—and I want the truth Gabriel, I realise that you've had enough time to make up an excuse—and if you don't tell me the truth I'll have no choice but to go and ask Nathan."

Gabriel frowned, he'd been waiting for this question, and as he looked down at her face he was in no doubt that she would go and ask Nathanael if he didn't tell her the truth. "Look, Nathan made it sound worse than it is," he said then smiled slightly at her frown, "I swear I'm telling the truth—hand on my dead heart," he frowned for a moment and then sighed. "Vampires have a few laws, that I haven't told you about, one being that we do not kill our own kind without just cause—the penalty, of course, is death—another being that new vampires, such as yourself, are not allowed to have any kind of relationship, until their maker releases their ownership—and even though you are not bound to him, he still has a lawful right—if he comes back he could insist that the council take my head, or he could take my head with no consequences for himself."

"Why would they have a law like that—how stupid," Miranda said frowning.

"No it isn't, not really," he said shaking his head, "as vampires we are very, very protective over what we see as belonging to us—just imagine creating something only to have it stolen away—the seconds set this law for the sake of peace, in the seventeen hundreds, if I remember right, after a feud that lasted for over four decades."

Miranda looked at him and frowned again, "why, what happened?"

"It's a long story, there were two vampires that wanted the same woman, a fight ensued, armies were created, the whole thing got very messy and the council were forced to intervene—they had no choice but to kill the two that cause the problem and then the legion of vampires they had made had to be hunted down and destroyed and that was when they decided that there had to be some kind of law to prevent it ever happening again, feuding vampires is something the world should never be exposed to," he said and frowned.

"So you're telling me that I still belong to him?"

"Yes but only by law—and like I said, Nathan made it sound worse than it is—because the chances are that he will never come back for you, considering he just left you there," he said pulling her closer, "anyway you don't have to worry about it."

"I don't have to worry about it—until he comes back you mean," she said slipping her arm around him.

"Even if he comes back—you're a first Miranda, the council wouldn't even consider killing you, being the only first in existence, I can guarantee that the council will do their utmost to protect you—I am the only one that would be held accountable for this relationship—you are perfectly safe."

"You think I'm only worried about myself—you think I'm only worried about my own head," she said pulling away from him angrily. "You could die for this, for us—well I won't let that happen, I will not let them take you away from me Gabriel, I will not survive without you, I don't want to live without you, how could you think I would live without you."

"Miranda, please calm down," he sighed putting his arm around her and pulling her close again, "you can't interfere. If you did—well if you did—you can't interfere, it's the law—I won't let you interfere."

"I don't care about their laws—if they kill you they might as well kill me, so let them come, because I will not let them take you away from me, I am not going to live without you," she said as a tear escaped and rolled down her cheek.

"Please don't say that," Gabriel said wiping the tear away gently, "I couldn't bear it, Miranda this time I've spent with you has been the best of my life—and Nathan was right, I am willing to die for you—I would die a thousand deaths for you, because no matter what they do, you have loved me more than I've ever deserved. I won't allow you to interfere."

Miranda wrapped her arms around him tightly, "I will not live without you, death will be kinder," she said quietly, as she did she projected the memory of how she'd felt the day he'd left, she felt his whole body tense and she looked up at him, "I cannot live without you," she repeated in the quietest whisper and then she kissed him passionately.

35

Gabriel sat staring at his paper, he was aware that Nathanael was sat opposite staring at him, but he wasn't going to get into another argument; he still hadn't totally recovered his energy from yesterday, so he ignored him.

"Where's Miranda?" Nathanael finally asked.

Gabriel frowned as he realised he was going to have to answer him. "Sleeping," he said shortly.

"You really should try and control your sexual habits if this is the effect it has on her," Nathanael said trying to force a grin onto his face, but he was pretty sure it looked more like a grimace.

"I think you will find it had more to do with your antics in the library, rather then our sexual habits, that have worn her out," Gabriel said closing the paper slightly to look over at his brother.

"I wasn't the only one in the library yesterday," Nathanael said calmly rapping his fingers on the table.

"No that's true, but I was the only one in her bed," Gabriel said returning his attention to the paper.

Morana moved slowly towards the kitchen door, any minute they could start fighting again, and she didn't want to get caught in the middle of it. As she moved it attracted Nathanael's attention. "What was that you thought?" he asked looking up at her.

"I didn't—" she started to say, but Nathanael interrupted her.

"Yes you did—don't lie, you still think after all these years, that you can block me you stupid bitch," he shouted standing up.

Gabriel looked up at Morana as she hovered by the door. The woman looked uncertainly at him for a second before Gabriel turned back to

Nathanael. "Nate—sit down and leave her alone—you really shouldn't delve if you don't like what you find."

"Who the hell do you think you are?" Nathanael shouted moving towards her.

Morana backed up to the door, and realised her efforts to escape would be useless. Gabriel looked around at her again, and frowned at his brother. He stood up and moved quickly in front of Morana, "I said sit down and leave her alone."

"And I don't give a damn what you said," he shouted reaching around Gabriel and grabbing a handful of the woman's hair. Morana shrieked as he yanked her head forward savagely. Gabriel was knocked forward unexpectedly by the force with which Morana's head hit his back.

"Let go of her!" Gabriel shouted reaching for his arm, but Nathanael punched him hard on the chin. He stumbled backwards into Morana making the woman yell in pain as the hair he had a hold of was ripped painfully from her scalp.

Gabriel turned to Morana and pushed her from the room as blood trickled down her face, and he turned back to Nathanael and pushed him back into the room, as he tried to go after her.

"What the hell is the matter with you Nate," he shouted trying to hold him at arms length.

"I'm going to kill that stupid bitch," Nathanael yelled, as he tried to get past Gabriel.

"You're not killing anyone, for god's sake—just sit down," Gabriel shouted pushing him forcefully back towards the table.

"Get your GOD DAMN HANDS OFF ME!!" Nathanael shouted drawing back his fist and hitting out at Gabriel. The force of the punch pushed Gabriel back towards the door and Nathanael ran at him, he sunk his teeth into Gabriel's arm and tore the flesh from the bone savagely.

Gabriel growled with pain and quickly wrapped his arms around Nathanael, he lowered his head to his neck and bit down as hard as he could, Nathanael yelped with pain. As Gabriel jerked his head away, crimson liquid flowed from Nathanael's neck, and spread quickly down the front of his shirt but Nathanael recovered quickly. He pushed against Gabriel with all of his strength, sending him flying back across the table; he hit the floor on the other side with a deafening thud. Gabriel jumped to his feet quickly as Nathanael sprung through the air towards him, and there was a loud crack as several chairs splintered into pieces as their bodies slammed into them.

Nathanael again sunk his teeth into Gabriel's shoulder, as they rolled around the floor. Gabriel grabbed his head viciously and pulled it back and bit down into his neck for a second time, and before Nathanael had time to recover Gabriel brought his head back and butted him hard in the nose. The sound of the bone cracking was lost in Nathanael's shriek of pain.

Miranda's eyes snapped opened as Libbi burst into the room, "you gotta come and stop them," she screeched.

"Stop who," Miranda said jumping out of bed quickly.

"Gabe and Nate, they are fighting again—it sounds real bad," the girl said lifting her hands to her head. "Oh please stop them—they're going to kill each other," she shouted.

Miranda dressed quickly and hurried out of the room. As she descended the stairs she could hear them fighting, she didn't hesitate to talk to Morana or Michael as they hovered by the door. She shook off Michael's hand and frowned at Morana's bloodied appearance, before she rushed into the room.

She almost lost her footing and slipped with the amount of blood on the floor, it was absolutely everywhere. There didn't seem to be one single place that was blood free. Both men were covered from head to toe in the claret liquid.

"Stop this now," she shouted as both men sank their teeth into the other. The gurgled cries of pain from them drowned out her voice for a moment. Gabriel lifted his head and opened his mouth to bite Nathanael again, and Nathanael pulled his fist back to hit Gabriel. "I said stop!" she shouted again lifting her hands towards them; they were forced apart as she pushed the energy towards them, they both rose a few inches into the air and she held them there as they both struggled.

"Let go of me!" Nathanael spat as he glared over at her.

"No!" she shouted angrily, "not until you've calmed down—have you both gone completely insane!"

"I'm not the insane one," Gabriel yelled as he tried, in vain, to kick out towards his brother. "Put me down I'm going to rip him to pieces."

"I'd like to see you try," Nathanael hissed.

"Let me go Miranda," Gabriel raged as she moved them a little further apart.

"No I won't, not until you've both calmed down."

"Well you may find you'll be waiting a long time," Nathanael shouted renewing his efforts to escape her hold. "I'm going to kill him."

"I can keep this up all night if I have to," she said calmly looking from one to the other.

"Let go of me Miranda; he has been asking for this for centuries—I've finally had enough—do you hear that brother? I'm willing to put you out of your misery once and for all," Gabriel shouted at Nathanael.

"Come on then—COME AND DO IT, YOU BASTARD," Nathan raged.

Gabriel put all of his energy into trying to break free of the hold Miranda had on him, and Nathanael followed suit. Miranda watched them both for a few more seconds, then she moved back and rested against the counter; she folded her arms and continued to watch them.

"LET ME DOWN, GOD DAMN IT," Nathanael yelled again.

She shook her head, then looked over at Gabriel, "I'm not letting either of you go, like I said I can keep this up all night—by which time you'll both be too weak to fight, and judging by the amount of blood the pair of you have already lost, its not going to take to much longer for the two of you to wear yourselves out—so you can both carry on as long as you like."

Gabriel frowned over at her but stopped struggling instantly, he knew by the look on her face that she was deadly serious; he was also in no doubt that she would indeed keep them both there for as long as she thought necessary. He closed his eyes for a moment, trying to calm the anger that bubbled away inside of him, and then looked at her again.

"I'm calm now, you can release me—I promise I won't try anything," he said silently towards her.

"If you do Gabriel, I will just confine you again—promise me that you're completely calm," she said silently looking at him.

He closed his eyes for a few more seconds, then looked at her and nodded his head, "completely."

She slowly moved the energy away from him and he dropped to his feet.

"LET GO OF ME—LET ME GO," Nathanael raged as Gabriel moved further away from him under his own volition.

"NO!" Miranda yelled looking back at him. She turned to Gabriel and frowned, "you need to clean yourself up—and rest."

Gabriel frowned and shook his head, "I'm not leaving you here alone with him for one second."

"I'm not arguing with you—go," she said, turning towards Nathanael. She stared at him for a second and he stopped struggling momentarily as he moved involuntarily towards the table. He was forced down onto one of the two remaining chairs.

Then she turned back to Gabriel, "are you still here?" she asked and he shook his head. "I'll be fine Gabriel; I want to talk to him."

Gabriel shook his head but walked to the door, "if you touch so much as one hair on her head, I will tear you apart piece by piece," he said venomously towards Nathanael and then left slamming the door behind him.

Miranda picked up the only other intact chair and placed it at the table opposite Nathanael; then she walked over to the cupboard and took out a bottle, she poured some into a cup then walked back to the table.

She placed it in front of him then took the seat opposite him. "I want you to promise you will behave yourself before I release you," she said simply looking over at him. He glowered at her for several seconds, but then nodded slowly. "You are aware of the power I possess Nathan, so give me your word that you won't try anything—I really don't want to hurt you—but I will if you force me too."

He frowned for a second then lowered his head, "you have my word," he said quietly. She slowly released him from her hold and he sat back in his chair.

"Drink it," she said looking down at the cup.

Nathanael looked down at it then shook his head, "I don't want it!"

"You may not want it, but you need it—unless you plan to bleed to death right in front of me," she said looking back at his face.

"Vampires don't bleed to death—so don't bother with your false concerns for me," he said sarcastically. "Tell me would it upset you—me dying—would it really break your heart?" he asked cynically.

Miranda looked at him for a moment, "yes it would upset me," she said honestly, "please drink it Nathan."

Nathanael looked at her for several minutes more before he reached out and took hold of the cup.

"Nathan whatever it is that you're going through, I want you to know, that no matter what happened between us, I'm still your friend and I want to help," she said staring down at the table.

"Friend," Nathanael repeated quietly. Miranda nodded keeping her eyes on the table. "Well it seems that your friendship doesn't suit me anymore," he said and she looked up at him quickly. "I love you Miranda, and I don't want just your friendship—I want you."

Miranda frowned and shook her head, "I love Gabriel, we could never be anything more than friends Nathan—I'm sorry if I ever gave you reason to think otherwise, but I belong with Gabriel—I love Gabriel."

Nathanael closed his eyes for a moment, it was exactly what he had expected her to say, but the pain that gripped him was unbelievable, "I don't believe you, you felt the same as I did when I kissed you—I know you did, tell me—I dare you to tell me that you felt nothing when we stood in the garden and I took you in my arms, I dare you to tell me that you felt nothing when my lips touched yours."

Miranda looked back down at the table, "I'm sorry, but I felt nothing," she said quietly.

"YOU LIAR," he shouted as his eyes snapped open, "you can try and tell yourself that you felt nothing but I know that you did—you felt something so stop lying and tell me the god damn truth."

Miranda moved uncomfortably in her seat, how had she thought that she could get away with such an obvious lie. The memory of how it had felt in his arms sprang into her mind and she closed her eyes for a second. "Ok the truth is that for a moment I did feel something, but it was fleeting—it was the smallest whisper of a feeling compared to what I feel for Gabriel—Nathan, I'm sorry for all of this—it was never my intention to hurt you—but I will only ever be your friend."

He reached over and took her hand gently, "please don't do this—please—choose me, I love you so much, if you choose him, it will kill me," he whispered as tears started to fall from his eyes. "I will do anything, just please—don't do this to me."

"Nathan I—" Miranda stopped talking as tears welled in her eyes, she couldn't bear the pained expression on his face. "I could never love you," she almost whispered as she pulled her hand away from him and stood up.

"Please, I'm begging you," he said jumping to his feet; he moved around the table and took her hands in his, "please—I need you, I could make you happy, I will make you happy, all you have to do is give me the chance, please," he said pulling her closer, "I never wanted to love you, I never thought I could love you, but I do so much, if you feel anything for me at all, please consider it—please let me prove how much I love you."

She looked up into his eyes as he stood there and faltered for a second as his pain and sadness threatened to overcome her. "I'm sorry—I can't—Nathan I don't and never will love you."

"But you haven't even given me a chance—you're killing me Miranda—I don't want to live without you—please," he whispered lowering his head to hers.

She knew she should pull away as his lips gently touched hers, she knew she should turn and run away as his arms snaked around her and pulled her closer. But she couldn't, she stood immobilised, as he held her close and kissed her deeply.

He pulled away slowly and looked down at her, "please Miranda," he whispered.

She moved further away and shook her head and frowned, "that is the last time you'll ever touch me Nathan—I'm sorry, but I could never love you."

Nathanael slumped back down in his chair; the night had been far too much for him to cope with. He couldn't take it anymore. All the pain of losing Sophie didn't even come close to the pain of Miranda's rejection. He'd known even before all his words, before all his begging that this would be the outcome, but he'd had to try. He loved her more than he'd ever thought possible, but he was now left in no doubt that she would never love him. After all his plotting and scheming, after all his plans and after all these years of waiting, he wasn't sure that he could do what he'd set out to do.

And now as the emptiness spread slowly through his aching body, he realised that his chosen path could only have led him to this moment. This moment, where he had to decide the outcome of the whole affair. He had two choices. The first being to carry out his newly revised plan to its final conclusion, or the second, pack a bag and leave as soon as the sun set tomorrow night and never come back. He wasn't sure he had the strength to do either.

He stood up and groaned quietly at the ache in his legs, and slowly walked up the stairs to his room. Sophie smiled at him as he opened the door, and he tried to smile back at her, but his face showed only the smallest grimace.

He closed his eyes as she reached out her pale ghost like hand and stroked his cheek.

"Yes I know," he said opening his eyes and frowning at her. Sophie frowned back.

Nathanael turned towards his bed, "yes I know that—please stop going on at me, I've had a hell of a night," he said quietly sitting down on the edge of the bed, "please just give it a rest, I know all this—you don't have to keep on at me all the time—my head is pounding and you're just making it worse," he said, undoing the buttons of his shirt. He pulled it off and threw it across the room and frowned again, "for god's sake woman—if you insist on carrying on you can just do it your god damn self—see how far that gets you," he said standing up and moving over to his wardrobe, "yes I am going to pack now."

He pulled out several pairs of trousers, then he pulled out a handful of shirts and walked back to the bed, he stooped down for a moment and retrieved a large bag from under the bed, he shoved the clothes into it and dropped it to the floor, then he finished undressing and got into bed.

He tried desperately to ignore her voice as he lay there; he tried desperately to ignore her as he succumbed to the agony. He closed his eyes as the tears fell silently onto his pillow, "please stop," he begged as he wiped at his face, "please—I'll do it—I'll do anything you want as long as you just stop talking—please stop talking," he whispered looking up at her as she floated above him.

"Promise me Nathan," she said, her voice the faintest whisper in his mind.

"I promise," he said quietly, then she faded away leaving him staring up at the ceiling.

The next week passed by in a haze of pain and anger and the only time he left his room was to hunt. Only after ten human lives had been exhausted in his quest to find some small semblance of peace, did he feel strong enough.

36

"To the forest it is then wench, but be warned, feeding isn't the only thing on my mind," Gabriel chuckled as Miranda pulled him down the stairs.

"Mine either," she replied with a sly look. As she pushed open the kitchen door she hesitated at the sight of Nathanael sitting at the table. None of them had seen him for a few days and she'd felt sure he must have left after their last conversation. But there he sat, staring down at the table.

Gabriel tensed at the sight of his brother, but Nathanael didn't show any signs of recognition towards him or Miranda, he just remained staring down at the table.

Michael looked up and smiled awkwardly at them; Morana hovered at Michael's shoulder and managed the slightest of smiles.

"Perhaps we shouldn't go," Miranda said silently into his mind.

"I'm hungry—Morana and Michael will be fine as long as they stay together," Gabriel replied silently, he looked towards Morana and after a moment the woman nodded uncertainly at them. All the time Nathanael's eyes remained on the table.

"See you later," Gabriel muttered as they walked out of the house.

Nathanael looked up at Michael as the backdoor closed and smiled slightly, "I'm sorry," he said quietly looking back down at the table.

"Sorry for what?" Michael asked as Morana placed her hands on his shoulders, he turned slightly and looked up at the woman for a moment and she frowned.

"For everything," Nathanael said looking up again briefly, "for everything I've ever done, I realise that I haven't been what you'd call friendly to either of you since we've known each other, and I am totally at fault for that," he said dropping his head again, "I just wanted to apologise," he said running his fingers through his hair and frowning.

Morana moved uncomfortably behind Michael.

Nathanael looked up at her and smiled slightly, "you have every right not to trust me Ana, I know I've never given you any reason to," he sat back and frowned, "I realise no amount of apologising can make up for the way I attacked you the other night, it was unforgivable—but I really am sorry—I was just—well, I was just—I'm sorry Ana," he said sitting forward a little.

"Apology accepted," Morana said quietly.

"I've made the decision to move on, I've decided to leave for good—by this time tomorrow I will be gone—I realise that this as probably come far to late, but I was hoping we could part on slightly better terms," Nathanael said standing up. He smiled at them both again, "I really am sorry for everything," he said quietly then left the kitchen.

Nathanael opened the door to the lounge and smiled over at Morana, "Ana I can't seem to find my leather jacket, I don't suppose you know where it is do you?"

Morana frowned over at him, "It's in your wardrobe, I put it in there a few months ago," she said.

"I've looked in there but I can't find it," Nathanael said and smiled again.

Morana stood up, as Michael continued to flick through the channels on the TV, and followed him up to his room.

"I'm sure I put it in here," she said looking around at the state of the room as she walked over to the wardrobe.

"Don't worry I will make sure it's nice and tidy before I leave," he said and smiled as she turned and frowned at him, "sorry, I didn't mean to delve—I guess I have to stop doing that," he said.

Morana searched through the wardrobe for a few minutes then pulled the jacket out and handed it to him.

"Thanks Ana," he said taking it from her and dropping it onto the bed, "and not just for finding the jacket—thank you for all the years you've taken care of me, for all the years you've done things and not got any thanks," he said quietly taking her hand.

Morana looked a little suspicious as he dropped his head for a moment, when he looked up again there were tears in his eyes and she faltered, he looked genuinely sorry. She moved closer and put her arms around him.

"I'm sorry," he said quietly burying his head in her neck as he wrapped his arms around her.

Michael looked up as the door opened and Nathanael walked in, he frowned slightly, "where's Ana," he asked looking past him.

"You know what Ana's like, my packing is nowhere near her standards—she has just unpacked my bag and is now repacking it correctly," Nathanael said grinning.

Michael smiled knowingly as Nathanael sat down next to him, "I thought I'd just leave her to it for a minute while I apologised to you again Mike," he said frowning, "I realise I have been an insufferable pain in the rear for such a long time, I know that I'm all alone because of my inability to let go of the past—I'm fed up of being alone—I'm fed up of watching everyone else's happiness and never feeling any of my own," he said his frown deepening.

Michael smiled as Nathanael stood up again, "anyway, take care Mike," he said holding his hand out to the man. Michael considered him for a moment and then stood up and took his hand.

Libbi looked up as Nathanael entered the kitchen and smiled. He walked over to the cupboard and took out a bottle; he flipped off the lid and took a long swig from it, then walked over and sat opposite Libbi. "So where have Mike and Ana gone?" he asked smiling over at the girl.

"I don't know," she shrugged.

Nathanael sat back and frowned over at the girl, "for heaven's sake Lib—look at me!" he shouted as she played with her doll.

She looked up at him quickly and sunk back into her chair as he sat forward. He looked deep into her eyes and she sat there mesmerized. "Ana and Mike left for the city shortly after Gabriel and Miranda went hunting—do you remember they asked if you wanted to go with them." Libbi nodded. "You wanted to stay here with me and we went into Miranda's room and you played guitar for me for a while and then we got hungry—so we came in here."

Libbi blinked as Nathanael sat back, "I'm not hungry," she said quietly.

"Well of course you're not, greedy, you drank nearly all this bottle," he said picking up the nearly empty bottle and waving it in front of her face.

Libbi looked guiltily at the bottle for a moment, "were we going to share—I'm sorry I didn't leave you any—I wonder how long Ana and Michael will be in town—they only went hunting last night," the young girl said still staring at the bottle.

Nathanael shrugged and smiled at her, "I could really do with a hug about now Lib," he said.

Libbi jumped up from her chair and walked around the table to him, he wrapped his arms around her and kissed her forehead, "I love you Lib."

"I love you, Daddy," she said resting her head against his chest.

"I'm sorry that I shouted—I didn't mean too," he said as he stroked her hair. "Do you forgive me?"

Libbi nodded as the backdoor opened and Miranda and Gabriel walked in. The girl reached up and kissed his face gently then she jumped off Nathanael's lap and ran towards Miranda. Miranda chuckled quietly and opened her arms as Libbi jumped at her, Libbi giggled and kissed her lightly on the cheek, and then she reached over and did the same to Gabriel.

Nathanael sank down into his chair and tapped his fingers lightly on the table; he resisted the temptation to look towards them as they greeted each other. It was far too much for him to handle, the scene would be burned into his memory . . . . and this was one scene he didn't want to remember.

"So I played guitar for Nathan and he said I'm getting good—will you come and listen," Libbi asked as Miranda lowered her to the floor.

Gabriel glanced towards his brother, but Nathanael didn't look up.

"Sure I will," Miranda said also glancing at Nathanael, and still he didn't look up.

"And you?" Libbi asked Gabriel.

He shook his head and smiled. "Sorry Lib I need to talk to Nate—so you two go ahead and I'll see you later."

They left the room hand in hand, Miranda glanced back at Gabriel and smiled, she looked fleetingly at Nathanael but he continued to stare down at the table. "You have broken him" a little voice whispered in the back of her mind.

Gabriel sat opposite Nathanael at the table. "Where are Ana and Mike?" he asked.

Nathanael shrugged, "they went to the city," he said as he sat back in his chair.

Gabriel frowned, "the city, why, they went hunting last night?"

Nathanael frowned back at him, "do I look like their keeper—they said they were going to the city and I didn't care enough to ask them why."

Gabriel considered him for a moment, of course he didn't care about them; he didn't care about anyone. He sat back and folded his arms and regarded Nathanael for a moment. "We want you to leave," he said after a minute.

Nathanael showed no emotion at all as he sat forward and placed his hands on the table, "the word we is such a generalisation, don't you think—so is it just you, or does this word we encompass everyone in the house."

"We, does mean all of us," Gabriel answered.

Nathanael considered him for a moment then sat back and smiled, "do you really think I give a damn what any of you want, this is my home—I will leave when I'm good and ready to leave and not when you tell me too—now tell me brother, don't you regret not killing me when you had the chance."

"Truthfully—yes I do, is that what you want me to say—is that really what you want to hear, I regret that I didn't have the strength to kill you—but you were my brother and I loved you, but not anymore, I haven't felt anything for you for a very long time—Nate you need to leave, you need to find a life of your own and move on."

"Oh yes, you would love that wouldn't you, for me to just disappear—your life here with Miranda would be wonderful then wouldn't it, your perfect world with a perfect little family—I had a perfect world once, I had the perfect family—do you remember that Gabe—I had a wife before you killed her."

Gabriel shook his head and frowned. "You won't make me feel guilty about the past anymore Nate, it happened centuries ago—I did everything I could to make it right, but that's it now, its over, I can't do anymore—I won't do anymore."

Nathanael sat there for a moment and smiled slowly, "and if I leave—what do I get Gabriel—what can you possibly give me that will convince me to leave?"

"Anything you want—just ask and it's yours," Gabriel said moving a little uncomfortably.

"Anything I want," Nathanael said standing up, "sorry Gabe but you don't own anything I want—but I will consider your request," he said walking from the room.

Gabriel watched him leave and frowned at the door. That had seemed almost too easy . . . . but he didn't believe for one minute that Nathanael would leave. He stood up and walked to the library; he stopped outside the music room and wondered how Miranda was coping with the noise that Libbi would be making, it was quite fortunate that Michael and Morana had the insight to sound proof the room.

Nathanael stood silently at the top of the stairs and watched as Gabriel disappeared into the library. Sophie was whispering quietly in the back of his mind driving him to distraction.

"Shut up or else I will change my mind," he whispered then frowned. Her voice was getting on his nerves, so was the way she kept telling him what to do all the time, why couldn't the dead just stay dead? He took the dogwood darts out of his pocket and looked at them for a moment before replacing them. He walked slowly down the stairs to the music room and popped his head in; Miranda looked up as he glanced quickly from her to Libbi. "Lib can I talk to you for a minute?" he asked quietly.

Libbi smiled and put down the guitar as Miranda put the earphones on and turned up the music. He knelt down in front of Libbi and smiled, "I need you to go to your room for a little while Lib, while I sort some stuff out with Gabe and Miranda," he said and Libbi frowned at him, "don't worry my love, we're not going to fight or anything like that, I want to make friends with them—I don't want to fight with Gabe anymore," he said and smiled again. "Will you go to your room and stay there until I come and get you," he asked. Libbi nodded and smiled back at him, and then turned and ran upstairs to her room.

Nathanael stood there for a moment then pulled one of the dogwood darts out of his pocket. He hoped the tomes had been right about the power this small twig had on the firsts and seconds. He wrapped his fingers around it then pushed open the door to the music room.

He stood looking at Miranda as she lay with her eyes closed listening to the music that drowned out every other sound. For the tenth time this evening he wondered if he should just get his bag and leave, but he had no choice, she had always been his means to an end, he couldn't back down now, he had to see this through in its entirety, no matter how much misery it would cause him in the years to come. This was the only way he'd ever be free.

He walked around the couch to stand behind her and again looked at the piece of wood in his hand then he closed his eyes for a second. When he opened them again he thrust the stick as hard as he could into the skin on her exposed neck. He acted quickly, dipping his head and she hardly struggled at all as he sunk his teeth into her flesh. He instantly got a mouth full of deer's blood; he'd had to wait for them to feed, and as he swallowed the blood in his mouth he knew without doubt that his venom was rapidly circulating through her veins.

He lifted his head and looked at the puncture holes in her skin. The tomes, he mused, had been a mine of information, going into fine detail of exactly how long it took to render another vampire unconscious when you'd sunken your teeth into their flesh. He pulled off the headphones and let her go.

Miranda's body flopped lifelessly down onto the couch. He stood up and walked around the couch to look at her. She looked as if she were sleeping peacefully. He crouched down in front of her and brushed the hair away from her face, she looked so beautiful, lying there, that for a moment he considered again just forgetting the whole thing. He didn't know if he was strong enough for this anymore. He lent forward and kissed her lips. He stayed there for many minutes with his lips against hers with his eyes closed.

He pulled back suddenly and frowned, "yes I know, I'm doing it aren't I, I just wanted a few minutes—oh shut up for god's sake, alright I'm going," he stroked Miranda's face then stood up and turned to face Sophie as she floated towards him. "You know you really go on for someone who's been dead for so long—what is it to you who I kiss, I'll be so glad when this is all over, then you can go haunt someone else and leave me in peace, my sentence is served after tonight, I owe you nothing after this and you better leave me the hell alone or so god help me I'll kill you again," he frowned as he walked towards the door. "No I won't make you any kind of promise—I'll kiss who I damn well please—now let me get on, I've got an awful lot to do before sunrise."

He walked out of the room closing the door quietly, and then walked over to the library; he paused for a moment, and then pushed down the handle.

Gabriel looked up expectantly then frowned as he saw Nathanael smiling at him. "What do you want?" he asked looking back at the computer screen.

"I've decided to grant your request—I am leaving tomorrow, after tonight you will never see me again," he said walking over to the desk.

Gabriel watched as Nathanael drew level with him, and sat back in his chair. "What's the condition?" he asked eyeing his brother suspiciously.

"It's hardly a condition, but Libbi will be leaving with me, she's upstairs packing a bag as we speak."

"You can't possibly be serious, how can you look after Libbi—no Libbi stays here."

"I'm afraid if Libbi stays so do I, so you really haven't got a choice—you said anything I want—and I want Libbi with me," Nathanael said smiling.

Gabriel stood up and frowned at him, "yes, well I don't own Libbi, she isn't mine to give away—and it isn't open for debate, she stays here."

Nathanael moved away from him and sunk his hands into his pockets; he took one of the darts in his hand and then turned back to face his brother. Gabriel walked towards him then stopped as Nathanael glared at him. "I am not debating anything, but I will be damned if I'm going to let you take Libbi away from me—you already have Miranda—you won Gabriel, you've taken so much from me already, Libbi is coming with me."

Gabriel frowned. "You can't possibly think that a life with you would be good for her—you have nowhere to live, no roots—maybe if you sort yourself out we can discuss it, but until then she stays here with us," he said turning back towards his desk.

Nathanael ceased his chance as Gabriel turned his back on him; he pulled his hand out of his pocket and stabbed the dart into the middle of Gabriel's shoulder blades. Gabriel grunted and stumbled forwards. "You should never turn your back on me Gabriel; more than three hundred years and you're still so dumb," Nathanael said as he jumped onto his back. "This is the only thing I've ever wanted from you—the only reason

I would ever leave my home—I've waited three hundred and twenty years for this day," he whispered wrapping his arms around him, "now you're going to pay for all the suffering you've caused me—like I would ever let you win," he said and then sunk his teeth deep into his brother's flesh.

Gabriel thrashed around momentarily under his brothers hold, but Nathanael's strength was far superior to his, it hadn't taken very long for the dogwood to strip him of every power he possessed. The venom pumped quickly into his body as he fought hard to remain conscious. He struggled until blackness engulfed him.

37

Nathanael stood in front of Gabriel and slapped him as hard as he could across the face. The sound echoed around the room.

Miranda flinched at the noise. She tried to will the energy out into the room but nothing happened. She tugged at the chains that were bound around her wrists, but they were fastened tight. Her fingers were already starting to tingle as the feeling began coming back. She looked down at the chain around her waist; it too restricted any kind of movement.

Gabriel's head lobbed to the side and Nathanael frowned, he put a hand under his brother's head and lifted it, he slapped him hard again, Miranda cringed at the sound and Nathanael turned to look at her then smiled.

"You know I think I may have killed the son of a bitch," he chuckled then turned back to look at his brother has he slowly started to regain consciousness. "Ok maybe not," he said looking into Gabriel's dazed face. "Well hello sleepy head—you had me slightly worried for a moment—I was beginning to think the combination of venom and dogwood had killed you—and killing you so quickly would have spoilt all my fun," he said smiling widely.

Gabriel frowned then shook his head; he couldn't understand what was going on. His body felt numb and his head felt as if it was going to explode, he opened his eyes wider for a second and saw Miranda. He smiled sleepily at her but couldn't understand the look of horror on her face. What was burning? He turned his head to the right and stared at the chains that bound his arm to the metal cross, he turned to look at the other arm, and it too was bound. Wisps of smoke floated into the air as the silver burnt his flesh; that explained the smell. But it didn't hurt, he couldn't feel anything. He glanced down at his bare chest, chains crossed his torso, it should be hurting like hell his mind told him, but he couldn't feel a thing.

"So by the look on your faces, I guess you're wondering what's going on," Nathanael said moving away from him and over to a table. He turned around to face them both and smiled. He glanced over at Gabriel and chuckled. "Are you with me brother dear," he looked toward Miranda, "I think I may have over done the venom you know."

Miranda was starting to get the feeling back in her hands, the silver chains were starting to hurt as they burnt her flesh but even so she tried to pull against them and free herself.

"I think you'll find that you're not all that strong anymore—dogwood you see," he said holding up one of the darts. "It is absolutely amazing the effect this has on you two, don't you think—taking away all your powers—leaving you so vulnerable—it must be such a drag being a first and second."

"Why are you doing this?" Miranda asked again pulling at the chains. Nathanael ignored her question.

He picked something up from the table and walked back to his brother and lifted the bottle to look at it. "Do you have any idea how long it took me to get this," he said frowning slightly, "actually not that long—did you know they have a website that you can actually order the stuff from, all the way from Lourdes—today's technology hey bro—absolutely amazing—of course I'm not all together sure that it's bona fide holy water—tell you what, lets have a little look see."

He took the top of the small bottle and splashed a little of the water into Gabriel's face, his flesh instantly bubbled and blistered. "Well I'll be damned—it really is genuine, well worth the money." Gabriel's head lobbed to the side again and Nathanael sniggered, "well that's gonna sting like a bitch when you get the feeling back—I cleanse you of all your sins, demon be gone," he said as he made the sign of a cross with his hand, "I could have been a priest you know—I think I missed my true vocation in life."

He walked back to the table and threw the bottle onto it and then he turned around to face them again. "I think I'm going to have to wait a little while until either of you can feel any of this—it's no good torturing you if you can't feel it, no good at all," he said smiling over at Miranda, "so now lets get on with some explanation as to why you're both trussed up like turkeys."

"Does it have anything to do with the fact that you're insane," Miranda said pulling against the chains again.

Nathanael looked at her for a moment and frowned; he walked over to her and stooped down beside her for a moment then raised his hand and slapped her hard around the face. Tears streamed from her eyes as he stood up and walked back to the table. "Don't interrupt me—women should be seen but never heard," he said turning to face them again. "It has nothing at all to do with my sanity, I am simply exerting my lawful right," he said folding his arms and smiling slightly, "you know, you made a complete mess of my plans—I had to re-think everything—whoever would have thought you'd turn out to be a first."

Miranda frowned at his words; she didn't understand what he was saying.

"For heavens sake, you're so slow," Nathanael grumbled. He walked over and knelt down in front of her and smiled wickedly. "Poor little Miranda—I'm sorry for your pitiful little life, I'm sorry that you will never age beyond your eighteen years—and so on," he finished.

He turned to look at his brother, but Gabriel still seemed oblivious to the things going on around him. Granted he had counted longer as he'd sunk his teeth into his skin, but even so it was no fun without his full attention. He looked back at Miranda for a second, "wait there won't you," he said standing up again and going to his brother. "Will you please get with the programme Gabe—I haven't gone through all of this for you to miss it—come on wake up!" he said slapping him hard around the face a third time.

Gabriel's head jolted to the side and remained there for a moment as he blinked rapidly, he closed his eyes and squeezed them together, it felt as if the fog that had been clouding his mind had suddenly lifted and he looked up at Nathanael. "What the hell are you doing!" he said straining against the chains.

Nathanael laughed when Gabriel grimaced at the pain it caused him. Then he walked back over to Miranda and stooped down beside her. "Now where was I—oh yes, have you caught up yet—sorry about your miserable life—sorry you won't get the funeral you want—blah, blah, blah, so on and so forth."

Miranda looked at him and frowned.

"And there I was hoping I'd made a good impression on you the first time we met," he said shaking his head, he sat down beside her and reached over to brush a stray hair out of her eyes, "oh come on Miranda—I said I was sorry for your pitiful little life, that I was sorry that you wouldn't age beyond your eighteen years and so on just before I bit down into your tender human flesh and nearly sucked you dry—surely you haven't forgot the wind and the rain and the empty street, surely you haven't forgotten my arms wrapped so tightly around you that you couldn't breathe—surely you haven't forgotten my teeth sinking into your tender flesh."

Miranda looked at him horrified.

"Ha, and now the penny drops," he said standing up. "Oh brother—you really did miss a treat by not changing her yourself, her blood was so sweet, so rich and warm, it took a considerable amount of willpower on my part to stop, I can tell you," he said walking to the table. "Imagine it, I was thanking my lucky stars when you asked me to look out for her—I just couldn't believe my luck, I waited patiently all those years just watching and waiting, just hoping for that one time when you wouldn't be watching her, I spent so much time just watching you watching her . . . . her disgusting human stench almost killed me a few times, you really were a vile creature in those days," he said picking up the small bottle again. He glanced at Gabriel and smiled then walked back to Miranda.

"So now bro—place your bets, how many drops of this will drip onto her beautiful vampire skin before she screams, do you think," he asked as he unscrewed the top. He held the bottle above Miranda's head.

"Get away from her," Gabriel shouted desperately pulling at the chains. "If you touch her I'll rip you apart."

Nathanael laughed loudly as a drop of the liquid fell from the bottle and onto her cheek. She flinched at the pain as the drop rolled down her cheek, leaving a trail of little blisters on her skin.

"How do you intend doing that—if you haven't noticed you are some what incapacitated—now shut up, or else I'll pour the whole damn thing over her," Nathanael said grinning over at his brother. Another drop fell from the bottle and Miranda bit down on her lip to hold back the scream that threatened to escape from her. "So that's two drops—shall we go for a third?"

"Please stop," Gabriel said quietly as he looked down at her. "I'm begging you don't hurt her—do whatever you want to me, but leave her alone."

"Not to proud to beg—I like it, you would do just about anything for her wouldn't you?" Nathanael said tilting the bottle a little more, another drop fell onto her face and this time the scream did escape.

"Please don't—come and take your revenge out on me, she hasn't done anything to you, Nate PLEASE," Gabriel begged as a tear rolled down his cheek.

"Just wait your turn—I'll get around to you in my own good time," he tilted the bottle further and the water trickled down her face. "Anyway you're wrong—she broke my heart—I mean she did choose you and after my heartfelt declaration of love too."

Gabriel looked at Nathanael and then back at Miranda.

"She didn't tell you about it did she—bad Miranda, not telling him about our little talk in the kitchen, she didn't tell you how her body melted into mine as I held her in my arms, or about the way my lips felt against hers—what other secrets as she been keeping from you brother? I mean your relationship won't last very long if she's already started lying to you."

"We don't have any secrets—she probably didn't tell me because she knew I would have killed you."

Nathanael laughed again, and a few more drops of water dripped onto Miranda's face. She sobbed as the burning became unbearable, she could feel the blisters as they formed on her skin. He dropped down besides her and smiled. "Don't you wish you'd accepted my offer now, all of this could have been so easily avoided, all you had to do was leave with me and let me love you—but no you chose him—you broke my heart, and now—well someone has to pay for all my sadness and pain!"

Nathanael stood up and looked at the bottle for a moment then threw it onto the table. "Does it hurt you to see her pain brother—does it hurt to know that you are completely powerless to help the woman you love," he paused for a moment and stared at Gabriel. "Imagine how it feels to live with that pain for over three hundred years—but of course you don't have to imagine how it feels do you because if either of you did you wouldn't be able to stand it—you know I'm still undecided which one of you to kill first."

Miranda closed her eyes and tried to concentrate—tried to will the energy into her body but it was useless.

"So I realise I haven't finished telling you my side of the story—where was I—honestly I'm so easily distracted," he said leaning back against the table. "Oh yes, my original plan had been quite simple, turn Miranda and then take her for myself, leaving you broken hearted, but of course nothing is ever that simple is it, turned out she was a first and therefore I had no hold on her—can you imagine my annoyance when I found out that little snippet of information, trust you to fall in love with a descendant—so it left me with only one other option, that being to kill you both, as I said a shame really—" he sighed then stood up straight. "At least I will show you the mercy that I wasn't afforded," he said turning back towards the table. "Now whose turn is it next," he said donning a glove and picking up a silver stake.

38

Libbi hovered at the top of the stairs, where had everyone gone . . . . the house was so quiet. Nathanael had told her to wait in her room until he came for her, but that was ages ago . . . . and Morana and Michael hadn't come back yet . . . . they had never been away so long before. She strained her ears to see if there was any sign of anyone downstairs for a moment, then she walked quietly down the stairs.

She stood outside Miranda's music room then pushed down on the handle and she frowned . . . . no-one was there. She walked quickly over to Gabriel's library and poked her head in . . . . no-one there either. She ran back upstairs and knocked at Miranda's bedroom door and when there was no answer she popped her head into the room, then she did the same with Gabriel's room . . . . still no sign of anyone. She stood outside Morana and Michael's room and frowned, it sounded as if someone was in there, she reached out and tried the door but it was locked, her frown deepened . . . . something was wrong, Morana and Michael never locked their door normally.

So what should she do now, she stood there frowning for many minutes, and then she smiled as she remembered there was a spare key to their room in the kitchen. She went to get it quickly: she felt sure that something was going on but she didn't know what it was . . . . she was never left alone . . . . but where had they all gone . . . . where had Nathanael gone. She hovered by the cellar door as she heard a noise . . . . someone was down there; she reached her hand out and froze as she heard voices.

"Please stop," Gabriel's voice said quietly, "I'm begging you don't hurt her—do whatever you want to me, but leave her alone."

"Not to proud to beg—I like it, you would do just about anything for her wouldn't you," Nathanael said. Libbi backed away from the door horrified as Miranda screamed in pain . . . . she needed to find Michael and Morana, they'd know what to do.

She ran up the stairs to their room and unlocked the door. Morana and Michael appeared to be sleeping, but as she walked further into the room she noticed the chain wrapped around them, she reached out her hand to touch the chain as Michael opened his eyes.

"Don't touch it Libbi, its silver—it will burn you," he said and the girl withdrew her hand quickly.

"Who did it," she asked quietly.

"Nathan," Michael said trying to move. He looked at Morana's sleeping face. "Ana wake up—Ana please, WAKE UP!"

Libbi hovered at the bedside as Morana slowly opened her eyes. She looked at Michael for a moment then frowned. "What the hell!" she gasped as she tried to move away from him, she looked down at the bed and her eyes widened as she saw the chain wrapped around them.

"I couldn't find anyone—Nathan said you had gone hunting in the city—but Miranda and Gabriel are missing too—and Nathan has gone—and I was all alone—and I think they are down in the cellar—I heard them and Miranda screamed—and Gabriel sounds hurt—and Nathan said he should beg—something is wrong—it is, isn't it, that's why Nathan told me to lie to Gabriel, but I didn't I promise—and now they are down there—but I didn't lie—I promise I didn't," Libbi said as tears started to roll down her face.

"Oh sweetie, we know none of this is your fault," Morana said as she tried to push against Michael.

"Libbi I need you to look and see if there is some kind of lock on this chain," Michael said as Morana's elbow dug into his ribs. "Ana can you just keep still, I can't think straight with your bony elbows digging into me."

Morana stopped moving immediately.

"Yes I can see it," Libbi said, reaching out and touching the lock; she wrapped her hands around it and tugged at it. "It's very big—I don't think I can break it," she said frowning.

She stood up and looked around the room, "there isn't even anything to open it with," she said looking back at the pair. "I need the key, oh I need the key, I can't do it without the key," she said quietly hopping on one foot as more tears fell from her eyes.

"Libbi calm down sweetie—the silver is making you weak—we'll think of something," Morana said quietly.

"Libbi think. Where would Nathan have put the key?" Michael asked. "Think Libbi where would he have put the key?"

"Maybe in his room—in his room—he might have put it in his room," the girl said excitedly.

"Libbi, quiet," Michael said quickly. "Go to Nathan's room and look for the key, but you have to be really quiet."

Libbi nodded then left the room, she tiptoed across the hall and opened Nathanael's door quietly, and crept in. She hated his room, it was so cold . . . . she hated the way Sophie stared down at her, the portrait always seemed to frown at her and she didn't like it . . . . she didn't think that Nathanael's wife had been very pretty at all.

She looked quickly around the room, then walked over to the bedside table and opened the drawer . . . . the key wasn't in there. She walked over to the wardrobe and opened it slightly then looked over at the bed. She walked over to it and looked down at his jacket, she picked it up and shook it gently and heard the keys jangle. She smiled proudly at herself as she dipped her hand into the pocket and pulled out the two keys. She looked back at the painting and frowned, she hated this room and she hated that painting. She left the room quickly.

"I got it—I found it," she said walking quickly around the bed and putting the key into the lock, the lock clinked as it opened and she pulled it free of the chains. "OW!" she wined as the chain brushed the skin on her hand, and then she clamped her hand over her mouth and looked apologetically at Michael.

"Careful," he said, then he smiled and added, "good girl Lib," he looked at Morana for a second, "Ana, we are going to need to roll—slowly—careful—that's it," he said as they moved together, they rolled off the bed and hit the floor with a loud thud. Michael frowned as he listened intently for a moment, for any signs that Nathanael was coming up the stairs.

Morana reached around him and grabbed the chain, and tried desperately to ignore the pain as the chain burnt her hand. A small sob escaped her as Michael rolled away, and got unsteadily to his feet. He stood looking down at her for a moment as tears streamed down her cheeks and then helped her up, careful not to touch her injured hand.

He wrapped his arms around her and held her for a second as Libbi hovered at their side. Morana looked up at Michael and frowned, "what are we going to do, he's not just going to let us down there—heaven knows what he's doing to them," she said, pulling away from him slowly.

Michael frowned then looked at Libbi. "You have to do something else for us Lib, we need you to get Nathan out of the cellar, tell him that you can hear me or Ana shouting, tell him that he needs to come and see us, say anything you can to get him to come up here—can you do that for me."

Libbi looked uncertain for a moment, she didn't want to get Nathanael into trouble, but she couldn't bear the thought of Miranda being in pain. Nathanael was going to be so angry with her for doing this but she nodded.

"Good girl," Michael said then looked at Morana. "We need to be quick—Lib, where's the key to the door?"

Libbi took the key out of her pocket and gave it to Michael. "You have to go and put these back where you got them from," he said taking the key out of the lock on the floor and handing the two keys to her. He turned and walked from the room and Morana and Libbi followed him, he locked the door and turned to Libbi, "Hurry Lib," he said silently and the girl disappeared for a moment into Nathanael's room.

"Right, are we ready?" he asked silently looking from Libbi to Morana as the girl joined them again. Libbi looked at Morana hesitantly as the woman nodded, then back at Michael and nodded.

Gabriel's skin was on fire, he couldn't remember a time when he'd felt so much pain. His brain felt foggy again as he tried desperately to remain conscious. He looked up at Nathanael as he walked back to him and smiled.

"Jesus Christ Gabe, you're bleeding all over the place," he said looking at the crimson liquid that seeped from the wounds in his hands. He rolled his hand into a ball and punched the end of the stake and it sunk further into Gabriel's right hand. "You have a bit of a stigmata thing going on here bro."

He laughed loudly as Gabriel grimaced in pain. "How are the feet doing—hurting like hell I suppose—who would have thought it would be so difficult to get a stake through the feet, I actually thought I was going to break into a sweat—in hindsight I probably should have sharpened them a little more," he chuckled again.

He stood smiling at him for a moment longer then turned and walked back to the table, he pulled the glove back on and picked up the sword, he stood there for a moment examining it and then walked back pointing it towards Gabriel; he traced a line from his chin down to the hollow of his throat and smiled, "I haven't sharpened this at all, so I will probably have to hack your head off, should take me about three or four attempts to remove it completely—five if I'm lucky," he said running the blade across his Gabriel's neck.

"Nathan stop," Miranda yelled frantically. "Please don't, I'll do it, I'll come with you, you can have me—please don't kill him—please—I'll do anything you want—just please don't kill him."

Nathanael turned to look at her for a moment, then frowned, "you think I would even consider taking you now—it's far too late for that—but don't worry I'm not going to kill him just yet," he said dropping the sword to Gabriel's chest. He thrust the blade deep it into his flesh; Gabriel let out a pained cry as Nathanael pulled it out again and chuckled.

"You're sick—a sick lonely man," Gabriel spat at him, tiny spots of blood splattered over Nathanael's face and he frowned, he removed the glove and wiped at the blood then looked at his hand.

"Would you please try and conserve what little blood you have left bro—you'll just bleed out too quickly," he said reaching out and pulling Gabriel's bottom lip out to inspect the deep grooves left there from biting down into his lip so hard. Nathanael chuckled and pulled away quickly as Gabriel snapped viciously at his hand. "I need you conscious for this next part—I need a little audience participation," he said as he walked back to the table, he dropped the sword onto it and then he picked up another silver stake.

He chuckled as he stood looking at it, "do you know, when I ordered these, the silversmith didn't believe me when I told him I was going torture a couple of vampires with them—he looked at me as if I was quite mad—and then as if that wasn't enough I had to endure a long lecture about silver chains not being the strongest chains in the world—I tell you, I was so happy when I finally got the chance to put an end to his endless chattering—mind you there was an upside to the whole thing, at least I didn't have to pay for all of this," he laughed as he reached over and picked up one of the smaller dogwood darts. He considered them for a moment then turned to his brother.

"So which one shall I use bro—large silver," he said waving the stake towards Gabriel. "Or small dogwood—which do you think Miranda would prefer—you choose."

"Neither," Gabriel groaned looking towards Miranda.

"You have to choose, that's the game Gabe—choose one or I will stab both of them into her beautiful flesh," he said waving both objects at him.

"USE THEM BOTH ON ME—COME ON YOU BASTARD—I'M THE ONE YOU WANT TO KILL—USE THEM BOTH ON ME AND LEAVE HER ALONE—COME ON!" Gabriel shouted angrily.

"Don't you listen to anything," Nathanael said shaking his head. "THAT WASN'T ONE OF THE OPTIONS—looks like you're getting them both Miranda and you have my brother to thank for that," he said moving towards her.

"NO!" Gabriel shouted, "get away from her—ok—dogwood—USE THE DOGWOOD," he shouted panic in his voice.

Nathanael stopped and turned his head to look at his brother and smiled, he turned back quickly towards Gabriel and thrust the silver stake deep into his shoulder. Gabriel shrieked with the pain.

"I knew you'd choose dogwood given a choice—but personally I think it should be silver stake," he smirked walking back to the table and throwing the dogwood stake down, he reached over and picked up another silver stake then walked calmly over to Miranda. "I realise this torturing lark is becoming a little one sided, however will you know the true extent of my brothers suffering unless you have experienced it yourself."

"Just kill us and get it over and done with," she shouted glaring at him. "Come on what are you waiting for—you're going to do it anyway."

"Yes, that is true—but would you really begrudge me my last little bit of fun before you both die—how very selfish of you Miranda. After all my years of torture and anguish—you have to scream and bleed a lot more before I've had my fill—before I allow you any sort of release from the pain—remember how it feels Miranda when the person you love more than life itself leaves you—six months you went without him, just six months—imagine it for three hundred years, what I'm doing to you now doesn't even cover the first century," he said grabbing her left hand and placing it over her right one, and then he drove the stake through both palms. The pain was unbearable, but she didn't scream, she wasn't going to give him the satisfaction. Instead she bit down hard on her lip, so hard that her mouth was instantly filled with blood.

"Get away from her," Gabriel said weakly as tears streamed down his face.

Nathanael frowned at her for a moment then walked back to the table, "this isn't a one way street Miranda—however will my brother truly know the extent of your suffering if you don't scream out nice and loud—come on play the game," he said picking up another silver stake and moving towards her, "be a good girl and scream nice and loud, I do so love the look on his face," he said plunging the stake into her left thigh. Miranda's teeth met through the flesh of her lip as she bit down into it, but she wasn't going to scream again no matter what he did to her.

"Leave her alone," Gabriel shouted his face contorting in agony.

Nathanael sighed and folded his arms, ignoring Gabriel's pleas. "So refusing to play along are you—well, that's fine—I still have plenty more tricks up my sleeve, now what's next?" he mused for a moment. He glanced over at Gabriel. "Glad you're still with us brother—I wouldn't want you to miss a single minute of the next hour or so," he said sitting down next to Miranda and running his fingers down to the opening of her blouse.

"Get away from her you bastard—DON'T YOU DARE TOUCH HER—GET AWAY FROM HER!" Gabriel shouted, trying to pull at the chains again, but the pain that it caused him was crippling, he couldn't do anything to help her, he was totally incapable of moving.

Nathanael glanced at Gabriel and grinned as he undid the buttons on her blouse slowly, exposing her flesh. She flinched as the chains touched her bare skin. He ran his hand under her skirt and pulled at the flimsy fabric of her underwear and tore them off quickly. "So beautiful—I can understand why you couldn't keep your hands off her Gabe—she is simply perfect in every way isn't she?" he said running his fingers slowly across her perfectly flat stomach.

"Get away from her—LEAVE HER ALONE," Gabriel yelled again.

Miranda pulled desperately at the chains as Nathanael dropped his head and traced his tongue over her exposed flesh. "Umm, you taste as good as you smell," he said lifting his head slightly to look at his brother.

"Please stop," Miranda begged as he dipped his head again and moved slowly up her body towards her chest. "Please Nathan, don't do this."

He stopped for a second to look at her blistered face, he watched as tears streamed down her cheeks, "it won't hurt—I'm a very considerate lover, ask my wife—oh that's right—you can't because she's dead, well you'll just have to trust me," he said pulling his shirt off quickly and lowered his head again.

"Please don't—stop—please," Miranda sobbed as he moved over the top of her. He ran his hand gently down to her breast then followed it with his tongue, then swapped to his teeth, Miranda jolted as he bit softly at her nipple, and she tried desperately to contain the shudder that ran through her body as he moved back up her body towards her neck.

"But I don't want to stop," he whispered softly against her skin.

"Please—stop," she whispered as he skimmed her skin with his teeth. He lifted his head slowly and looked into her face.

"I couldn't even if I wanted to—oh Miranda, the times I've dreamt of this day," he sighed kissing her again.

"Get away from her," Gabriel said, his voice no more than a whisper as tears rolled down his face.

"It's such a shame that he can no longer hear your thoughts, I will just have to make do with the fact that he has to watch, I will just have to be content with the fact that I will be the last man that ever makes love to you," Nathanael said quietly running his hands down the length of her body and pulling her hips towards him.

She realised that Gabriel had stopped shouting, all she could hear now where the broken sobs that escaped from him as he stood there with his eyes closed. She tried so hard to block out everything as she lay there, unable to do anything to stop Nathanael as he slowly worked his way back down her body. Suddenly he stopped, and she heard Libbi calling from somewhere above. Nathanael rolled away from her quickly and stood up.

"For god's sake—what is it Libbi—I'm kinda in the middle of something here," he shouted walking to the bottom of the steps.

Miranda heard a door open and Libbi's voice became louder. "Michael's shouting—he sounds real mad," she said looking down at him.

"Just ignore him—he'll quieten down in time," Nathanael said turning away from her.

"But he's shouting real loud and he's swearing something terrible—and I heard a loud bang too—you gotta come and see, I think there's something wrong with Morana cause he keeps shouting at her, please you gotta come and see," she said walking down a few steps.

"Stay there—do not come down here," he said turning back to the girl, "god damn it—ok, I'm coming."

He looked at Miranda and smiled, he walked over and stooped down to pick up his shirt and kissed her gently. "I won't be long my love . . . . then we can pick up where we left off," he said pulling on his shirt, and then he turned and ran up the steps and out of the cellar, slamming the door.

Miranda kept her eyes closed; she couldn't bear to see the look on Gabriel's face.

"Miranda look at me," he pleaded. "Please look at me."

Miranda shook her head as a fresh wave of tears fell from her eyes. She couldn't bear the way his voice cracked as he spoke to her, couldn't bear to see the pain etched on his face.

"Please we don't have very long—please look at me."

She opened her eyes slowly and looked up at him. Her beautiful strong man, nailed to his cross.

"You said that you could forgive me anything—please Miranda—forgive me this," he said quietly lowering his head as tears welled in his eyes.

"How can I forgive you—when there is nothing to forgive Gabriel," Miranda said quietly.

"Yes there is, this is all my fault—everything that you are going through—everything that Nathan is doing to you is because of me—if I hadn't loved you so much, if I hadn't wanted you so much you wouldn't be going through all this now," he said as a sob escaped him. He dropped his head; it was more than he could stand to see her naked, bloodied body lying before him. It was more than he could stand to see the pain and fear on her blistered face. It was more than he could stand, knowing that he was completely powerless to help her.

"Gabriel please—please don't say that—I love you," she whispered.

Gabriel raised his head and looked at her, "I love you—I will always love—" he stopped talking as his voice abandoned him and a sob choked off anything else he wanted to say.

Miranda closed her eyes as the cellar door opened again. He was coming back and he was going to kill them both. And neither of them could do anything at all to stop him.

The footsteps descended quickly and she didn't know whether to laugh or cry when she saw the concerned faces of Michael and Morana appear through the darkness.

39

Nathanael stood outside the bedroom; there wasn't a sound coming from inside. He thrust his hands into his pocket and fumbled for the key, then remembered he'd left it in his jacket pocket. Now where had he left his god damn jacket?

He couldn't think straight for a moment, images of Miranda's blistered, tear, stained face as she'd pleaded with him to stop ran through his mind. He'd wanted her so much and he just couldn't resist the temptation when it presented itself. If Libbi hadn't interrupted, he would be making love to her now, he frowned at the though . . . he was going to have a serious discussion with the girl once he'd finished down in the cellar. It had been a most unfortunate and quite inappropriately timed interruption he mused; a few seconds later and Libbi would have seen things an eight year old should never see.

His jacket was in his room, he remembered, he walked quickly and opened his door. The portrait smiled down at him wickedly. He smiled as he picked up his jacket. "Yes it's going well—it's been a lot easier than I thought it would be—but then, hate is so much stronger than love isn't it," he said walking towards the door, and then he frowned and turned to face Sophie.

"I knew you wouldn't like that—but what can I say—you're dead babe and a man has needs." He shook his head, "for god's sake shut up and get over it—like I said you're dead."

He folded his arms across his chest as Sophie drifted closer. She stopped a few inches away from him and frowned. "Yes I know that, yes I know that too—oh shut up, you should be content with the fact that she and that disgusting excuse of a brother of mine will soon be dead, so will you please just let me get on with it."

He frowned down at the floor for a moment, and then looked back at her, "Of course I'm still going to kill her, what would the point be of letting her live, you know what we vamps are like for vengeance—she'd kill me in a blink of an eye, I just want a little fun before I do, it's been so long since I last—" he stopped talking and frowned again, "ok—stop shouting—it hurt's my head when you screech—you begrudge me just the smallest amount of pleasure, when all this is for you—god damn it Soph—ok I promise—I have to go now, Michael is being a pain in the ass as usual—looks like I'm going to have to knock the son of a bitch out again—I'll be back later."

Morana looked quickly from Miranda's naked body to Gabriel and back again. "Oh my god what has he done?" Morana said grabbing a glove from the table and kneeling by Miranda's side. Miranda turned her head away; she couldn't bear the look of disgust in the woman's eyes. Morana looked at the stakes, and then the dart and frowned. "I'm so sorry sweetie but this going to hurt," she said wiping the tears away from her own face; Miranda stifled the scream that rose up in her throat as the woman grabbed at the dart in her neck and pulled it out. She put the glove on quickly and grabbed the stake in her leg and grimaced. "Miranda I'm sorry," she said quietly.

"Do it," Miranda said simply, bracing herself for the pain she knew was coming. Morana yanked at the stake, and it popped as it exited the hole. Miranda again bit down into her already damaged lip, but even so couldn't stop the small scream that escaped. Morana stood up and wiped the tears away from her eyes again as she grasped the stake in Miranda's hands.

"Oh god, I am so very sorry," she said as she yanked the stake out, Miranda bowed her head as the tears flowed freely from her eyes.

Michael moved towards Gabriel and frowned, "we don't have long before he's back." He stood there for a moment trying to decide where to start, as he pulled the glove on. Gabriel clenched his teeth as Michael grabbed the stake in his shoulder and pulled it as hard as he could, the sound as it clattered to the floor was so loud that Michael froze for a moment and listened for signs that Nathanael was returning. Gabriel dropped his head to hide the pain on his face as Michael took hold of the stake in his right palm, if he had thought it was painful as they went in, he discovered quickly that it was nothing compared to the pain of having them ripped out.

"Sorry," Michael said quietly as he pulled it out, and moved on to the next hand, "I'm so—"

"Don't say sorry," Gabriel croaked closing his eyes. He bit down into his lip again to stifle the scream, and his eyes watered with the pain.

Michael moved down to his feet and shook his head; he looked up at Gabriel for a moment and frowned.

"Just do it," Gabriel said trying to brace himself for the agony, but he couldn't help but cry out as the man tugged at the stake.

"I can't get it," Michael said releasing the stake for a moment, "Ana you're going to have to help me—I can't do this alone," he said glancing towards the woman.

Morana frowned down at Miranda for a moment, and then she grabbed the chains and yanked at them quickly.

"Don't move yet—I'll be back in a minute to help you," she said getting to her feet and moving over to Gabriel. Miranda smoothed her skirt down with very shaky hands and managed to re-button her blouse and she tried to move towards Gabriel, to help him in anyway she could, but she was just to weak to do anything, instead she had to sit there and watch his pain.

Morana hovered by Michael for a second then stooped down and took hold of Gabriel's feet. "I'm so sorry," she muttered quietly as Gabriel winced at her touch.

Michael quickly pulled the glove off his hand, it restricted his grip on the stake, and looked up at Gabriel, "You ready?" he asked, Gabriel simply nodded. Michael wrapped his hands tightly around the stake trying desperately to ignore the searing heat on his skin, he pulled at the stake and it popped loudly as it exited the hole.

Gabriel screamed with pain. Michael and Morana snapped the chains around his arms, then Michael released him from the chains around his waist, and he fell to the floor in agony. Michael crouched down beside him and removed the dogwood stake from his back quickly. The pain was so bad from everything else that Gabriel didn't even notice.

Michael stood and moved out of his way. Morana moved over to Michael and put her head into his shoulder and cried silently.

Gabriel crawled slowly on his hands and knees towards Miranda; he just needed to get to her. He wrapped his arms around her and held her as her tears fell onto his skin. All the pain he'd gone through meant nothing compared to the pain her tears caused him. How could he bear what his brother had done to her, how could he bear the thought that he hadn't been able to help her when she'd needed him most, after he'd promised that he wouldn't let anybody hurt her.

"I'm so sorry my love," he whispered wiping away her tears; he kissed her gently, and then got unsteadily to his feet. He helped Miranda to her feet and then turned to Morana and Michael, "thank you," he said quietly nodding his head slightly.

Michael produced a bottle of blood and handed it to him, he opened it and drank deeply, it didn't stop the pain but it dulled it somewhat. He turned to face Miranda and wrapped his arms around her again. "I love you," he said as he kissed her gently on the lips.

"What are you going to do?" she asked as he pulled away from her.

"Something I should have done three hundred and twenty years ago," he said walking to the table. He picked up the silver sword that lay there and held it up, ignoring the burn on his skin. He glanced over at Michael and Morana and then at Miranda, "take care of her, this won't take long," he said as he turned and limped towards the steps. Miranda ran behind him, and he turned back to her, "I said stay here, he's my problem—and I'm going to deal with him—he's going to pay dearly for this."

Miranda shook her head and frowned, "you're still too weak, and he's not just your problem anymore, I'm coming with you."

Nathanael stood outside Michael and Morana's room. There still wasn't a sound, Libbi must have got it wrong, stupid girl. And now when he went back down to them, he'd promised not to touch Miranda again. Having a dead wife hanging about was starting to really cramp his style, as if it wasn't bad enough, having to hear her constant chatter in his head, now she had put a stop to the most pleasurable thing he'd done in years. He couldn't wait until all of this was over.

He reached into his pocket for the door key, he frowned then slipped his hand into the other pocket, he was sure he'd put both keys in the right hand side, but now they were in the left, he took both keys out and stared at them for a moment. He was still frowning as he put the key in the lock; had Sophie fried his brain so much that he couldn't remember the simplest of things, he pushed the door open and walked into the room.

He looked down at the chains laid scattered on the floor; he frowned down at the rumpled blanket. He knew he should have just killed them. He walked around the bed and picked up the open lock, he stared down at it for a second and threw it across the room. He swore under his breath.

"LIBBI!" he shouted, she had let them out. How stupid he had been, trusting the girl, he stood there for a moment weighing his options. No doubt they were already in the cellar, freeing Gabriel and Miranda as he stood there debating what he should do. He rubbed his head, "think Nathan," he growled at himself.

Gabriel would still be weak; he still had a chance, would he be fast enough to kill him before Miranda regained her powers. Would there be time enough to do so and escape before she summoned enough energy to kill him. He ran to his room, enough time to collect his bag before they found him, he thought slipping his jacket on.

"Oh I know I've cocked it up, but what did you expect? Shut up—you're not in the least bit helpful—shut up I said," he shouted as she glided towards him. He shouldn't have trusted Libbi, he should have tied her up with the rest of them . . . . he was so god damn stupid thinking that the young girl could be useful . . . . he should have just killed the lot of them when he'd had the chance. The last year spent with Miranda had softened him so much . . . . and now he had the feeling that he was going to pay the price for his idiocy.

"I said shut up, god woman—do you know I should be grateful that Gabriel killed you when he did—imagine the life I would have had to endure, even in death you won't give it a rest." He stood at his door for a moment, listening for any sign of life. He didn't have much time, he couldn't risk walking through the house, and without a doubt they would be free by now.

He walked over to the window and opened it; he sniffed the night air and jumped up onto the window ledge. He looked around at her near transparent figure, "well, it seems this is goodbye my love," he said turning away again.

He jumped gracefully from the window, and dropped to the ground quietly. He thought about taking his car, but he moved faster than any vehicle ever invented, and no doubt Gabriel would soon be hot on his trail. He ran silently toward the gate and leapt into the air clearing it easily. As he hit the ground he turned one last time to look back at the house.

Miranda followed Gabriel swiftly up the stairs. Gabriel slowed to a stop at the door of Michael and Morana's room and peered in . . . . no sign of him. He moved quietly towards Nathanael's room. He paused for a second and turned towards Miranda.

"Stay out of the way unless I need your help—I don't want you to get hurt," he said silently into her mind.

Miranda nodded but entered the room right behind him. Still no sign of him. Gabriel scowled as he looked up at the portrait smiling down at them. He lifted the sword and slashed it straight down the middle. The fabric of the canvas curled outwards towards the edges of the frame, and the image of Sophie disappeared.

"Where the hell is he?" Gabriel growled as he turned and left the room.

Miranda followed as he opened every door upstairs. He paused for a moment in his room to pull on a shirt and to slip his bloodied acing feet into his shoes, and then Miranda followed him quickly to Libbi's room.

Libbi cowered in the corner of her room as Gabriel threw the door open. Tears streamed down her face as Miranda rushed over and picked the girl up in her arms and held her close.

"I'm so sorry," the girl sobbed into her chest. "I didn't know he was going to be bad—I didn't think he could do that sort of thing to you—I heard you down there—I knew he was doing something bad—and then I opened the door and I saw you there—and I couldn't do anything—and he was so mad that I'd interrupted him—I'm so sorry that I didn't help you sooner—oh I'm sorry."

Tears fell from Miranda's eyes as she looked down at the girl, "you did well Lib, you saved us," she said trying desperately to smile at her.

"I saved you—but he still hurt you terribly—and I should have known something was happening because he told me to lie—and he sent me to my room—but I heard you—I heard that he was hurting you—but I was so frightened," she sobbed looking towards Gabriel, "and then I heard you shouting at him to leave her alone—and I knew for sure it was something really bad."

Gabriel dropped the sword and then fell to he knees at Miranda's side and put his arms around the pair of them. "Libbi none of this is your fault—we are alive because of you, you really did save us, please stop crying."

"But I feel so bad for what he did to you—he was going to kill you—after he'd done all those bad things—I hate him," Libbi said wrapping her arms around Gabriel's neck.

He kissed the girl gently on the cheek. "Do you know where he is?"

Libbi frowned then shook her head, she looked up at Miranda, "I think he's gone, I heard him in his room talking to Sophie—he shouted at her to shut up—he said goodbye to her and then it went quiet," she said looking from Gabriel to Miranda.

"Talking to Sophie?" Miranda asked puzzled as she looked at Gabriel. He shook his head and looked down at Libbi.

"Sophie's dead Lib and she has been for a long time."

Libbi looked slightly exasperated at Gabriel's statement, "I know that—but he talks to her a lot—and I think she talks to him—because he has long conversations with her sometimes—I've heard him—I can never hear what she says—I think, only Nathan knows what she's saying."

Gabriel stood up and frowned, was it possible that his brother had left. He needed to search the rest of the house, he bent down and picked up the sword and flinched slightly at the pain the silver caused as it touched his skin.

"Stay with Lib," he said to Miranda as he left the room. He met Michael and Morana at the bottom of the stairs. They stared up at him as he rushed down towards them.

"I want every room opened down here," he ordered as he walked into the library, he re-appeared after a few seconds and disappeared into Miranda's music room.

"Keys," he shouted as he reached one of the locked doors. Michael threw them to him. He turned the key in the lock and pushed the door open, disappearing into the room quickly. He emerged with a frown; he repeated the process with the other three doors in the hall.

He walked out of the last room and dropped the sword to the floor; the pain in his hand eased the instant the sword clattered to the ground. He frowned towards Michael and shook his head at the questioning look on the man's face.

"DAMN HIM TO HELL," Gabriel shouted throwing the keys across the hall in anger. He turned towards the front door as Michael reached out and grabbed his arm.

"Where are you going?" he asked trying to pull him back.

Gabriel swung around to face Michael and Morana; the woman shrank back slightly at the look on his face as he scowled at them both. "I'm going to find him, and then I'm going to make him wish he'd never been born—I'm going to rip the son of a whore to pieces," he said quietly as he shrugged Michael's hand away. He didn't stay long enough to hear their words of protest; he ran at great speed from the house and didn't stop running until he reached the city.

40

Miranda walked to the library window . . . . Gabriel had been gone so long, she was worried. He hadn't been at his strongest when he'd left and gone after Nathanael and now as the sky started to lighten she was terrified that he would never come back. Morana opened the door and walked quietly up to her, she handed her the mug, "no sign yet?"

Miranda shook her head as she took the cup and drank the liquid. The sky lightened all the while the women stood there looking out down the drive towards the gates.

Morana shifted uncomfortably as the sun rose slowly in the distance; she turned to look at Miranda, "we need to close the curtains," she said quietly, but Miranda shook her head. She moved closer to the window and narrowed her eyes as a dark shape approached the gates. She recognised Gabriel's stance as he stooped down and jumped nimbly over the gate. She ran out of the library then out of the front door, ignoring Morana's plea's for her to stay in the house.

She ran into his arms as he opened them out to her. "I was so worried—thank god you're back, I just couldn't stand it if anything happened to you," she said frantically kissing his face.

He smiled weakly at her and walked unsteadily with her towards the house. He still felt so weak; he didn't even have the energy to talk as Miranda helped him up the stairs and into his room. She pulled off his shoes has he flopped down onto the bed and closed his eyes. He barely managed to roll over and wrap his arm around her as she took her place next to him, but he did manage a light kiss on her cheek before his eyes closed and sleep overcame him.

Miranda stared at his exhausted sleeping face; the tears brimming in her eyes. Everything she had been through, all the pain, all the torment was nothing to what he'd had to witness. She'd heard the pain in his voice, heard it in his sobs, and seen it on his face . . . . and she couldn't stand it. Nathanael had used her in the worst possible way to torture his brother . . . and it had worked with the optimum effect. How could he possibly love her anymore . . . . how could he possibly bear to look at her ever again?

Gabriel rolled over and opened his eyes. He couldn't ever remember a time when he had felt so tired. Libbi smiled down at him as he sat up slowly, and she handed him a cup. He took it and drank quickly. He placed the cup on the table and looked back at her as she hovered by the side of the bed. "Where is Miranda?" he asked quietly.

Libbi frowned and shifted her weight from side to side. "She's in the kitchen—she's very sad—she needs you to tell her everything's alright—she's very sad," the girl sadly, moving uncomfortably as Gabriel frowned at her. "She thought about leaving—and you have to go and stop her Gabe—else I think she might just go—and I don't want her to, do you?"

Gabriel shook his head and tried to swallow the lump that had risen in his throat. How could she even consider leaving after all they had been through, how could she think that he would ever just let her go, after all his words, didn't she know just how much he loved her.

He swung his legs off the bed and got unsteadily to his feet, and more or less stumbled down the stairs. He stood outside the door and listen for a moment to Michael and Morana's hushed voices, he could hear the strain in their tones, and he rubbed his aching head . . . . Libbi said he had to stop her . . . . that he needed to tell her that everything was alright . . . . but what was there that he could say to her. No words could take away the things she'd had to suffer at the hands of his brother . . . . what could he possibly say to heal her pain . . . . when everything she'd had to endure was because of him.

Miranda glanced up as he walked into the kitchen and instantly dropped her eyes back to the table, as he hesitated in the doorway. Morana and Michael looked at each other and stood in unison, they walked past Gabriel and out of the kitchen. Michael put his hand on Gabriel's shoulder for a split second as he passed by, and tried to smile reassuringly.

He stood there for a moment looking at her. "Libbi told me you've been thinking of leaving," he said walking slowly over to the table.

"I think I should—maybe for a little while," she said quietly keeping her eyes on the table.

He sat opposite her and took her hand in his, "I realise that this is difficult for you, and if you think it would help, maybe we could spend a little time apart—but you don't need to leave—perhaps you could go back to sleeping in your room—" he stopped talking for a moment, the pain in his throat from trying to stop the sobs that threatened to escape at any moment, was making speech difficult. "I know the fact that we're twins can't be an easy thing to cope with—after all he put you through—but I'm not him Miranda, I'm not him—" he stopped talking and frowned down at the floor, he couldn't carry on as she looked up at him.

"You are nothing like him—is that what you think? You still think that I compare you to him—I love you Gabriel, and I will never stop loving you," she said as tears started to fall from her eyes.

"So what reason is there for you to leave—I don't understand—why, if it's not for the fact that every time you look at me you'll see him—why, if it's not because every time you look at me you're reminded of what he did to you?" he asked reaching out for her hand.

"Because I can see it in your eyes Gabriel—I see it on your face, every time you look at me—I see all the pain—after what he did how can you want me—how can you love me—when every time you look at me you'll remember everything he did, you'll remember the way he kissed me the way he touched me, you'll remember every single thing—every single detail—how could you ever want me again after that?" she said pulling away from him quickly.

He stood up and walked around the table to her, he pulled her to her feet and held her close, "don't ever think that—I love you Miranda—I couldn't love you anymore than I do—if you leave he will win, because I wouldn't survive without you, I can't live without you," he whispered as he lowered his head and kissed her tenderly. "We can't let him destroy what we have—even if it takes the next century I will wait for you, just please don't leave me, I will die without you."

Miranda looked up into his eyes as a single tear rolled down his cheek. She lifted her hand and gently wiped it away, and then she wrapped her arms around his neck and kissed him fiercely.

41

Gabriel walked slowly down the stairs, he'd been slightly surprised when he'd turned over and Miranda's side of the bed had been empty. She'd appeared minutes later with a cup and ordered him to get out of bed, and then she'd chuckled and moved away quickly as he'd tried to grab her and pull her back into bed.

Morana was stood at the bottom of the stairs, waiting for him, "there is a letter for you on the table—it has—it's from the council," she said then turned towards the kitchen. She opened the door and Gabriel followed her into the room.

Miranda was sat looking down at the envelope, and she flinched slightly as he touched her shoulder. She turned to him as he sat next to her, and the expression on her face could only be described as panic. It was bound to happen, with her now being over two years old, but she hadn't expected it so soon. She looked back down at the envelope, and couldn't help the involuntary shiver that crept down her spine.

Gabriel took her hand and tried to smile reassuringly; he had expected some form of communication from them and he had expected it sooner, but now it had arrived he couldn't help but feel a little surprised by it.

"Are you just going to sit there looking at it all night or are you going to open it?" Morana asked looking down at the envelope.

"Be my guest," Gabriel said motioning towards the letter.

Morana snatched up the envelope without waiting for another invitation. She ripped it open and unfolded the single piece of paper, read it and then frowned.

"So?" Gabriel asked. Morana handed him the letter then sat down.

Gabriel read it and smiled, he handed it to Miranda, and she too read it.

Dear Gabriel,
We will arrive soon.
Raphael.

She sat there staring at the writing for a moment, and then turned the paper over; she looked at Gabriel and frowned. "It doesn't say when they will be here," she said looking back at the paper.

"They are already here," Gabriel said standing up. He bent down and kissed her lightly on the lips, then smiled, "you have nothing to worry about," he said quietly then walked from the room.

Morana reached over and patted her hand, "he's right—you have nothing at all to worry about," she said reassuringly as she stood up and moved to the counter.

Miranda froze as she heard a light tap on the front door; she dropped the letter onto the table and stood up quickly. She walked over to Morana and stood at her side. "Miranda, you are far more powerful than any of them and this is your home—please calm down—I can feel the panic radiating off you—Gabriel wouldn't let any of them hurt you," Morana said taking her hand, she squeezed it lightly then released her and smiled.

Miranda could hear them in the hall; she closed her eyes and concentrated on the small ball of energy that bubbled away in her stomach. She opened her eyes again as the kitchen door opened and Gabriel walked in ahead of the visitors. He walked around the table and put his arm around Miranda's shoulder; he smiled down at her for a moment and then looked back at the council members. Miranda watched as eight strangers walked into the room and regarded her with curious eyes.

"I'm glad to see the letter arrived before we did," one of the men said smiling down at the paper on the table.

"Only just," Gabriel said glancing at him.

"Introductions are called for Gabriel," the same man said and then smiled at Miranda.

Gabriel nodded. "Miranda this is Raphael, to his left Azrael, to his right Anngela." Miranda nodded and the three of them moved forward to shake her hand, then Gabriel spoke again. "The rather large one is Saraph, the one to his right is Uriel, and the one to his left is Sammael." They did the same, moving forward and shaking her hand. "And lastly the young man is Zachariel, and the young lady is Evangeline."

Zachariel inclined his head a fraction, but made no attempt to shake her hand. Evangeline however, moved forward and shook her hand vigorously. "Oh it's so good to finally meet you Miranda—you can call me Eva—Evangeline's such a mouthful—I know, I should change it right, it make's me sound so old really doesn't it—I mean I am old, but doesn't mean I have to sound old does it—you have such a beautiful name—I—"

"Eva—please," Zachariel said quietly, his eyes remaining on Miranda's face. The woman stopped talking immediately and moved back to his side.

"Zachariel—won't you please sit down," Morana said motioning towards the table.

He looked at Morana and again inclined his head towards her, "Morana—thank you—please call me Zach," he said; he removed his jacket and handed it to the one called Uriel, then moved towards the table and took a seat. Evangeline sat at his side as did Raphael, Azrael and Saraph stood directly behind them and the rest remained where they were.

Gabriel pulled Miranda over to the table with him and they sat opposite them.

Zachariel's eyes remained on Miranda's face for a moment, and then he looked at Gabriel, "I wonder brother, is this house of yours big enough to accommodate my family and me for a while," he said sitting back in his chair.

Gabriel considered him for a moment and then nodded his head, "we have enough room for you—but first will you do me the courtesy of telling me why you should need accommodation—why you and your family suddenly descended on our home."

Zachariel sat forward slightly and frowned, he regarded Gabriel for a moment then spoke quietly, "it has recently been brought to our attention that Miranda is not the only first in existence, there are others—three others to be exact—three others that are, let us say, not as friendly as Miranda here," he said and again inclined his head towards her.

"Who are they and why would they mean to harm you?" Gabriel asked frowning.

"I fear it is not us that they mean to harm—but you and your family are not safe Gabriel—word has reached us that they intend to kill you, Miranda, your brother Nathan and anybody else who gets in their way,"

Zachariel said quietly, "and as kith and kin, we feel we cannot stand idly by and let this happen."

"Who are they?" Gabriel asked again.

"The eldest of the three was one in a long line of Decastell's letters—I am afraid to say that we missed it—he changed his family at some stage, before we were created—and unbeknown to us he gave us false information—we missed the fact that he'd named his old family of letters and not the new one," Anngela said looking at Gabriel.

"He lied," Gabriel stated looking up at the woman.

"Yes it would seem so," Azrael said looking slightly uncomfortable when Gabriel looked at him. "The onus is on us brother—we did not expect them to lie—we were foolish not to investigate—but alas the damage, as they say, is now done."

"Didn't any of you think to read the tomes before you passed them on to me?" Gabriel asked. Azrael simply shook his head.

Miranda was highly aware of Zachariel's eyes on her while the rest of them sat talking, and it was making her uncomfortable. She was drawn to him and his hypnotic stare, and although she tried to drag her eyes away from him, she found her eyes returning to his face time and time again.

"I will ask once more," Gabriel said slightly agitated, as he looked back at Zachariel, "who are they?"

Zachariel frowned and looked away from Miranda to Gabriel, "her name was Sophie Lambrick—that was until she married your brother."

Miranda felt as if her eyes had opened as wide as saucers and when she glanced around at Morana, the woman looked as shocked as Miranda felt. Gabriel however didn't react the way she thought he would, he simply sat back in his chair and folded his arms, and there wasn't even a hint of surprise in his voice as he spoke again. "Does Nathan know about this?"

"We have been having a little trouble in locating your brother," Evangeline said and smiled uncomfortably at Miranda, "seems this particular Pride is one slippery character."

Gabriel glanced around at Morana, "would you mind opening the rooms for our guest, make sure they are comfortable—Miranda will help you," he said standing up.

Miranda stood up and looked at him, "where are you going?"

"I have to go out for a while—you will be quite safe here, with our house guest," he said moving closer to her.

Zachariel stood up quickly, "we feel it is not prudent for any of you to leave the house—until we have confirmation of their whereabouts," he said raising his hand slightly.

Gabriel looked over at him for a moment, "I will not be held captive by anyone—this is my home—and not to sound disrespectful—but I will come and go as I please—that is unless any of you have a mind to try and stop me from leaving."

"We have no intention of stopping you Gabriel," Azrael said standing up quickly. "But we think it wise that you take someone along with you, Sammael and Saraph will accompany you on your outing."

Gabriel frowned but nodded his agreement at the arrangement, then turned to Miranda. "If you need to hunt while I'm away, do not go alone, I'm sure Zachariel will make sure you're safe," he said glancing at the young man. "Please just stick to the forest if possible—feed quickly then come straight back to the house, stay inside when possible—and that means no running around the maze with Libbi."

Miranda looked at him and frowned, "I don't mean to sound disrespectful—but I will come and go as I please," she said moving away from him.

Gabriel took her hand and pulled her out of the kitchen and away from prying eyes, then frowned at her, "please Miranda, promise me that you will do as I ask, I will worry enough while I'm away without the thought that you're running around all over the place—please promise me," he said taking both her hands in his.

"Why do you have to go anywhere, Gabriel?" she asked pulling away from him.

"Because I do," he said looking down at the floor.

"You're going to find Nathan, aren't you?" she asked quietly.

"I'm sorry, but yes—she's a first Miranda, a very old and very powerful first—and I think Nate's actions may have had something to do with her all along," he said taking her hands again, "I know what he did was unforgivable, but we need to know everything Miranda—and the best way to find out is to ask Nate in person—he should also know that she's out there—please Miranda, please promise me that you will do as I ask."

Miranda looked at him for a second then nodded, "I promise—I will do as you ask."

Gabriel wrapped his arms around her and kissed her tenderly, when he raised his head he added silently, "you have to promise me one more thing—if Sophie should turn up here while I'm gone, don't stay and fight—leave her to them—you get Libbi and run as fast as you can, don't even worry about Ana or Mike—just get away from here, you are not strong enough to fight her, they will act as a distraction, and when they do you just run—promise me."

"I can't do that Gabriel, how can I just leave them—she will kill them," Miranda said into his mind.

"She will probably kill some of them, yes—but they are not my concern—you are and I would sacrifice them all ten times over to keep you safe—now promise me Miranda," he said tightening his hold on her.

Miranda considered for a moment then nodded again as the kitchen door opened. Zachariel walked out followed by Sammael and Saraph. "We are ready if you are," Sammael said quietly and glanced at Miranda.

"I'm ready," Gabriel said looking down at Miranda, again he kissed her. Miranda clung onto him as long as she could, until he finally pulled away from her and turned towards the front door. "I will see you when I get back," he said quietly as Sammael and Saraph walked past him. He turned to her once more and tried to smile, "I love you," he said and then he was gone.

Epilogue

Nathanael slipped his hands into his pockets as he leant up against the lamppost, he considered the young girl huddled up in the shop doorway, she was pretty enough though nowhere near as beautiful as Miranda. He frowned as thoughts of her entered his mind.

He missed her so much that it caused a dull ache in the place where his heart should be and no amount of blood could rid him of it. He thought that after this long, lonely year away from home, away from her, it would become easier, but instead everyday seemed a little harder, a little lonelier. He was fed up with being alone. He pushed himself away from the lamppost and walked confidently towards the girl. "Hi, my name is Nathanael—but you can call me Nathan, or even Nate if you prefer," he said stooping down in front of her, "you look so cold Charlotte—how about I take you to get a nice hot cup of coffee before you freeze to death," he said and smiled at her.

She looked at him for a second and then smiled brightly as he offered her his hand.

He looked into her eyes for a moment and flinched involuntarily at a forgotten memory in the girl's mind; he breathed in and smiled again at the scent that still lingered on her. Once touched by a vampire the smell was not easily removed . . . . why hadn't Miranda killed her?

He pulled Charlotte to her feet and looked down at her for a moment. "Do you know I'm totally alone in this world—no one to love me, no one to love—I've had enough of being alone Charlie, would you like to keep me company for a while?" he said carefully wrapping his arms around her.

Charlotte giggled quietly as Nathanael lowered his head and kissed her gently, "we are going to be such good friends Charlie, we are going to see the world together, we are going to do so much, we are going to have so much fun—and you will never be cold or hungry ever again," he said taking her hand with a smile. "But first that coffee—and maybe a bite to eat," he said as they started walking down the street.

Nathanael couldn't see the bright green eyes that watched his every move intently, nor could he see the cruel smile that curved the seductive red lips. Sophie turned her back to the window and smiled at the young man and the woman stood in front of her, and then looked at the various lifeless bodies that were scattered around the room.

"Gabriel and Nathanael Pride—the bane of my life," she said and frowned as a low groan escaped one of the bodies that lay in the corner, she smiled wickedly and moved over to the man as his eyes opened slowly. "Yes, yes wake up—come on wake up everyone, time is wasting and we have so much to do, so much to prepare," she said pivoting on her heal and turning to face the man and woman again.

"Gabriel and Nathanael Pride messed with the wrong person—but soon they will pay for what they did," she chuckled kicking the closest body to her viciously. "Soon they are going to wish they'd never even heard my name," she added dancing manically as the dead at her feet started to move again, at last.

Lightning Source UK Ltd.
Milton Keynes UK
UKOW051608311011

181223UK00001B/45/P